Praise for Ali Vali's F

Carly's Sound

"Vali paints vivid pictures with her words...*Carly's Sound* is a great romance, with some wonderfully hot sex."—*Midwest Book Review*

"It's no surprise that passion is indeed possible a second time around"—*Q Syndicate*

The Devil Inside

"Vali's fluid writing style quickly puts the reader at ease, which makes the story and its characters equally easy to get to know and care about. When you find yourself talking out loud to the characters in a book, you know the work is polished and professional, as well as entertaining."—*Family and Friends*

"Not only is The Devil Inside a ripping mystery, it's also an intimate character study."—*L-Word Literature*

"*The Devil Inside* is the first of what promises to be a very exciting series...While telling an exciting story that grips the reader, Vali has also fully fleshed out her heroes and villains. *The Devil Inside* is that rarity: a fascinating crime novel which includes a tender love story and leaves the reader with a cliffhanger ending."—*MegaScene*

The Devil Unleashed

"Fast-paced action scenes, intriguing character revelations, and a refreshing approach to the romance thriller genre all make for an enjoyable reading experience in the Big Easy...*The Devil Unleashed* is an engrossing reading experience." —*Midwest Book Review*

Deal With the Devil

"Ali Vali has given her fans another thick, rich thriller...*Deal With the Devil* has wonderful love stories, great sex, and an ample supply of humor. It is an exciting, page turning read that leaves her readers eagerly awaiting the next book in the series."—*JustAboutWrite*

Calling Out the Dead

"So many writers set stories in New Orleans, but Ali Vali's mystery novels have the authenticity that only a real Big Easy resident could bring... makes for a classic lesbian murder yarn."—*Curve*

By the Author

Carly's Sound

Second Season

Calling the Dead

Blue Skies

<u>The Cain Casey Saga</u>

The Devil Inside

The Devil Unleashed

Deal with the Devil

Visit us at www.boldstrokesbooks.com

BLUE SKIES

by
Ali Vali

2009

ISBN 10: 1-60282-077-5
ISBN 13: 978-1-60282-077-7

THIS TRADE PAPERBACK ORIGINAL IS PUBLISHED BY
BOLD STROKES BOOKS, INC.
P.O. BOX 249
VALLEY FALLS, NY 12185

FIRST EDITION: MAY 2009

CREDITS
EDITORS: CINDY CRESAP AND STACIA SEAMAN
PRODUCTION DESIGN: STACIA SEAMAN
COVER PHOTO BY BARB KIWAK (WWW.KIWAK.COM)
COVER DESIGN BY SHERI (GRAPHICARTIST2020@HOTMAIL.COM)

Acknowledgments

The more I write, the more it becomes clear that the final product takes a team, no matter how long I spend at the keyboard. That was definitely true this time, and I have to thank Radclyffe more than ever for her steady, unbending support. I'm lucky to have found such a good home with BSB, and such a great person to work for.

A million thanks to my editor Cindy Cresap. Cindy made this process easy during a difficult time, and for that I'm forever grateful. You're a good and patient teacher.

If I consider this book a cake, the definite icing is the cover art by Barb Kiwak. Thank you, Barb, for your talent and vision as well as your friendship. Thanks also to my first readers Kathi Isserman and Connie Ward. Your enthusiasm for more is a great encouragement to keep writing.

Thanks to the readers. Each word is written with you in mind.

Thanks to my parents for teaching me what true dedication and commitment are all about. These past few months have been hard, but you've chosen life, love, and laughter. It makes the battles easier to fight, and if there's one person I'm confident will win whatever battle is put to her, it is my mom.

Thanks to my partner, who fuels my imagination and makes my life fun even when laughing is the last thing I think I'm capable of. I love you with all I am.

Dedication

For C
My love, always
&
For Mami
Each day is a gift

CHAPTER ONE

White House Situation Room, Washington, DC

"Sir, I don't mean to argue with you."

"Then don't," newly inaugurated President Peter Khalid said in as calm a voice as possible without being overly threatening. "I know I'm new to the job, but let's get something clear right now. The election is over and I don't give a damn how many of you endorsed the other guy—he lost. You ended up with the one who isn't the war hero, so learn to live with it or get the hell out."

"Sir—" Admiral Rodney James tried again.

"I'm not finished." The president stood from his seat at the head of the table in the situation room. "I'm the candidate who promised change, and that's what the American people are going to get. They're going to get it even if I have to fire everyone in this room to get a more receptive audience. Do we understand each other, gentlemen?"

A chorus of "yes, sirs" came from the military leaders around the table except for Admiral Rodney James in his stiff blue dress uniform. The four stars gleamed against the dark fabric as if he spent a good bit of time lovingly buffing the symbols of his success, and they showed Rodney's commitment to service. Everything about him practically screamed tradition, honor, and most importantly, the status quo.

Peter saw how his shoulders stayed rigidly straight as if someone was pressing their knee to the middle of his back. The defiance in his eyes held the message "don't rock the boat, especially on my watch, asshole."

"Admiral, do we understand each other?" Peter repeated.

"With all due respect, Mr. President, if you aren't interested in my opinion, then why am I here?" Rodney put his hands on the oak table and leaned forward in a way that showed he was a man used to giving orders and not getting any flack about it. "What we have is a serious situation here, and it calls for men to make a serious response. It's no time for publicity stunts or an implementation of radical changes. What you need to do is let us handle this, so the message is clear. You may be new to your job, but everyone in this room is highly trained and totally capable of handling it. All we need from you, sir, is a green light."

"You're dismissed, Admiral James." Peter rested his weight on his fingertips as he leaned forward. "Vice Admiral Garner," he said to the naval officer standing behind Rodney close to the wall. "When can you carry out my orders? Or do I go down to the next eager beaver looking to be promoted? And I mean that even if I go down to the person cleaning the toilets on the smallest dinghy in the Navy."

Vice Admiral Sawyer Garner opened his briefcase and removed a file. "A bit young, but an excellent candidate for what you have in mind, Mr. President. Captain Sullivan comes from a Navy family, and I don't see a problem getting the job done once we decide on a course of action. The *Jefferson* will be in capable hands."

"That takes care of the Navy," Peter said looking down the line to the next branch of the military.

An hour later Peter had gotten what some would refer to as a token change, considering the size of the armed forces, but change to level the playing field for those who wanted to serve had to start somewhere. Placing talented, capable people who'd previously never been considered in positions of authority would either blow open the doors of the military old boy's club, or blow up in his face, but either way Peter was committed to providing the chance.

"Thank you all for your cooperation." Peter signaled his staff to dim the lights. "Now let's get to why we're here."

"The situation *is* serious, sir, but it can be easily defused if you're willing to send a message," Garner said from his new seat at the table.

"I believe I've demonstrated I don't have a problem with that, so let's hear everyone's suggestions." The screens in the room suddenly displayed an array of maps and satellite images.

These were the moments the military personnel trained for and that defined presidential legacies. Peter took a deep breath and felt his hair turning gray. There was already a conflict in the Middle East involving U.S. troops, and what they were contemplating had the potential to start a fire that would make the Iraq situation seem like a mere grain of sand in a vast desert in comparison.

❖

Top Gun Facility, Fallon, Nevada

Blue skies. The expanse of them made Commander Berkley Levine smile and think momentarily of the games of hide and go seek she played as a child. This was the same concept, but with a day like this it was more of a game of sitting duck if you didn't know what you were doing.

It was the slightly panicked voice in her ear that put the memories aside.

"Are you all right, ma'am?" The young navigator sounded concerned. "I don't know if you've noticed, but we're starting to drift a bit off course."

"Tell me what you see, Lieutenant."

"Ma'am?"

"Look around and tell me what you see." She aimed them farther north and was confronted by even more blue skies.

"Nothing, ma'am." If his breathing was any indication, her relaxed chuckle ringing in his helmet had driven his nerves up a couple of notches instead of reassuring him. "Blue skies, Lieutenant. It's the one thing God made for all of us to enjoy no matter what name you call Him by."

"All that wonder confronting you, and your answer is nothing?"

"I'm sorry, Commander." The answer was tentative.

"Do you see anything else?"

"No clouds?" He sounded as if this was a test that none of the crew in the simulator told him about before sending him out with Berkley.

"That'd be a great answer if I'd asked you what you don't see."

"Sorry, ma'am."

"Sorry won't bring your pilot back when you don't also see the bogey coming up on us at five o'clock either, Harvey." Berkley heard Lieutenant Harvey Whittle gasp as she went into a set of rolls to get away from their pursuer. When she leveled off their bogey was now in front of them.

One quick press of the trigger on the throttle and the computer eliminated the slick young hotshot trying to sneak up on them. She then banked again hard to the left and avoided the trap the young fliers had set. Their objective had been to sacrifice one in order to get their main target, which was her. It was a game, after all, and they could land that afternoon bragging how one of them had done the impossible—brought down the one flyer who had yet to be caught in the crosshairs during these training sessions.

"Still with me, Harvey?"

"I'm trying my best, ma'am, but I'm getting a little dizzy. That's usually not a problem, but none of the other pilots I've gone up with have put so many moves into their flying."

"Uh-huh." She pitched them forward into a dive that made it seem like they were on a roller coaster more than a jet. "You haven't christened the seat back there, have you?"

"No, ma'am."

"Good. Keep an eye on that guy on our ass, will you please? Trust me, Harvey, it'll keep your mind off your breakfast." The mountains of northern Nevada got very close as she flew lower to the ground than their commander liked, but she knew she wasn't about to hit one of the protruding rocks.

"Cletus, get your ass above fifteen hundred feet," the tower broke in.

"Aye, aye, sir." It felt like she slammed the brakes on and Berkley could almost hear the plane that had been on their tail scrape the glass when they overshot them. "Ask and you shall receive." She then climbed in a hard bank to the right trying to draw her opponent out in an attempt to get him to start thinking like a seasoned combat pilot. With the move she had just put on him, it would have been the easiest thing in the world to just finish him off.

"What are you waiting for, ma'am?" Harvey now sounded more engaged in the process.

"You sound impatient."

"Sorry, I didn't mean to tell you what to do."

"I didn't say I didn't like it, did I?" She laughed again. "Good to hear you've gotten over a major bout of timidness and started to open your mouth."

"He's circling back around, ma'am."

"Good job. Now keep your eye on the bouncing ball." Before he could ask what she meant they went into another dive, flying through a canyon that Berkley was sure the hotshot behind her wasn't going to follow her into.

Pilots like Lieutenant David "Blazer" Morris were good, but most of the time they were predictable. It was Berkley's job to knock some of that cockiness away and teach them to be better than good. It was her job to make them Top Guns.

"Still with me, Harvey?"

"Yes, ma'am, and I still have Blazer in sight. He's behind us but hasn't entered the canyon." A wall of rock was coming up, and she had no choice but to gain some altitude. When she did the young pilot behind her would have a clear shot. "He's locking in, ma'am."

"Of course he is. Are you a gambler, Whittle?"

"I like playing poker. Why?"

She laughed again and accelerated a little. "Well, we have to gamble that we can fly out of here before we hit those rocks, not hit Blazer, and not get shot down." While Berkley could hear the computer's warning of the lock Blazer had on them, she was more interested in something else in the front of them. Seemingly only inches from their demise, Berkley saw what she was after and pulled back on the stick, bringing them shooting out of the canyon like a bottle rocket on the Fourth of July.

A soft "fuck" came through her headset from Harvey when they heard Blazer and his navigator celebrating their kill, having gotten off a shot before Berkley could take any more defensive maneuvers. "I'm sorry, ma'am. I feel like I've let you down."

"I appreciate that, but don't be so quick to count us out."

"Cletus." The radio cracked to life again.

"Yes, sir." She started back to the base taking the long way around for a few more minutes of flying time to work on her craft. Way out of sight of the brass she did a series of rolls that she was sure made Whittle wish he'd skipped the Spanish omelet that morning. Flying was her religion, and just as those who prayed to demonstrate their devotion to

God, she showed her devotion to flying by trying to become as perfect as she could, no matter the situation.

"Let's call it a day. So bring Whittle back before the boy has a nervous breakdown."

"Yes, sir."

The F-18 came to a stop and the ground crew was waiting with the ladder to help them out of the cockpit. A hundred yards from them, Blazer was being congratulated by his peers for being the first to score a kill against the legendary pilot they'd chased all day.

The backslapping continued as Berkley's feet hit the tarmac and she shook out her short dark brown hair. Even if she had been perturbed by the display, she wouldn't let them see it in her eyes, and she covered them with Maui Jim sunglasses.

"In the conference room, ladies, unless the party has already begun and you can't spare the time," Berkley said as she walked by.

All the students snapped to attention and gave her a rousing, "No, ma'am."

CHAPTER TWO

Blazer, what did you learn today?" Captain William Percy "Rattler" Jepson stood at the front of the room in a uniform so starched it seemed it would crack when he moved. Will had been the commander of the Top Gun school for fifteen years and rarely took to the skies anymore. He did have an eye for talent when it came to combat pilots and culled the best of what the armed services had to offer to help him teach the next generation to be exceptional.

"If you keep at it, sir, any bogey can be brought down." Blazer cut his eyes toward Berkley. "No matter how good they *think* they are."

"Boy, stop talking before I ground you until the next millennium." The monitor at the front of the room came to life and the computer records of what had happened that day were cued up. "You thought you'd sacrifice your wingman for the glory of the kill. If I were Cobra, I'd request never to be sent up with you again." The first pilot taken out that day at the end of Berkley's computer guns nodded slightly. "The score you were after learned a long time ago that teamwork is what gets the job done. Impressive flying trying to keep up with her, though."

His words belied his statement as the footage from the camera in Berkley's plane was cued up. More than one of the pilots in the room cringed when the onboard monitor showed just how close the canyon she had flown through actually was. No one's eyes were wider than Harvey's. He was pressing his hands so hard into his desk his fingers were purple.

"Answer me one more question, Lieutenant Morris. Can a ghost shoot someone down?"

"Sir, I'm sorry. I don't understand the question."

"Am I speaking in tongue, boy? Can a fucking ghost shoot someone down?"

"No, sir, not that I know of." Blazer's face flushed scarlet and his hands clenched to fists. Will stared at him, and Berkley could tell the young pilot wasn't used to being made fun of and that the laughter around him was starting to piss him off.

"Then you can apologize to your fellow fliers for bragging about bringing Cletus down."

"I shot her fair and square. That you can't take away from me."

The computer cut to some different footage showing both Berkley's and Will's computers in a split screen. Just before she came screaming out of the canyon, Will's smaller and faster plane had zeroed in on Blazer and knocked him out of the game. "If you're dead before you get the shot off, it don't count, boy. Cletus used the same tactics you used on her to give her wingman the shot. Because in the end she knows dead is dead no matter who pulls the trigger."

"So you see, Whittle, why I don't want you to ever take your eye off the target," Berkley whispered to her navigator sitting next to her. "Had you been looking back, if we'd been in his situation, you'd have spotted Rattler before he was able to get that shot off. You'll always be the eyes in the back of the head of any pilot you fly with, so don't let them down."

"Thank you, ma'am." Whittle straightened up in his chair. "Would you mind if I had lunch with you, Commander?"

"Sure, the chipped beef around here is better tried with backup."

They stepped out into the heat of Nevada and headed to the mess hall. The khaki uniforms helped with the dry, hot air, but still it could be felt through the cotton material. They finished going through the line and picked a table next to the wall of glass that gave them a good view of the mountains in the distance.

"Can I ask you something, ma'am?"

"You can give it a shot, but I'm not promising I'll answer."

He pushed the mashed potatoes around on his plate and didn't look up after that. "Why'd you pick me to go up with you today? I'm not exactly in your league."

"My dad flew for the Navy with a young guy named Whittle, and I believe his first name was Harvey. He told me it was like having someone glued to your ass the whole time they were in the air, and it made him feel like he had a guardian angel on his butt." Her knuckles wrapping on the table made him finally raise his head. "Is he a friend of yours?"

"He's my dad, ma'am. He saw some action and he got hooked on the adrenaline rush, so it took him a while to settle down and have a family. The way he speaks about the military made me feel he would be disappointed in me if I didn't give it a shot. Unfortunately for him, I inherited my mother's coordination, so it kept me out of the cockpit."

"I'll tell you a secret." She leaned forward and staged whispered her next line. "The person in the hopper seat is just as important as the pilot. Don't let people like Blazer or Cobra tell you otherwise. If their backseats had been giving good advice today, we'd still be out there trying to outmaneuver each other."

"Thanks for that, ma'am."

"We need to do two things before you head back to the barracks today, Whittle."

He grinned and sat up straighter in his chair. "Whatever you like, ma'am."

"First." She held up her finger and pointed it at him. "You can call me Cletus or Berkley. If you're going to be my backseat, I can't have you wasting time trying to get out Commander or ma'am." Another finger went up and she smiled to soften the reprimands. "We need a new name for you."

"You can call me Whittle, ma'am. I really don't mind." She shook her head, and he backtracked. "Sorry, Berkley."

"I'll give you until the morning to pick a flyer name. If not I'll do it for you."

"Can I ask you one more thing?"

"Sure, I'm in a generous mood today."

"With the way you fly, why didn't you pick some name like Viper or Killer? Cletus isn't exactly very menacing sounding." She leaned in and told him the story behind the name, enjoying the way his head fell back when he gave her a big belly laugh.

"Thanks for telling me, and I promise I'll work on the name tonight."

"See you in the morning, and don't forget to pay attention during the rest of today's classes. Blazer got his ass handed to him in that conference room today, so he'll be really gunning for us tomorrow."

❖

"How'd it feel up there today, boss?" Berkley put her feet on the desk in Will's office and looked at the pictures covering his wall. More than a few had her father's smiling face as he stood next to Will in front of a slew of different planes.

"Like it did when I could keep a hard-on for more than two seconds."

"Ever hear the expression too much information, sir?" She laughed at his straightforward nature. If she had to guess, Will never really noticed that she was a woman, and had never treated her any differently than any other pilot who had come through the program.

"Fuck off, Cletus, and tell me what you thought of the new group, since I figured this first exercise would've stretched past an hour. Imagine my surprise that my ass hadn't warmed the seat yet when we were done."

"A lot of egos to contend with, but when isn't it like that? Tomorrow we'll go through some maneuvers before we head back to the chase. Should make them start to think like part of the wheel instead of one of the cogs."

"I was looking at Whittle while you were up there today. The boy was a shade of sickly green for most of the flight. Want to admit you were wrong on that application and change out tomorrow?" He picked up a file on his desk and opened it. "There's a kid from Lincoln that's supposed to be pretty good."

"You leave Whittle alone. He'll be fine. He's a bit nerdy, but he'll turn out to be a great backseat. You'll see."

"Get your ass out of here, then, and I'll see you in the morning. If you're not busy, Rose wants you at our house tomorrow for dinner. She's trying a new recipe for enchiladas."

"Mexican food?" Berkley put her hand on her stomach and felt the need to stock up on antacids. Will's wife Rose wasn't known for her skill in the kitchen.

"Mexican food, and I'm not going in alone, so don't think about making any excuses of why you can't come."

"The last time she tried that we were out for a couple of days.

I love Rose to death, but would it kill you to give the woman some cooking lessons for her birthday?"

"And admit to her that she can't cook? I'm not that brave, wiseass. Get out of here before I find some way to sneak my food onto your plate. We'll meet in the morning to map out the exercises for tomorrow."

"If they go anything like today, you might consider a few days in the classroom as a way to get their attention. Nothing brings some of these little ones into line faster than taking their toys away."

"That's true, since you pout better than any two-year-old, and before you think of a smart-ass reply to that, remember that you could be sitting in there with them."

She stood and gave him a casual salute before heading out to the old Jeep she drove. It was a purchase she'd made at an army surplus auction and had spent a few summers restoring it. From what the previous owner had said, the 1943 vehicle had seen action in France during the war.

Rebuilding the engine and getting her hands dirty had allowed her to get her mind to focus on the task instead of on the demons that haunted her thoughts when she sat idle. After getting her wings and serving six years in every dangerous situation Uncle Sam needed taken care of, Berkley had given up the live ammo for the computer-simulated rounds of Fallon.

The position at Top Gun was coveted but perfect for Berkley, who in her career had never turned down any assignment and never failed to put herself in any position to get her team home safe. In Fallon the constant pressure situations they practiced had elevated her talent to a point that no one had brought her down yet.

At this point in her life the moments in the cockpit were enough to make her forget what she didn't have when her feet were on the ground, and it's where Berkley planned to finish her naval career since she knew the life of a naval pilot was over almost as fast as the planes they flew. The day your eyesight weakened and your reflexes slowed was the day you had to leave the cockpit to the younger, more able pilots.

But a naval career had been something she'd worked hard on for a very long time, and while she still had a passion for it, the same wasn't true for most everything else. Like Harvey, the choice of enlisting hadn't been difficult for her since her father's life in the service was something he had used as bedtime stories. She'd wanted the same excitement he'd told her about when he was known as Fearless. That was his nickname in the cockpit, and what he'd tried to instill in her.

Her parents had been *gifted* with four daughters, as her father liked to say. That they didn't have a boy was never an issue of disappointment for him from the moment Berkley arrived with a head full of brown, poker-straight hair, screaming like the room was on fire. The story was that when the nurse on duty had come out and handed Commander Levine the newly born Berkley, it was the first time the macho guy had shed tears in public. She was followed by sisters Ann and Willow, all of them eleven months apart, and when Berkley was five her parents had come home with Suzette.

Commander Corbin Levine had been a devoted father to all his girls, but everyone knew how attached he was to the one brunette in his brood. His gangly kid, who'd topped out at six two, had become a star athlete, model student, and talented pilot. His friends teased him unmercifully for the size of his smile when Berkley graduated top in her class from the Naval Academy, assuring she would follow in his footsteps into the cockpit of the meanest machines on the planet. She wasn't the Navy's first female combat pilot, but she was one of the best they'd ever trained.

Berkley's sisters, Anna, Willow, and Suzette, went on to work for their mother's family in New Orleans when her father was stationed at the Belle Chase Air Station to finish his career. All of her siblings were married with children, and the next generation was still populated with red hair and green eyes, leaving Corbin and Berkley as the only two with pale blue eyes that contrasted nicely with their dark chestnut hair.

The large family had given Berkley a sense of place that had been important because her father's assignments had moved them enough that she had trouble remembering all the locations. Her father had taught her honor, service, and commitment to country—all the things that defined him and his duty, but had also encouraged her to choose what was important in her life.

Her mother had given her the thirst to expand her horizons beyond what she found in the cockpit, and also the example that even though she'd picked the life of the wanderer, as her father had done, there was the possibility for a great love affair. Both of her parents bragged about them in different ways, and when her mom talked about her, the best description was that Berkley had an outlook on life that both thrilled and terrified her because she feared so little. But it was what had attracted her mom to her father when they met, so when it was Berkley's turn to love, whoever it was would be damned lucky. It was that lesson in risking her heart that had brought her to Fallon.

❖

After stopping at the grocery store for a steak and ingredients to make a salad, Berkley drove home to the ranch house she was leasing right outside of town. When the Jeep came to a stop, her golden retriever jumped off the porch and ran to the vehicle, putting his two front paws on the side.

"Hey, Junior," Berkley grabbed her bag and kept it out of his reach. The dog had been a gift from her father and was the great-grandson of the best hunting dog her father had ever owned.

With the front gate closed, Berkley went to change so she could fire up the pit. While the coals got hot she spent some time throwing Junior his ball. When she put his toy in her pocket Junior went inside and pulled open the fridge by the towel Berkley kept on the handle and carefully clutched a beer in his teeth and brought it out. He knew this kind of fetching game would get him a treat later. He gave the beer to her and sat away from the fire to watch Berkley cook. Their menu was limited because of Berkley's cooking talents, but anything tasted better cooked over an open flame—at least that's what her mother had told her when she'd come out and helped her set up the house.

Her mom had spent a month with Berkley on the pretext of helping her unpack and to teach her a few things now that the Navy wouldn't be providing every meal. Berkley had enjoyed having her around as much as her mom had needed to feel like the self-sufficient sailor she'd raised still needed her. When her mother left, the closets in the house were in order, the boxes unpacked, a new grill sat in the backyard, and in the kitchen she'd left a list of things Berkley could throw on the grill and instructions for how to season them.

She ate her meal in silence, splitting her steak with Junior and watching the sunset from the back deck. After she washed the dishes and refilled Junior's water dish, Berkley sat in the backyard with another beer and looked up at the stars. Her life wasn't full, but it was enough for now. In the quiet moments like this she not only missed her family, but missed having someone to share her time with. That would have to wait until the sting of her first serious relationship was forgotten, and then there was that little hiccup that the Navy frowned on her telling them all about what she desired in a partner. Up to that point they hadn't asked and she hadn't told.

"You know, Junior," she said as she scratched the dog behind his ear, "I can sense when I've got someone trying to fuck me over up there," she pointed at the sky with the bottle in her hand, "but when that great instinct really mattered, I pretty much put myself in the crosshairs and didn't know it until the bomb hit."

The phone rang. "Levine," she answered, surprised at the late hour.

"Make sure you polish your shoes before coming in tomorrow," Will barked at her. "I just got word we're getting a visit tomorrow from a Captain Sullivan. He's heading up the newest carrier the Navy put in the water and he's shopping for crew. The suits feel like there's a situation brewing in the east and the USS *Jefferson* is going to be sailing right into the middle of it." The suits he'd referred to were the idiots in the Pentagon who liked to play war but had never donned the uniform. For men like her father and Will who'd seen more action than they cared to in a lifetime, the suits were the bane of their existence.

"I'll make sure I look all nice and shiny, then." She hung up the phone and leaned against the wall, releasing a long breath. "It couldn't be, but with my luck it is. Shit."

CHAPTER THREE

The next morning Berkley headed to her office down the hall from Will's to get some paperwork done. If the brass was here looking for crew, they'd want updated files on the pilots they had on hand.

"They're ready in the small conference room, Commander." The secretary the instructors all shared poked her head into Berkley's office and gave her the notice.

"Thanks. Let Will know I'll be in as soon as I'm done with Blazer's file." When she finished printing out the reports, Berkley stood and smoothed down the front of her uniform, having made sure to put on all the ribbons and commendations for exemplary service the Navy had given her through the years. She knew her audience and decided to play her part of the perfect naval aviator.

When she stepped into the room the only other people present were her fellow instructors. Before she could say good morning, Will's assistant stepped into the room and snapped everyone to attention. "Officer on deck."

Berkley saw the arms of her crewmen quiver as if they were coming down from their salutes when a very feminine voice said, "At ease, please take your seats."

Just as it had on the day they met, the first thing that struck her about Captain Aidan Sullivan was that she was short. She was short and resembled a California surfer more than she did a naval officer with her blond hair, tanned skin, and blue eyes. Her only other distinguishing feature was the hard set to her mouth as if she found very few things in life humorous.

"Thank you for giving me a few minutes of your day," Aidan started, giving each person in the room a brief look, her eyes straying in Berkley's direction just a bit longer than the rest. "I'll try to be as brief as I can since Captain Jepson has informed me you have training flights this morning. The Navy has allowed me to hand-pick my personnel for the upcoming mission, and I thought I'd start at the greatest talent pool."

"Captain Sullivan would like volunteers from the instructor pool first, then with your help she'd like a frank evaluation of the students we have on hand as well as past participants. We're looking at about a three-month hop if all goes according to plan, but even if it takes longer, your position here will be secure should you decide to go," Will added. From the way he clipped his words, Berkley could tell he was pissed with the news, but would follow orders.

"This information doesn't leave this room, people. We have a situation off the North Korean coast at the moment that the Pentagon might order some action on before it gets any further out of hand. This could all come to nothing, but for now we're treating this seriously," Aidan said. The two officers with her put the first picture on the screen at the far side of the room.

"We're thinking of sending in a team of perhaps six pilots to take out this target." A laser pointer in Aidan's hand circled a building in the upper right-hand corner of the satellite image, then to the building to the west of it, each on a small island. "Within these facilities the regime has moved its nuclear program and the scientists who have it on the fast track. The Pentagon figures from recent intelligence, if left unhindered, the North Koreans will have launch capability in less than eight months. If action is warranted after all diplomatic means have failed, taking out the facility as well as its personnel would put them years behind in getting to that point."

"Those islands belong to the North Koreans?" Will asked. "From the reports I got on this, there was a question about that."

"During recent talks between the UN inspectors and the Korean ambassador, their government insisted for the first time in history the islands were the property of China, but it's North Korean personnel in the boats regularly patrolling the waters around them, so we figure it's only a tactic to delay anyone from inspecting the facilities for as long as possible."

"According to CNN, the North Koreans are cooperating with UN demands to dismantle their nuclear program," Berkley said, her eyes on the screen, working out scenarios in her head for how it could be done. She wasn't going on this mission, but it was hard to turn off that part of her brain.

"Don't believe everything you see on television, Commander. What I'm sharing with you now is the latest satellite photos we have, so we know the intelligence is sound."

Berkley could feel Aidan's eyes on her, but she refused to give her the satisfaction of acknowledging her. "That's comforting, but I hope you realize the ramifications from any action in this region. You try and fail, and they will retaliate with something like a dirty bomb in the middle of Manhattan. This isn't your average nutcase you're dealing with here, it's more like a heightened case of crazy."

"Thank you for your concern, and I, as well as the U.S. government, understand all the reactions that could come from any actions on our part."

"Good. What's your plan of action, then?" Berkley asked.

"The *Jefferson* will sail in under the pretense of an invitation from China and South Korea to participate in some naval exercises since both countries don't want to see this program any further along than our government. Once we're in place if it's still a go we'll launch from the Sea of Japan. It'll be up to the team leader to fly across South Korean airspace undetected to the two locations in the Yellow Sea since we believe North Korea monitors any movement in the sky, even to the south." Sullivan got to the point in short order and waited for questions.

"Ambitious, but doable," Berkley said.

"Thank you for the information, ma'am," Will said. "My crew has a ten o'clock training hop this morning. So if there's anything else they need to know we'll meet after lunch to go over it." Will's comment was a clear dismissal to the instructors in the room. "After what happened yesterday, I'd like the gloves to come off today, gentlemen. If this is the *Jefferson*'s first mission it'll be hell to pull off, so let's get them sharp." His eyes never left Berkley as he spoke. "Are you up for it, Cletus?"

"I'm always up for it, sir." The men sitting with Berkley laughed since they knew how lethal she was in the sky. "How about you, boss?"

"With the arrival of our guests, I wasn't planning on it. But then again, how better for Captain Sullivan to observe everyone's skill level up close and personal?"

"Ma'am," Berkley said as she headed for the door.

"What do you say, Captain Sullivan, how about a short flight today?" Will asked.

"I suppose you're right. There's no better way to see what your people are capable of than from the air." When she heard both Berkley and Will chuckle, Aidan turned her head from one to the other. "Is there something humorous that I'm missing, Commander?"

In her time in the Navy Aidan had developed a tolerance for pilots, but people who laughed at her expense shortened her fuse. More than one seaman had learned the meaning of swabbing the decks after a run-in with her. The men in her command attributed her bitchiness to keeping control in a male-dominated world.

"No, ma'am." Berkley gave Aidan her best smile. "If you're going up with Rattler, going up on BE day is a good day to do it."

"Should I even ask?" Aidan turned to Will.

"The students who make it here are the best of the best. These young people are the top one percent when it comes to talent, and with that comes a certain amount of ego."

"I know what the *E* stands for, then, so what's the *B*?"

"Breaking their egos only helps them elevate their game. Something like when you were a kid and told someone, 'you're good but I'm better.' Knowing that there's someone better than you motivates you to try harder," Berkley said.

"And is there anyone better than you, Commander?" Aidan's mouth turned up ever so slightly in a smile, but just as quickly it disappeared as her eyes stayed locked to Berkley's.

"No, ma'am, there isn't. There can be only one king of the mountain, and in Fallon, Nevada, her name is Cletus." Her parting salute was sharp, but the smile never left Berkley's face.

"Are all of you egotistical maniacs?" Aidan asked Will.

"My definition of an egotist is someone who can't back up their claims except in words. That definition, ma'am, would in no way apply to the pilot who just walked out of here."

"We'll see."

"What'd you come up with, Harvey?" Berkley asked. They had all geared up and were walking to their planes carrying their helmets.

"What do you think of Raven?"

"I think it sounds like a Poe piece." She slapped him on the back before heading up the ladder and getting situated in the cockpit. Not wanting to be obvious, she barely glanced at Aidan who looked incredibly attractive in her flight suit climbing into Rattler's backseat. Berkley could tell that Captain Sullivan had taken them all by surprise since everyone from Will on down was expecting an older man with the swagger that came from getting his own carrier commission. "I'll give you one more chance, then I'll come up with something. Stay away from the bird family. It's been overdone."

"Yes, ma'am." Harvey gave the ground crewman a thumbs-up to close the hatch.

"You ready to go hunting, Whittle?"

"Yes, ma'am, happy to be here."

"Keep your eye on our ass. Rattler is joining us again today, and when we land we'd better have more kills than him. I'd hate to take it out on you by tying you to the back of my Jeep for a jog tonight."

"Not going to happen. I've got you covered, Cletus."

"Cletus, this is the tower. You're cleared for takeoff whenever you're ready."

"Roger that. Heading out on runway two." She lined them up and punched the throttle, slamming Harvey and her into the seats as the plane picked up speed. Behind her, ten planes followed, holding students and their navigators.

Berkley had given them all assignments that if followed would make it difficult for her or Rattler to start picking them off one at a time. The problem was if they would stay together. The previous day's performance didn't give her a lot of confidence her orders would be followed. When everyone was a star, no one was willing to bring up the rear.

"To our left, Cletus," Whittle reported. At his warning she banked hard and was able to take both planes out in the middle of a roll. Just as quickly as she came out of it, they were facing Blazer and she pulled the trigger again before gaining altitude. She'd taken out the semester's biggest hotshot in what amounted to a game of chicken and quicker reflexes.

The next three were flying in the formation she'd ordered them to fly in. Slowly, she drew them south and toward the mountains. "Cletus, the deck today is ten thousand feet. Go below that and Rattler will take you out of the game." The tower's warning came as she leveled out at fifteen thousand feet. No one hugged the ground better than her, but today she would have to contend with the expanse of blue skies with not a cloud in sight, again giving every team still up there essentially nowhere to hide.

"Roger that." She turned a little to the west looking for Rattler. "Tell me what you see, Harvey."

"Three at five o'clock and Rattler directly behind us, just not in range."

She went into another set of rolls and was able to take out one of the wingmen in the formation before Rattler took out the other despite the other pilots' attempts to outmaneuver them and engage. Dropping too close to the deck minimum, she picked up altitude just as quickly and surprised the last man in the now dead formation. "That makes six."

"The computer shows Rattler took out one other one," Harvey said, sounding like he was getting more into his role.

"Three to go, then, let's go find them."

❖

"Holy shit," Aidan said, obviously amazed at Berkley's display of acrobatics. "She still flies that thing like it's an extension of her body."

Less than an hour later the only two planes left in the air were Berkley's and Will's. When he flew past her, Berkley was more than happy to take his wing, ready to follow him wherever he wanted to lead.

"Captain Jepson?" Aidan said.

"Yes, ma'am?" He waved as Cletus took the lead and headed south. "You doing okay back there?"

"Just fine, but I was wondering if you were going to land this thing anytime soon?"

"One more thing, then I promise I'll put you on the ground safe and sound."

"I just thought..." The words died on Aidan's lips as Will banked hard to the left and Berkley's plane came close to theirs as she flew in from the other direction. Aidan was able to strangle the scream before it came out at the sudden unexpected move, and had only relaxed her hands when Will reversed their direction and rolled until their plane was flying with its belly facing the sky. Below them Berkley and Whittle gave them a salute before dropping their elevation enough for Will to even out.

"Was that necessary?" Aidan asked.

"To the victor go the spoils, Captain, so yes, it was totally necessary," Will said before radioing the tower they were headed back in.

Aidan and Will spent the rest of the afternoon in his office going over personnel files, including his instructors' information. The posts at the Top Gun facility were some of the most coveted because everyone who aspired to fly knew what the title of Top Gun meant, and the positions were given up only when an instructor was ready for something new. With the changing times, though, the government was willing to cull from wherever to win the war on terrorism.

The engine of the Jeep starting outside made Aidan's head pop up and she watched as Berkley drove away. "I'm sorry, what?"

Will turned to see what she was staring at and laughed. "I asked if there was anything else you needed before your briefings tomorrow?"

"Just one more thing," she said, her eyes never leaving the fading vehicle.

CHAPTER FOUR

On impulse, Berkley turned in the opposite direction from her house and headed toward the café in town for dinner. The day had been not a complete surprise since Will had mentioned Aidan's name the night before, but seeing her again had brought back the flood of memories from the time they'd shared.

In the booth facing the back of the restaurant, Berkley couldn't help but dredge up the time she'd spent stationed in Hawaii—a time in her life that she spent an inordinate amount of energy trying to forget.

Pearl Harbor Naval Station, Eight Years Before

The transport plane came to a stop in front of one of the big hangars near the fence line at the southern end of the base, and Berkley's new commanding officer was waiting for her and the other four pilots who had made the trip from Pensacola with her. This was going to be her first assignment after all the training she'd had to undergo.

"Welcome to Pearl Harbor, people," the captain said and shook hands with all of them.

"Glad to be here, sir," Berkley said.

"We have a little exercise set up this afternoon if you all are up to it." He looked at his watch and nodded. "It'll give you enough time to drop your stuff off and grab some lunch."

"Just name the time, sir." Berkley spoke for her group. She was sure the option was there to turn him down, but her father had warned her from the day she'd applied to the Naval Academy that the way to make the time easier was to start off on the right note. "We'll be there."

By 1400 they were in the air and going through patrols and exercises with evasive maneuvers with some of the senior pilots, and the captain had assigned Berkley to fly point. She glanced at the outline of the islands and the blue water of the Pacific, and then to the radar to try to find any sign of the beta team.

"Anything behind us, Killer?" Berkley asked the pilot bringing up the rear.

"Not yet."

She was in the process of swinging away from land when the instruments lit up momentarily, meaning that she'd been shot down by the computer and it hadn't come from the sky but from the water. "What the fuck was that?"

"I don't know," her backseat said, "but just look for the shithead bragging about it and you'll know who did it."

The person going on about it at dinner that night was the newly promoted Commander Aidan Sullivan. Any bad feelings about getting sidelined so easily evaporated, not because Berkley found herself instantly in love, but because she took a good look at the braggart.

"Were you able to reach the trigger or did you need a step stool?" she asked Aidan. That immediately sent the teasing remarks in another direction until Berkley told everyone to stop.

By morning she knew Aidan's history and just who her father was. Asking the daughter of Admiral Preston "Triton" Sullivan out for coffee the day after she met her wasn't the smart choice, as her father would've warned, but Berkley was curious. Triton was the man in charge of the Pacific fleet, and if her curiosity was misinterpreted then she was sure Aidan would have permission from the self-proclaimed son of Poseidon to shoot her down using live rounds.

"Why?" Aidan asked the next morning.

"Why not?" Berkley said after the short response to a coffee date. The little blond dynamo had her hands on her hips and was staring at her like the ulterior motive she obviously had for asking was being scrolled across her hairline.

"I get off duty at six," Aidan said and then wrote her address on Berkley's hand and dismissed her.

Coffee was changed to dinner that they ordered in that night at Aidan's apartment off base, and if asking a superior officer wasn't the smart choice—sleeping with her on that first date certainly was grounds for pleading insanity at your court-martial.

That was what had happened, though, and it didn't take much longer for Berkley to give away her heart to the woman who not only could be trusted with it, considering their positions, but who understood her. When you knew why someone served and what the consequences could be, it was a good foundation to a lasting relationship.

It's what Berkley had wanted even if she had to hide it from the world. It had been worth the risk because Aidan was the one her mother had promised would come along. She loved Aidan with no reservations until Aidan asked her to dinner that last night and said they had to break it off.

Berkley had listened to the reasons, then requested the reassignment. After a few years she landed in Fallon. It was the one place she didn't have to worry about seeing Aidan again until she was ready. Only now Aidan hadn't even given her the gift of what she felt was an adequate time to heal.

❖

Fallon, Nevada

Junior didn't come running right away, but it was dark and Berkley figured he was asleep on the sofa. She headed inside even after hearing the car door slam behind her. The only invitation she provided was to leave the front door open as she headed for the deck outside for some stargazing before bed.

"Is this why you threw your career away?" Aidan said. Berkley took the beer that she offered before looking up at her. "You never mentioned the house and the dog in any of your letters."

"Not all of us are so career-minded, Captain Sullivan, but if you think it's easy becoming the lead pilot here, then I suggest you try and see how it works out for you." She held her bottle up in salute before she took a long swallow. "The dog and the house I didn't mention because I realized you wouldn't be interested in something so…mundane."

"I saw you up there today, Cletus. You still love the chase—up there with your hair on fire and your ass in that seat. That kind of passion is hard to hide. You may be a teacher now, but you're still the best the Navy has in the sky and you should be using that talent to make a difference, especially in the times we live in."

"I don't mean to sound rude, but what the hell do you know about me? You think just because you got one brief glimpse today that you know all about me? When you sail off to find that glory you're so interested in, the pilots who are going to get it done for you will do so and hopefully get back safe, and it will be because of something they learned here from someone like me, so save the sermons."

"Something traumatic must have happened then, because once upon a time you craved the chase that wasn't simulated and you were more career-minded than I was. And that's saying something."

"No one actively serving is as career-minded as you, Captain. If you need it explained to you, all I can say is shit happens, and it changes your perspective on what's important. For me it was simple."

"All right, I'll play along. What happened to make you change?"

"Easy, I wanted to be somewhere that I made a difference and there was no way I'd have to see you again. Is that a good enough answer for you, Captain?"

Aidan felt as if someone had pushed her into a cold pool. "That's not fair, Berkley."

"Now that's something we can both agree on. What happened was fucked up and definitely not fair, but I didn't get a vote. If your memory's faulty, let me remind you that all of it was your idea."

Aidan drummed her fingers on the bottle and leaned back on the deck railing. "I thought *our* decision was mutual."

"Mutual? Are you kidding? When someone tells you to fuck off because they have better things to do, it's not a joint decision. That's your superior officer putting you back in your place once the fun was over."

"If you felt that way you should've called me and I would've come and set things right so that we were both okay with it." Aidan took a breath and Berkley remembered that it was her way of reining in her emotions. "It wasn't forever."

Berkley laughed and slammed her drink on the deck floor hard enough that it echoed across the emptiness of the yard. "I must be pretty dense, then, first for falling for the bullshit you fed me for months about what a great future we'd have, then for not catching the fact that your dumping me was only temporary. Aidan, I'm not interested in scratching your itch whenever you find the time to see me, then go back to you pretending you don't know me. It's been four years. I figured you found another scratching post."

Aidan dropped into the seat across from Berkley and said, "Ouch."

"I'm taking lessons from your playbook and ripping the bandage off quick. I don't mean to hurt your feelings, but let's be frank. Things have changed." She finished her beer before turning and giving Aidan a smile. "I'm not going to lie to you and say that I don't care about you anymore. I do. What we had was special and you were a lot of fun, but that's over. And I know for damn sure I don't fit into your life, and I'm way past begging even if that were a possibility. It's not."

"If you give me a chance, you might find that I've changed from the ambitious naval officer you once knew."

Berkley laughed and reached over to brush away the hair from Aidan's forehead. "Twelve years after graduation and you get the helm of the fastest and best carrier in the fleet. I don't think you've changed too much." When Aidan lowered her head Berkley reeled from the criticism. In reality the hurt had gotten to a point she felt she could close this chapter of her life and move on. Forgetting was an impossibility, but she'd show Aidan a hell of a lot more compassion than she'd gotten. "Ambition isn't a bad thing, darlin'. What we had together was something I'm never going to forget, but you have to admit that it would've gotten in the way of the career you've built for yourself. If there isn't anyone questionable in your life, then there's nothing for you to tell, and nothing for the brass to give you shit over."

"You haven't called me darlin' since that night in Hawaii," Aidan said.

"I haven't done a lot since that night, starting with not believing anything you say when it comes to commitment or what you feel for me." Then again perhaps she wasn't as big about this as she'd thought, as she couldn't help taking another shot at Aidan.

"Do you hate me that much?"

"I don't hate you, but after you left me, I don't owe you any explanations on my feelings at all."

"That's not exactly the way I remember it," Aidan said with heat.

"Close enough though, right?" Berkley said and sighed. "Look, I'm proud of you, and you're going to do great. Having a woman at the helm had to happen sooner or later, and I'm glad the Navy chose you. Having you break down the barriers that seemed impenetrable means it'll be that much easier for the next talented officer who wants her chance. It was worth the sacrifices you had to make, even if I'm one of the things on that list. So I don't hate you, but when I got that first letter from you, writing back was easier. I stepped away because I knew the Navy would always win over me, and playing second fiddle isn't in me, Captain."

Berkley was sure that Aidan still didn't realize that the part of herself she'd given away so freely when she'd fallen in love was something no woman before her had come close to getting from her. But that's what you did when you found the person you thought would be the one common factor in the rest of your days. She'd never thought to question what her future was going to be because she'd believed Aidan when she said she loved her. It's why what had happened had totally blindsided her.

They had made plans for a romantic dinner, but that morning Aidan received word of her next promotion. The lure of eventually having those four gold bars and silver eagle on her uniform had erased a lot of other things from her mind, Berkley being the first on the list. At least it was the impression she'd given Berkley at the time with some of the idiotic things she'd said during their meal. She'd led off with what a problem their relationship was going to be if she were asked about it.

But Berkley was right, Aidan wanted to be truthful about her personal life when the brass asked before they gave her the rank she'd need for her own ship one day. Now the USS *Jefferson* was her reward for giving up the one person who'd stolen her heart, but it was a hollow victory. She felt like shit that she didn't figure it out before Berkley flew out of her life, literally. Berkley hadn't returned a phone call or request to see her again after their last night together, no matter how many times she'd asked.

Their only communication was the letters that came often enough to make her feel like Berkley still cared, but sporadically enough to send the message that there was no going back. She'd kept a stack of them and she'd read them enough to have memorized every line, hoping to glean some hidden message that Berkley was still in love with her.

"Does it help you to understand any better if I told you I was wrong?" Aidan asked. "And that I'm sorry?"

"Thanks for coming out here and saying it. It does help, but why waste your time? What we had seems like a lifetime ago and now we're in different places." Berkley stood and offered Aidan a hand up, intent on walking her to the door. "I'll help you assemble the team you need to stock the *Jefferson*, then I'm going to stand on the pier and wave good-bye."

Aidan looked at their physical link and remembered how Berkley's large, warm hands made her feel. For the profession they had chosen it was forbidden, but temptation sometimes was like the song of the Sirens—impossible to ignore. It stripped away your reason and called to the part of your heart that wanted the comfort that came from giving in when you were this close to the person who owned you.

"We're in the same place now," Aidan said. She moved closer and ran her other hand up Berkley's chest until it came to rest at the base of her neck. "I've missed you, baby. Please don't turn me away. You're the reason I'm here."

"Am I? Why?" Berkley let her go and took three steps back.

"I love the sea. I'm not going to deny that. And the fact the Navy trusted me with the *Jefferson* was an honor, but honor doesn't make me feel alive." She moved closer until their bodies were touching. "Not the way I felt when I was in your arms. I miss you. Besides, I only got this as a gimmick to show what an equal opportunity organization the Navy is. I know better than to think I got it on merit. The new president promised change, and he rammed it down their throats."

"That's not true, and this isn't going to happen." Berkley was up against the railing, so she gently backed Aidan up.

"It is true, but I plan to give it my best no matter why they gave it to me." Aidan didn't try to touch her again, but she did move closer. "That's not what I'm here to talk to you about, though."

"I'm not interested, Aidan, so back off." Berkley stepped around her and faced the open land behind the house. "I'm many things, but I'm not an idiot. You only get one chance to throw me away, and you did it in spectacular form."

"That was the worst mistake of my life, and I've paid for it every day since. I didn't understand what losing someone truly was until I stupidly gave away what we had."

"You didn't lose me, Aidan, you laid it all out for me over a plate of shrimp so that I couldn't make a scene and mess up your perfect little script of how things should be," Berkley said. "I felt like an item on your to-do list you had to check off before you left for more important things. It's like I came between you calling a moving company and turning off your utilities."

"That's not true."

"I was there, so I'm not making this shit up." Berkley turned and glared at her so intently it made Aidan drop her gaze. "I do know what losing's all about. You educated me so well that it's hard to forget, so get back to your successful job and leave me the hell alone." Almost as suddenly as Berkley's temper flared, it quickly died. "Just get out. you're not worth getting upset over anymore."

Aidan didn't back down and took a chance since there was no way Berkley was going to make the first move that would get them past the hurt. She stood on the tips of her toes and kissed Berkley, slipping her tongue into her mouth when Berkley opened it a little to protest. The moan Berkley released made Aidan's nipples tighten, and she took one of Berkley's hands and put it on her chest as encouragement to explore. There had been no one else after Berkley and there never would be if she could help it, but her dreams weren't enough anymore.

"Please, baby, I've waited so long for you," Aidan said.

"Am I supposed to roll over and give you what you want because of a few pretty words?" Berkley pushed her away with a little more force this time. "That's more insulting than breaking up with me in a restaurant." Berkley's face appeared set in stone, and if the kiss had softened her any, her emotions were back in place.

"I know you don't have any reason to believe me," Aidan said, then laughed. "Jesus, that sounds so clichéd. You don't, but if it takes me turning in my resignation to prove how serious I am, I'll do it." Nothing she said made Berkley change her expression. "I'm serious."

"There's no need for grandiose gestures or flowery promises. You're going to sail the *Jefferson* and I'm going to stay here and teach spoiled little boys who think they have something to prove." Berkley stared at her so intently that Aidan felt as if she was looking right through her. "I don't have shit to prove to anyone, especially you."

"You can say you don't, but you really do hate me, don't you?" Aidan let loose some of her self-control. The tears started slowly, but soon they turned to sobs, and before she could turn completely toward the door she found herself back in Berkley's arms. The only one who had ever seen this side of her was Berkley, and being strong all the time was tiring.

"Aidan, I'll tell you as many times as it takes to sink in," Berkley said as she ran her hands up and down Aidan's back. "I don't hate you, but you also don't get to walk back into my life four years after you decided I wasn't worth another thought, and expect to pick up again just because you think it's time."

"I've thought of nothing else from the first morning I woke up alone."

"And yet you show up about twelve thousand days later. I'm sure you put more thought into getting promoted to captain," Berkley said and dropped her arms. She didn't push Aidan away, but she did let her go like she was too fatigued to deal with her anymore.

"I tried to call," Aidan said and pointed at Berkley. "You can recall every mistake I made, but you don't get to conveniently omit the things I tried to do to make up for my mistakes."

"You manage to promote yourself into the helm of the *Jefferson*, and I'm sure you could tell me about every rivet on that monster, not exactly the kind of energy you put into making anything up to me. It's time to give up that dream. We've been apart so long you don't know if you'll even fit into my life now."

Aidan tightened her arms around Berkley's waist like it was a life preserver in rough seas. "I know where you were from the moment you left, and I know you well enough that there's no way you change the most essential part of yourself to the point that I wouldn't love you. I tried, Berkley, I really did. I tried to make what I did right, but all you ever responded to were the letters." She reached up and placed her fingers under Berkley's chin to make her look at her. "If you felt that strongly about it, why respond in any way at all?"

"You know why," Berkley said as if to utter the words meant defeat. "From the moment I met you I knew we'd be linked somehow until one of us was dead. I wasn't the one who tried to sever it, but despite the hurt I couldn't let go completely."

"If even a little part of you feels like that now, could you let me in just that little bit? I swear on all we both believe in that you won't be sorry."

"This conversation has gone on long enough to make me sorry, Aidan." Berkley tilted her upper body away from her. "If I give in now, all this would turn into is a one-night stand, and I'm not that desperate. Like I said, I'm not stupid enough to think I'd win out over the ambition that drives you, so I'm not going to set myself up for you to knock down again."

"One night is the last thing I want." Aidan caressed the side of Berkley's face. "I'm selfish in that I want them all, but forever has to start somewhere." She felt Berkley relax enough so she could bring her down for another kiss.

Berkley had been right that it had taken her almost no time to realize Berkley was the one person she wanted. That first day they'd met in Hawaii was all it took, and no matter how hard she worked to erase Berkley from her heart, it had been impossible.

"I know how controlled you are when you're flying, even if it doesn't look that way, but what I'm asking is for you to let some of that go and trust what your heart's telling you."

"Are you sure you want me to do that?" Berkley laughed. "Because for once my head and my chest are in total agreement, and it's to show you the door."

"I'll go easy on you, then." Aidan brought her hand to the front of Berkley's waist. "You tell me you don't want me and I'll go."

Berkley didn't answer her and didn't make a move to stop her when Aidan unfastened her belt. In the stillness of the night the zipper of Berkley's pants sounded unusually loud. "Tell me you're not as turned on as I am and I'll leave. It'll kill me, but I'll do it."

She briefly lost eye contact with Berkley as she opened the khaki pants enough to see the white underwear underneath. "Tell me to stop." Since Berkley hadn't moved away yet, Aidan reached inside and slumped against Berkley when she discovered how hard she was.

"See? Not all of you forgot me." Seeing Berkley shiver in the cold night air, Aidan took Berkley's hand and led her into the house. She pushed Berkley against the kitchen counter, then followed Berkley's pants and briefs to the ground. When she glanced up she felt like she'd gone back in time when she saw what appeared to be adoration on Berkley's face. "When I'm alone I think of you like this, and I remember how much you wanted me and my touch."

Berkley's head screamed what a mistake this was. Aidan had been almost impossible to forget, much less get over—that was actually something she was still working on, and she willed herself to act. She lifted Aidan off her knees and meant to push her away again before the situation got any further out of control. It was the tears and the soft "please" that put the first cracks in her resolve, but the anger was hard to let go of, and she forced herself to move Aidan's hand.

"You need to go," Berkley said, and felt exposed in more ways than just having her pants around her ankles.

"I'll beg if I have to," Aidan said and reached behind her to unzip her skirt. It fell around her plain black shoes and Berkley couldn't help but laugh. Along with her body's response to Aidan, there was something else that hadn't changed.

The Navy might have issued all parts of her uniform, but the underwear was where Aidan was rebellious. Silk, navy blue bikinis were definitely not government issue, but they were incredibly sexy.

"What do you do on the days you have to go in for a physical?" Berkley asked.

"Don't worry. You're the only one who knows about this particular quirk of mine. The doctor thinks I'm as plain as everyone else in their Navy whites." Aidan stripped off her underwear and reached for Berkley's hand. "Touch me."

Berkley gave in to the request but held back the gentle touch she once shared with Aidan, and after kicking her feet free she picked Aidan up, carried her into the living room, and laid her on the sofa. She could've insisted that Aidan leave, but she'd been out in the cold so long that she'd almost forgotten what it was like to have the warm skin of a lover under her fingers.

With one hand Berkley unclasped Aidan's bra and let it fall to the ground. She paused to enjoy the two pink and very alert nipples before sucking one into her mouth. She was holding herself just above Aidan, and when she sucked a little harder Aidan tipped her hips up seeking some relief. Her wetness painted Berkley's stomach, but Berkley wasn't ready to stop the slow torture she'd started.

"Please touch me," Aidan said.

"You may outrank me, but you're going to have to be patient. I'll touch you, but the way I want." The rocking of Aidan's hips was starting to speed up, so Berkley let go of the nipple with a pop. "If you come you're going to be sorry."

"That's what you think. I'm close enough that it won't take much, so touch me." Aidan finished her plea with a pinch to Berkley's nipple as motivation. She then lowered her hands and opened herself to Berkley. "See what you do to me? Come on, I'm wet and it's all for you."

The sight of Aidan like this was too good to ignore. Berkley left her perch and moved down. She held Aidan's hands in place, liking the access it gave her. She lowered her head and put her hands under Aidan's firm bottom. Aidan moaned when she dragged the tip of her tongue from the opening up and around the hard clitoris.

"Stop teasing me," Aidan said when she lifted her head and met Berkley's eyes. Not another coherent word came out of her mouth when Berkley did as she asked and sucked her in. As much as she had wanted it, Aidan was disappointed that it was over so fast. She had wanted Berkley from the moment she saw her snap to attention that morning, and she couldn't hold back the orgasm.

The next thing she knew she was wrapped up in Berkley's embrace and she was sobbing. "I've got you," Berkley cooed to her. "It's all right."

"I'm sorry, I didn't mean to fall apart on you. It's nothing you did, I just missed you."

"Either I'm better than I remember or you haven't done this in a while." Berkley swept away the hair that had matted on Aidan's forehead and then wiped away her tears.

"I may've been a bitch, but you can't seriously mean that. I haven't done this since the last night we were together."

"Been that busy, have you?" Berkley said, unable to hold back her sarcasm. She drew small circles with her finger on Aidan's chest.

"Don't make light of it. I have been working hard, but there hasn't been anyone else." Berkley's inhaled breath could only mean she was about to disagree with her, so Aidan lifted up a little and placed her hand over her mouth. "It has nothing to do with the military and their archaic rules. We could flip burgers for a living and it would be you that

I'd still be waiting for. I missed you, so it made having someone else in my life impossible."

Berkley's eyebrows rose as if the admission had stunned her.

"I might've been raised on the water, but it doesn't come close to how free I feel when we're together like this." Aidan swept her hair down Berkley's body. "How privileged I am that it's me you've picked to share yourself with," she said as her fingers slipped inside.

Berkley closed her eyes and lost herself in the pleasure Aidan gave so willingly in that one moment, but it wasn't the same as when she was in love with her. Her body relaxed after the orgasm, but Berkley had held back for good reason.

This was one night, and she wasn't crazy or naïve enough to hope otherwise. Thinking like that would only lead to complications and self-inflicted wounds when she watched Aidan sail away. Again.

CHAPTER FIVE

"Commander." Will's assistant casually saluted Berkley when she stepped into the building the next morning. "Captain Jepson would like to see you, ma'am."

Berkley was still a little tired from the hours of sleep she'd missed, but she felt the pleasant ache in some of her muscles and put the slight fatigue aside. Her body was sated, but the nagging feeling that she'd made a colossal mistake had been gnawing at her since their night had ended with her walking Aidan to her car and kissing her good night at around midnight.

Aidan had made more than one promise as the night progressed, but Berkley wasn't putting too much faith in any pretty words Aidan spun about the future. Experience had been lesson enough on that score, and if Aidan had been driven before, now that she was the poster girl for the "new Navy" she'd be relentless to be the perfect naval officer and to hell with anyone who got in the way of that.

"No, now I keep my pants on until she leaves, and she will leave, and I'll be fine," she said to herself as she made her way to Will's office.

"Good morning, sir," she said to Will. "Ma'am," she said as she saluted Aidan. "You asked to see me."

There were files scattered over Will's desk of the candidates who had attended Top Gun the last two years. Most were now serving on carriers scattered around the globe with a few assigned to shore bases after tours in Iraq. Berkley followed Will's line of vision when he didn't respond, surprised to find her name on the top folder.

"Captain Sullivan has expressed her strong desire in recruiting you to be her team leader on the upcoming mission," he said.

"Did she?" Berkley said and brought her shoulders back.

"Berkley—" Aidan said her name, but Berkley talked over her.

"Funny how this is the first I'm hearing about it." She would never embarrass Aidan, but somewhere between their first kiss and getting dressed hours later would've been a good time to broach the subject. "Sir, could you give us a few minutes?" Berkley said to Will.

"I was going to tell you…" Aidan just fell silent when Berkley glared at her once they were alone.

"Save it. Save the lies and the come-ons because you're wasting your breath. You want to save the world, have at it, but leave me out of it. I'm not some project for you to fix, Aidan. I told you last night why I'm here, and you believing I'm wasting my talents isn't going to change what happened and how I'm dealing with it."

"I have the authority to pull you—"

"Do you really want to finish that statement? You do and you prove me right about what a liar you are. I'm such an idiot." Berkley shook her head. "You're going to pretend you're the perfect officer now. Your have the ability to erase the most interesting things from your memory when it's convenient to you, doesn't it? What would Daddy have to say about that?"

"That was uncalled for, so leave my father out of this." Aidan's eyes closed to slits, and just as quickly her anger died away. "Berk, listen to reason. I need you with me on this. I don't trust anyone else to do this right."

"Is that what last night was about? Fuck good old, stupid Ber—" The slap snapped her head to the side.

"Try that with someone else, Commander, but with me you know better. I may love the Navy, but I'm not about to whore myself for it."

"Yes, ma'am." Berkley snapped to attention and saluted. There was no need for a formal dismissal, and she wasn't waiting for one.

"Damn, that went well." Aidan sat and picked up Berkley's file. Her hand still stung from the slap, but the real sting was to her heart. She knew it wasn't going to be easy when she decided to make this trip, but the level of hostility Berkley displayed was not what she was expecting. All her life Aidan had excelled at everything she'd tried, and the only thing that had ever derailed her was Berkley and the swell of emotion she was capable of creating within her. "Only now it feels more like root canal work than anything remotely romantic."

❖

Berkley headed for the hangers and tried to slow her breathing to a rate resembling something normal. She hadn't believed the promises from the night before, but having Aidan play her so blatantly was something she hadn't expected either.

"Cletus, will you slow down, goddammit?" Will called after her when she ignored him the first three times.

"You could've shot her down before I even got here this morning, so what's this shit about me leading this crap?"

He took off his cap and scratched his forehead. "That wasn't my call, it was yours, and I guess you just made it." She was so pissed that she didn't respond. "You know every crew around here would trade their left nut for something like this, and it wasn't going to come from me that you didn't want to go. It makes me sound like I think you're a little woman who needs a man thinking for her. Fuck, had I done that you know you'd have been the first one to put my ass in a vise."

"If this were for anyone else, I might," she put her finger up, "*might* consider it, but I will not fly for that woman under any circumstances. And if you want to ask me why, you aren't going to like the answer, so I suggest you steer clear of that one."

He put his hand on her shoulder and gently squeezed. "Like I said, I told her that it was up to you and not to put the screws to you no matter how badly she wants this. I'd do that for any of my people, so it wasn't charity for a kid I love like my own. Let me know if Captain Hard Ass in there gives you any more shit about this. She may outrank you, but no one's going to be whistlin' up my ass."

"That's what I love about you, sir. Your way with words."

"Fuck off and get back to work."

❖

The methodic clicking sound of weights as Berkley lifted and lowered them in chest presses was helping her concentrate on something other than how her day was going. The room was empty except for another pilot jogging on a treadmill.

"It's good to know you're still somewhat predictable," Aidan said in a soft voice, not wanting to be heard by anyone but Berkley.

"Which part of me?" Berkley sat up after placing the bar back and wiped her face. "The part that fell for what you were selling last night or the part that likes to exercise when I'm upset?"

"The first insult was enough, Cletus, you don't have to belabor the point." The bench next to Berkley's let out a woof of air when Aidan dropped into it. "Can I invite you out to lunch just to talk?"

"There isn't anything to talk about, Captain. You told me over and over again from almost the first moment we met that your life is made up of the choices you make. They define you, your honor and your code, and I eventually learned that nothing or no one will get in the way of that. We both made choices that have led us to this point, and in my mind they aren't wrong. They might hurt like hell, but they weren't wrong. I'm just asking you not to punish me for mine, and I'll return the favor." She threw the towel in the hamper and stood. Her gray shorts and T-shirt were damp with sweat.

"Just lunch, and we don't have to talk at all. Don't make me beg, please."

"Meet me outside in twenty minutes and then you can get back to the job you're here to do. Trying to change my mind is a waste of time, and I'm sure the Navy has you on a tight schedule for what needs to be done as far as your assignment goes."

Aidan watched her head for the showers but stayed on the weight bench after she glanced behind her to see if the man was still there. He was still running at a good clip, not paying any attention to anything but his workout. "The future is what I want to talk about, Berk, and I need you present for that conversation."

CHAPTER SIX

The diner only had a few other customers scattered throughout the place since it was still early for lunch, but the hostess still seemed happy to see Berkley as she held the door open for Aidan. She gave them the most private table she had available after asking how Berkley had been.

"Come here often?" Aidan asked.

"I like the fries."

"Still eat them with salty ketchup and a plain burger?"

"I do, but everyone in my family picked up some of my dad's strange eating habits, so it's not as unique as you think." Berkley leaned back and smiled at the waitress who put down the two iced teas they'd ordered.

The bowl of peanuts on the table held Aidan's interest. She didn't want to look Berkley in the eye since she practically bristled from anger. "I never got to meet your family, so I'll have to take your word for it. Maybe we could rectify that soon."

"Why would you want to do that?" There was no sarcasm in Berkley's voice—only a bit of curiosity. "Our lives are on different paths is why I'm asking."

"You say that like it's a bad thing."

Berkley slowly stirred her tea, her eyes on the open window beside them. "I used to think that it was."

"The operative word being *used* to?"

"When someone is passionate about something and works hard to achieve it, I now see that as something to be admired, Captain. Your path and mine split, and while part of me is proud of you, the part you threw away so easily has been slow in catching up."

"If that's what you think, that it was easy, then I really did fuck up worse than I thought. It was anything but." Aidan pressed back into her chair but kept her hands wrapped around her drink. "Thank you for being honest, though, and I guess this really is lunch."

"What were you expecting here?"

"Nothing but silly hopes, but I see now there's no forgiveness for the stupid."

The waitress interrupted them to take their order, leaving Aidan's statement hanging between them. She had sounded so bleak that Berkley quickly gave the girl her order ready to be rid of her.

"What happened wasn't all your fault, Aidan. If I'd tried harder to change your mind, who knows where we'd be, but it's different now. We had a great time, and it's been great seeing you again, but last night is all there's going to be between us."

"Is it because of that one night in Hawaii?"

Berkley sighed before taking a sip of her drink. "Yes and no. A lot has happened to me in the time we were together and I can honestly say I'm not the same person. Eventually, my feelings will fade to something that doesn't give me a massive headache when they cross my mind, but I haven't made peace with the past that belonged to us. I know that and I can accept it'll get better with time, but it isn't your job to get me there."

Aidan reached across the table and put her hand on Berkley's forearm. "What about having someone in your life?"

"I don't know how to answer that." She pulled back wanting to distance herself from Aidan's touch. "It doesn't help that I picked a career that makes that possibility something to fear."

"You're a pilot. There are other choices."

Berkley laughed but not out of humor. "You're a sailor, so I could say the same of you."

"You could and my answer would be to say you're right. It all comes down to what you want and what'll be most fulfilling." Her hands went back to her glass. "Maybe when I make those choices, then I'll have time to reflect on the mistakes I made when I got my priorities mixed up. Then maybe you'll believe I'm serious."

"That's up to you. I just want to concentrate on getting you prepared as much as possible for what you have to do. That's all you should have on your mind, and what I think or believe about it all isn't important." Berkley smiled up at the waitress as she put down their food.

"Like I said, Commander, there's no forgiveness for the stupid. Not really anyway."

"I'm sure you'll be fine, at least that's the impression you always gave me."

Aiden didn't respond, not wanting to start a fight that would land them back at square one. They ate and returned to the base. The rest of their afternoon started with another training flight, and Aidan again rode with Will so she could observe the team in action. At Will's request some of their other past outstanding students who were close enough to Nevada flew in to join in on the fun. With the priority status the Pentagon had placed on Aidan's mission, she had the right to transfer anyone she wanted to the *Jefferson*.

At the end of the day all the pilots landed again complaining since there was only one plane left in the sky. The better the talent pool in the sky, the more Berkley seemed to excel, but it made no difference in changing her mind.

❖

"Are you free for dinner tonight?" Aidan asked when Berkley had changed out of her flight suit and returned to the office.

"I was going out to a local pizza place later, but you can join me if you want," Berkley said, to Aidan's surprise.

"I'd like that. Want me to pick you up?"

Berkley shook her head and picked up her bag. "I'll swing by and get you. That way you can change. This place's pretty causal."

Forty minutes later Berkley stopped in front of the barracks Aidan had been assigned to where she was waiting outside talking to Will. "Stay away from the spicy sausage, Captain, and you won't be up all night," Will said. "Cletus, your buddies in the maintenance hangar asked that you stop by in the morning if you have the chance. They're tearing down the engine on the old Russian MiG and they need some opinions."

"Let them know I'll be there early. Thanks for letting me know," Berkley said and shook her head slightly when Will kept staring at the back of Aidan's head and lifted his eyebrows as if asking if he needed to talk to her on Berkley's behalf.

"Ready to go, Captain," Berkley told Aidan.

"I'm not complaining that I have you all to myself for a little while anyway." As they pulled away Aidan put her hand on Berkley's knee and smiled when Berkley made no attempt to move it.

"At the threat of sounding like someone who doesn't want to confuse you, I'm not complaining either. I may still be smarting over what happened between us, but it's been nice seeing you again," Berkley said as she turned into the pizza place. Aidan's smile only widened when she told her to wait while she went in and ordered to go.

With dinner on the backseat, Berkley headed out of town and turned off on a dirt road. Less than a mile down the wooded road opened up to a small lake, and when she shut the engine off it was utterly quiet.

"This is one of the few places I've ever been that proves to me there's a God." Berkley leaned on the steering wheel and spoke softly. "Not even the cockpit is this peaceful and beautiful."

"Thanks for sharing it with me."

"I've used this place to try to put my life back in order a brick at a time, as it were. Before you ship off I thought you might need something like this to remember in the coming days. What they're asking you to do, Aidan, could lead to something big if anything goes wrong. I wasn't just telling you that to give you a hard time."

"Are you trying to talk me out of it?"

Berkley laughed at the answer. "I'm not delusional. When it comes to you, if there's a choice between something or someone and the Navy. The Navy will always win out."

"The Navy has gotten the last sixteen years of my life if you count the Academy, and after this assignment they'll get no more. I'm going to sail the *Jefferson*, get the job done, and retire." The scenery held her attention as she spoke. "That's why I came here to talk to you. I could've sent my second to select the flight crew, so thanks again for agreeing to have dinner with me."

"Talk to me about what?" Berkley wrapped her fingers around Aidan's wrist trying to get her to face her.

"You're my greatest regret, Berk. When I left Hawaii, I kept trying to convince myself it was for the best." She laughed as she shook her head. "I figured we were young and it would've never worked out, but damn if I can erase you from my mind. You're imprinted in my heart."

"Our lives are different now. We're different people, and I don't know how we reconcile our differences to plan a future together." Berkley tightened her hold on Aidan's wrist. "Are you sure you want to retire? The helm of the *Jefferson* was given to you. Does it really matter why? You should be asking yourself what can come of it instead of considering quitting. You're spectacular at what you do, so don't throw your career away on romantic notions."

"Is that what we were together? A romantic notion?"

"We were great together, but like I said, that was then and we were two very different people."

Without losing contact with Berkley, Aidan moved closer and pressed her lips against hers. Her kiss was readily accepted and when they parted she put her palm against Berkley's cheek.

"Maybe I should use my time with you reminding you of that young naval aviator. That *was* then, but we're still the same when it comes to our feelings. You just need some reminding. Lucky for you I'm nothing if not persistent in getting the things I want."

"That kid has a lot of miles on her, and she sure as hell isn't as idealistic anymore."

Aidan caressed her cheek before she opened her door. "We'll see."

The only response Berkley gave her was a laugh before she reached for the pizza box. They ate sitting close to each other, cuddling close beneath a blanket Berkley had brought along, talking about the scenery and how Berkley enjoyed the area, Aidan wanting to give her a little time for what she'd said to sink in. The sun had gone down when they returned to the base.

A vehicle pulled up next to them as Aidan got out of Berkley's Jeep and a young man hopped out of the driver's side. "Commander, sorry to disturb you, ma'am, but you have some visitors at the gate. Captain Jepson wanted me to tell you he's going to escort them to the mess hall for coffee."

"Thanks, Sergeant."

"Expecting someone?" Aidan asked.

"No, but it's my lucky week for visitors. It's probably some more guys wanting to impress you, Captain, so if you're not tired you can come with me and I'll make the introductions."

They walked since they were so close, and Aidan almost tripped over a chair when she saw the man seated and talking with Will. There was some graying around his temples but it didn't take away from how handsome he was. Next to him sat a petite redhead laughing at something Will had told her. The woman had to be Berkley's mother, though there was no resemblance to her. That couldn't be said of Corbin Levine.

The naval pilot still retained that rigid posture the military had perfected in him, and when he turned and looked in her direction Aidan found the genetic origins of Berkley's appearance. They shared the same strong jaw, straight nose, tall build and blue eyes.

"Aidan, this is my dad, Captain Corbin Levine," Berkley said after she hugged both of them, "and my mom, Maggie."

"It's a pleasure to finally meet you two. Berkley's told me so much about you over the years, I feel as if I know you."

"How about we get acquainted, then?" Maggie said when Corbin just stood silently next to her looking at Berkley.

"Come on, Mrs. Levine, I'll get us a cup of coffee."

"Take a walk with me, Cletus," Corbin finally said.

"I'd ask what you're doing here, but I have a feeling I'll be wasting my breath since you'd never give Will up." She pointed him in the direction of the parked planes once they were outside, knowing how much he loved admiring them. "Are you here to make sure I don't go, or to make sure I don't screw up the opportunity to go?"

"I'm here so that you don't make the decision for all the wrong reasons."

"I don't follow."

He put his hand on her shoulder and jerked her to a stop. "You're damn right you don't. I raised you to be a leader no matter what the situation, and up to this one moment I've never been disappointed in you."

"You're upset that I'm not going, then," she said and let out a long breath.

"I didn't raise you to hide in a little pond. You've been the shit around here, but it's time to decide if you want to continue to be the big fish or move on. That goes for the Navy and for all the other reasons you're here. I've gotten a slew of calls about this and the guys who make the decisions want you, so it's not all about the little woman trying to get you on that boat. I just thought it'd be better coming from me."

"I don't mean to be disrespectful, Dad, but back off. If you're on a recruiting mission give the spiel to someone else."

He stopped and crossed his arms over his chest. "Are you done, or do you need to add a fuck you to the end of that?"

"I'd never do that, but accept that we handle things differently and I know that the bit about the little woman has more of Mom written all over it than you."

"You think whatever you like, Cletus, but your mama isn't the only one interested in your happiness. Life kicks you in the ass sometimes, and it's how you get up and fight back that makes the difference." He starting walking again and put his hand on her shoulder. "You tell me right now that you aren't the best the Navy's got and I'll leave you alone."

"And if I tell you I'm not?"

"I'd tell you that you're lying to your father, and if you're okay with that, then I'll guess I'll have to accept it."

"Thanks, Dad, I'll keep that in mind, but it's not going to change how I feel. The big fish has a little more swimming to do. Eventually the right assignment will put me back in the field, but for now I'm happy here."

"Before you say that and they pass you over, take a little more time, Cletus." Her father walked out of the hangar to Berkley's Jeep and crossed his arms over his chest. "For once don't give a damn as to what everyone else wants from you. You do what you think's right and the rest will fall out if not this time, then the next. The world's become a dangerous place, so there'll be other chances."

"You flew here just to tell me that?" Berkley laughed, but it was more sarcastic than humorous.

"I flew out here because you're my kid and I love you, and because an old friend asked me to help do some training. Do you honestly think I'd push you into doing something you don't want to? Your job is to bury me with honors, not the other way around." He placed his hand on the front of the Jeep. "If this girl clouds your mind that much, then skip this go-round, but don't use that as an excuse to not do something you want so bad. Hell, I can taste it."

ALI VALI

"How do you know that?"

"Same way I knew you weren't going to throw up on me when you begged me to take you on that roller coaster when you were six."

"Sorry, Dad, but I'm getting tired of people doing my thinking for me."

"Let me add my nickel to that pile, then I'll take your mother and get the hell out of here if you want." Berkley laughed and relaxed a little at his words. "Taking what this girl's offering you is what *I* think will make you happy, but that's not what you should be thinking of now."

She leaned against the vehicle and copied his pose. "So what should I be thinking about?"

"When I was a young obnoxious pup in that white uniform, I only thought about one thing."

Berkley laughed knowing what kind of response she usually got in the uniform. "How many girls you could pick up?"

The crack earned her a slap on the back and his deep, heartfelt laugh. "Yeah, besides that." He moved closer and put his arm around her. "It's what I had trained for all that time and I was ready to go because it was my duty, and why I'd signed up." With a squeeze he released her and turned so they were facing each other. "Unless you feel exactly like that, you tell them to shove this assignment right up the ass. If that's what you do decide, I'll be happy to back you up."

"A little part of me wants this, but it's smaller than the part of me that thinks I'm not ready to balance what needs to be done and who I'll be doing it with. And if I have any doubt, I know I should turn it down."

"Who's king of the mountain here, Cletus?"

Standing before her now was Captain Levine, not her father. "Me, sir," she didn't hesitate to answer.

"Ain't no fucking higher mountain in the world, Commander, so don't talk about not being ready. You're my kid and I trained you to keep your word and do your job." He put his hand on the side of her neck and softened his tone. "Just know that I'll be proud of you no matter what."

"Thanks, Dad." She put her hand over his and knew he was sincere by the peaceful appearance of his face.

"Then take your time and give Captain Sullivan an answer *you* can live with."

"Are you sure *you* can live with my answer?"

He nodded and stood to start their walk back. "Like I said, Cletus, you make this decision for you and only you. If you do then I'll be a happy son of a bitch because I'll know you made it from your heart and your gut. Either way, you make me proud."

Berkley nodded in return and they walked the rest of the way in silence. Inside the mess hall her mom stood and joined her dad when he announced it was time to turn in and Berkley's guest room was waiting.

After she said good night, Aidan accepted Berkley's offer to walk her to her room. "You okay?" she asked when they were finally alone.

"My father's here to give me a trip to the woodshed, Corbin Levine style."

"Is this a regular thing, or does it have to do with the evils of blondes in the Navy who want to date you?" Aidan said as a joke.

"One of the things you and my father have in common is the strict code of duty you uphold for the position you have. He came to remind me that I'm here by choice and it's time I remembered that."

Aidan stopped Berkley by grabbing her forearm at the front door of the building. "The last thing I want is for you to come with me out of a sense of obligation to him, the Navy, and especially me."

"You should be happy. He's trying to make me see what I'm passing up if I turn you down."

Aidan didn't say anything but led Berkley to her room and shut the door. "I want you to listen to me, okay?" She stood close to Berkley but didn't touch her. "The reason I came was for me first, and you don't have to say anything after I'm done. Leaving you was the worst mistake of my life, and I intend to make it right. You and I are meant to be together, because if we weren't, this feeling of something important missing from my heart would've disappeared by now. I don't know if that's the case for you, but I know what I need to be happy, and I'm going to keep trying until you either agree with me or tell me there's no chance."

"What if I tell you there isn't?"

"Then I'll have to accept that and live with the certainty that the rest of my life will be manageable but incomplete." Aidan still didn't move to touch her, but looked directly into Berkley's eyes. "What I can't accept is your agreement to come with me unless you're absolutely sure that the piece of your heart that makes you the best in the sky is there and beating strong. If I can't have you, I'll try to learn to live with it, but I'll take comfort in knowing you're somewhere doing something you love. I wouldn't survive it if you don't come back."

"The best answer I have is to tell you that I'll sleep on it. I know you don't have a lot of time so I'll let you know in the morning."

Before Berkley turned to go Aidan stopped her again and kissed her. "Would it be too much to ask for you to think about the rest of what I want?"

"I'm not sure about the rest, Aidan. It's flattering to know how committed you say you are, but it's a lot of history to overcome."

"Not all the history was bad, though."

"No, it wasn't, and it's what made that missing part you talked about impossible to recreate." Berkley smiled after she said it. "That's the best I can give you for now."

"That's good enough." Aidan lifted Berkley's hand and kissed her knuckles. "The thing I have going for me is you might not totally like me, but your heart hasn't forgotten me."

"Good night," Berkley said and kissed her forehead. "I'll see you in the morning."

CHAPTER SEVEN

Berkley headed back to the base at ten after five the next morning after her restlessness drove her out of bed. The trip was quick, with few other cars out in the early morning. After she returned the guard's salute at the front gate, she drove to the building where Aidan was staying.

The door to Aidan's room opened quickly after she knocked almost as if she was expected. "Is everything all right?" Aidan asked, her hand still on the knob as she stood there in her pajamas.

"I've been up for an hour and I got tired of staring at my ceiling. I hope I'm not bothering you." The room was small, so Berkley took the desk chair after Aidan let her in.

"Are your parents okay? It didn't sound like you were expecting them," Aidan said, and sat on the end of the bunk.

"They're fine. They're only here for the reasons I told you last night. My dad lives to give advice when it comes to the big decisions." Berkley ran her hands down her thighs to her knees. "It's nice since he doesn't expect me to just fall in line. Then there's the chance to climb back in the cockpit for a couple of days of fun."

The comment made Aidan feel that she would be leaving alone. Berkley had made her decision and she'd have to do her best to accept it. "You said no," she said as a way to give Berkley an out. "What help did you need with that?" The question was an observation that held no malice. "I meant what I said. As soon as I'm done, I'll be back to finish our talk."

"I'll need all the information you have on this because I know for security reasons you held back some," Berkley said and held up her index finger. "I want the list of pilots you've already recruited." She held up the next finger. "And I want your word that the ship is yours, but the flight mission and the few pilots I'm bringing are my responsibility."

"Are you sure?"

"About which part?" Berkley asked and rubbed the middle of Aidan's forehead with her thumb. "Relax, Captain."

"I mean are you sure you want to do this? You weren't interested before yesterday."

"If you're willing to take a chance on me I'm not going to let you down, if that's what you're worried about." She accepted Aidan's hand. "Three years here is enough and I'm ready to move on."

Aidan squeezed Berkley's fingers and placed her other hand over her heart. "You have my word I'll respect your judgment, and I'm going to do whatever it takes to make this easier for you."

"I'll give you my best, but I appreciate your support."

"That's good enough for me, but I want you to be sure this is what you want," Aidan said again.

"My dad's right. My life here has become too complacent." Berkley glanced away as she admitted that.

"Your life's been what it's needed to be, and there's a lot of pilots out there that are better for it."

"Say things like that, Captain, and I almost believe you do understand me," Berkley said with a smile. "The other good thing about taking this job is that we'll have plenty of time to get to know each other again. After it's done you might not like where I end up."

Aidan nodded and laughed. "Yeah, I'm sure that's true. But the only way I see that is if you became a serial killer in your spare time, so get used to the fact that I plan an all-out attack."

"Duly noted, but hold off for now since we have a lot to do." Berkley pointed to the window where the sky was starting to lighten. "When can we go over your intel?"

"Let's meet today in the conference room before your first training flight. After you see what needs to be done I'll accept whatever answer you have for me, but I want you to be sure because this isn't going to be easy. If it's yes, then how much more time will you need?"

"Depends on who makes the final cut and on the best way to get to the Korean facilities in the spots you showed us already." She took a moment to study Aidan's face before she let go and stood. "Another week should do it, so if you want to, shove off and the team and I will be right behind you."

"I'll stay on for a couple more days, then I have to go. There are some Pentagon meetings I have to attend next week." Wanting some contact with her, Aidan stepped closer and put her arms around Berkley's waist. "Thank you for even considering this. In the end the world probably won't know how brave you are, but I will. And I also know you aren't doing it for the glory."

"I have enough shiny stuff on my uniform, you're right about that."

"I just feel better with you in the lead up there. Anything that goes wrong will only escalate an already bad situation, and you know what kind of nut we're dealing with. I want to get in and out without starting a war that'll keep me from the life I want."

"That's my plan as well, so no worries." She kissed Aidan's forehead almost as a reflex response to something her heart remembered, but for once the memories brought no pain.

"What life do you want?" Aidan asked.

"One lived with little regret that makes me look forward to tomorrow."

"If you promise to take me on a date I might have some suggestions for you."

"You do, huh?" Berkley asked.

"That I do, and the thing you should concentrate on is how fun I am on a date. But only do that when your feet are on the ground. When you're in that hell machine I want you to pay attention to what you're doing so you stay in this great-looking package."

"I'll go so you can get ready." Berkley kissed her forehead again and released her. "I'll see you later on to go over everything."

CHAPTER EIGHT

As I mentioned at our first meeting, you'll have two targets."
Aidan put a satellite photo on the large screen at the front of
the room. "With constant satellite surveillance on the two locations,
we know that Kim Jong Il has concentrated his research and testing to
these two areas."

"Were the radiation tests positive from the test Jong Il said he
already conducted?" Berkley asked.

"The radiation levels did rise in the mountain section we pinpointed
on the mainland, and from the intel we've collected, we think he has
enough material to conduct perhaps seven more rounds of testing."
Aidan clicked to the next photo that showed trucks hauling material
after being loaded on the large docks on the northern side of the islands.
"What President Khalid understands and is afraid of now is a North
Korean sale of nuclear material and intelligence to a country like Iran.
A move like that would destabilize an already bad situation in Iraq. I
don't have to tell you how that situation would change if the suicide
bombers start using dirty bombs."

"Has the Chinese government been briefed on this?"

"Those talks have taken place, I just wasn't privy to them." She
turned the projector off and went to sit next to Berkley. "Now that
you've seen all this, what do you think?"

"I'm coming with you, Captain, no need to hard sell me."

Since they were both aware of the guard Aidan had posted on the
door and instructed not to let anyone in, she threaded her fingers with
Berkley's. "I'm going to hard sell you on getting you to admit that you

still love me, but not this. I need you to be as sure of this as you'll need to be when it comes to giving me an answer about our future."

"I'm sure about this job, Aidan. As for us, these past few days reminded me a lot of when we first met and how. It also reminded me of the things I think are important. I'll do everything in my power to make sure you pull this off without a problem, and the rest will come in due time or not at all, but like this mission, it can't be forced. I'm coming with you, though, and while you're sailing us around we'll have time for all those talks you keep going on about. But trust is a fragile thing, and once it's broken it has a way of showing cracks no matter how well you think you put it back together."

"Uh-huh." Aidan squeezed her fingers and leaned over and appeared ready to kiss her but stopped at the very last moment before their lips touched. "If the other night proved anything to you it's how good we are together, so we'll see who cracks first."

"It's not going to be me, so behave."

Aidan did give her a quick peck before pointing to the northern site again. "In my opinion, and after watching you again this past week, this one plays to your strengths in the air. But I'll trust you to choose who you want with you on this and who hits what."

"That's it?"

"I'm giving you total control of the team, so yes, that's it."

Berkley leaned back in her chair and smiled. "There's *nothing* you want to add to that?"

"I came here for two things," Aidan said as she gripped the remote for the monitor if only to have something to do with her hands other than put them down Berkley's pants. "I wanted you with me on this."

"What else do you want?"

"The most important thing is to have you with me even after all this is over." She finally let go a little and slid her hand down Berkley's collar to press her palm to the back of her neck. "I just wanted you to realize that I understand what you've been through and I know what kind of position I'm putting you in by asking you to come with me, and it's not something I take lightly."

"Don't feel guilty for something I want to do." Berkley pulled her hand free and kissed Aidan's fingers. "The rest we'll see as this plays out."

"I'll accept that."

"If you're so easily willing to accept that, then perhaps you have changed." Berkley offered her a casual salute. "If there's one thing I've learned in our time apart, it's that the best expectation in life is to have none. My mother was right about the fact that you're more pleasantly surprised that way."

"Happy flying, then, and I see a lot of good surprises for you once you land." Aidan put her hand in Berkley's and smiled in a way that made it clear how she felt about her. "We'll start with dinner tonight with your parents. That is, if you'll lend me your kitchen."

"You learned how to cook?" Berkley asked incredulously.

The laugh Aidan let out did earn her a brief kiss when Berkley acted as if she couldn't hold out any longer. "You learned and you're going to ask me that? Let's just say that eventually I want to be as good a partner as I've been a sailor." Wanting more contact with Berkley but remembering where she was, Aidan stepped closer and put her arms around her waist.

"My kitchen is yours if you tell me what you're making."

"The first thing I learned to make was Southern fried chicken. You fall for those tall Southern types, and it's a must-have in your culinary scorecard. Still your favorite?"

"Still my favorite."

"Get going, then. I need you to be perfect so I get you back in one piece once we're done."

❖

When Berkley changed and stepped out to the tarmac there were twice the usual number of planes. The pilots Will had put out a call for had started to arrive, and they were lined up and ready for whatever test Berkley threw at them. She wasn't surprised that her father was one of those wearing a flight suit and standing with Will.

"Have you decided to give up the desk job?" Berkley asked her dad.

"Rattler tells me it's been a while since someone knocked you on your ass," he said with a laugh. "So I thought the two old men would give it a try."

"Emphasis on the word try, old man," she teased back. "Isn't that right, Whittle?"

Harvey had joined them and nodded at Berkley's question. "No way are we going down, Cletus."

Behind them the planes started to take off. The training had changed to a constant dogfight mentality. Their goal was to bring Berkley down, along with the other two pilots she had picked out that morning.

Commander Lake "Killer" Goram and Commander Sonny "Vader" Forche had gone through the Academy with Berkley, and she trusted them both at her wing or leading her into combat. Sonny had actually inherited her backseat when Berkley was on a carrier. She now had a couple of days to pick the final pair.

After introductions she and Harvey were the only ones left. He looked like a man who was waiting for bad news.

"How's the nickname coming, Whittle?"

"I wouldn't think it'd be important now." He had to yell his answer as her father and Will hit the sky.

"I'm leading this mission and I need a good pair of eyes behind me, so I figured that'd be you. You telling me you're not interested?"

"I just thought you'd want to bring someone with more experience."

"My dad trusted your father with his life, and he came through." She slapped him on the shoulder and pushed him in the direction of the plane. "I figured you Whittles are good luck."

"Cletus, your targets have been painted and you're given a go," the tower operator said once they were lined up for takeoff.

"Roger that." She punched it down the short track they used to simulate carrier takeoffs. "Killer, Vader, are we locked and loaded?"

"We got your ass, Cletus," Killer said from her right wing. Following her lead, they shut off communication after that.

A hundred miles to the north in the mountains the computers had simulated a target in terrain similar to what they would find in the field. The rules of elevation wouldn't be in play. Their job now was to disappear from the radar by any means possible, whenever possible.

In less than twenty minutes, Vader had taken the shot to eliminate their first target with no mishap. Their second target was farther south in a heavily wooded area.

"Cletus, five o'clock," Harvey yelled as Will's plane came closer with an impressive set of rolls. Without moving too far away from her, Killer took him out in a move that made it look easy.

"His buddy's at ten o'clock," Harvey informed her.

"And he brought friends," she said as six other flyers joined the fun. "Vader, keep heading for the target."

"Want me to help even the score?" Vader asked.

"Killer has my wing, so get going." She banked left, her finger on her guns the whole time, taking out two planes. No matter what moves she made, Killer stayed on her wing taking shots of his own.

Soon there was only one plane left to face down.

"Cletus, I could use some help here," Vader radioed over. "There's a mess of hornets defending their nest around the second target."

"Killer, you're on backup at T-2." She dropped her altitude abruptly when the plane chasing them locked on them briefly. "Eyes open back there, Harvey."

"He's still on our ass. He dropped his elevation and so did two of the others."

The three remaining planes were heading directly toward them, the sixth dropping off to follow Killer. "How about you keep your eyes on the guys behind us, Whittle?"

"They're still there." Berkley could tell he was trying to keep his voice calm, but the elevation of tone gave away just how nervous he was.

"Good, because the three ahead of us are still there too," she said and laughed. "Let's see how good everyone is at the game of chicken."

She kept her eye on their surroundings but also on her instruments, which showed that one of the planes behind them and one in front had them locked in. Now it was a matter of waiting for them to pull the trigger.

"Cletus?" Whittle asked.

"Hang on, Harvey." According to the computer, both planes that had targeted them had released their missiles. They were now locked on to their target—her and Whittle—but Berkley had other ideas. In modern dogfights like this, it was all about making someone else the target.

Waiting until the very last moment, Berkley sent them shooting up like a cork released from a bottle of agitated champagne. Her quick reflexes gave the missiles no chance to follow. Missiles were made for one reason, and that was to destroy. With their plane now above their pursuers, the missiles had to find something else to bring down.

One of the young guns was the first plane to go down and Berkley laughed as she imagined the emphatic "fuck" over how he'd been taken out. "Vader, give me an update," she said as she came around. With all the planes in front of her, she quickly got off some of her own missiles.

"We've taken out the second target and are heading back with company. You need us to come back?"

"Keep going for the green zone, and I'll try and shake my admirers." Now it was just a good old-fashioned game of chase. As much as she loved the fight aspect of her daily flying, the mission training had more to do with an in-and-out mentality. Once the targets were eliminated, it wasn't their job to engage the enemy any further.

"Two hundred miles, Cletus, time to put the moves on these guys."

As they closed in on what was considered the green zone, Berkley actually kept on the straightest course she could find. In a realistic setting the ship would be their final backup if the need came.

When she got to the target zone, Vader and Killer joined her at her wings. The show of force made the enemy planes break off.

"Good job, people. All we need to do now is recreate this in the field," Berkley said as she broke off from her team. Just as quickly, her father and Will took their place and followed her toward her usual southern sightseeing route.

"Let's get back, Whittle."

After Berkley landed she headed to her Jeep wanting to enjoy the time she had left with her family.

CHAPTER NINE

"Do you know where Berk keeps her flour?" Aidan asked as she opened cabinets, not having any luck finding the ingredients she was looking for.

Maggie Levine sat at the counter shelling the beans she and Aidan had shopped for that afternoon in the open market in town. The chicken Aidan had cut up was marinating in the spices that would be locked in when it was dipped in buttermilk and coated with flour to deep-fry. Chicken, beans, and corn—Berkley's favorite Sunday meal growing up.

"In the refrigerator, since she doesn't use it much. I've taught her how to barbeque because, like her father, the thought of cooking anything over an open flame is too good to pass up, but I think the stove and hot oil still intimidates her a bit."

"She would die if she heard you saying that." Aidan got the flour out and poured some in one bowl and buttermilk in another. The chicken went into the buttermilk first, then she dredged it through the flour. "Great warriors of our day are seldom intimidated by anything."

"One of my best days was the morning they finally pulled Cletus out of my womb after what felt like thirty-six days of labor. She screamed so loud from the minute the air hit her that I really thought the doctor was going to drop her."

"Maybe it was because she was comfortable where she was," Aidan said.

"I don't think that's why. From that first moment of her life I think that she wanted what came next. That screaming convinced me that she'd inherited Corbin's wandering soul as well as those good looks, and the patience God gave a two-year-old."

Finished with the chicken, Aidan cleaned her hands and leaned against the counter. "But I thought the reason the commander accepted this final assignment was to be with you and his family since there'd be no more transfers? It's nice to know that love can tame the wanderer in him."

"Before we met, his time in the Navy was his own and he enjoyed making the decisions that shaped the man he became, but he eventually came to see that he needed something more if he was going to lead a complete life. When we found each other, I was lucky that he was ready for whatever came next. He loves me and our girls, and he's never strayed from the day he walked me down the aisle, but I know that I'll never tame his soul. That part of him that takes chances most people wouldn't dream of is what makes him the man who keeps my interest, and because of that, I would've followed him to hell and back."

Aidan nodded and turned her eyes to the refrigerator covered with pictures of Berkley and her family. "You sound like a very lucky woman who found what she wanted and wasn't stupid enough to let it go."

"I wasn't telling you that story to make you feel bad, sweetheart. You were right in that there isn't much that intimidates our modern-day warriors."

"You may have a warrior, but I can't make that claim."

"Cletus may have come out with her hair on fire like her father when it comes to chasing down adventure, but there's only one thing that can cut them so deep it makes them careless in the face of battle." She slid off her stool and came to stand in front of Aidan. "Why are you here?"

"I'm cooking dinner."

"Don't bullshit me. I've lived with sailors too long to not know what it sounds like when it's being shoveled my way. Why are you here?"

"I'm back for another chance."

"If it were up to me, there wouldn't be another chance." Maggie grabbed Aidan's hand and squeezed her fingers to the point of pain. "You take that chance and then walk away again and I'll hunt you down and kill you if something happens to her out there. You make promises you have no intention of keeping and it clouds her mind, and Corbin will beat me to it." With one more squeeze, she let go and smiled.

"She told you about us?"

"If you're asking me that, then you don't know Cletus as well as you'd like to think. She didn't have to tell me, I saw it on her face when she came home after you left." Maggie laughed and went back to her beans. "You made her skittish for the first time in her life and she wasn't the same. Not that you killed her spirit, but she wasn't the same and now she holds back a big part of herself no matter how hard I've tried to bring back the kid I raised."

"Would you prefer someone else for her?"

"I wouldn't imagine picking something so personal for her. Only Berkley can decide who to give her heart to, and if it's you then we'll welcome you into our family. I only told you what I did because while Corbin or Berkley will never tell me exactly what she's signed up to help you do, I'm not an idiot. I'm sure she's not leaving to fly in some parade over the capital. It's going to be dangerous and if something happens to her because someone else is better, then that's the life we signed on for, isn't it?" Maggie's eyes filled with tears. "But I won't have her shot down because she's licking her wounds because you broke her heart again. If you're here, then it better be for good, or leave now."

"I'm here for good, Mrs. Levine, of that I can assure you."

"Then start frying chicken. They'll be home soon and I'm guessing this is a good night for comfort food."

❖

After dinner that night Berkley drove Aidan back to the base and walked her to her room. Aidan was leaving in the morning and they wouldn't see each other until just before the *Jefferson* pulled out of Virginia.

"That was a great meal." Berkley stood in the doorway with her hands behind her back. She came close to losing her balance when Aidan pulled her inside by the belt and closed the door.

"This is your last chance, Commander."

"Last chance for what?"

Aidan laughed when Berkley stood before her at parade rest. "Your last chance to stay here and wait until this is done. I'm not going to think any less of you if that's what you want, and I'm still going to come back here when I'm finished."

"My mom talked to you, didn't she?"

"Your mother loves you, but she's not why I told you that."

"It's not, huh?" Berkley grabbed the wandering hand that had started at her stomach and was heading upward. "Then why'd you say it?"

"Because I need you to know that you don't have anything to prove to me in the air or on the ground. I just want you to be happy and believe in the possibilities of dreaming again." She kissed the part of Berkley's chest she could reach through the khaki shirt of her uniform. "And I want you at my table for years to come telling me how much you love my chicken and how it reminds you of your mother's."

"Go to your meetings, Captain, and when you stand on the bridge to sail off for this mission, I'll be standing on the deck below you ready to carry off my part."

With a slight tug she freed her hands and put them behind Berkley's neck so she could pull her down for a kiss. "And when we come back?" she asked when they pulled apart.

"I'm sure we could get court-martialed for this behavior, but I'm willing to think about it." Berkley started the next kiss and pulled Aidan so close her feet came off the ground. "If you did talk to my mom, I'm sure she told you that the future has a way of taking care of itself. When we get back we'll see where the possibilities we talked about on those beautiful Hawaiian beaches can take us."

"I'll see you in a couple of days, then."

"You bet. I just need to pick my last team members and we'll be ready to fly."

❖

"I won't let you down if you give me the chance, ma'am." Lieutenant David "Blazer" Morris stood at attention in front of Berkley as she geared up for one more training flight.

"You're the one who sacrificed his wingman the first day here hoping to get me in return for his sacrifice. Why would I trust you enough to take you? What's going to prevent you from doing that again when it really counts, only it's me up there with you?"

"Because I'm the best in the Navy after you. I'd think you'd put past mistakes aside for that reason alone."

Berkley zipped up her flight suit and laughed. "Cocky sons of bitches don't impress me, boy. Let's see what you got up there today and I'll let you know, but even if I pick you, just remember one thing."

"Anything, Commander."

"If I pick you, you'll be flying wingman this time and you should start praying I'm not in a sacrificing mood when we're flying over the Korean countryside."

❖

The next morning her mother stood on the porch of the house and waved good-bye to Berkley. Junior sat as her side, his paw in the air, waving as well.

Her father drove her to the base to see her onto the transport plane that would take her and her team to Washington. There were seven people standing with Will when he brought the Jeep to a stop in the hangar. Their attention turned to the Levines as Berkley lifted her duffel out of the back.

"Lieutenant Whittle, a word with you please," her father said, staying next to the vehicle.

Berkley threw her gear up to be stowed but didn't interrupt the two men who had their heads together. When they rejoined the group there was only a little time before they had to be in the air.

"I'm proud of you, kid, and you do what you have to, but you come home to your mama. In and out, remember that," Will told her as he hugged her.

"Yes, sir."

"Just remember the Levine golden rule of flying and you'll be okay," her dad added.

"Land because I want to, not because it's someone else's idea," Berkley said when Whittle shrugged. "Take care, Dad, and I'll see you."

"I'll see you and your backseat as soon as you've finished the job. Heard the kid didn't have a name, so I took care of it." He pulled her close and kissed her. "I love you, Cletus, and you be careful."

"I will, Dad. I love you too, and tell that to Mom while I'm gone."

"You got it."

CHAPTER TEN

The transport plane was loud and the passengers all closed their eyes and got as comfortable as they could for the long flight. Berkley stared out the window until the clouds obscured the ground. It was time to leave something else she loved behind in search of the next chapter of her life.

Her time in Fallon had been overshadowed some by her memoires of Aidan and the years of happiness she'd missed out on. As hard as it was to get through, she felt she had succeeded in burying her personal life deep enough that she'd been able to give Will her best. It's why she felt she owed it to herself to get wrapped up in the excitement that was starting to build in her gut.

The fact that she was ready wasn't a question she had to waste her time on since she'd felt different every time she climbed into the cockpit in their training flights in the last few days. Her confidence was quickly changing Harvey too. Their relationship was staring to gel on the ground as well as in the air.

The only factor that made her feel unbalanced was her feelings for Aidan. It had been two days since Aidan had left, which had given Berkley the opportunity to clear her head when it came to the woman that she knew was the opiate of her life. Not that she'd ever considered taking drugs, but she could see how people fell easily back into a habit no matter how long they'd gone without.

Aidan Sullivan had been a young naval officer when they'd met, and it had been an instant attraction strong enough to short-circuit her defenses. For two years, that attraction had grown into a relationship Berkley was so certain of that she concentrated on the life they'd have together that would end with them picking cemetery plots, and on little else. She never once thought that Aidan would one day be gone of her own volition.

Her problem now was that no matter Aidan's mistakes, she'd never gotten to the point of hating her, no matter how hard she'd tried. Aidan hadn't left because of someone else, so there was no sense of betrayal to fuel her ire, and because Berkley had started from that position, what Aidan was saying was like rain to land scorched from drought. Those pretty promises of what could be had sunk in no matter how hard she fought against it, but the numbness she'd felt for so long was being replaced not by hope, but by fear.

Love was easy to fall into but hard to maintain because it took trust and commitment, Aidan had that in abundance, only it was for the Navy. As they said their good-byes before Aidan left for her meeting in Washington, Berkley had come close to believing the promise in her eyes.

If you're honest with yourself you'd walk away, she thought as she joined her group in closing her eyes and stretching her legs. *But if I'm even more honest I'd just give in because there isn't any other choice.* The latter thought was more accurate since it summed up the reasons why she hadn't moved on.

For every heart there was only one perfect home, and she had found hers in a cocky officer who'd shot her down in more ways than one. And it didn't matter to her heart that Aidan had been the source of great pain; there was no denying she'd also been the source of her greatest happiness. It was those memories that were starting to win out.

"Hey, Cletus," Harvey said, stopping Berkley from wandering any further down the road of her past. "Do you think during our time off you'll have a few minutes to meet my parents? They'll be in town."

"Are you two getting married or something?" Blazer asked. "If you are, which one of you is wearing the dress?"

"Fuck off," Harvey said.

"Ooh, I guess it's going to be you, Whittle," Blazer said and his partner, Alan Lewis, laughed.

"Listen to me." Berkley put her hand on Harvey's shoulder as she stood. "I'm already regretting picking you, and it's not too late to change my mind, ass wipe," she said to Blazer in as menacing a voice as she could. "So why don't you concentrate on what you need to do to fit in as a part of this team, and if you can't, then now's the time to let me know. I'm not as impressed with you as you are, so it won't be a difficult decision to find a replacement. Either way, when we get back I owe you a comeback for the stupid remarks, and it's going to involve you losing some of those pearly whites."

"My apologies, ma'am," Blazer said. It sounded like the three words had been a struggle for him.

"Just keep your mouth shut and we'll be fine." Berkley stared him down and cut him off when he went to say something else. "I'd take that advice starting now."

Berkley walked to the back of the plane and got a Coke. As she popped the top Vader joined her and pointed to the storage area in the next section back.

"Are you sure about this kid, Cletus?"

"He's got attitude to spare, but he's good if he follows directions." They sat away from the others when the plane hit turbulence. "I'd worry about it," Berkley said in a low voice, "but he wants it too much to fuck this up."

"I remember what that was like," Vader said.

The liquid in the can fizzed a little as they were jostled by more turbulence. "Me too. That's why I gave him the chance he asked for. He's a hotshot, but the thing Will taught me is they're all redeemable. He'll be fine, and since he'll be coming with me I'm not going to give him any other choice but to fall in line."

"It's good to have you back. We all know what a taskmaster Will is, but you still have a lot of field work left in you. After that you can go back and play with obnoxious pups."

"How about you? What's been on your plate besides bombing rocks in Afghanistan?"

"I got a girl planning a wedding for December, so clear your schedule and bring the dress whites. She wants all the pomp that goes with having a bunch of sailors wearing their shiny ribbons."

"Anyone who said yes to you is worth meeting." Berkley laughed.

"All I can tell you is that she's a crazy from your hometown and after spending time with her when I went down there after Katrina, I understood you better. It must be all that gumbo that makes you all a little nuts."

"It's not the food, buddy, it's the heat, so December was a good choice. Sounds like she's crazy for saying yes, but not completely."

"She tells me I was the crazy one for asking." He bumped shoulders with her. "What I found is that life can be better when you mingle the insanity with someone else. Remember that, Cletus. It's not too late, my friend."

"Yeah?" Berkley laughed. "You have anyone in mind?"

"I'll let you know if I meet anyone nuts enough to hook up with you."

They continued their talk as they looked over the information Aidan had left with Berkley. She had started to develop her plan during their training runs. Vader was to lead one team and she the other. She trusted Vader to carry out what needed to be done as much as Aidan trusted her with the overall mission.

Their friendship had started in flight school where they were way ahead of their classmates thanks to fathers who'd put them in cockpits as soon as they were old enough to start training for a license. But it wasn't only the mechanics of flying that they taught. Like her father, Vader's dad had access to jets and taught his son what was possible at the stick.

When they finally got their chance in the seat of an F-18, all their time in the air came together and they were evenly matched. Vader was someone she trusted not only on her wing, but to carry out orders without a glitch.

"You know what the crappy thing about our job is?" Vader asked.

"What's that?"

"None of these idiots ever learn from experience." He pointed to the soldier in one of the satellite photos. "They play at war with kids like this, and I don't think they ever stop and realize they aren't toy soldiers. That when their stubbornness makes the world react, this guy isn't going home once I blow the shit out of this place."

"I believe love is changing you." Berkley accepted the pictures back.

"You think I've lost my edge?"

"Some people do because they go into these things thinking more about the life that's waiting for them than the mission."

"I'm in love, but I'm not in that category yet."

"I know," Berkley said as she buckled in. "If you were you wouldn't have agreed to go."

"I'm coming along, and when it's done the beer's on me."

CHAPTER ELEVEN

Washington, DC

When the plane landed, Berkley took a cab downtown and checked into the Essex House next to the Capitol. They weren't set to sail for another week and she didn't want to be stuck in a barrack in Norfolk where the *Jefferson* was moored. She left the room in her khaki uniform and headed to one of her favorite spots in the city intent on enjoying her days off.

She was standing in the main room of the Smithsonian National Air and Space Museum admiring the planes hanging from the ceiling when Aidan found her.

"Think you could have done rolls in that one?" Aidan pointed to one of the older ones in the exhibit.

"If I wanted to crash and burn, maybe. That's not what would've worried me, though. I would've been a nervous wreck thinking I was going to shoot my propeller off." She took her eyes off the relics and looked at Aidan in her dress whites. "You do the Navy proud, Captain. You *are* beautiful in white."

"You say that like you mean it."

"Wanting to go slow doesn't translate into blindness. The president made a good choice if he wants to recruit as well as put a new face on the Navy." Berkley winked and moved to the next exhibit. When she attended the Academy she'd spent a lot of weekends visiting museums and historical spots. Her father was a pilot, but her mom was an American history professor who instilled a love of the subject in all her children.

"I don't mean to be such a pain, but could you define slow?"

"Last time around we went at warp speed and look where that got us." Berkley walked her to the World War II exhibit.

"Considering I slept with you on the first date, I think you need to cut me some slack," Aidan whispered into Berkley's ear after she pulled on her arm hard enough to make her bend down. "And if you tell me you don't remember that I'll hurt you."

"Of course I do, and that I'm here at all is testament that you're getting some serious slack." Aidan gazed at her with such loneliness that Berkley's chest hurt. Chances weren't like buses, her mom said all the time. If you missed one, sometimes that was all you had on your schedule. "Come on." Berkley offered Aidan her arm.

Outside, the weather was cold but sunny and the mall wasn't overly crowded with tourists. "I'm probably freaking you out, I know that, but—"

"You decided on your course and you don't want to wait," Berkley finished for her. "Don't give me that face," she added and poked her finger gently against the middle of Aidan's forehead. "Do you want me to be brutally honest with you?"

The question made Aidan hesitate and sigh. "Probably not, but go ahead."

"That night you told me you had to leave for this," she tapped the symbols of Aidan's rank, "hurt me more than anything ever had. I wanted so much from you and you didn't feel the same way. That kind of hurt changes you in ways you don't realize until you start to get over the crushing effect of it."

"Do you think you can get over what I did? I know you won't ever forget."

"You're wrong," Berkley said with conviction and stopped moving. "I loved you, Aidan, and because you left didn't mean it stopped. It's why I answered every letter and it made me think about you every day."

"You still love me?"

"I do, but to be honest, it's different. All I can compare it to is flying after losing your nerve. Just because you can't force yourself into a dangerous situation doesn't mean you've lost your ability to fly the plane. That's the part that's ingrained into your brain to the point that it's second nature."

"I know that going in, baby, and there's only one way to prove myself to you." Aidan looped their arms together again and started them walking. "Actually, two things."

"Don't feel like you have to get crazy on me."

"I'm not." Aidan smiled. "The first thing is consistency, and the other thing I need your consent for."

"Let's hear it." Berkley walked slowly and tried not to stare at Aidan.

"Did you bring the monkey suit?"

"According to you, I owe you a date, so I took the dress uniform out of mothballs. I figure if you wanted to collect, a pizza joint wasn't going to be good enough."

"Careful talking like that, Commander. You could turn a girl's head." She laughed, relaxing her features enough that it reminded Berkley of when they first met. "I do want to go out, but tonight I'd like to do something different."

"Is it kinky?" Berkley asked with a laugh. "Even if I was up for it, I'm sure that could be dangerous so close to the Pentagon."

"Maybe after dinner in the privacy of your hotel room, but tonight I'd like to have dinner with my parents."

The wind was blowing down the mall, and it ruffled through Aidan's hair as they started back toward the Capitol. "Call me when you're done, then," Berkley said, trying to sound light despite the fact that Aidan was already trying to blow her off.

"I meant I want *us* to have dinner with my parents."

"You want me to have dinner with the admiral?" Berkley stopped to stare at Aidan as if to see if she was serious. "Do you think that's a good idea?"

"He's mellowed some after taking the teaching job at the Academy, and I think it's time he and mom meet the one thing in my life that's more important than the Navy." Knowing there were too many people around and how much trouble they could make for themselves, Aidan just smiled up at her but made no move to touch her more than she was already. "I really want them to meet you, honey."

"You don't have to do that. I believe you want to try again, so there's no reason to get crazy."

"My parents don't work for Naval Investigations, and this *is* important to me."

"If you're sure, then let's get changed. I want to make a good impression, so I need to polish my shoes. Just tell me when and where."

Aidan squeezed Berkley's arm. "You do realize what this means, right? At least that's what my father's going to infer from you coming, and he'd be right because that's what it'll mean to me." She put her hand up to block out the sun. "Are *you* sure?"

"What it'll mean is dinner and meeting your parents, nothing else. That's it, Aidan, so don't go shopping for those rings just yet."

"Then why go?"

When an elderly couple passed them and the gentleman gave them a look of what Aidan took to be suspicion, she started walking again. "Because I said I was willing to try, and to do that means giving in even when I don't think we're ready for whatever your timeline is. But we have to remember one thing. We had something that we walked away from."

"Don't you mean *I* walked away from?"

As they reached the Lincoln Memorial, Berkley led her up the stairs. "Do I strike you as the kind of person who's going to beat you over the head with mistakes? I meant what I said. It was both of us, and this time around I want us to take it slow so that we get it right." She stopped them at the top and glanced out at the reflecting pool. "I want you to be as sure as I am this time around."

"What if I'm already there? I was the first night we spent together at your house, only this time it was my idea to rip your clothes off."

"You weren't that shy the first time around, so don't give me that," Berkley said and laughed. "Besides, the choice might be out of my hands."

"What are you talking about?"

"It could be that after meeting with the admiral I might not have any choice but to go and buy you a ring if he finds out what I did to you on that first night together, or he might not find me worthy enough for you."

Aidan stopped her again. "Promise me that you won't let my father scare you off. He's my dad, but that doesn't mean he's not a little intimidating."

"Let me walk you to your room and don't worry about that."

"How do you know I checked into a hotel?"

"Because your only other choice was staying with your parents, and I have a feeling you didn't want to do that."

"I actually have an apartment here, but I do have one question for you. Are you on the fifth floor?" Aidan asked.

"Some traditions are hard to break, baby, and maybe all your wishful thinking is contagious."

"Good," Aidan said and felt feather light. "It's those traditions that have kept me going, Commander."

Berkley patted her hand where Aidan still had it resting on the bend of her elbow. "Same floor makes it easier to sneak into your room once the halls are quiet."

"Still feel like sneaking around with me?"

"Let's see how dinner goes first before we starting thinking about dessert."

CHAPTER TWELVE

I'm here to meet the Sullivan party," Berkley said to the host of the hotel's restaurant.

"Welcome, Commander." The man led Berkley to the table toward the back. Aidan was sitting so she was facing the dining room, and her father was sitting across from her making Berkley notice his thinning hair as he studied the menu.

"Sir." Berkley held her hand out to retired Admiral Preston "Triton" Sullivan. He was about five inches shorter than her but more than made up for it in bulk. He took her hand in a firm handshake, and Aidan covered her mouth to hide her laugh at the extra effort he obviously put into it.

"Commander, have a seat," Preston ordered. "We were getting ready to order without you."

"Ma'am, it's a pleasure meeting you." Berkley offered her hand to Mary Beth Sullivan after she sat down. "I apologize if I'm late. Aidan told me eight."

Aidan smiled at Berkley, then glared at her father. "It was eight, which means you're fifteen minutes early."

"You certainly know your audience, Commander," Triton said. "The Navy obviously thinks highly of you." He pointed to the honors on her jacket.

"Thank you, sir, but once you get to know me you'll realize the last thing I am is a glory hound."

"My daughter tells me you'll be leading the air combat part of the mission she's getting ready to head out on," Triton said as a conversation starter.

"Yes, sir, I am."

"That would've been unheard of ten years ago."

"It's a good thing for me that I was born in the right year. I'm going to be able to make the same contribution that my father has before I return to Nevada."

"Please, Berkley, don't get him started on that. We don't have that much time with Aidan, and I'd like to enjoy it without reliving military strategy gone wrong in American history," Mary Beth Sullivan said as she took Berkley's hand in hers. "Why not tell us something much more interesting, like where you met our daughter?"

"We met in Hawaii during a drill our units were invited to participate in. Aidan was able to lock onto me and knock me out of the sky with her ground crew."

"That's my little girl," Triton said.

"It did knock the ruffle out of my feathers, especially when I realized how short she was."

Aidan reached across the table and slapped Berkley's arm. "Not all of us are giant Amazon warriors, Cletus."

"We became good friends after that and she helped me focus so that getting shot down even in a simulation hasn't happened again," Berkley finished her story for Mary Beth.

"Once is all it takes to get what you're gunning for," Aidan said smiling at Berkley in a way that let her know she wasn't talking about planes or anything to do with the Navy. "Tell us about your classes, Dad," she said, steering them into safer waters. There was no reason to let her parents in on just how much she cared for Berkley.

Triton launched into one of his lectures that lasted through the appetizers, and only stopped when Berkley asked a slew of what he called probing and intelligent questions. "Today we covered some dogfights that took place during a misunderstanding of airspace during the cold war, and the name Corbin Levine came up as one of the pilots who did their job but also kept his cool. Seems he not only provided air cover to a group surrounded by enemy fire, but he saved the lives of two airmen who'd been hit and were having trouble gaining control of their planes. It earned him quite a few commendations." He picked up his drink and took a long sip. "Friend of yours?"

"Captain Levine is Berkley's father, Dad. I had the honor of meeting him recently when I was in Fallon," Aidan answered.

"I'm sure Commander Levine won't have trouble answering my questions, Aidan." The conversation stopped while their entrees were being served. Triton's reprimand hung in the air like a bomb waiting to go off. "So, Corbin Levine's your father?"

"Yes, sir, he is. He's currently the commanding officer at the Belle Chase Naval Station outside of New Orleans. In another year he'll be retiring to work in the family business my grandfather started. It's an airfreight operation that'll keep him in the air like he wanted, even though they're much slower planes than he's used to." Berkley took a sip of water and mentally counted to ten before going on. If this guy went off on her dad, she was going to have do something about it, and Aidan wasn't going to like it. "Why? Is there a problem?"

"The only problem is that I haven't met the man yet. One of the pilots he provided air cover for that day was my little brother Gary. The boy got a little nuts after that, but he started that way, so we can't damn well blame it on the stress of his service, but the reason he came back at all was because your dad was so accurate. Your father took a hell of a lot of chances so that Gary and a couple of his buddies could limp back to base." He lifted his glass and waited for Berkley to do the same. "I looked up who it was that day that gave Gary the chance to get out of there with his butt intact. Tell your dad that I look forward to shaking his hand and having him come and talk to my class whenever he's in town. You come from good stock, Commander."

"It really is a small world, isn't it? Thank you, sir. I'll have to tell him when I talk to him tonight. He doesn't talk about those days much, but I'm thinking he'd love to reminisce if you give him the chance. He taught me everything I know, so I've heard all the stories. If you could talk him into it, your class will be in for a treat."

"I have to tell you that knowing who Aidan's got watching her back makes me feel a whole lot better. I'm not privy to the goings-on at the Navy anymore, but I'm smart enough to know what you two are headed out to do is not only important but dangerous. I want your word, Commander, that you'll keep an eye on my little girl. She might be a captain now, but that's how I feel about her."

"That's why I'm here, sir, and I won't let you down."

"Are you as faithful as you are dutiful, Commander?" Mary Beth asked.

"Mary Beth," Triton said with an edge in his voice.

"It's a simple question, honey, so calm down," Mary Beth said.

"There's nothing simple in its implications. Don't you know it's a don't ask, don't tell policy now?"

"Every bit as faithful, ma'am. You don't have any worries on that front either. You don't have to worry about Aidan at all." Berkley didn't think she had to elaborate any further.

"I'm so glad you all are having such a good time without me," Aidan said when her father looked like a pot that was getting ready to boil over. "Let's change the subject."

"Why? To make your father happy?" her mother asked. "The Navy he believes in and still misses is the one that would have kept you in the secretarial pool, dear. If I were you I'd wake up and take some action no matter what the stodgy oldsters like your father think. Unless you're blind, you have to have noticed just how dashing Commander Levine looks in that uniform. Keep playing hard to get and the woman at the next table in the little black dress will deliver her hotel keys wrapped in her underwear before dessert."

Triton had to slap Berkley on the back when she swallowed wrong at the end of Mary Beth's observations. "Sorry," she gasped as she reached for the water again.

"I may be stodgy, Mary Beth, but Aidan can't go around noticing how dashing anyone looks in their uniform, especially if they're serving under her. She's a captain in the U.S. Navy, and they still court-martial you for shit like that," Triton said in a harsh whisper.

"Guys, no one's getting court-martialed, so calm down." Aidan ran her hand along Berkley's back, trying to get her to start breathing normally again. "Are you all right?"

"Fine, just went down the wrong way," Berkley got out in a wheeze.

"I'm sorry if I embarrassed you, Commander, but while my husband is interested in Aidan's career, I'm her mother and I'm more interested in her happiness." Her mother looked at Aidan and nodded her head in Berkley's direction. "I know just how smart you are, baby, but I want you to take a good look at the sailor next to you. That's what we used to call six feet of happiness just waiting to happen. It's what I got in your father, just in a shorter package."

"I appreciate the vote of confidence, ma'am," Berkley said.

"No need to apply for the job I'm hoping you're interested in. I have every faith in you to do right by Aidan, and that starts with forgiving her for her past misjudgments." She reached for Berkley's hand again. "Am I right about that too?"

"Aidan isn't to blame for anything, ma'am. We've both made mistakes, but this time around we're going to take it nice and slow so that we don't repeat any of the mistakes you mentioned," Berkley forgot about her pride and spoke for Aidan's parents' benefit.

Mary Beth let go of her hand and sat back in her chair and took a deep breath. "I see. Is that how you go about flying, Commander?"

"What do you mean?"

"What I mean is, do you take those expensive toys the Navy lets you play with and go about your missions nice and slow, with no plan to make sure you're successful?"

"No, I wouldn't say my time in the air could be described as slow," Berkley said, followed by a small laugh that made her sound nervous.

"Then how about you get with the program when your feet are on the ground as well? Life is short, and when you find something or someone worth your heart, you shouldn't dally. Even though Triton is a major pain at times, taking the gamble on spending my life with him has been more than worth it."

"Thank you for the advice, and I'll do my best not to disappoint." Berkley smiled and glanced down to find Aidan's hand in her lap. She was sure the squeeze she received to her thigh was Aidan's way of saying she appreciated Berkley playing along and not just getting up and leaving.

"See that you don't and that's good enough for me." Mary Beth let go of her again and reached for her wineglass.

They spent the rest of the evening talking about Aidan's new commission and Berkley's time in Fallon. The evening stretched out to dessert and a few cups of coffee before Aidan and Mary Beth excused themselves to the ladies' room.

"Finally," Triton said as if this was the opportunity he'd waited for. "You seem polite enough, and your parents obviously taught you some manners."

"But, and I'm guessing here, you don't think I'm right for her. The policy might mean you can't ask me, and I'm not obligated to tell you what I want in a partner, but I also know you're not stupid, so I'm sure I'm not what you had in mind when it came to someone in Aidan's life."

"Mighty presumptuous of you, Cletus." He pulled a cigar out of his coat pocket and stuck it in his mouth but made no attempt to light it. "Do you mind me calling you Cletus? Your father's not the only one mentioned in some of that military history I read about. Impressive career so far, and now this assignment."

"Not at all, sir, and I'm sorry if I jumped the gun. As for impressive commissions, we both know Aidan wins that competition hands down."

"You're a little right." He leaned further in to keep their conversation private. "I don't want my daughter hurt, and it's not for the reasons Mary Beth accuses me of. I'm sure those manners of yours will keep Aidan out of any embarrassing situations when it comes to her service to her country."

"I would never put her in a situation that would blemish not only her name and reputation, but yours as well, sir. Both you and my father served with honor and courage, and I'll do everything I can to respect that. I just met you, but I feel like you're no different from my father in that regard."

"Like I said, that's the least of my worries."

"Is there anything I can say to help ease your mind about this, sir?"

"I remember Aidan coming home from Hawaii after you two met and her talking about this young flygirl who had hung the moon, to hear her put it. As a parent, it's a big part of your job to accept not only who your children are, but who they will become." He sighed and moved his cigar to the other side of his mouth. "As high as you had her flying is as low as she's been since you two went your separate ways."

"I didn't—"

"I know what happened because Mary Beth finally wrangled it out of her, but that makes no difference now, does it? She left because staying would have meant betraying me, or at least that's what she thought at the time. I love the Navy, Commander, and I'm sorry if what I've been preaching all these years has hurt you in any way because Aidan thought I put all that I believe about honor and service over what she wanted. Because let's face it, what she wants is you, but she walked away from you because of me. If you're going to blame anyone, don't let it be her."

"I'm not going to lie and tell you that the separation didn't hurt me, but I'm willing to try again. It's one of the most important reasons I'm here."

"You'd better put your heart and soul into it is all I'm saying. You hurt her trying to make yourself feel better and I'll make chum out of you."

"Duly noted, sir, and I can safely say I'd never do that to her. Aidan is one of those women you think of every day and wonder what if. No amount of time would've made me forget her even if we didn't have this chance."

He laughed and slapped Aidan on the back. "She's like her mama when it comes to driving you crazy. Mary Beth got under my skin from the minute I laid eyes on her, but don't worry, in a good way. When it finally hit me that she was the one, damn if she hasn't given me the time of my life ever since. Aidan's also like her mama when it comes to making up her mind as to just how quick she wants the ring and the commitment that comes with it. You're still thinking about how great she looks in a skirt, and damn if she hasn't planned the rest of your life for you," he said making Berkley think he wasn't talking about Aidan.

"I'll keep that in mind, sir."

"You're it for her, so you might as well go ahead and accept that and get with the program, like Mary Beth said. Trust me when I tell you it'll be better for all of us involved, especially me. My wife has made me a happy man, but she's hell to live with when she's upset about something. Her daughter's broken heart," he said and laughed, "yeah, _her_ daughter, because this somehow is my fault. So her daughter's broken heart upset her. Sitting here, though, is the cure for that." He pointed at her with his cigar. "Whatever you do, don't screw it up for yourself, but more importantly, for me."

Berkley laughed with him. "I'll keep that in mind, and thanks, sir. It makes a big difference that you and Mrs. Sullivan are so supportive."

"That we are, and when you get back let's see if we can do something about bringing your father up here for some of his war stories."

"After this mission I'm sure we'll have some R and R, and I'd love to introduce you to my father. I'm sure you'll have a lot in common."

"It should be close to the Fourth of July when you two get back, so that'll be a great time of year for family." Triton stuck out his hand again and nodded when Berkley didn't hesitate to seal their deal.

"You didn't just demand their firstborn, did you?" Mary Beth asked Triton when they returned. She and Aidan exchanged smiles when their dates jumped to attention as soon as they spotted them.

"Just making polite conversation while you were gone. Don't worry about it," Triton said, removing the cigar.

"Don't worry, I'll wheedle it out of you later, but for now it's time for the parents to make a graceful exit." Mary Beth leaned toward Aidan and kissed her cheek. "Good night, Commander. It was nice to finally meet you after hearing about you for so long. You lived up to the hype."

"The pleasure was mine, ma'am, and thank you for dinner, sir."

"If you two are free, maybe we could have lunch as well before you push off," Triton said. "There's a great restaurant right across from the Academy if you like crab cakes."

"That would be great," Berkley said trying to ignore just how good Aidan's nails felt on her leg.

"We'll call you," Triton said and put his hand on Berkley's shoulder and squeezed. "Don't forget a word I said."

"Yes, sir, not a one."

CHAPTER THIRTEEN

Aidan walked her parents outside and saw them into a cab while Berkley stood back and waited. The night was clear and crisp, and once the Sullivans were gone Berkley pointed to the sidewalk.

"Captain, would you like to join me for a walk?" Aidan didn't answer, but fell in step with her. "That was fun."

"I know I owe you for that, and I'm sorry my bladder couldn't hold out until the end of dinner. Leaving you alone with my father wasn't intentional."

"Who wouldn't want to have a talk with the son of Poseidon?" Berkley said and laughed. "I'm kidding. I happen to like Triton, so you don't owe me anything." They stopped and waited for the light to change so they could cross the street to the Capitol. "After leaving you alone with my mother, I'm sure we're even."

"I think Triton's in a category of annoyance your mom will never reach." Aidan walked but Berkley caught her staring at her hand.

"The last thing I want is to betray your dad's confidence, but all he needed me to know was how much he loves his daughter, and how much he cares about her happiness." Berkley took her hand long enough to convey she knew what Aidan was craving but because they were in public it was impossible. "That he cares that much isn't annoying."

"You're a good sport, Cletus."

"Sometimes it depends on the game and what's at stake," Berkley said and glanced up at the dome of the Capitol before she looked in the opposite direction.

In that building, the people elected to it had made decisions that had changed the course of history. Some of those had been commemorated in the monuments that surrounded the area, from the wall of names of those who'd died in Vietnam, to Lincoln, who'd seen his country through a civil war.

Whatever the conflict, there were those who made the decisions to fight, and those whose responsibility it was to go into harm's way. They were called and they went because it was the life they chose.

"Can I ask you to say something one more time for me?" Berkley asked. Life was like the snap of your fingers—quick and over with no do-overs for the things you got wrong if you died before you were ready. And because of the decisions made by others on their behalf, dying was a real possibility for her in the coming days.

"What?"

"Tell me you don't plan to leave again if we try."

Aidan placed her hand over her heart. "I'm yours and I'm here to stay, but like I said, I don't want you to believe me. The proof won't be in my words but in my saying them day after day until my actions and my presence become my proof."

Berkley knew what her mother meant. Chance had sent her another bus, and in this moment the door was open. The only decision was to get on or not. There was a small part of her that still thought it was too fast, but Aidan wasn't new to her heart.

"I almost believe you," Berkley said as she gave herself permission to release some of the pain that had been such a good companion for years.

"You do?"

Berkley laughed and it made Aidan smile. "You aren't lying, are you?"

"No, but—" Aidan stopped when Berkley briefly pressed her fingers to her mouth.

"You're still ahead of me, but I've been emotionally stagnant for too long, and I'm ready to move on." Berkley turned them around and started back toward the hotel. "If I keep you at arm's length that only punishes both of us, and I'm not into voluntary misery."

"You won't be sorry, I promise."

"Come on. It's time for good captains to go to bed."

❖

When they made it back in through the revolving doors of the hotel, they walked to the elevators without talking. On the fifth floor Aidan put her hand on Berkley's forearm but didn't make eye contact with her.

"I don't think I could bear it if you were anywhere tonight except my bed."

"You promised slow," Berkley said.

"I also promised persistent, and if I have to beg I will." She finally looked up. "You can't blame me for wanting the things I want no matter how stupid I've been. We have a week, then even if we want to move faster, we'll be on a carrier headed east."

"Then maybe we should do something about that before we head out to sea. I'm looking forward to being back on the water, but not the fact that I can't do this," Berkley said practically picking Aidan up and carrying her into her room so she could kiss her.

"Are you sure? Because if you keep doing that I'm not going to be able to stop, and I don't want you to freak out in the morning."

"I've gone over in my head what it'd be like seeing you again, and this isn't how I pictured it." Berkley dropped her arms and sighed.

"If I had to guess, your plan had more to do with giving me a hard enough kick that I would've landed back where I came from without the help of a flight." Aidan looped her fingers into the front of Berkley's pants.

"No, but I did think I had more willpower than this." She took Aidan's hands in hers. "Once I would've never thought to be afraid of you, but now I can't help but freeze up when I'm this close to you."

"I don't want to push you, but thank you. I want us to enjoy tonight and all the nights we have before I have to let you concentrate on the mission." Aidan pressed herself to Berkley's body so that they were touching everywhere possible. "Just swear to me when you're up there, you'll be careful. I've been out in the cold alone for so long, baby, and I don't want to go back to that kind of life. You might not be ready for what I feel for you, but I love you and I'm tired of missing you."

"You're so far ahead of me, and I can't..." Berkley didn't know how to go on without ruining the night.

"If you think I'm leaving because you need more time to say the words, I'm not. I'll be happy right now with what you can give me, and the rest will come in time."

"Don't sell yourself short, Aidan." Berkley pulled the clip from Aidan's hair, wanting to feel the blond curls through her fingers.

"I'm not." The buttons of Berkley's jacket came undone easily under Aidan's determined fingers. "I see this as an investment in my future, so I can be patient." She smiled as she took the time to hang her jacket in the closet, not wanting to wrinkle it. "Besides, eventually you'll come to realize what I know for sure."

Berkley sat on the edge of the desk in the room and watched Aidan take off her uniform one piece at a time. She laughed softly when the beautiful set of panties and bra came into view. Aidan might have inherited Triton's short genes, but hell if the sexy curves didn't make her crazy.

"What do I need to come to realize?" Berkley asked as she stepped behind her and unfastened Aidan's bra with one hand.

"That you can't live without me," Aidan said. With a little assistance, her bra fell to the floor and Berkley had wasted no time in cupping her breast while her other hand slid into the navy blue bikini panties she was wearing. "Oh shit," Aidan said when Berkley pinched her clitoris between her fingers.

"Want me to stop?"

"Not unless you want me to shoot you down again, and this time it won't be simulated."

Aidan slumped against her and rested her hand behind Berkley's head to try to keep herself upright. With Aidan's hard clitoris still between her fingers, Berkley rocked her hand just enough to provide a little stimulation. "This is to pay you back for driving me crazy through dinner."

"Thanks for humoring my father and not choking to death after my mother's insightful comments." Berkley laughed at the coherent sentence because the more she touched Aidan, the wetter she got, so the fact that she was able to still string words together meant she had to kick it up a bit. She bit down on Aidan's earlobe as she squeezed her clitoris harder.

"Anytime," Berkley whispered in her ear.

"You have to go inside…I want you inside," Aidan was able to get out as she wrapped a hand around Berkley's wrist. "I want…oh."

"What do you want?" Berkley stopped her hand, not wanting Aidan to come like this. "Tell me what you want."

"Please, I need you so much." There was so much want in Aidan's voice that Berkley turned her around and picked her up so that her feet came off the floor and wrapped around her waist. "Your pants, honey," Aidan said as she painted the front of Berkley's uniform with the evidence of her desire.

As soon as Berkley sat on the bed Aidan pulled her forward and pressed her cheek to the top of Berkley's head. To Berkley's disappointment it took only sliding her fingers in to trigger Aidan's orgasm.

"Jesus, that felt good." Aidan shivered and clung to Berkley as she pulled her fingers out. "I missed you for so much more than this, but it was in my top five."

Berkley laughed as she stood again and gently laid Aidan on the bed so she could finish taking her clothes off. "You mean to tell me there wasn't anyone who tried to usurp my place in all this time?"

"There's been plenty of interest," Aidan said as she held the corner of the blanket for her.

"I'll just bet." Berkley couldn't believe just how much the thought of Aidan with someone else bothered her, but then Aidan was the only woman in her past that had sparked any jealousy in her at all.

"There was, but you can't have forgotten what my mother said tonight."

"You want to narrow it down for me?"

Aidan ran her finger down the middle of Berkley's chest as she kissed her shoulder. "There was only one sailor at the table who looks dashing in a uniform, honey, and it isn't me. There might have been interest, but nothing compared to what you must have gotten in the time we've been apart. I didn't forget how women react to you in or out of the uniform." She stopped her teasing and laid her hand flat on Berkley's abdomen. "Not that I can blame any woman for looking. You're still gorgeous. It's all the touching your admirers are fond of doing that I've never been able to get used to."

"Aidan Sullivan, you can't have been thinking all this time that people have been lusting after you for no reason. What'd you think all those sailors were interested in? Getting in your pants so the admiral would let them drive the boat?"

"You don't drive a boat, you loon, and we both know that I'm way out of your league. Compared to you I'm just ordinary."

"I swear, for such an accomplished woman, you're blind sometimes to the most basic things."

"I am not." Aidan went willingly when Berkley rolled her onto her back so she could hover over her.

"You're blind if you can't admit to just how beautiful you are," Berkley said before she kissed her. "If you haven't, then it'll be my pleasure to make sure you're sure of that fact for a very long time to come."

"Promise?"

"It's an easy one to make, and an even easier one to keep no matter what happens with us. Don't worry."

Since they both officially had the following day off they spent the rest of the night trying to piece together their connection.

As she held Aidan as they got ready for sleep, Berkley's heart was starting to take notice of what had been missing for way too long. It was the first night in years that Berkley drifted off into a peaceful and dreamless sleep. Aidan might have hurt her more than any other woman, but she also was the one who brought her peace.

For that reason alone Berkley's heart was willing to unlock the door for the possibility of a lifetime of that.

CHAPTER FOURTEEN

I gave everyone the next couple of days off since once we sail, there'll be no communication going out unless it's to Naval Command," Aidan said the next morning as they sat enjoying the coffee and breakfast Berkley had ordered from room service.

"Are you telling me you're actually going to take your own advice?" Berkley was wearing the robe the hotel provided and her hair was slicked back and wet from her shower.

Aidan lifted her leg and poked her in the chest. "I did a walk-through yesterday morning with Erika, so unless someone decides to take her out for a joy ride, there's nothing else to do. So yes, Commander Levine, I'm taking my own advice and enjoying every minute of my shore leave."

"Erika? Who's Erika?"

"My assistant." Aidan stood and sat on Berkley's lap. "She came with my last commission and she was good enough for me to want for this job."

"Is Erika one of the people you mentioned in showing an interest?"

This time Aidan understood the tone Berkley was using and why. It made her so happy she almost laughed. No one got jealous unless it mattered. "Can I tell you something and not have you think I'm totally sappy?"

"I'm willing to chance it."

"It didn't matter who was interested. They couldn't compare to you." She pressed her lips to Berkley's neck right under her ear and enjoyed the way Berkley pulled her closer. "I'll admit to being busy since we were together, but not with my social life. It's hard to beat perfection once you've had it."

"I'm hardly perfect, and that did come off as a little whiny." Berkley turned her head so they could kiss. "So what are you planning to do with your time off?"

"If I get my wish, it's to spend it all in this room with you, but I'll let you out every so often. How about we start at the Smithsonian since I know you love it and don't get to come often."

As Aidan started to rise the phone rang, but she figured it was either Corbin or Maggie checking in so she waved on the way to the bathroom. When Berkley answered, "Yes, this is Commander Levine," Aidan stopped. "Yes, sir, I can be there in an hour." When Berkley put the receiver down, Aidan's cell phone started ringing.

"Shit," Aidan said as she looked at the number.

"Ever take the Pentagon tour?" Berkley asked with a laugh as she kissed her forehead.

❖

Pyongyang, North Korea

The meeting was mandatory, so Jin Umeko's plans would have to wait until she was granted leave again. "It was a lousy day for a motorcycle ride anyway," she whispered as she gazed out the window of Central Command in Pyongyang, North Korea, to an overcast day.

"Captain Umeko, General Lee will see you now," the young receptionist said with a slight bow of her head.

The large room had maps adorning the two longest walls and pictures of the late President Kim Il Sung, the hero of the revolution and father of the current ruler Kim Jong Il. General Pak Kwang Lee was sitting at the head of the table along with Pom Su Gil and Chun Doo Samji.

"Good morning, Captain Umeko," General Lee said as he pointed to the seat to his right.

"Good morning to you, General. It's good to see you again in such good health," Jin said, though her voice bore no sign of warmth. She was merely being civil for the sake of the other two men in the room.

He nodded then handed her a stack of papers marked confidential.

"These were delivered this morning from government intelligence." He waited as she scanned the papers. "I'm having you transferred immediately since the airstrip is finished."

"As you command, sir."

"It's remote, but it poses the greatest threat if anything should go wrong," he continued. "Having China at our backs makes the security of the largest plant extremely important to Chairman Kim Jong Il. You're our best pilot, Captain Umeko, so you'll set up constant air patrols starting this week. We need at least three planes in the air at a time, twenty-four hours a day."

"I'll have trouble carrying out that extensive a mission with the fuel shortages." Jin never lifted her head as she spoke, scanning the folder the general had handed her.

"The crew and the fuel will be there on your arrival, the Great Leader guarantees it. This location is central to our future plans, so no expense will be too great."

She flipped the pages quickly until she reached a short report written under the press photo of the *Jefferson*. "China agreed to exercises with the Americans?"

"The *Jefferson* is set to sail at the end of the week. From our intelligence reports, its first assignment is in the Sea of Japan, but until her course is set we don't know where the new carrier is headed. That's why I want extra security. Should she come near our shores, we will step up the air security where you're going and Major Gill and Lieutenant Samji will move extra ground troops to the coastline."

"Would they dare to come after any target within our borders?" Pom Su asked.

"It's your job to see that they don't and to capture anyone who tries. The Great Leader wants to show the world what a pack of butchers the Americans are, and there's no better way to display that than with a war criminal caught in the act of carrying out atrocities against North Korea. I imagine the price of failure should there be a threat is something I don't have to review. Am I right?"

All three soldiers stood and saluted at his question, the two men left right after, and General Lee knocked on the table to make Jin sit. "How's your mother?" he asked.

"She's returned to Hungnam to tend to her ailing parents, but we had dinner before she made the trip."

Pak sighed. "I heard she was ill recently. That's not the case, then?"

"What exactly is it you want to know, Father? She was sick and I used part of my leave so Yong and I could help her."

"Then her trip to Hungnam isn't about taking care of her parents."

"The surgery to remove both her breasts has left her weak, but I had no choice but to have her true family take over her care." Jin laughed. "Duty calls, after all, does it not?"

"I know you blame me for leaving, but I had no choice."

"Everyone has choices, General, even you."

"For your sake, and for your career, I had to sacrifice my happiness. How do you think you became the best pilot in North Korea? Are you still flying with Yong?"

"I've told you she's off-limits unless it has to do with orders from our Great Leader."

"What you're doing could jeopardize your career. If that happens, where will you go? That's if they don't execute you for the crimes you're committing against the state."

Jin stood ramrod straight to make the most of her five feet six inches. "I don't care if I end up in the fields with the farming peasants starving or in front of a firing squad. At least it's better than ending up alone and shunned by my family." She gave him a salute. "I hope at the end of your life you still feel that the sacrifices were worth what you lost."

"Just worry about your job and serving our Leader, and forget about me."

With one last glance at him she started for the door. "I wouldn't lose sleep about that. Unless I'm ordered to come here, I usually do forget about you."

She was vibrating with anger by the time she stood on the street. To try to defuse her feelings she decided to forgo a cab and walk the two miles to the small apartment she shared with Lieutenant Yong Nam.

The city streets were crowded, but no one came close to touching Jin as she made her way along open markets that were mainly empty. She figured people still came out just to escape their houses and to congregate with friends. With any luck they could also find a treat with one of the vendors, though that seemed more and more infrequent.

"He didn't order me shot, did he?" Yong asked as soon as Jin walked in.

"Not yet, but with any luck my honorable father will have me shot first and forget about you. It's only fair I guess for sullying his reputation and name by committing such horrible crimes against the state."

With a walk that reminded Jin of a jungle cat, Yong made her way across the room and put her arms around Jin's waist. "Not if I can help it, and that's why you took your grandfather's name. He's as proud of you as your mother is."

"Thanks, but we don't have time for you to flatter me. We've been reassigned to start protecting the coast. We have to fly out as soon as possible."

Yong ran her hand down Jin's side until she was able to slide it between her legs. "Sex now, pack later. Because unless the base close to where I think we're going has changed much since the last time we went, it's a rock with nothing to do. If everyone is bored, then they'll definitely notice if I do this," Yong said as she dropped to her knees, taking Jin's pants with her.

CHAPTER FIFTEEN

Northern Virginia

"Commander Levine," Deputy Secretary of Defense Jerry Teague said as he held out his hand. He had a firm grip as he shook her hand and just as quickly let go to welcome Aidan. "And, Captain Sullivan, thank you for coming."

"It's our pleasure, sir," Berkley said trying to keep Aidan from saying anything she'd regret later since she'd been steamed all the way over. "What can we do for you?"

"What she meant to say is what can we do for you that I didn't cover in all the days I've spent here lately?" Aidan asked. "I'm sorry to sound a little put off, Mr. Teague, but we sail in a matter of days and I wanted my crew to enjoy the time we have left."

"As you know, we're undergoing change here at the Pentagon and President Khalid has decided for now, under the circumstances, to keep some of the old guard until his team is up to speed." He waved them to the sofa in the room and took the seat across from them. "Secretary of State Henley took over for his predecessor and opened dialogue with the North Koreans via the UN Security Council."

"Any luck?" Berkley asked.

"Some people need things proven to them, Commander," Jerry said as he picked up a bowl of peanuts and started shelling them without offering them any. "These people are lunatics with a hatred of our way of life. There's no negotiating with that."

"I thought the UN wanted no part of the North Korea problem," Aidan said.

"The UN isn't exactly useful in situations like this because they move at glacial speeds no matter what's at stake." He kept shelling peanuts like it was part of his job, and before too long there was a circle of litter around his chair. "For once, though, they seem to be somewhat motivated since this could be a nutcase with a nuclear weapon, so they want us to exhaust all diplomatic avenues. They're also trying to pressure China and Japan to go in there and talk some sense into this wingnut." As if someone had flipped a switch, he let go of the peanuts and moved to the coffee service, only this time he played the perfect host.

"Are you going to be our contact on this?" Berkley asked after she waved off the cup he held up.

"They'll have to drag me out of here at gunpoint once we bomb the crap out of their facilities, because no way is my replacement going to be trained by then." Teague's voice rose enough to make him sound unbalanced and he seemed to realize it when he drained his cup instead of saying another word.

"We'll be dealing with Naval Command, Commander," Aidan answered for Jerry.

"Getting back to the UN and the coalition the president wants to build. We have a few more meetings with the North Korean diplomatic corps, then we'll go to the UN with our findings. It's our hope that the UN Secretary General will announce any actions deemed necessary in about two months."

"We'll be pushing it to be in the area to participate in naval exercises in that short a time. Why take the chance of tipping our hand by moving too fast?" Aidan asked.

"Your job is to have the *Jefferson* in position before the UN meets, so your orders are to sail full throttle. As soon as the Secretary General makes the announcement they're in agreement that military action is necessary, the plants are to be blown. If they're not, we feel that'll give Jong Il time to put countermeasures in place, retaliate, or sell this material to other rogue states. None of these options is acceptable."

"So as the UN makes the announcement we're supposed to be airborne and ready to launch," Berkley said. "The information Captain Sullivan gave me already stated that, so I'm confused as to why I'm here on a weekend to review."

"I want you and Captain Sullivan to be sure you understand that when the decree is made we need to hear instant explosions, Commander. We want you in and out with nothing fancy. The United States wants no repercussions from this that'll require any kind of sustained military presence. That isn't something anyone seems to have a stomach for anymore, and it was the only way to get China and Japan to agree to military action. We gave our word nothing would go wrong, so I need you to understand exactly how grave this is before you go in." He stared at her as if she were simple. "I felt it was important enough to go over it again no matter what day it was."

Berkley smiled and glanced over his head to the diplomas hanging behind his desk in very tasteful frames. "What branch of the military did you serve in, Deputy Secretary?"

"I did a few summers in the air national guard, why?"

"Missions are by nature dangerous propositions. If just anyone could do it they wouldn't need Captain Sullivan or me to carry it out, would they?"

Teague put his cup down with a little bit of extra force. "What does that have to do with anything?"

"It's just that we can plan and prepare for just about anything, but like in Iraq, a well-thought-out plan, no matter how brilliant, can fall short of its goals. I'm planning to fly in, carry out the mission, and fly out, but I can't guarantee there won't be a glitch along the way. Anyone who tells you differently is lying, because life holds no guarantees."

"Doesn't sound very optimistic, Commander," said the new arrival, who stood at the private entrance to Teague's office.

"I'm being realistic, sir, so you all can plan for any contingency. That's the advice my father gave me that's served me well."

"My advice is to trust your teammates and you'll be fine." He held his hand out to her but enough out of reach that she'd have to stand to take it. "Adam Morris," he said when Berkley had no choice but to comply, "and I tell you that about your teammates because I know what my son is capable of in a plane." David "Blazer" Morris looked like his father. Blazer had inherited his dad's blond hair, height, slim undefined build, and pinched mouth. Both men gave Berkley the impression that someone in their life had convinced them that they were misplaced royalty who'd have to suffer walking among the hoi polloi for the rest of their lives.

"With any luck all he'll have to do is take my wing and have a good story to tell someday." Berkley smiled as she looked down on him, taking advantage of the few inches she had on him.

"The Morris men aren't followers by nature, but everything in good time," he said but didn't elaborate. "You concentrate on carrying out the orders and we won't have to worry about contingencies."

"I'll give it my best shot, sir." Berkley turned toward the door briefly to give Aidan a hint that she'd had enough of the company.

Teague stood as well and slapped his hands together. "Excellent, and thank you for coming. We'll meet a few more times before you sail, but you should consider this a go unless you hear otherwise." He patted Berkley on the back. "Once you're in position, blow those plants back to the Stone Age, Commander."

"Yes, sir." Berkley gave him a salute. "Mr. Morris," she added as she turned to leave, "pleasure meeting you."

"Captain, you'll get an updated report as soon as today's round of meetings are finished," Teague said as the tension in the room became palpable.

"I'll look forward to it," Aidan said, then stayed silent until they boarded the Metro.

"Can you believe they give those jobs to the person who made the biggest campaign contribution?" Aidan asked. "Then you can't get rid of them even when there's a change at the top. And you were wondering if I'm ready to retire. I'm tired of these meetings with people who know nothing about military strategy and never bothered to put on a uniform. I never wanted to take up cluelessness as a hobby."

"Morris was a pilot, but he's interested in different conquests, it seems, and he's found a good ally in Teague. Call me crazy, but there's something off about this whole thing."

"The odd thing is that they've kept some of these guys in place, but I've got a theory about that. I'll tell you about it later, but right now I need you to feed me then show me some old stuff at the Smithsonian."

"How about after that? Want to catch an Imax or something?"

"Later you'll be busy, so don't make any plans."

The subway train stopped and Berkley moved aside so Aidan could exit first. "I am, huh?" she whispered.

"Yes, you are. Just keep thinking non-standard issue underwear."

❖

"My son was right," Adam said when he was alone with Jerry. "The world we know and love is dead and it's our job to revive it."

"America thinks it wants change, Adam, but the idiots who vote it in don't know what they want."

"Sir." The voice of Jerry's assistant Sergeant Nelson Alexander came over the intercom. "I'm sorry to disturb you, but your guest is here."

"Should I go?" Adam asked.

"Only if you didn't mean what you said about reviving our way of life." The door opened and the newly retired Admiral Rodney James walked in wearing a suit that didn't appear right on him. "Thank you for joining us, sir."

"There are only so many models you can build before you go insane, so I appreciate you asking me." Rodney took the seat Jerry had occupied during his meeting with Berkley and Aidan. "Though I'm surprised you'd work for our new fearless leader."

"My replacement is being trained, so we don't have a lot of time to rectify some of the things going on around here." Jerry hesitated but took his place on the sofa. "With your recent and unfair retirement I thought you'd be available to give us some advice on how best to do that."

"What do you have in mind?" Rodney asked. "And who is this?"

"Adam Morris, sir," Adam said and stood to shake his hand. "My son will be a pilot on the *Jefferson*."

"That's the best ship the Navy has ever floated, and it's become nothing but a joke. It's a shame your child has to be a part of that."

"That's what we want to talk to you about, Admiral," Jerry said. "I've given this a lot of thought and if there was some way for the *Jefferson*'s maiden voyage to be unsuccessful, I believe the president will have no choice but to change the ship's leadership and return some of the old guard."

"Short of Aidan Sullivan running the damn thing aground, I don't see Khalid doing that," Rodney said.

"You left before you were informed of where the *Jefferson* was going and what the mission is when they get there. If Sullivan succeeds, the Navy you served and gave most of your life to will be a memory," Jerry said and paused. It wouldn't take much to hook Rodney's interest, but he didn't want to come across as too eager lest he lose control of the situation. "The new Navy will have Sullivan's face on it and will be backed up by someone like Berkley Levine."

"Levine is on the *Jefferson*?" Rodney slid to the end of his seat. "That's the girl who's been serving at Fallon?"

"That's her, and she's going to *lead* the flight team on this," Adam said.

"Everyone thinks that's such a hot spot, but considering she's been the best out there for a couple of years shows how much the military has fallen with everyone giving in to all these factions who think they deserve a fair shot. Defending this nation has nothing to do with giving in to anyone, but making the hard choices and carrying them out with the people most able to do what needs to happen to annihilate the competition. Women aren't emotionally suited to serve in combat positions. Putting them there does nothing but endanger lives," Rodney said, outraged. "What do you two have in mind?"

Adam stayed quiet as Jerry laid out his plan. To deliberately sabotage a mission would be considered treason, but sometimes sacrifices were necessary. All that mattered to Adam was that Blazer would be in the middle of the action. The chance they were taking was huge, but the rewards were too big to not be involved.

"If you repeat what I've just told you Adam and I will have no choice but to deny it, and with both of us sticking to the same story yours won't hold water," Jerry said. "So if you want time to think about what I proposed, I'm willing to give you that."

"Meet with your son," Rodney said after Jerry had talked for over an hour. "Give him the details we discussed today and tell him to expect a call from me. There are ways to go about this, but he needs to be prepared to act if the opportunity arises. Is that answer enough for you?"

"Yes, sir."

"Any responsible serviceman would be court-martialed for coming up with this madness, but the president is untouchable? I don't think so. Gentlemen, it's up to us to show the American public he can't be trusted with their national security."

"Do you think we need more than Adam's son to carry this out, Admiral?" Jerry asked.

"It depends on if his son is capable or not," Rodney said and stuck his finger in his shirt as if his collar was too tight.

"Blazer is more than enough," Adam said. "We want things to return to normal, but we can't bring that about if we're in jail. He'll do his part in a way that can't be traced back to us."

"Well said." Rodney nodded slightly in his direction. "We'll go with one for now, but I'll need a list of the crew in case we have to alter our plan. Even if they're at sea you'll have the authority to contact the ship," he said to Jerry. "Thank you, gentlemen. I feel better about our country, and failure isn't an option."

"This is the last time we can meet here," Jerry said. "From now on we'll meet at the office, so as not to arouse suspicion."

"We have a week to prepare," Adam said.

"More than enough time," Rodney said. "The *Jefferson* will go down in history, but not for what Khalid has in mind."

CHAPTER SIXTEEN

"Where'd you run off to?" Aidan asked without uncovering her head from the layer of blankets when she heard the door to her room open. "I'm not used to waking up alone."

"I had a coffee date with two guys named Harvey, and I figured you'd rather sleep than join me," Berkley said as she got back into bed naked. "My backseat wanted me to meet his dad and this was the only time they could squeeze me in."

It had been a quick week and by this time the next day Aidan would have the *Jefferson* well out to sea. As excited as she was about that, it meant another long span of separation from Berkley. And it would be harder because she'd seen her across her pillow every morning during their leave.

"I wanted to wake up with you since it's our last day," Aidan said and tried not to whine.

"You did, and I was in the bed two minutes later," Berkley said softly as she pressed up against her. "Besides, that won't be the only time you wake up today."

Aidan turned around and held her breath when Berkley put her hand between her legs. "What do you mean?"

"You're wet, hard, and I'm going to have to do something about it. Once I do you're going back to sleep, and when you wake up I promise I'll be right here."

"It's a miracle you were still single," Aidan said before she gave in to Berkley's touch. It was maddeningly slow, but she knew why. Like her, Berkley wanted to commit to memory every moment because there would be no more mornings like this until they returned.

When it was done Aidan felt like an idiot when she started to cry, but Berkley held her without saying anything. Berkley's humming in her ear was the last thing she remembered as she dozed off, and as promised, Berkley was there when she woke the second time.

❖

The next afternoon they met Triton and Mary Beth in a café not far from the Norfolk Naval Station for their last meal on shore. They had planned the lunch so there'd be plenty of time to take a tour of the *Jefferson* with Aidan as their guide. Berkley enjoyed watching Triton inspect every nook and cranny as he made his way from stem to stern. As he ran his hands along the gray steel of the ship it was easy to see where Aidan had inherited her love of the open water at the helm of something like this.

"Who's your backseat for this, Cletus?" Triton asked as they stopped in front of Berkley's plane.

"Lieutenant Harvey Whittle, sir. He's a little green, but I trust him with my ass up there. My father served with his dad years ago, so he comes from good stock as well."

"Just make sure you follow the advice I gave my daughter. You get back here in one piece. You owe me a dinner in New Orleans."

"What is it with owed meals and your family?" Berkley asked Aidan with a laugh.

"Maybe it has to do with loving to spend time with you," Aidan said in a whisper, not wanting any of the crew to overhear her.

"I'm sure that has to be it." Berkley smiled as she leaned back against the plane. "When we get back we'll try our best to get together with my folks. I'm sure my dad will like getting to know you, Admiral." She pointed to the stairs that would take them back to the deck and led the way up. When Aidan headed for the bridge Berkley put her hand on Triton's shoulder to stop him. "I wanted to ask you a favor if I could."

"Ask away."

"Once we sail there won't be any communications allowed. You might not have met my parents yet, but they know this drill, and I'd like you and your wife, if you're inclined, to call them and keep in touch. I think my mother especially would appreciate hearing from your wife."

"I'd be glad to do that for you, Cletus. It's what families do when things are tough."

"Thank you, sir." She smiled and didn't contradict him, and he smiled back as he put another unlit cigar in his mouth. "Now let me deliver you back to Aidan so you and Mrs. Sullivan can spend some time together. We have an hour before they clear the ship of visitors and another hour before we get going."

"You just remember to take care of Aidan and get back safe." From the pocket of his jacket he pulled out something and kept it hidden in his fist. "Like your dad, I served, and my father gave me this before I left on my first tour. The pictures have changed over the years depending on which Sullivan was carrying it, and I thought it was time to put it back in service. For a long time it had a picture of my family in it, then I replaced it with one of Mary Beth, but this one has been my all-time favorite." He opened his hand and in it sat what appeared to be an old watch.

"Sir, I couldn't let you part with that, especially if it's a family heirloom. Aidan and I aren't at that point yet."

With a press of the release on the side he opened it and Berkley saw it wasn't a watch but a compass with a place on the other side for a picture. She hadn't seen many of Aidan's baby pictures, but the toddler in the picture with her hands on her hips and her head cocked to the side had to be her. "Damn if she couldn't stop you in your tracks even when she was four. Always quick to steer me in the right direction, even if that was really my job."

"I've had that pose and that face directed at me on more than one occasion, and you're right, it'll stop you cold."

With one last look he closed the compass and pressed it into Berkley's hand. "How about you keep it for a while? I'm positive you'll take care of it and be proud to hand it off to the next generation. No matter where you think you are in this relationship, I'm betting on you. I see how you look at my daughter, and that means your heart realizes something that your head isn't ready for."

"Are you sure?"

"I'm as sure as Aidan. Use it to find your way home." He opened it again and pointed to the picture. "The compass will point you in the right direction and the picture will remind you of the destination."

"Thank you so much, sir. I'll take good care of it."

"Brought me luck when it counted. I'm sure it still has a lot of luck still left in it, and the salt in my blood tells me you're going to need it."

"It's going to be a little tricky, but I guess it's time for the Navy to reap the benefit of the millions they've poured into my training," Berkley said, slapping him on the back. "Come on. There's a captain around here who I'm sure wants to give her dad a hug before she takes this thing out for a spin."

"You know something, Cletus?"

"What's that, sir?"

"Aidan was right about you."

She laughed and couldn't begin to imagine what he meant. "I wish that I had time to play twenty questions with you, so you're going to have to explain that to me."

"When she first met you and she'd called home, she couldn't stop talking about you." Triton put his hand on her shoulder and Berkley stopped walking. "I finally called her on it, and she told me that no matter what came to pass I was really going to like you. The reason she said was because we're a lot alike. I'll have to get to know you better to see if that's true, but she was dead on about the first part."

"The main part of us having something in common is we both care about her."

"I can see that, so make sure she sticks to her guns this time around."

"Aye aye, sir."

The bridge was fully staffed and they were at their stations getting ready for Aidan to order them away. For the moment, everyone was in their dress whites getting ready for the ceremony that the Secretary of the Navy was there to preside over. The *Jefferson* was the Navy's future, and her captain was the woman who would sail them to it.

Berkley stood back as Aidan bid her parents good-bye and accepted a hug from them before they disembarked. As the dignitaries started their long-winded speeches, she ducked back into the bridge and called her house.

"Hi, Dad."

"Cletus, how's it going?"

"The talking heads have started and this is my last chance to call you. How is Mom holding up?"

"She's doing fine and talking with your sisters, so don't worry about us. You have enough on your mind so keep it clear of things that are under control."

She laughed at her father's ability to compartmentalize just about everything in his life. "I'll try my best. Tell them that I love them and I'll see them soon. I hate to cut this short, but Aidan's giving me the look that means I have to go."

"I love you, Cletus, and you keep your ass in the air, you hear me?"

"I hear you, and I love you too."

The ceremonies lasted about an hour and then the lines were cast off and Aidan sounded excited as she ordered the engines started. With the speed they were going to maintain, they'd be in position in twelve days. It could have been faster, but their orders were to be there on time but not to seem over-anxious. As soon as they were clear of the base everyone took the opportunity to change into their standard uniform so they could start their duties.

Berkley called an hour-long meeting with her pilots to review again the terrain they'd be flying over and how best to approach their island targets. When they were done she took advantage of the clear day to take a jog with Harvey on deck. They had to work as a team and she wanted to relax him so that he'd be at the top of his game when she needed it the most.

"Are you sure about this?" Harvey asked as they headed back to the mess hall.

"Sure about what?"

"That you want me with you on this. This is some serious shit and I'm not exactly the best qualified."

She stopped him while they were still outside and leaned against the rail so she could enjoy the smell of the salt water as long as she could before heading back to work. "Why do you think you landed at the Top Gun school?"

"My father called in a few favors and they found me a slot. It's not because I'm the best. I couldn't fly and Dad thought this would be the next best thing for me to have some sort of aviation career."

"Let me let you in on a little secret," she said as she moved closer to him. "No matter how much stroke your father thinks he has, no one just gets in because their old man makes a call. After you met Will you should've figured that out. You got in because of merit, but if you have one doubt then you have a couple of days to figure it out. If you flinch, it's not just my ass you knock out of the sky, but yours as well, and I don't know about you, but I really don't want that to happen."

"I'm sure, ma'am. I just wanted you to be sure."

"If I had doubts about you, Whittle, I'd have left you back in Nevada. Just keep to your schedule so you get plenty of rest and everything will be fine. Whatever you do, don't let someone like Blazer get into your head."

CHAPTER SEVENTEEN

Off the Northwest Coast of North Korea

"You are cleared for landing," the man in the tower radioed to Jin as she circled the airstrip they'd built on shore close to where the plants were located. Her partner Yong was right that the area was remote, and from the air Jin could see where'd they'd conducted some of their underground testing. There were already signs of tree die-off.

Yong radioed back since Jin was still studying the terrain from the cockpit. They made four more passes before she headed to the airstrip that had been finished the week before, complete with hangar. Until they were ordered elsewhere, they'd be working from there every day and living in the barracks set up right on the beach.

"Welcome, Captain Umeko," the ground crew member who'd rolled the ladder to her plane said as she opened the cockpit glass. The Russian fighter jets they flew were older, but smaller and faster than what the Americans had in their arsenal.

Jin just nodded and stepped out to cold temperatures from the sea breeze. "Have our supplies arrived?"

"Yes, ma'am." He bowed and almost appeared to be expecting a blow. "My humble apologies, ma'am, but we've had to place you and Lieutenant Nam in the same room due to accommodation shortages with the extra personnel the general has sent to the area."

"I guess we'll have to make do then, won't we?" Jin said as she glanced back to Yong. "Have the others arrived?"

"Not for two days. General Lee left word that you're to use the time to set up the schedules and flight patterns you'll be utilizing."

Jin got into the front seat of the waiting jeep and wished not for the first time that her father would stay out of her life for good. "Of course he did. General Lee is nothing if not thorough."

The available quarters were as utilitarian as the government could make them, with two small cots and no windows. Thankfully, there was a small bathroom in the room so they wouldn't have to share the communal showers down the hall. It was designed for sleep and hygiene and nothing more. To spend idle time here would be to lose one's mind, and that's how the Great Leader wanted it. Idle time was for powers like the evil Americans, not for the never-ending revolution.

"Think they bugged the room?" Yong asked.

"Want to chance it?" Jin asked in a way that put an end to any romantic notions. "This is a test from the general, so we have to show some restraint and do our duty to the best of our ability. If we pull this off and the Americans are dumb enough to try something, we'll finally be out from his heel."

"We could be here for months, though." Yong unpacked her bag and put her things away before starting on Jin's.

"I'm not made of stone, darling. We'll manage something, just not here." She whispered right into Yong's ear just in case her father had put any kind of surveillance in the room. "Now that we're settled let's get back to the airstrip and get things going. I want to be prepared for whatever is coming."

"No one is in your league, so I wouldn't worry about it," Yong was quick to say.

Jin laughed at the decisive defense and thought that while Yong was loyal in her bed, she still had a lot of the revolution's ideology in her head. "If I thought like that I would've given this up by now. If they come they'll send up some worthy adversaries, so we have our hands full, I'm sure."

And Jin hoped the chance would come. One of the things her father had taught her that had been worth retaining was to think ahead so that you stayed a step ahead of your opponents. If she could defeat the Americans on a stage where the world was watching, it would be the opportunity to escape from under her father's heel, but she couldn't be that lucky.

"If there's one person I agree with in all this, it's Pom Su. The

Americans wouldn't dare carry out any kind of military option against us after they went into Iraq with hardly any backing. Considering the obstacles their military already faces because of that conflict, it would be suicidal to try."

The temperature had dropped as the sun started to set, and Jin pulled her uniform coat closed as they stepped outside. "You read the reports just like I did, and China and Japan, if pushed, will not side with our right to do what the Great Leader Kim Jong Il is doing."

"Jin, if anyone hears you say that—" Yong started.

"I'll be court-martialed?" Jin asked with a great deal of sarcasm. It wasn't the first time Yong had given her such a warning, and it always made her think of something else her father told her constantly when she was going through her training. "Never trust anyone, no matter how close to you they seem." It was the only other thing of any value he'd ever told her. "Are you the one who'll tie my noose, darling?"

"I would never betray you. You must realize that by now."

"Then take my grandfather's wisdom to heart and think for yourself for once. Just because the government says something is so, does not make it fact. I think that holds true for any government out there, but more so here. Continue believing all the hype and it'll get you far in the military, but you'll only be a part of continuing the lies."

"I just worry about you and your beliefs. If you continue to defy so openly where you can be overheard, I'm afraid that they'll take you somewhere that even your father won't be able to find you."

With a pat to Yong's back, Jin continued toward the jeep. "Given a choice, I'll live my life the way the man who raised me taught me to live it, and his name wasn't Pak Kwang Lee. My service isn't a question. I'll do that gladly, but my mind and heart will never belong to anyone but me. And I'll share them with no one I think unworthy of them. If you can't accept that, it's best you tell me now before we waste any more time."

"Just like in the plane, I'll always have your back, so you needn't worry about me."

With her father's warning still ringing in her head, Jin nodded. "Let's just get started on what we were sent here to do."

❖

Onboard the USS *Jefferson*

"Uh, now I remember why I detest boats," Berkley said as she stretched for their usual afternoon run.

The *Jefferson* was sailing through some rough seas that were common in the late summer and early autumn in the Southern Hemisphere. Harvey was standing next to her, and the rest of the pilots were making their way along the corridor. They had decided to join Berkley and Harvey to pass the time after their daily meetings since there'd be no flying until they reached their destination.

"If any of you falls off this damn thing, I'm not fishing you out," Berkley warned as they stepped outside to a driving rain.

"Explain to me again why we're doing this here instead of the state-of-the-art gym they have inside," Blazer said as he started blinking furiously.

"Because we're Navy men, Morris," Killer explained with a roll of his eyes. "Getting wet should be essential to your everyday activities. Or did you miss that part of the program at the Academy?"

"Quit your yapping and get running," Berkley ordered.

From the bridge Aidan put her binoculars down and shook her head at the crazy people on her deck. They skirted weather systems like the one they were in the middle of whenever possible, but with their tight timeline she had no choice but to sail through the worst of it.

They'd been sailing for over twenty days, and watching Berkley run was one of the few times she'd actually seen her aside from meals. But even then the ace of naval aviation was surrounded by the other pilots on board trying to get a few minutes of Berkley's time to talk and to ask her advice.

"She certainly is easy to spot in a crowd," Lieutenant Erika Gibson commented as she stood next to Aidan. "I haven't gotten a feel for her, though."

"Do you think you need to?"

"Permission to speak freely, ma'am." She waited for Aidan to nod, which she did. "When you hear about military legends and then you actually get to meet them, they usually aren't the shining stars the stories make them out to be. With the gravity of what we're facing, I think we should've recruited someone with more combat experience than Commander Levine. There's a long list of pilots with hundreds of hours over Iraq that we could have gone with."

"Don't you mean *I* should have recruited someone better? Thank you for sharing your thoughts, but this might be a subject we'll agree to disagree on. The commander has my full confidence, and not to slight the others you mentioned, but most of them learned their skills from the officer you see running out there. She'd probably argue with you about the legend title, but this is a different mission than what the pilots are doing in Iraq and Berkley's more than qualified to carry it out." She pointed out the window as the groups made another pass under the bridge. "She's done more for the Navy than fly in Fallon, so I'm happy with my choice. If I didn't feel that way I would've gone elsewhere."

"Sorry, Aidan, I didn't mean to second-guess you."

"Of course you did." The exercise group reached the bow and started back. Aidan stopped to admire Berkley's stride. "But that's what keeps me at my best. I trust your opinion, but you're going to have to trust me on this."

"I do, but I had to ask."

Aidan scanned the horizon again out of habit and found the sea still rough but clear of other ships. "I know, and feel free to share anything else." The one good thing about Erika aside from her competence was she knew when to quit when she couldn't win. They sailed in silence after that with Aidan glancing at the runners every so often. An hour went by and the weather only got worse, but before she could order Berkley's team inside, they came to a walk.

She looked around one last time to make sure everything was in order as Berkley disappeared through one of the hatches. "If you need me I'll be in my quarters reviewing the packet from the Pentagon."

The crew members she encountered on the way back gave Aidan a casual salute but none of them stopped her. One of the wonderful things about the *Jefferson* was the small strategy room just off her office in the captain's quarters. The room also had another door and led to the lead pilot's office, then to the quarters beyond. The only way to access the room was from either her office or Berkley's, and at the moment both doors were locked.

When she entered Berkley's quarters she heard the shower running and smiled as she started to remove her uniform. It would be a tight fit, but she was willing to chance it to spend a few moments alone with Aidan.

"I don't want to know how many regulations we're breaking by you being in here," Berkley said as soon as Aidan's hands landed on her back.

"Is this the same flygirl I met who painted the commanding officer's car bright pink when we were in Hawaii?" Berkley already had her pinned to the wall of the shower and her lips were pressed to her neck.

"I remember who was holding the paint can for me." Even though Aidan had joined her, Berkley was shielding her from the bulk of the spray.

"That's because you're a bad influence on me."

Berkley laughed in that deep joyful way that Aidan loved and still dreamt about. "Should I remind you whose shower you're in? You're not fooling anyone with that angelic face and the all-American looks, Sullivan."

"You can't blame me."

"I can't, huh?" Berkley reached behind her to shut off the water.

"You know how much I love you in those shorts, so yes, it's your fault." She stood as Berkley took her time drying her off. "And you've been avoiding me since we lifted anchor."

"I'm not avoiding you." Berkley made quick work of drying herself off.

"Sweetheart, you've barely spoken to me since you boarded."

"That's because," the towel landed in the sink after Berkley threw it so she could scoop Aidan off of her feet, "I didn't want the crew realizing how much you want me."

The egotistical comment made Aidan bite her on the shoulder. "I'm glad to see time hasn't tempered that naval aviator mentality." Aidan bit Berkley's shoulder again to keep her quiet. "Just remember that I have some big guns at my disposal and I know how to use them."

"Are you threatening me?" The cot the room held was small for Berkley's frame but Aidan fit perfectly when Berkley laid her down. "You are so beautiful." The teasing died away as Berkley seemed to study every inch of Aidan's face.

"You're the only person who's ever told me that and made me

believe it." Even from Berkley's quarters Aidan could hear the hum of the ship's engines. She could just make out the rough seas as she and Berkley rocked against one another. But the reminders of where they were and what they were doing didn't matter. "You're the only one who didn't treat me like the admiral's kid."

"That's because I'm not militarily ambitious. All I wanted was you."

The hair at Berkley's neck tickled against the tips of Aidan's fingers as she ran her hands up to the longer strands at the top. Though the temperature of the room was comfortable, the intimate act puckered Aidan's nipples and doubled the wetness between her legs.

"So Triton didn't scare you away?"

Berkley pulled her closer and bit down gently on the nearer nipple, making Aidan hiss. "Do you really want to talk about your father right now?" she asked before treating the other nipple to the same pleasurable stimulation. "Because right now I'd really like to talk about something else."

"What do you want to talk about?" Aidan was able to ask the question, but the feeling of Berkley's fingers skimming down her abdomen, then down her thighs was making her lift her hips hoping that she'd land between her legs. It was funny to her that after going without sex for so long after she'd lost Berkley, she could so quickly be so ravenous again.

"I want to talk about just how long I can make love to you and achieve two things."

"What?" The end of the word rose in pitch as Berkley finally spread her open and ran her middle finger through the wetness and just barely skimmed over her throbbing clitoris.

"I want to see just how long I can make it last before you come." Berkley followed with a firmer pass along Aidan's clitoris, making Aidan moan. "And I want to see just how quiet you can be since I don't think it's a good idea for us to get court-martialed this far into the mission." She sounded like she was joking but covered Aidan's mouth in a kiss anyway.

It was all Aidan needed to get swept up in the passion that Berkley had done such an excellent job of starting, then fanning the flames. She pulled her head back from the kiss when she needed air but just as quickly bit Berkley's shoulder again when she thought she was going to have no choice but to scream as she felt those talented fingers stroking away her thoughts and worries.

It might not have lasted as long as Berkley had wanted, but Aidan figured she didn't care as she felt the orgasm take her over. She moved her hips in time with Berkley's hand and at the pinnacle moment she grabbed Berkley's hair with an insistent pull and dragged her head down to her nipples, which had gotten hard as she came.

Above her, Berkley was panting. While Berkley's fingers were still in her, Aidan reached down and started the dance all over again, only this time she wanted to watch as Berkley got lost in what they shared for each other. Berkley started to rock her hips, driving the fingers Aidan still had buried in her that much deeper.

"Let go for me, honey, and don't stop." Aidan was the one panting now. Her fingers were soaked from Berkley's sex, but she was anything but gentle. They were both past the moment for gentle, so she gave Berkley what she wanted. "Oh God, I'm coming again." Aidan's whisper made Berkley's hips speed up and they both orgasmed together.

"You do have a good work ethic when it comes to making up for lost time," Aidan joked a little time later as they were in the shower again actually showering.

"That's easy to do when you love what you're doing." Berkley helped Aidan wash her hair, then opened the door and handed her a towel so there was enough room for her to finish.

CHAPTER EIGHTEEN

Ten minutes later they were both sitting at the table in the strategy room going over the latest papers from the Pentagon. But Aidan's mind was on something else, and she figured she had a few minutes before her job would again take precedence over her personal life.

Aidan put her hand over the papers in front of her. She rested her head on the soft leather of her chair and stared at Berkley's expression. "I should've understood the kind of commitment you wanted from me and that it's what made my life complete a long time ago and not been so goddamn stupid."

"I'm not sure where that came from, but don't dwell, Aidan. We agreed to start again, and we have."

"Sorry, I can't help the insecurity that kicks me in the ass every once in a while. It's been going great, but the future's a scary place all of a sudden."

"You're not sure where you fit in now?" Berkley asked.

"I'd like not to worry about it, but I can't help it."

Berkley didn't say anything for what seemed like an eternity to Aidan, but then she reached across the table and picked up Aidan's hands.

"If anything, the future holds no dark rooms for you and no uncertainties. It won't all be easy, but it won't be lonely."

Aidan lowered her head and kissed Berkley's knuckles. "When all this is over I want two things from you."

"Name them."

"I want you to take me flying. In all the time we've known each other, we've never done that."

Berkley let go of one of her hands and reached up to place her palm on Aidan's cheek. "That's one, and sure, I'd love to. What else do you want?"

"I want you to come back to me in one piece, Cletus. You earned that swagger of yours because you're the best the Navy has up there, so you prove it to me. You come back and give me the life I want, and don't you dare let me down."

Her chair scraped on the floor as Berkley stood and saluted. "Ma'am, yes, ma'am. I have some plans of my own for the first time in a long time, so don't you worry about that." The knock on her office door ended their conversation, but they both smiled in a way that spoke of healing past hurts.

"These are the latest reports from Command," Erika said as she walked in followed by Berkley's group of pilots. She placed the folders on the table, then went to sit at Aidan's right. At the other end of the table, Berkley sat studying the screens in the room that showed their position in the Indian Ocean.

"They've moved the UN speech up two days?" Aidan asked as soon as she glanced at the page. "There's no way we're in place by then even if I open the engines up full throttle. Not if we have to set up for the games they want us to participate in as a cover."

"That might work to our advantage, so don't worry about it," Berkley said. She walked to the screen and placed her finger on the farthest target. "Calculating the miles in from the coast, and the capacity of fuel, we need to be about here for us to be able to carry this off." She moved her finger out to sea and tapped the screen lightly. "If the powers that be want the element of surprise, that might do it if we put our birds in the air before the cavalry shows up, don't you think?" She turned and looked at Aidan. "You should have us to this point by then, won't you?"

"If something goes wrong, I won't have us in position to provide cover for you."

"Then we'll have to make sure nothing goes wrong," Berkley said as if she could make it happen just by saying the words.

Erika shook her head and turned to the next page of the report. "I'm sure that'll be the case, Commander, but you might want to read page two of what they sent. The satellites have picked up movement from the North Korean military. They're now running air cover over the northwestern-most site, and there's a battalion of men moving to the shoreline. It would seem to me that they're expecting us."

"It's more like they're anticipating us," Berkley said, not turning her eyes from Aidan.

"There's a difference?" Erika asked.

"It's like this." Berkley turned to her. "If you know your friends are throwing you a surprise party for your birthday, then in the back of your mind you anticipate walking through the door and people shouting. You know about it, so it isn't a surprise at all. But you know what? When the day comes and you walk through the door, you can't help but be shocked at the precise moment you hear those yells."

"How do you know how I'd react, much less the pilots guarding the nest?" Erika asked, watching Berkley move closer to her.

"Because, Lieutenant." Berkley stopped three feet from her and smiled before lunging at her and slamming her hands on the table. She didn't laugh when Erika pulled back so quickly her chair hit the wall from the sudden fright. "It's human nature. Knowing something and being confronted by it are two different things."

From the way Erika's chest was heaving, Berkley could tell there was a curse simmering inside her.

"Who told you that bullshit?"

"Commander Corbin Levine, and to this day I haven't found a smarter guy around. We're going in there and blowing this thing, and I don't give a shit who's in the air with me. They aren't going to stop me from doing my job."

"I hope you're right," Erika said. "Because God help us if you're wrong."

"Did you come along for the rousing pep talks?" Berkley asked and this time her crew did laugh.

The humor didn't penetrate Erika's cool façade. "I'm here to do a job just like you. I'm sorry if you don't appreciate my point of view."

"What I don't appreciate is your counting us out even before we start. I'm not an idiot, so of course they've put some countermeasures in place considering the movement going on off their coastline. That's to be expected."

"Don't you mean you're anticipating that they did that?" Erika asked.

"If I'd meant to use the word 'anticipate,' I'd have used it. I'm sure their air cover is in place, and my educated guess is the best they have is stationed at the location you just mentioned."

"Why's that?" Erika looked not at all perturbed that she was dominating the conversation.

"Because it's the closest one to their shores, and whoever Cletus sends up there, their pilots will have the most time to chase and shoot down," Killer answered for Berkley.

"Like I said, that's my educated guess, but we'll make sure we're ready for whatever we find. We'll go over some countermeasures in our meeting after this," Berkley said to her group of pilots, then pulled Erika's chair back to the table enough so that she couldn't stand up. "Everyone is dismissed. I'll meet you in the situation room on the second deck." The pilots stood and gave her a salute, and Berkley could feel Erika trying to pull her chair out so that she could leave as well. "Not you, Miss Gibson."

"Cletus," Aidan said almost in question.

"A few minutes if you would, Captain. I'd like to talk to your assistant."

"What? You can't take constructive advice?" Erika asked as soon as they were alone. "And I'd appreciate you addressing me by my title."

"And I'd appreciate you not being such a bitch, but we don't always get what we want, do we?"

"Are you trying to bait me, Commander?"

Berkley laughed and didn't move. "Bait you into doing what exactly?"

"Into giving you the excuse to bring up insubordination charges against me? My daddy taught me a few things as well, and I'm sure he'd tell me getting rid of the fly in the ointment is the easiest solution." She pushed back on her chair again, but Berkley wasn't letting up the pressure. "Don't worry, though. Unlike some of the crew you brought aboard, I do have an iota of restraint. You won't be getting the satisfaction of me losing my cool with you."

"Let's try this." Berkley moved and sat in the chair Aidan had occupied. "What is your suggestion of what we should do? You have an opinion on how we'll do, so you must have some idea of how we could do it better. If you have a better plan, let's hear it."

"It's too late for my suggestion, Commander. Captain Sullivan should have gone with more experience, and in my humble opinion, that's not you."

"Why do you think the captain went with me, then?" There was a definite picture forming in Berkley's head when it came to Erika, and it painted the attractive officer in bed with Aidan. At least that's what this woman was hoping for from the bristling attitude coming off her. "You and I both know what the price of failure will be if I screw this up, so why not someone else?"

"That she didn't share with me. I'm sure she had her reasons, even if in this case because of personal issues, she's wrong." Erika straightened her papers and hesitantly pushed her chair back. "But that's none of my business."

"I see that you don't have a problem baiting me, Miss Gibson." Berkley smiled as Erika stood holding her folder close to her chest. She kept quiet until Erika's hand landed on the door latch. "And I'll make sure Aidan puts that you left a meeting with a superior officer without being dismissed into your file. Not an offense punishable by time in the brig, but I do think they frown upon things like that when promotions are being considered." Berkley stood and opened the door and stepped out into the corridor. "Just my humble opinion, anyway."

"Commander, may I have a word in my office, please?" Aidan said as soon as she saw Berkley walk past her door. "Problems?" she asked as soon as her office door closed.

"Erika is in love with you, so you tell me. Is that a problem?"

"Don't—"

"Be ridiculous," Berkley finished for her. "I'm not being funny here, darlin'. You may not have noticed it, but that's what her problem is, with me at least. You might have never shown an interest before, but you're showing one now. Only it's not directed at who she sees as the right person."

"I never—"

"Encouraged her in any way," Berkley cut in again. "I know that. We may have lost out because of duty, but I never questioned your loyalty. It might not be protocol, but I'm telling you that she's dying to ask if you're willing to tell her that you want her in your bed."

"Stop finishing my sentences for me, Cletus, and you don't have anything to be jealous over, so lose the pout." She laughed as she put her hand on Berkley's chest and scratched the skin she could reach through the open top button. "You want me to talk to her? Set her straight, so to speak?"

"Fighting my battles for me, Captain?"

"It's more like proving myself to you and just how seriously I take your happiness. I'm sure she'll understand since I've seen her eyeing you on your morning runs right along side me." Aidan moved closer when Berkley's hand landed on her butt. "You might have it all wrong. Did you consider that? Erika just might have her sights set on you."

"It's more like she's got a thing for authority figures, and that ain't me." Berkley kissed her forehead and slapped her gently on the ass. "Face it, you're adorable and I'm not the only one who's noticed."

CHAPTER NINETEEN

"How do you want to do this, Cletus?" Vader asked as soon as the team assembled in the situation room.

Berkley brought up a map on the large screen of the Sea of Japan and North Korea. "When we reach this point," she used a laser and flashed on a spot south of both places, "I want us in the air."

"How do you want to play it?" Killer asked.

"Tight formation while we're over water, then I want you and Vader to peel off and fly east."

She brought the laser to the point she had in mind only to be interrupted by Blazer. "You want them to head away from the drop?"

"How much do you know about North Korea, Lieutenant?"

"Enough to know it's in the opposite direction?"

"See? Already I'm regretting bringing you, so tell me why I wouldn't want to replace you with one of the other pilots onboard?" The others in the room kept quiet. "I asked you a question, Lieutenant."

"You many not like me, but you saw what I can do in a plane. That's why I'm here and why you won't replace me this late in the game."

"That sure of yourself, are you?" Berkley laughed and stared at him long enough to make him turn away first. "Trust me, don't be. Since Lieutenant Morris needs more information to understand our best strategy, let me explain myself. Junior." She nodded to Harvey, who brought up the graphics she wanted.

"The players in the region know we're coming for a training exercise, so a small formation won't be immediately suspicious. When we reach the split point, Morris, you'll be flying at my wing, and I need you close and vigilant. As soon as we see the coast I want a four-thousand-foot deck. Think you can handle that?"

"Cake walk," Blazer answered.

"Uh-huh." She pointed them to the animated planes heading northwest on the screen. "Vader, you'll be flying point, and, Killer, same thing as Blazer—tight and vigilant. No radio communication for any reason until Morris and I are two hundred clicks from our target."

"Two hundred should give us plenty of time," Vader said.

"For what?" Blazer asked.

Killer laughed and shook his head. "Do you need to take a nap?"

"It was a legitimate question," Blazer said as he glared at everyone in the room.

"Sure it was," Vader said, "for a rookie pilot. So try thinking before you open your mouth from now on. This isn't all that complicated."

"Rein it, guys," Berkley cut in. She pointed the laser at the two animated planes at the bottom of the screen. "Two hundred miles from our target will give our second team time to swing it back toward the southern target." She looked at Blazer and hiked her eyebrows. "Any other questions?"

"No, ma'am."

"Good. Take it easy from here on out, but be ready to go. We're hot as soon as we reach our hop point." She pointed to Harvey to flip the lights back on. "If you have problems, you have until then to stop by my office. I'd rather hear it now than when we're in the middle of this."

"Think you can order up some apple pie for us?" Vader asked.

"Tonight in the strategy room next to my office at six. Don't be late or you're not getting milk," Berkley said.

"Apple pie? And there's no way I'm getting that no matter how much I think about it," Blazer said.

"Finish a meal with the thing that'll make you want to come home, Blazer. For us it's apple pie, and it's been lucky so far, so no sense fucking with what works," Vader said.

"Till then, dismissed," Berkley said.

❖

Off the Northwest Coast of North Korea

"This is going to get old fast," Jin said as she pointed her plane back to the airstrip. "With our luck we'll be stuck here for the next two years flying this shit route for nothing."

"Captain, you're cleared for landing," the ground crewman cut in.

"Maybe we can just put one plane up at a time," Yong said as she scanned the area one more time.

"Maybe." Jin lined up and touched down with no difficulty even though the area was covered by a fog bank. "This is too close in for anyone to attempt an attack. They might get close, but then we'll be free to punch back without diplomatic repercussions. There's no way they'd make it back to any carrier before we scramble."

"If we do that it'll give us time to explore the hot springs that are supposedly around here." They continued their talk as they walked to the cinderblock cell they were living in. "You know how much I love adding new places to our list."

"We'll have to trade with Su Yu for afternoon sessions for the next week or so." Jin winked at her as they closed the door to their room. "What could happen?" she asked before going back to pretending she barely knew Yong and ignored her.

The showers were empty, but Jin didn't linger under the surprisingly hot water. She cleaned up and headed for the small rec room that had a small collection of books and a television that caught only the station that constantly expounded on Kim Jong Il's greatness. Jin wasn't interested in his exploits or in any reading material, just the lone phone in the corner. After fifteen minutes of trying, she finally got through to the party leader's home in the small town where her grandparents lived. Luckily, the man with one of the few phones in the area lived only three houses from her grandparents.

"Father, I hope you're well," Jin said when her grandfather's voice came on the line. In her opinion, Pak might have fathered her, but it was her mother's parents who had shared the duty of raising her.

"Older than the last time we saw each other, but well. It's been too long, my child."

The endearment made her take a deep breath as a way to control the sudden swell of emotion. "It has, but hopefully after this assignment I'll have time for a visit. How's Mother?"

"Mr. Lee and his sons are helping your grandmother bring her over." Jin could hear voices over the phone, as if something exciting had happened. "She's been waiting to talk to you," her grandfather went on, not really answering her question.

"Jin." A female voice came through the line before she could ask him anything else.

"Mom, how do you feel?"

"I'm fine. Don't worry. Tell me how you are."

"General Lee has sent me away again and I'm not sure how long I'll be, so you take care so we can walk through Father's garden when I see you again."

"That gives me something to look forward to. What about the other?"

If anyone was listening in, and if Jin knew her father, there was, the question probably made no sense to them. "It goes well despite everything. I always remember you said that anything can bloom even in the most barren soil if you're persistent enough," she said, referring to Yong.

"Good for you. My greatest wish for you is that you're a luckier gardener than I've been. If you are, then the coming pain will have some outlet, but don't waste your time worrying about the inevitable. In a way, I welcome it."

"I know it isn't easy, but try to wait for me. I miss you."

"I feel bad about making promises I can't keep, so just remember what we talked about the last time we saw each other. I love you, and my life has been blessed because of you."

The tiredness in her mother's voice was as clear, and it made Jin want to bolt from the desolate place and rush to her side. She wanted to spend her mother's last days in her grandfather's small garden holding her hand, not doing her father's bidding.

"I love you too, Mom," Jin said even though she wasn't alone anymore.

"That's what I've been waiting to hear."

"Just hang on a little while longer and I'll be there for that walk I promised you."

"This is all I needed to find peace. You just remember to mind your garden and keep it thriving until you can enjoy your harvest. I may not live to see it, but my spirit will always be with you. I love you and I couldn't be prouder of you."

It was their code for calls like this when Jin knew there was nowhere to hide. Her mother in her own way was telling her to mind her father until her service was done and she could return home to her grandparents to live out her days in peace, however she chose to live them out and with whomever she wanted. For her real family there was never any shame in being who she truly was.

"Take care," was all Jin could get out before her grandfather came back on the line.

"If you can, hurry home, but if you can't we'll take care of everything."

"Thank you, Father."

As she gripped the receiver Jin noticed the soldier who had joined her in the rec room never glanced up from his book. Her mother's voice rang in her head and she suddenly had an overwhelming urge to hear it again since she knew it would be silenced forever in too little time.

"Captain, the men are waiting for your briefing," another soldier informed her.

"Five minutes." She would be as brief with them as she planned to be with her father. She would give this mission another week of her time, then she was going to join her mother. Pak would have to learn to accept the consequences of her decision. The revolution would get no more sacrifices from her.

Chapter Twenty

Onboard the USS *Jefferson*

"Tell the comm room to be extra vigilant tonight. We're entering dangerous waters, so we need to keep our eyes on the air and the sea." Aidan was giving direction as she made her way to her room for the night. The weather had cleared considerably, and after another week of sailing full throttle she'd taken their speed down a notch since they were still on schedule to be in their target area on time.

What was burned into her brain like a big red X was the spot Berkley had pointed to as they went about making plans. By her calculations, they'd hit that point in the morning, and for once in her life, fear was soaking into her bones. The worst of it was that her belief that Berkley would prevail wasn't making her fear go away.

"Do you want me to bring you the hourly report?" Erika asked when they stopped at Aidan's door.

"Not unless there's something out of the ordinary. We've got a stressful day ahead of us tomorrow, so a quiet night would be good."

"I'll do my best to make it happen, Captain. See you in the morning."

Aidan laughed when she stepped through her office door into her private quarters and saw the candle burning next to her bunk. In the chair across from the bed Berkley smiled back at her, sitting in her skivvies.

"It's a good thing you didn't invite your admirer in with you," Berkley said as she crossed her legs. "That would've been uncomfortable."

"Where'd you find a candle?"

"Just a little contraband I snuck into my bag when we boarded. I knew you're a sucker for candlelight, so I thought it was worth making you happy."

To subdue the urge to immediately put her hands on Berkley, Aidan pressed them to the cold metal of the door. "Just so you know for the future, while I do love candlelight, finding you in your underwear in my room goes a long way in making me happy."

"Is that the line you give all the sailors who wander in here in their underwear?"

"And what if I said yes?"

Berkley put her feet on the floor again and pushed herself out of the chair. "Then I see a lot of fistfights in my future." She picked up a plate covered with a napkin from the footlocker in front of the bed and held it out to her.

"You saved me a piece?" Aidan asked when Berkley lifted the cover. "I think I'm wearing you down."

"Since you baked it, I thought it was prudent to save you some."

"I don't think you have any worries about going pieless."

"Sounds promising." Berkley fed her a piece, then tapped the tip of the fork on Aidan's nose. "I just thought if I came bearing gifts I might be able to bribe you into spending the night with me."

"Again, honey, for future reference, you just have to show up and ask."

"That's good to know too." Berkley handed her the plate so she could start helping her out of her uniform. She finished the pie while sitting on Berkley's lap after they moved back to the chair. "You've done a good job on the dessert and on getting us this far, Captain."

"With talk like that I could use you as a reference."

Her teasing made Berkley laugh, but she didn't stop her hand from roaming up and down her naked legs. "Depends on what job you're applying for. Tonight I have an opening for someone to hold."

The way Berkley said it made Aidan lean back and study her face. She found none of the hesitancy that had plagued her since Berkley had come back into her life. This time she had no problem asking for what she wanted, and it made Aidan ecstatic that it was her that Berkley asked for. "You won't be gone that long, so I'm hoping it's more than a one-night assignment."

"That island is too close to enemy lines, and I'm not saying it's impossible, but it's no gimme. If something happens—" The rest of what Berkley was going to say stopped when Aidan pressed her hand to her mouth.

"No talking like you aren't coming back, Cletus. You're going in there and you're coming right back out. No detours, no problems, and no excuses, you hear me?"

Berkley pulled her hand away and kissed her fingers. "You know my motto, baby—make a work plan, then work your plan." She stood and carried Aidan to the bed. "Part of covering my bases is making sure I don't leave anything to chance." The surface squeaked when they both lay back, Aidan in the circle of Berkley's arms. "If something happens, all the stuff you'll need is in the top drawer of my desk."

With just the tips of her fingers, Aidan scratched lightly down her chest until she reached the elastic of her underwear. There she stopped. "Would it help if I gave you an incentive?"

"Does it have anything to do with that hand?"

"Since you asked so nicely." She lifted the elastic of the white jockeys and snapped them against Berkley's skin. "I'm going to stop right here, then when you get back I'll head down this way." She snapped the elastic again and laughed.

"That's the kind of incentive they should use on the recruitment posters." Berkley wrapped her hand around Aidan's wrist and brought her hand up so she could bite down on her fingertips.

Berkley looked down at Aidan's face when she didn't laugh at her joke. The last thing she expected was tears. "Hey now, what's wrong?"

"Nothing." Aidan sniffed and pressed her face into Berkley's T-shirt. "Shit."

"I've known you for a long time, Aidan Sullivan, and you don't cry over nothing. Tell me what's wrong."

"I didn't want to do this in front of you…not tonight."

The bed creaked again when Berkley placed Aidan's head on the pillow and leaned over her to see her face better. "Don't be afraid. Tell me."

"That's just it, I'm scared," Aidan got out softly. The way she forced it out made Berkley think that the answer wasn't an easy confession.

"You sail the boat, babe, and I'll find a way to get back on it."

"Sorry that I'm picking now to freak out on you." Aidan pressed her fingers to Berkley's mouth again when she took a breath to say something. "And don't say it's all right, because we both know it's not. The last thing we need is for me to jinx you."

"It's not true, and I'm not going to argue with you about that, so let's get some sleep." She kissed Aidan's forehead and got as comfortable as they were going to get on the bunk. "I don't want to freak Harvey out by falling asleep in the cockpit tomorrow."

Aidan fell asleep to the hum of the powerful engines churning them toward the dangers that needed to be faced to bring about peace and to the steady sound of Berkley's heartbeat. Even during her time at the Academy, she found it humorous that no matter how hard they tried other options, peace had to be garnered by the most violent means man could devise.

❖

Pyongyang, North Korea

"General Lee?" The young woman standing at his door appeared as if she'd rather be teaching cobras to line dance than be in his presence. "I'm sorry to disturb you, sir, but Captain Umeko is on the phone for you."

Pak waited until the door to his office was closed before even glancing at the phone. In reality, he hadn't given Jin much thought after shipping her to a position that was beneath her. It was the only thing he could think of to drive her and Yong apart. Being under the microscope of such small base was just the stressor his daughter needed to bring her back in line.

He took a sip of his hot tea then picked up the receiver. "Jin, do you have a progress report?"

"My mother is dying and I'm leaving tomorrow night to be with her before she does."

The china cup on his desk rattled when he pounded his fist on the wooden surface. "You desert your post and I won't be able to protect you anymore. Do you understand the consequences of that?"

"I'm sure you'll be the first in line to start the inquisition against me, and you'll volunteer to drive me to the work camp once I'm found guilty. We both know your devotion to service."

"Your mother's life is at an end, so think before sacrificing everything for such a lost cause." His mouth clicked shut as he took deep breaths, trying to center himself. As she stayed silent he studied the picture on his desk of a much younger Jin taken on her first day of school.

Back then he had just started on the fast track of his military career. It was a year later that his service was brought to Kim Jong Il's attention. The day Jin had proudly given him her school picture was one of the last times he remembered her calling him Father.

"It isn't worth what we've worked so hard for?" Pak said.

The only sound that followed was Jin's laughter. "What we've worked for? Are you joking, or are you mad? After all this tireless devotion, what exactly will be your reward, General Lee?"

"Should I remind you that I'm your father?"

"That sad reality has nothing to do with the answer to my question. The power you think you have will vanish as quickly as dog piss on a hot street. You'll be forgotten so fast that not one cadet recruited to continue your work will even know your name."

He pushed his tea away impatiently to do something with his hands, sure that if Jin were standing in front of him he'd have slapped her. "How can you be so sure?"

"Because as you just reminded me, I'm your daughter, and after today I'm going to try my best to forget you. The saddest thing is that you so easily dismiss the love that you have left in this world, and you won't ever go out of your way to change that."

He laughed at what he knew was a blatant lie. "Since when do you love me?"

"I couldn't care less about you. I'm talking about my mother. You threw her away to a barren life, but she still defends you and cares about you. And you think her life isn't worth acknowledging since it's about to end. You're beyond pathetic. I'm leaving tomorrow, so feel free to do whatever you like to begin my punishment."

"There's no stopping you when you make up your mind, but just remember that I can't protect you any longer." His last sentiment was whispered to the empty room and the dial tone. Jin had hung up. For once in his life he felt the pain of such an empty life, but there wasn't anyone to turn to who could ease the hurt.

"Tell my driver to be ready to go in an hour," Pak told his assistant as soon as he had gathered himself.

In his opinion, a trip to the village where he knew his ex-wife was living was in order. It was too late to beg her forgiveness, but it had been a long time since he'd been at the center of someone's true adoration. If he played this right, it was his surefire way back into Jin's good graces.

He needed that to happen so that even after his time at the top of the military chain, he'd still have influence. Having Jin back under his control would guarantee that he wouldn't be forgotten, and to him that would mean his life wouldn't end in vain.

CHAPTER TWENTY-ONE

Onboard the USS *Jefferson*

Berkley opened her eyes and the red glow of the clock clicked to 5:32 as she focused on it. Aidan lay quietly in her arms, but from her breathing Berkley could tell she was awake. Back home it was already late afternoon and she could just picture the head of the United Nations sitting in his office going over his speech.

"You know what I'd like?"

Aidan lifted her head at the question and kissed her. "If it has anything to do with making love you can forget it, flygirl."

"Should I be worried that you aren't interested?" Berkley asked, enjoying the banter, realizing after another glance at the clock that it would come to an end in a few more minutes.

"I'm plenty interested." Aidan kissed her again. "But it makes you relax to the point of lethargy. Today I need you bright eyed and bushy tailed."

"Then we should go with the big cup of coffee in bed I was going to ask for before you threw my thought process to more pleasurable pursuits." The bunk was warm since Aidan was practically wrapped around her, but it was time to get going. "You'll just have to owe me a cup when I get back." She quickly kissed Aidan again and waved as someone softly tapped on the door. "See you in a few, Captain."

There was no need to rush, Aidan thought as she watched Berkley disappear; it was just Erika with the morning reports. The sun wouldn't be up for another few minutes, so she took her time pulling out a clean uniform and tossing it on the bunk. "I wonder what it's going to be like when all I have to worry about is getting a table full of cute kids off to school in the morning."

She smiled at the fantasy and mentally ticked off another day in the countdown to making it a reality. "Anything exciting going on?" she asked Erika.

"Interesting question for today." Erika put down the coffee and reports she'd brought with her. "Mike down in the comm room said he's ready with the link-up whenever you like. Think Command changed their minds about this?"

The reports from their satellite and visual surveillance held nothing that raised any alarms as she skimmed through them. "The brass changes their minds about a lot of things, but blowing someone like Kim Jong Il back to the Stone Age if given the chance isn't likely to be one of them. Especially if the rest of the world gives them their blessing."

"I just hope this preemptive strike," Erika made air quotes on the phrase, "doesn't turn into the cluster that Iraq has."

"We're just paid to sail," Aidan said as she grabbed her coffee and headed for the bridge. She wanted to see what the weather was that morning and check out the satellites for any incoming storms. This was one day she didn't want clear skies that meant miles of visibility. "So let's get to it."

They moved down the corridors and up the few steps to their destination, and Aidan was disappointed that she didn't cross paths with Berkley. The computer counting down the distance Berkley pinpointed for launch indicated they still had another twenty nautical miles to go.

Aidan gave everyone a casual salute as she sat in the captain's chair and looked over the instruments and then at the horizon. Below her the planes were being brought to the deck, and that was where she found Berkley. She was already in her flight suit. As she walked around her aircraft Aidan could see the easy smile and the way she moved. Berkley looked like an adventurer waiting for the next mountain to climb.

"Mike, hook me up," Aidan said into the phone. It was time to break their radio silence.

"Captain Sullivan, there are no changes to our exercises," the man's voice on the radio said. The transmission was coming from

Washington. "Keep the line open on the chance we add or subtract components."

"Understood," Aidan said. "My second will be on the line for the duration." When the executive officer acknowledged her order, she walked outside to the stairs next to the bridge.

"Captain, a moment please," Berkley requested when Aidan's foot hit the main deck. They stepped into the first corridor and Berkley slightly closed the door. Before Aidan could say anything Berkley kissed her for one long, passionate moment.

"Not that I'm complaining, but what was that for?"

Berkley kissed her forehead before letting her go. "Just wanted to make sure you don't forget me while I'm gone and Erika puts the moves on you." When Berkley laughed Aidan knew she was being teased. "Keep the light on and I'll see you in a little while, okay?"

"I expect you back in three hours, and that's an order."

"Aye, aye, Captain." Berkley looked over her shoulder before kissing her again. "See you in a bit."

When they stepped back out the flight team going with Berkley was waiting. When Berkley lifted her thumb they stood at attention and gave Aidan a sharp salute before heading for their planes.

"Junior, you keep your eyes open up there," Aidan said.

"Yes, ma'am," he said before turning for their ride.

Aidan stopped him. "One thing, Lieutenant. Why Junior?"

"It was the perfect fighter name if I'm flying with Cletus."

"You never did tell me why you picked that nickname," Aidan said to Berkley.

"I'll tell you when we get back. Let's go for a ride, Junior."

The engines started as Aidan made her way back to the bridge. As she turned and picked up her binoculars Berkley streaked off the carrier, followed quickly by her team. She glanced at Erika, who was watching the same thing. Erika made eye contact with her and shook her head, pointing to the radio.

Berkley flew point, heading east toward the South Korean border. They were flying low enough to see the whitecaps in the Sea of Japan. She had only the inner plane radio on so Junior could warn her of anything on their tail that the radar missed. Blazer was a little behind her right wing, with Killer and Vader behind him.

As they got closer Aidan radioed them the live feed coming from

New York as the members of the United Nations Security Council convened their meeting. A man who Berkley guessed was the UN Secretary General cleared his throat and said, "We call this meeting in the interest of lasting peace, and to bring to light a current situation that could have grave consequences if not addressed."

The onboard computer emitted a single beep and Berkley broke away, going a bit more north but making sure not to stray over the North Korean border. Her plan was to only cross that line when they flew over the islands where their target lay. She dropped their altitude a few thousand feet. Thirty minutes later they saw fishing boats dotting the surface of the water. So far their luck had held in that no other plane was in the air with them.

"Within the last three months we have evidence that the Kim Jong Il government of North Korea has successfully tested more than one nuclear weapon. This act is in direct violation of the agreement he signed just two years ago in consideration of eased U.N. sanctions. We meet today as civilized nations interested in a resolution to this matter before any other tests are conducted as President Kim Jong Il has promised."

Berkley lowered their altitude so they were almost skimming the water. When they were lying this low, the only alarm that could be raised was a call from some of the startled fishermen. Additionally, for this mission the planes had been stripped of their usual markings and painted black. Command's explanation was that everyone who voted for the Security Council's resolution could share in the success of the outcome. To Berkley it was more a case of covering their asses on the off chance something went wrong. Her computer beeped again, meaning Killer and Vader were starting their loop south to give her time to reach the farthest target.

"We will employ every option available to us to see that this nuclear threat to all our countries is eradicated in the interest of global security. I'll open the floor to suggestions." There was a pause. "The chair recognizes Germany."

The coastline came into view but instead of heading for it and her target, Berkley started to drift west. When she did she watched Blazer continue forward as if trying to take over even though he'd been delegated to wingman. If neither of them changed their direction they'd lose sight of each other within minutes. To Berkley it was Blazer's version of a game of dare.

As Berkley banked left even harder, followed closely by a now compliant Blazer, her radio came to life with the same feed Aidan and Erika were listening to. The detour had taken them off course enough so their timing would be right once she reversed her direction. Her plan was for both teams to hit their targets while flying in the direction of the *Jefferson* in case the Koreans were able to scramble planes.

She lined up the shot for the main complex and waited for the computer to confirm the target. Once she was locked she hesitated, waiting for the final okay.

After some discussion, the Chair said, "Everyone in agreement with the motion made by Germany and seconded by the Russian Federation that the price for North Korea's noncompliance with the wishes of this panel is the loss of its nuclear sites, signify by saying aye."

"Aye," said a group of people. It was the sign Berkley was waiting for. She pushed the trigger that released her destructive load and hoped Vader had gotten his off as well.

"Direct hit, Cletus," Junior said.

From the size of the fireball she didn't need his confirmation, but she appreciated his enthusiasm. "Time to get home," she said. Now it was a run for the *Jefferson*. She hoped without planes chasing them down.

"Cletus," Junior's voice went up so fast it sounded as if he'd sucked on a helium balloon. "They got a plane off. It's behind Blazer and closing fast."

"Just one?"

"That's all I see, and it's backed up by radar."

She tipped her left wing down for Blazer as a signal to stay on that side behind her. If they kept this course they'd make it to South Korean airspace before the pursuit plane could close the gap. If the Korean plane had to circle north, both teams would be on board the *Jefferson*, and if the lone pilot engaged there it would stir up the hornet's nest of the other pilots onboard. That would be suicide.

"Trying to lock on us," Junior said.

"Too far back to worry about that now." She flew but kept an eye peeled to the radar screen. In the upper right corner she could see two other blips coming directly at them, and she had a feeling it wasn't Killer and Vader. "Don't lose sight of our tail."

"Still behind us, and still trying to lock."

"My guess is that's what the cowboys in front of us have in mind too." She lifted the cover of her trigger and checked her altitude. "Time to turn the radio on, Junior, and hope it takes them a while to find the frequency."

"Go ahead," Junior said.

"Blazer, do you copy?"

"Copy, go ahead," Blazer responded. "Can you handle the two incoming while I back track and take out our tail?"

"Negative, stay on course and engage only if fired on. We're not that far from the coast, and I don't want to use any unnecessary force. Do you understand?" The roar of her engines couldn't drown out the static coming through her headphones. "Blazer, do you copy?"

"He's gone silent," Junior said. "And he's turning around."

"Fuck." The two planes that had been heading toward them climbed and passed them by. They'd acquired a new target and it was the insubordinate idiot with her. "Lots of chatter now, Junior. I need to know what's going on and if anyone's trying to crawl up my ass."

"Roger that."

They were both pressed into the seat when she banked hard to the right as she picked up altitude. She'd faced a hundred similar situations in the last couple of years, only the results had been tabulated by computer. Now they'd be tabulated by blood.

Blazer was trying to set up a shot on the original plane, but the pilot he was up against showed extraordinary skill, and if Berkley had to guess, the North Korean was only playing with him to drag out the fun. As she came around and had all the players in front of her, she could see it was the same scenario they'd played out on Blazer's first day of Top Gun school.

The North Korean lead plane had done its job well, leading Blazer right into the trap the two other planes were setting. "Nice to know Blazer learns from his mistakes," Berkley said.

Berkley punched them forward and took out one of the planes now after Blazer. The pilot of the second plane reacted by coming about, but no amount of maneuvering would save him as Berkley let loose this time with her guns. A barrage of bullets struck his fuel tank and he went down with a trail of black smoke, ending in a spectacular fireball.

Once the two planes were out of the way, she turned her attention to Blazer. The Korean he was up against was done playing and was going after him with serious intent. Blazer was doing a good job of holding him off, but the Russian-made plane was slightly smaller and faster. It was older, but obviously well maintained and made for short hops in dogfight situations.

The moves the pilot was making at the stick made Cletus admire his skill even if it was the enemy. It was like he had led Blazer to his death like a border collie with a herd of sheep.

"He's got him locked in," Junior said. "And we're now over North Korean territory."

"Got it." Berkley was looking for an opening, but Blazer was between her and the target. "Stay alert. That was just two, but we'll have more company soon enough."

"Cletus," Blazer's voice came though her headphones, and for once the superior attitude had signs of cracks. He sounded panicked. "Cletus, some help here. I can't shake this bastard."

"Drop and roll to the right. I can't get a shot with you in the way."

"Roger that." When he dropped and rolled to the left all Berkley could think was that in the heat of the moment he just got it wrong. The only problem was that to avoid Blazer slamming into her, Berkley had no choice but to take his place as the plane in the most vulnerable position.

"Cletus, we're locked," Junior yelled.

Berkley felt like everything had slowed down to a crawl. They were at twelve thousand feet and she tipped the right wing down trying to escape the infernal beeping of being in someone's crosshairs. The idea was to drop and try to come around to be in a more defensive position.

"They've fired," Junior said.

"Hang on." She fought to keep the plane under control in the fast steep drop. Since they were in the half roll she was blind as to what was coming after them, but she was confident they'd be able to drop under the missile and come back around.

Those thoughts shattered as the missile completely sheared off the tip of her right wing, making the cockpit panel light up like she'd hit the jackpot in Vegas. "Cletus," Junior sounded truly scared now.

The fire from the missile strike was headed for the missiles she still carried, leaving her no choice. With one press of a button, she ejected both seats, sending them shooting sideways and away from their plane. The position of the plane gave them some cover and kept them from becoming a convenient target for the Korean's guns.

As soon as her chute opened, she twisted around trying to find Junior. He was floating down a few hundred feet from her, but he was unconscious, or at least he seemed to be by the way his head was slumped back.

In the distance she could see Blazer making for the coast with the North Korean plane in pursuit. From the north there were more planes coming, but they were a good ways off, so hopefully they'd be on the ground before they were spotted. Below them there was a stretch of trees that would provide good cover while she assessed just how fucked they were.

CHAPTER TWENTY-TWO

W e don't have much time if we want to catch them," Yong
said.

"I guess we won't be lucky enough for this fool to turn around again and try to take us one more time?" The leather of the seat felt cool against Jin's damp shirt. They hadn't had the opportunity to put on the flight suits before taking off since they'd sped from the hot springs they were enjoying to the airstrip when she saw the planes coming in. The time off was her parting gift to Yong since she was going through with the plans she'd shared with Pak, and once she deserted her post she figured she'd never be allowed to see her lover again.

"At least we brought one down. The general will be pleased with that," Yong said.

Jin could see the water in the distance and knew her chances to engage were getting slim. Not that she was afraid of facing off again, but her backup was too far behind her for that to be prudent now if there were any other planes to come to his defense.

"From the size of that explosion we flew through to get here, we'll be lucky if the general only has us shot. The facility and everyone in it is gone." The burning building was something she saw destroyed as her plane's wheels left the ground, and the ramifications of not being in the air with the number of planes her father wanted was too much to contemplate at the moment.

She'd gambled by being lax and the rubble pile was a clear signal that she'd been wrong. While she and Yong were enjoying an intimate bath together at the hot springs Yong had found, Jin had ordered the two planes scheduled to patrol that morning to head farther south since that's where she figured the danger would lie, if there was anything to fear at all. All she'd wanted was a morning of peace and normalcy before she gave up everything she'd worked for.

Her only salvation was that they'd downed one of the planes. She had kept the plane she was chasing under her paw like a cat would with a wounded mouse while she watched the other enemy plane take out her fellow countrymen. The talent and the speed meant he was the lead pilot, and she was surprised by how easy it had been to take him out, but she had the pilot in front of her to thank.

"No amount of patrolling would have stopped that," Yong said.

"And the fact that the two other witnesses that could confirm we weren't in the air are dead doesn't hurt either, right?" They were over the water of the Sea of Japan and she was still too far away to take a clean shot.

❖

"They're still there," said Alan Lewis, Blazer's backseat.

"Don't sweat it, we'll be back to the *Jefferson* before they get anywhere near us." From what his radar was showing they were alone in the air aside from the idiot behind them. The sight of Berkley's plane exploding in midair was playing in an infinite loop in his mind.

"What you need to sweat is what's going to happen to us when we get back and the others find out what you did. We're screwed, I hope you know that."

Blazer rolled his shoulders, trying to relax the tension in them. "Listen to me. I'm not going down because of this, and if you try it I'll do everything in my power to see that you're thrown out of the Navy. What happened was an accident—nothing more." His conversations with Rodney came to his mind. The admiral would be thrilled with the outcome. Berkley had not only been downed, but behind enemy lines liked they'd planned.

"She said not to turn around and to roll right when we got our ass in a crack and you rolled left. It's almost like you set her up on purpose."

"You can't fucking believe that. Just shut it down. I don't want you talking about this with anyone. The great Cletus is dead and there's not a damn thing we can do about it now. See? I was right. No one is that good all of the time."

❖

Jin finally pulled back when she saw the two other black planes coming in from the east. Vader and Killer came around and were split enough apart and behind her for Jin to take a chance, even though, her position with her father would've been better had they brought down more than one plane.

"Find the nearest place we can land," she told Yong as she watched the two planes streak by. "We need to refuel and call Central Command to tell them what happened."

"There's a base fifteen minutes to the north," Yong said softly. "Our base just radioed and said the other nuclear site was destroyed as well." Jin realized that any plans to see her mother before she died would have to wait until it would be too late. "The dispatcher said that's where the general will be waiting for you. We're to refuel and return to our base as soon as possible."

"With any luck he left the firing squad at home."

❖

"Blazer, where's Cletus?" Vader asked as he flew on Blazer's wing.

The airwaves were silent for so long that Killer asked again. "Blazer, what happened?"

"She went down." Blazer's voice was soft. "One of the planes locked on me, then at the last minute it changed targets. It's like she didn't see it coming." In essence it was the truth.

"Are you sure she didn't eject?" Vader said.

"There's no way she had time. She's gone."

"Did you go back and check there was no parachute in the air?" Killer asked.

"The same plane that shot them out of the sky was on my ass."

"Then there's a chance they made it," Killer said.

"She didn't."

The *Jefferson* was a spot in the distance, and they let Blazer line up first since he was flying point. It wasn't the time to distract each other with any more questions, and for that Blazer was grateful. As long as he kept his story simple it would be harder to break him. Rodney had told him that over and over until he could say it backward.

❖

North Korean Countryside

After she'd rolled up her chute so no one would spot it, Berkley reached Junior where he was hanging ten feet in the air from a tree branch. A branch that was sagging precariously from his weight.

"Junior?" She hoped her voice wouldn't carry. They weren't alone in the area and she didn't want to attract attention. On the way down she'd seen a village and people pointing, but none of them looked military.

Above her, Junior moaned as he came around, then bit into his fist to keep from screaming. "What happened?"

"Did you pass out before or after I hit the eject button?"

He brought his head forward and just stared at her like a man trying desperately not to throw up. "Does it make a difference?"

She shook her head and turned her attention to how best to cut him down. "I just wanted to know how much detail you needed." With the way the branch was sagging, she thought her only option was to go above it and cut him down.

"I was fully alert when we got hit, but I think something smacked me in the unexpected exit."

"Is your head all right? No bleeding?" After years of practice in the mimosa tree in their New Orleans backyard, Berkley made quick work of the climb.

"No hits to the head or bleeding." He stared up at her as she hung by her knees from the branch above him with a pocketknife in her hand. "But," she brought the blade down and was about to cut when he let out a panicked, "Wait."

"It's just ten feet. I promise it won't kill you."

"A piece of debris hit me, but not on the head." He pointed to his leg where his flight suit had a large tear in it. "I'm not a doctor, but I think it's broken. If I had to guess, the pain is what knocked me out." Just as he finished his assessment and before Berkley could come up with another course of action, the branch snapped.

CHAPTER TWENTY-THREE

USS *Jefferson*

"Where's Cletus?" Aidan asked as soon as the pilots were safely away from their planes. She'd ordered up another team to fly security just in case there was any fallout from their actions.

Vader stepped forward and shook his head. "Let's go inside, Captain."

"Where is she?" Aidan asked, her voice so clipped it sounded foreign even to her.

"She didn't make it," Killer said.

It took every bit of discipline her father ever taught her when it came to her emotions not to fall to the deck in despair. *She didn't make it.* What kind of cruel joke was he trying to play?

"What?" Now she fought the urge to hit one of them. To inflict physical pain as a payback for the emotional death she was feeling after hearing those four simple words.

"We need to set up an inquiry, Captain, while it's all still fresh. Do you want to set up the usual format? I can get Lieutenant Gibson to get things going," Vader offered, referring to Erika. At the moment Erika was standing behind Aidan as if frozen in place.

"Mike, call Devin and have six separate rooms set up in the brig, and post an escort in each one," Erika said, clearly taking control.

"No communication between any of you staring now," Aidan said after a deep breath. "Have Devin meet me in my office in ten minutes and you'll escort each pilot and navigator to and from there until we're done," she said to Erika.

"We just flew through hell, Captain. Can't this wait till tomorrow?"

It was the first time she'd heard Blazer's voice since they'd landed. Aidan tried hard to remember what Berkley had said about Blazer—the precise words. Hearing him say the most stupid thing he could, given the situation, made it suddenly very important to remember verbatim Berkley's words on the subject.

"No, it can't, Lieutenant Morris, but if you're that traumatized by the whole ordeal then I give you my word to save you for last. Feel free to take a nap while I talk to the others." The brief glimpse of panic was all Aidan needed to know how they needed to proceed. Six of the crew stepped up behind her. "Hattie, make sure you escort Lieutenant Morris to his cell and let him sack out for a while and post someone on his door to make sure he's not disturbed." She said it loud enough for all six men involved to hear. "But have his navigator brought to my office first."

The walk from the deck to her office was one of the longest Aidan could ever remember making. Waking up with Berkley just that morning felt like the end of a lifetime. How very surreal that it took less than a day for every hope, dream, and fantasy for the future to cease so abruptly. The reality of what she had to look forward to was what made her tears fall as soon as she stepped into her quarters.

"Aidan?" Erika waited twenty minutes before knocking on the door. "Lieutenant Alan Lewis, Blazer's backseat, and his escort are waiting in the corridor. Can I come in?"

"No reason for you to." She knew her face appeared drained and somber. She'd been looking at in the mirror, but the need to break down and give in to her grief would have to wait. "Bring Lewis in." She nodded in Devin's direction.

"Are you sure?" Erika spoke as she looked between Devin and Aidan.

"Erika, I'm really not in the mood to repeat myself. Bring Lewis in, then wait in the hall. We'll take care of the interviews."

"Lieutenant Lewis, tell us what happened," Aidan said after the door was shut. He was standing in the parade rest position and Aidan had no intention of changing that. "Before you begin, I should inform you that this will be part of the official report. I'm sure you're familiar with the penalties for lying."

"Yes, ma'am."

"Let's hear it," Aidan said.

It didn't take long for Lewis to tell them what happened in what Aidan thought was a robotic-sounding tone. When he was done Aidan noticed that he kept his eyes on the rivets on the wall. She had never interrupted him from the time they started, but he had steadfastly kept his eyes front and center as if he was reading a script off the wall. It was the first story he'd tell them, but her gut suspected it wouldn't be the only version of it.

"That's it?" Aidan asked.

"That's all, ma'am."

"Just as long as you're sure." She knocked on the top of her desk to make him look down. "You're dismissed for now, but you'll be restricted to temporary quarters until we get this sorted out. I will personally throw you off this boat if you try and disobey that order and try to get past your guard. Understood?"

"Yes, ma'am." Lewis snapped to attention and saluted.

Devin Clark crossed his legs and tapped on the bottom of his boot with his index finger. He was the head of their onboard security and someone Aidan trusted implicitly. The fact that he was one of the shortest men serving on the *Jefferson* didn't matter; his forceful personality more than made up for any height disparity. He was the perfect man to head the MP unit they had onboard.

"That boy's like a phonebook that's ten years old," he said to Aidan.

"How so?"

"Got a lot of information between the covers, but it ain't worth shit. There's something he's not saying."

"I figured that out on the deck, but we'll get it out of him eventually. And we *will* find out. I can't go back and tell Corbin Levine that I lost one of the Navy's most valuable assets and his legacy and I don't know why. Have the others brought in, but have Lewis cued up the second we're finished with Blazer."

"And if he still refuses to talk?"

"Then I might just let you snap him like a twig."

"Don't get me all excited with talk like that, Captain. The next few shouldn't take long since they won't have any firsthand information. No matter why, though, we need to wait at least four hours before we bring Blazer in here."

"Bring a couple more in, then, but let me check one more thing out." Aidan picked up the phone and asked Erika to step in. "Get Mike in here, and, Devin, post some guards on those planes now."

It didn't take Mike Dyer, the head aircraft mechanic, long to arrive, and he saluted Aidan immediately. "Ma'am, I didn't mean to overstep my authority, but I went ahead and downloaded all the planes' computer logs for you."

"You saved me a call, Mike," Aidan said. "Let's see Blazer's first."

The regular black boxes had been removed since there was no way they wanted to give North Korea any ammunition against them, so Berkley's flight information wasn't available. Because of their mission if one of the planes went down, it was set to self-destruct. The only information they had available to them was the route Blazer had flown after the encryption code was put in, as well as the very brief radio contact he'd had with Cletus.

When the map came on screen Aidan watched and almost came out of her chair when Blazer's plane suddenly turned around and flew toward the shoreline. The route didn't become erratic until he was seventy miles in, and then he reversed his course again and flew a direct course for the ship, but mostly over enemy territory.

"Get Lewis back in here now," Aidan said and Devin snapped to attention.

"You need to call this in, Aidan. If she was shot down that far in, it could have serious repercussions, and the sooner Command knows it the better," Erika said when they were alone. "This isn't what they had in mind as an outcome, and I did warn you. But no matter what, I'll stand behind you."

"I'll call when I'm goddamn ready to call, and I'm not going to do that until I know what happened." Aidan felt her anger rise. "And you warned me?" She threw the words back at her. "Are you kidding me?"

"I know you're upset now." Erika put her hand on Aidan's shoulder close to her neck. "That won't last as long as the consequences from this if it turns into an incident that requires more military action. You need someone who'll help you through that who cares about what happens to you."

The touch made Aidan want to hit her. All the teasing about Erika being in love with her wasn't some fantasy Berkley had made up. "If you don't want to be transferred to the kitchen for the remainder of our time here, I want you to keep your opinions to yourself." She shrugged off Erika's hand and put some distance between them.

"Aidan, I'm only being honest because I care about you."

"You will address me as Captain Sullivan." Aidan glared at Erika's hand as she went to touch her again. "We aren't friends, much less anything else your imagination conjured up for you."

"She isn't coming back, Aidan."

"Captain." Devin had opened the door with Erika's words hanging in the air. "Are you ready?"

Aidan lifted her finger to put him off. "Erika, I want you to report to the kitchen and tell them you'll be responsible for supplies until we put to shore."

Devin pressed his hands behind his back as if he was ready to subdue Erika if that's what it took. "I think that was a dismissal," he told her.

"Captain," Erika said and hesitated before finally leaving when Aidan didn't respond.

"Thanks, Devin." Aidan took her seat. "Bring him in." Lewis appeared more nervous as he was brought in, his eyes darting around the room this.

"Ma'am, I don't have anything new to add."

Aidan kept her eyes on the computer screen as Blazer's plane made the loop from take off to landing. At the point where he turned north toward the coast, she added the brief radio contact he'd had with Berkley.

"You're not here to add anything new, so shut up." Aidan clenched her fists so hard she broke the pen in her hand. When she finally looked at him he was staring at her hand. "You're here because I've got something new to add." She turned the screen so he could see it.

The room was silent until the planes went into the obvious combat with the enemy. Aidan and Devin kept their attention on Lewis as the audio came on.

"Blazer, do you copy?" Berkley's voice made Aidan bite the inside of her cheek.

"Copy, go ahead," Blazer responded. "Can you handle the two incoming while I back track and take out our tail?"

"Negative, stay on course and engage only if fired on. We're not that far from the coast and I don't want to use any unnecessary force. Do you understand?" There was silence. "Blazer, do you copy?" Berkley's voice came on, but again there was no response.

"In case you missed it, genius, when she says negative," Aidan said and placed her finger on the blip that represented Blazer's plane, "that was a direct order to not head north. But from this information, your pilot chose to ignore that direct order from a superior officer. That was one ignored order." The plane on the screen then crossed into North Korean air space.

"Ma'am, I can—"

"No one asked you to speak, Mr. Lewis," Devin bellowed. "I don't think you understand the world of shit you're in here, so zip it and listen."

Aidan started the program after she'd paused it for the outburst. "The orders I gave before you left were to not breach enemy lines except for your brief flight over your target." She tapped the screen and the program showed their flight back to the *Jefferson* was mostly over North Korea. "This is proof you also ignored my order, and I plan to turn you over to be court-martialed as soon as we return."

"But—"

"Do not interrupt me again." Aidan spoke over him. "I plan to turn you over for disciplinary action for insubordination, and if I can prove you had something to do with Commander Levine getting shot down, I'll have them add murder charges to that."

"You should thank Captain Sullivan, idiot, for at least warning you," Devin said. "If it was up to me I'd throw you off the side and see if those water survival classes you probably slept through really work."

"Ma'am," Lewis said but snapped his mouth closed when Aidan took a deep breath.

"In this game you only get one turn before we move on. That means I talk to Blazer next and get his version of events. Only this time, I'm going to start with this program and the mistakes you two made out there. While you're sitting in your cell, start praying that he's as loyal to you as you've been to him." Aidan cued the program to run again so he could see it one more time. "I have a feeling, though, that Blazer is the type of person who'll gladly pass the blame onto someone else if given the chance." She added the part of the radio contact where Blazer asked for Cletus to help him.

"That's not fair," Lewis complained.

"You had your chance and you blew it. Not fair is having no chance at all." Aidan turned the screen away from him and looked at Devin. "Get him out of my sight."

When the two men stepped out Aidan started the program again and watched Blazer's plane head toward North Korea. In her mind she could imagine Berkley following him. Whatever came next was a mystery or whatever the crew wanted to call it, but all she knew was Berkley hadn't come back and it had something to do with Blazer and Alan Lewis.

"When you get back I'm going to kick your butt," Aidan said with her eyes closed. "Because I refuse to believe you're dead."

CHAPTER TWENTY-FOUR

Off the Northwest Coast of North Korea

"Comrade, the general is waiting for you in the common room," said the man who opened the hatch of the plane as soon as Jin came to a stop.

"Jin," Yong said as Jin turned to go down the ladder to the ground. "What if he takes you away?"

"The general might try, but you know I'm not without my own ways of fighting back. Get inside and wait in our room."

"The general is waiting," the man reminded her.

"Yong, if things don't go well, you have to leave and find your way to your family in Hyesan. From there you might have a chance to cross into China," Jin said softly and quickly. "There's no reason for both of us to pay for my mistakes."

She walked at a fast clip to the main building, ignoring her father's men as she stepped into the common area. The television had pictures of the facility to the east of them with a voice-over of Kim Jong Il screaming about the unprovoked attack, but no picture of the Great Leader was shown. Pak sat with his legs crossed and listened with what seemed to Jin to be the kind rapt attention only those filled with total hero worship were capable of having.

"My father was a farmer with seven children he couldn't feed, much less buy shoes for," Pak said without his eyes leaving the television set.

"I've heard this before."

"Shut up, you stupid girl." Though his voice rose, there was no other sign of anger as he sat in the same relaxed way. "You can hate me all you want. I don't give a damn, but I hope you know you've ruined us both. I grew up with nothing, so I know what to expect, but you…" He looked at her and laughed. "You have no clue."

"So you're here to gloat?"

"I'm here to try to salvage what's left of my life. With luck, our Great Leader will overlook my mistake in having any faith in you at all, and not cast me aside." He stood and smoothed his jacket down. "I want a full account of what happened, then I'll give you what you kept telling me you most desire."

"I doubt you've ever paid attention to anything I want."

"When I leave here I plan to never see you ever again. Whatever happens to you and your whore isn't my concern."

"Finally, you show your true colors, General."

Pak reached into his breast pocket and removed something but kept it hidden in his hand. "Your report, Comrade Lee."

With as detached a voice as she could manage, Jin told him what happened. "The planes were painted black, but I'm sure they were Americans. You should find the wreckage in the interior."

"Anything else?"

"The fact that we were able to down one despite the surprise attack should be enough."

He opened his hand and Jin took a step forward when she saw the jade circle her mother had always worn around her neck. "She wanted you to have this." Pak placed it on the chair instead of handing it to her. "She died early this morning in her sleep."

"Anything else?" Jin asked through clenched teeth as he walked away.

"Good-bye, Jin, and good luck. Starting today you'll be transferred to General Ling in the northern territory."

"Damn you."

"No, after today you've damned us both."

Jin saw Pak take a deep breath when someone opened the door without knocking. From what little she knew of Pak it was how he kept himself in control.

"General." The man who entered said the word like it was some bad taste in his mouth he had to spit out.

"Lowe, it's good to see you," Pak said and formed a smile before he turned to face him. Lowe Nam Chil was a small man whose father served with Kim Jong Il's father, and was most known for his viciousness. It was a talent he'd shared with his son from a young age so that the teacher paled when compared to what he'd created. No one held out for long when they were locked in a room with Lowe.

Lowe pulled on the leather coat he had draped across his shoulders to keep it in place. "You don't seem excited to see me."

"Your company is always welcome, but I'd think you'd have other things to keep you busy."

"The destruction of the only two nuclear plants we have doesn't sound like something that would interest me? This was our future, General, and our leader entrusted it to you." Lowe smiled, but to Jin it made him look cruel. "Considering what happened you can imagine our disappointment."

"From my understanding the attack was a surprise," Pak said.

"I'd hope so." Lowe laughed. "That our best would see this coming and wait to act would be unacceptable. And I believe you understand what happens when our Great Leader finds something unacceptable."

"And I would hope you and he realize the level of my loyalty," Pak said.

Lowe didn't answer him, but turned his attention to Jin. "The brief report I got on my way here was that you downed one of them."

"Yes, sir," Jin said. Her father might have climbed the military ladder, but it was her mother who told her never to answer any question with too many words.

"I've got a team on the way to see what we find. Before that happens, do you want to tell me anything else?" Lowe removed an unfiltered cigarette from his front pocket and acted as if he expected Pak to light it, which he did.

"That's what happened. There's nothing more to add."

"If you need a hint." Lowe blew a stream of smoke in Jin's direction. "You should be trying to impress me with your efforts to uphold our beloved leader's honor."

"The American attack was cowardly, Comrade. They waited until the patrol circled south to carry it out. When I got in the air I took out their best pilot. I'm sure of it."

"What our leader will remember is that both of his plants are now destroyed as well as the other two planes you put in the air. The life of one pilot doesn't seem like a good trade."

"Even if it was their team leader?" Jin tried to keep her voice calm, but she could see how Lowe's hands were twitching as he continued to fool with his coat. "I would think that would be a victory for us since the Americans pride themselves in their piloting skills."

"You're so sure of this that you'd wager you life on it?"

"I'm that sure."

The door opened behind Jin and since Lowe hadn't answered her yet she heard the heavy clack of someone's boots getting closer. It had to be one of her father's men since Pak only utilized women in what he considered lowly positions. That was one of the reasons she'd always blamed for him abandoning her and her mother so easily. Pak had been disgusted that she was a girl, and disgusted with her mother for letting him down. He had set her on the course of her career, but no matter how good she got, he never seemed proud of her.

"What is it?" Pak asked the soldier.

"We've found the plane, sir."

Lowe's eyes cut to the messenger momentarily before locking with Jin's again. "Tell us you've brought the bodies back so we can exchange those for the two piles of bricks," Lowe said. "And show the world how the Americans have no honor."

"The plane is scattered along the countryside, sir. The impact caused it to self-destruct, but I have men on the ground collecting every piece so we can reconstruct it. So far what we have isn't of any use in identifying where it's from."

"Any bodies among the wreckage?" Lowe asked.

"None that we've found so far. The seats haven't been found in the line of debris."

Jin didn't know Lowe well, but she couldn't believe the transformation on his face. He surprised her with a look of pure joy, a reaction she was sure came from the anticipation of being alone with her and his tools for hours of what he considered fun.

"Which of us wins our bet?" Lowe asked Jin even though he'd made no counter offer.

❖

North Korean Countryside

"Junior," Berkley whispered into Harvey's ear. The fall from the tree had knocked him out, not from the impact but from the pain in his leg. Berkley had taken advantage and carried him to a more secluded spot in the woods.

From her calculations and the brief glimpse of black smoke from their wreckage, the wind had carried them about six miles southeast. It was a head start, but Blazer's idiocy had driven them at least eighty miles into North Korean territory. Their best chance to survive was to make it not to the coast, but into South Korea.

The odds of that would've been somewhat manageable if they were both mobile, but Harvey would slow them down to the point that the search parties looking for them would have a better than average chance at finding them.

His groan was laced with what sounded like excruciating pain. "Where are we?"

"Eighty miles from where we need to be, so you feel up to a walk?" Berkley put her hand on his chest since she'd lowered his head to rest on her thigh.

"The best thing is to leave me," he said as he turned his head toward her feet. "No sense in both of us dying out here."

"I could do that, but then they wouldn't give me a medal for saving you." Berkley poked him in the head with her finger.

"You don't give a shit about that."

"Sure I do. They really make my dress uniforms pop. You don't want to take that away from me, do you?" Berkley chuckled. The sun was starting to set but the temperature was still warm, and she hoped for Junior's sake it would stay that way.

"How fucked are we?"

"Enough that if we dig out from this we'll be legends." Before it got too dark, Berkley took out the compass Triton had given her. Whether Junior was ready or not, they had to start moving. "I don't care about that either, but I do want to get back to beat the shit out of Blazer."

Junior nodded and tried to sit up. "Oh God, I think I'm going to throw up."

"When you were out I set your leg. I know it hurts, but give it time and it'll fade some."

"What's your plan?"

"We've got to cover at least five miles tonight, but since you can't put any weight on that leg yet, we'll go as far as I can carry you." The stillness of the area made it easy for Berkley to hear the helicopter in the distance. "Try and get some sleep and we'll move out after it gets fully dark."

She was deep in enemy territory, but Berkley wasn't completely empty-handed. Her father had flown for the Navy years before her, and though the military had trained her, it was her father who had taught her what she considered the most important lessons. She always kept a small bag in her flight suit that she hoped she'd never have to use.

Every item in it was on her father's list of essential supplies. The knife, small binoculars, energy bars, and handgun wouldn't seem like much to most people, but to Berkley it gave her a sense of hope they'd make it out if she kept calm. She moved up to the top of the hill they were lying against and focused on the site of their wreck. There was no way to make out exactly what was going on from this distance, but there was a lot of activity for a pile of small pieces of twisted metal.

The buzzing helicopters were the sign of what was to come. When the North Koreans found they weren't in the wreckage, Berkley had a feeling they would hunt them down if only to ease the sting of having been caught unawares.

"Shit," Berkley murmured. There was no choice, they had to start moving, and Junior would have to put the pain out of his mind.

She took out the compass, and the picture of Aidan filled her with regret for all their missed opportunities. The biggest one Berkley would take to her grave, if that was where this ended, was not ever telling Aidan again that she loved her.

"Of course I wait until now to figure out that I never stopped."

CHAPTER TWENTY-FIVE

Northern Virginia

"Sir." Sergeant Nelson Alexander spoke into the phone to Jerry Teague as the new secretary of defense stood rigidly in front of his desk.

Drew Orr had served in ROTC in college and gladly reported to active duty after graduation. But his years of service had not been what brought him to the attention of the new president. That had come on the first day of college and Drew had arrived at the dorm to meet his new roommate.

Once Peter Khalid had announced his candidacy, Drew had retired from active duty and hit the campaign trail with him. On election night Peter had recruited him for a new job, and since Drew had spent the last years of his career in the Pentagon, he was the perfect choice. The military was more political sometimes than the halls of Congress, but Drew had learned from his first day in the massive building to swim in those waters.

"What is it? I told you no calls," Jerry said in an irritated voice.

"Secretary Orr is here to see you." It was the only warning Nelson was able to give before Drew lost patience and walked in without invitation.

"Secretary Orr," Jerry said and stood with as broad a smile as his lips could stretch, or at least that's what it looked like to Drew. "I've been so busy I haven't had a chance to come by and congratulate you. Sorry about that, but hopefully you got my e-mail."

"What are you doing here?" Drew asked.

"Sir?"

"It's a simple question, and if you're going to stand there and play stupid, I'll have you hogtied and dumped in the parking lot."

"I offered to train my replacement," Jerry said slowly like Drew were simpleminded. "If anything, you should be thanking me."

"Lucas Rhodes has nothing to learn from you, and since he's in China at the moment, exactly how are you doing any training?"

The side door of Jerry's office opened and Adam walked in with a sheet of paper in his hand. "I finally heard from our contact," Adam said with his eyes on the paper as if it held the answer to world domination.

Drew's scalp tingled from the realization that his decision to personally deliver some background documents to the new deputy defense secretary had turned over a rock to expose the cockroaches underneath. Jerry's clearance had been revoked weeks ago, so there was no reason for him to be getting any messages from anyone unless it was a wireless company trying to sell him a new plan. "Let's hear it then, Adam," Drew said as he removed his phone from his belt.

"It's nothing, sir." The obvious shock of seeing Drew made it came out as a whisper.

"No one gets that excited over nothing." Drew punched in a brief message. "Read it," he ordered without looking up. "And before you lie to me, I recognized the tear sheet that makes it Pentagon property, so I'll be leaving with it." Drew pressed the send button and gave Adam his full attention. "Get to it."

"Mission accomplished—minor glitch on back end—Captain being difficult," Adam read in an even tone, but Drew noticed how his eyes darted to different spots on the page.

"Do you want to explain, or do we play the game you and your former boss perfected?" Drew asked Jerry as he held his hand out wiggled his fingers so Adam would hand him the page.

"We've been monitoring the situation on the *Jefferson*," Jerry said, then swallowed loud enough that Drew almost laughed when the MPs he ordered came in and stood at attention next to him.

"I doubt this'll be easy, but what the hell," Drew said with a smile that was hard to tamp down. This was his opportunity to deal with some of the people who'd been quick to send troops into harm's way even though it was the last thing they'd chosen even when there was a government enforced draft. "Who's your contact who gave you all this pertinent information?"

"Like Adam said, Secretary, this isn't anything important. I'm sure you're busy. No need to waste your time."

Drew read the note for the third time. The answer of the *Jefferson* was at least honest since it was the only situation that fit. The outcome of that was the main issue on the agenda of the meeting Khalid had scheduled that morning, and if it weren't for the last three words Drew might have taken Jerry's advice to ignore it. An hour before, Captain Aidan Sullivan had told him what happened and how she had Lieutenant Morris and his partner separated and confined to the brig.

The incomplete story told by the young pilot and the fact that his father now held this information left Drew's scalp still tingling. *Sometimes it's better to be lucky than good*, Drew thought, the quote one of Peter's favorites.

"Jerry, I want you to listen carefully. I want the name of the person who sent this to you—now."

"I'm not at liberty to say," Jerry responded just as seriously.

"Take these two into custody and have someone in here to lock all this down," Drew said to the MPs. "Don't forget Mr. Morris's office as well, and no phone calls or outside contact for either of them starting now."

"You can't do that," Jerry said.

"Sure I can. Remember how hard you and your friends worked to pass the Patriot Act? All I can say is thanks." Drew laughed at how red Jerry's face got. "I consider you both a national security threat, so I'm going to drop you in a hole until we sort this out."

"How dare you," Adam said and stopped after one step when one of the MPs mirrored his movements. "I served my country and don't appreciate you questioning my patriotism."

"I'm going to question a lot more before we're done. We're going to see how well you hold up when I do, because I was in all those meetings when you argued for tougher interrogations."

Jerry leaned closer to Drew. "Think about what you're doing, Drew. All this is revenge for policies you didn't totally agree with, and that Adam and I weren't responsible for putting into place."

"Of course you did, Jerry, but you're wrong on that. I didn't agree with the methods, but the results are what you pushed for in all those meetings: stronger and better interrogation methods. When someone doesn't want to talk we've become good at changing their mind, and that's hard to argue with."

"I want to talk to the president," Adam blurted out.

Drew shook his head in disgust at the visibly nervous man. "Take them in and tell Walby I'll call him in a couple of hours," he told the two MPs.

"Walby Edwards?" Jerry said the name and his voice rose comically at the end. The CIA operative had a reputation people like Jerry loved to brag about when they talked about his special ability to produce confessions. What Lowe Nam Chil was to North Korea, Walby was to the CIA, only it was people's heads Walby like to screw with, leaving all his bruising there.

"You're one of his greatest admirers, so it's only fair that you get to see him work in a way very few citizens get to experience."

"This is totally unnecessary and premature, don't you think? It's just a note, for the love of God." Jerry said and pulled his arm out of the MP's grasp.

"It might be, and if it is you'll have my sincerest apologies. But for now we have a situation brewing and I need to make sure it doesn't escalate to something we all don't want." Drew stood aside when the MPs escorted them out, then stopped in Jerry's assistant's office to talk to him. Nelson was locked in a staring contest with the MP standing in front of his desk.

"Is there something I can help you with, Mr. Secretary?" Nelson asked.

"Has our young friend called anyone?" Drew asked the guard, who shook his head. "I need the list of appointments your former boss had in the last six months, official and unofficial. Then I need you to be patient with me and agree to stay in the quarters here with an escort until I'm done going through the list. If you choose to side with Mr. Teague on this, I'll be happy to make arrangements for you to join him. That means if you make any attempt to contact anyone for him as a part of some pact you may have formed, you'll find yourself on the first plane to Gitmo, and it won't be to work on your tan."

"I'll get that for you." Nelson got on the computer and started printing. When it finished, he handed over twenty sheets.

"Anyone missing?" Drew asked casually.

"No, sir."

"No friendly visit that Jerry didn't see the need to record in his official log?" Drew kept scanning the names, many of whom worked in the building. The list would be compared to the visitor's log outside to see if Jerry's help came from outside, but if it was someone else like Adam it would be harder to track them down. "You're young and just starting out, so I want you to think before you answer."

"None that I can think of, sir," Nelson answered after a few moments of silence.

Drew nodded, then glanced up at the MP. "Thank you for your cooperation," he told Nelson. "Take him downstairs and put him in protective custody until further notice. Once I'm finished with the visitor logs and video surveillance we can let this young patriot get back to work."

"Video surveillance, sir?"

"Every space aside from private offices in here is monitored, son, but you've been truthful, so you've got nothing to worry about. I'm sure we'll have you reassigned before too long." The look of concern seemed to suck the vigor out of Nelson's appearance, but his lips stayed glued together. "Like you said, everyone I need to talk to is on this list. If someone's missing I'm sure you weren't here at your post, so how could you know everyone Teague met with?"

"Is that all, Mr. Secretary?" the MP asked.

Drew stared at Nelson for a long minute before he responded. "I guess so." When he was alone in the office, Drew picked up Nelson's phone and dialed the head of security for the Pentagon, Commander Mark "Rooster" Palmer'. "Rooster, get a small team together and get up to Jerry Teague's old office as soon as you can."

"Anything in particular you want to concentrate on?"

"I have a feeling we have a mole on the *Jefferson* giving the wrong people information, and Jerry has conspired with an undetermined number of people for something I'm not quite sure of yet."

Rooster laughed. "I see you have all the answers then, so our jobs should be easy."

"I'm having the office locked down, so start here and move to Adam Morris's office after and see what you find. Whatever it is, I think our friends are up to no good."

CHAPTER TWENTY-SIX

North Korean Countryside

Berkley's parachute was now in strips that she was using to fit a splint to Junior's leg. He'd insisted on walking part of the way, so while the sun went down Berkley fashioned some crutches for him. Their deal was that he could walk until he started to lag, then she would carry him.

"Ready?" Berkley asked once she had the last strip tied off.

"Lead the way." Junior stood on his good foot. He swayed a little but Berkley could see that he was trying to hide how much pain he was in.

"Remember," Berkley said as she folded the rest of the chute in case they needed it, "you tell me when the pain gets to be too much. I don't need you to hobble yourself any more than you are already." Before they started out she took an energy bar, split it in half, and offered him a piece.

"What do you think our odds are of making it out of here?"

Night had set in and Berkley was amazed at how dark and still the countryside had gotten. She'd seen in night satellite surveillance shots how a large section of land looked like it was swallowed by a black hole. Her world history teacher at the Academy had said it was the choice between progress and idiocy when you compared it to South Korea.

The silence and the darkness weren't anything to fear, though. It was the best-case scenario for them as they moved toward their goal, since any squad sent to hunt for them would stick out like a lit Christmas tree in a closet.

"A good chance if we work together, and with any luck it'll take them a couple of days to figure out we're still kicking." She started walking and glanced over her shoulder to see how well he kept up. "We'll stick to the trees and see how far we get tonight, and then tomorrow I'll give you a better answer."

At two in the morning Berkley stopped them, figuring they had gone about four miles, but Junior's breathing was more ragged and he was starting to grunt with every step. They were still in the tree line, which was thicker than their starting point so the ground was more uneven.

"Let's take a break," Berkley said softly and held up her hand. The half-moon provided enough illumination to spot a small structure with pens around it. This appeared to be a rural farm where the land was worked by either the animals in the pens or by hand; she didn't spot any equipment. "Stay put and I'll be right back."

She left the safety of the trees and walked halfway before dropping to her belly and crawling. It was no time to let a farmer raise any type of alarm, but she didn't want to kill anyone she had no fight with either.

The pens held only a few chickens, a cow, and small pigs, but she passed by those and headed for the well. A missing bucket and ladle would immediately be missed, so she took an empty bottle from the three near the back door. When she sniffed it all she found was the faint odor of milk, so she filled it with water and drank down the entire liter.

She returned to Junior the same way, but with a bottle of water for him. "We've made good time so far considering, but you've got to let me carry you for a while."

"All that's going to happen if you do that is that your back is going to get messed up," he said and wiped his mouth with the back of his hand. "I'll be fine on my own."

"You can go voluntarily or I can cold-cock you. Your choice. Let me know before we have to start moving."

He put his arm around her neck and pressed his crutches and their supplies between their bodies as Berkley shifted him to a more comfortable spot.

An hour later the trees started to thin, so she stopped and put Junior down carefully. The next patch of cover was at least two miles away and all downhill, which would be a bitch with a passenger on her back.

"It turns light in a few hours. Maybe we should stop," Junior said.

"The only way we can stay here is to turn back for more cover, and that's a time killer."

"You're already getting tired, so why chance it?"

Berkley helped him back up and made sure to distribute his weight as best she could with his leg sticking straight out. "We have to chance it because you have to understand the kind of people we're up against. They're starving and poor, but they'd gladly rip your heart out with a spoon to prove themselves to the killer who runs this place."

"You sound like a preacher when you talk like that."

"Ha," Berkley laughed. "I'm more of a sinner. All I'm saying is these folks are looking for a break no matter who they have to turn in." She stopped talking as the incline got steeper and she felt the sweat start to roll down her neck.

Close to them a dog started barking, and Berkley stopped to make sure it was only one. Even if it was, they needed to move so there was no hint of their passing. If possible she wanted to leave as little a footprint as they could to make it harder for their trackers to find them. She planned to keep moving even after the sun went up. The more distance she put behind them, the more she threw off the formula the trackers would use to pinpoint their search area.

The dog's barking got louder and Berkley had no choice but to put Junior down and investigate. "We're only halfway, Cletus. We can't stop here," Junior said.

"Let me see, because if this dog barks and ends up waking the neighborhood, it's not good for us." She helped him sit and took off before any more time was lost.

In the middle of the next hill there was another, more prosperous farm, with a tractor parked close to the living quarters. When she was close enough she saw the dog wasn't barking at their presence, but at the two horses moving slowly around a small enclosure. That attention shifted quickly when the dog caught Berkley's scent as he stopped and lifted his muzzle in her direction.

"Great, the owner isn't going to wake up because this mutt's barking but because he's not," Berkley thought. The longer he stayed quiet, the better the chance that someone would come out to investigate, so she thought quickly as she removed her shoes. "I've gone from pilot to horse thief."

She removed the boots that would have left a distinctive tread mark and ran in on bare feet. The dog went back to his excited barking when he saw her, but he backed up slowly instead of trying to attack her. His fear was to her advantage, so Berkley headed right for him and picked him up with the hope he wasn't going to bite. Before the dog could think about it, she deposited him in the pigpen, then stuck her hands into the muck at the bottom of the enclosure and pressed them briefly to the dog's nose.

The horses were next, and like the dog, they shied away from her, so she moved slowly with her hands up. Berkley had no experience with horses, but a horse provided a way to cover a lot more miles, especially with Junior's injury. She finally got a grip on the solid brown one and led him back toward her partner.

"Let's hope I don't end up with a broken leg," she said when she was far enough away.

"Why do you smell like pig shit?" Junior asked.

"I gave the dog a new scent to follow to right here," Berkley said as she wiped her hands on the grass so she could put her shoes on. "You know anything about horses?"

"You're talking to a summer camp alumnus," he said and accepted her hand up.

"Good, you can drive." She climbed up so she could pull him up in front of her.

"He'll do better in the open."

"I'm sure he would, but there's no time like now for him to learn to dodge trees." She gripped the sides of the horse with her legs when Junior got them going. "That way, Lone Ranger." She pointed in the right direction after glancing at the compass again.

"Does that make you Tonto, kemosabi?" Junior asked and laughed.

"Not unless you want me to break your other leg, so get your mosey on."

❖

USS *Jefferson*

"If that kid doesn't shut up soon you may not have to worry about trying to find out what he did," Devin said to Aiden.

They had anchored and started their military exercises as if nothing had happened. With every passing hour, the crew became more convinced that Berkley and Harvey weren't coming back. The night before, Aidan had closed her eyes, but the hum of the engines, which for so long had brought a sense of comfort, instead kept her awake and filled her head with thoughts of Berkley.

Hearing from Secretary Orr before the night watch had gone on duty was a surprise. He'd asked for Aiden to gather her most trusted crew for a briefing. With that order Aidan had called in Devin, her deck leader Mike Dyer, and her communications man Luther Oliver.

"We'll give him the chance to tell his version of the pack of lies his backseat was trying to feed us," Aidan said, referring to Blazer.

"We're ready to go, ma'am," Luther said before he punched the button that would bring in the live feed from the Pentagon.

Drew sat at his desk, and Aidan could make out a little of the view behind him, and that too made her think of Berkley and their brief visit to the Pentagon, adding to her heavy burden of guilt that she'd talked her lover into this mission. "Good morning, Secretary Orr," she said, looking into the camera on their end.

"And good evening to you all. I'll be as brief as I can, Captain, because I've got a feeling you've got plenty of work ahead of you."

Aidan introduced everyone in the room with her before asking, "What can we do for you, sir?"

"I need to review your communication logs, Mr. Oliver, and see if you can pinpoint who contacted Washington approximately two hours after the completion of our exercises. Once you figure out who that is, I need you to confine them to a cell as you did Lieutenants Morris and Lewis." Drew glanced at his notes and moved to the next page.

"Sir, I've got the log book here, and I can tell you no one on the ship made radio contact stateside until Captain Sullivan reported in," Luther said.

"Then we have a problem, folks."

"Could you elaborate, sir?" Aidan asked.

Drew's image was briefly replaced with the sheet he'd confiscated from Adam. "We've taken Jerry Teague and Adam Morris into custody for questioning, because my gut along with this cryptic message tells me there's a big problem and you've got a mole on board."

"Since the message was written when Adam Morris first got it, I'll check with my crew to see if one of them sent it by other means."

"I'll give you a day to investigate, then we'll compare notes again and I'll let you know what Teague and Morris cough up."

"Before you sign off, sir, could you tell me if Adam Morris is related to Lieutenant Morris?" Aidan asked.

"He's his father, and one of the reasons I think we've got trouble."

"Permission to share what you told us with Blazer when we question him?" Aidan asked.

"Use any means you have available to rattle his cage, Captain." Drew pushed the papers aside and leaned back in his chair. "Gentlemen, please step out. I need to speak to Captain Sullivan a moment."

When the door closed, Aidan mirrored his relaxed position. "What are we really looking at here, sir?"

"Please, Aidan, no need to be so formal. We've known each other too long for that. So tell me how you're holding up?" He'd been one of the leading people pushing for her commission, but not because of his long friendship with Triton. Through his relationship with her father, he'd watched Aidan grow up and become one of the finest officers serving in the Navy and knew she deserved the chance.

Aidan exhaled and rested her hands on the edge of the table. "I lost two of my people and because of the secrecy involved, I don't know why, and the two smart-asses who could tell me aren't talking."

"How many times did Jerry Teague ask to meet with you?"

"After a week of briefings I had with you and Naval Command, he called and asked to speak to me and Berkley. Because of his title, I never thought to question why he wanted the meeting." She closed her eyes briefly.

"Did he ask you to contact him?"

"All he said was to listen to the orders, and confirm when it was done, which you know I didn't do right away. And when I did,

I contacted Command. Had he asked to talk specifically to him, I would've demanded a meeting with you for clarification knowing that the new deputy secretary had been confirmed."

Drew nodded. "There's something going on, and the story is divided between here and the *Jefferson*. We need to work together so we can defuse this situation."

"I still have one pilot to question, and I'll get Devin to track where the message came from."

"Let's give it a couple of days then before I contact you again."

"Thanks, Drew." Aidan's lips turned up in a smile, but it was halfhearted. The monitor went dark and she sat in the silence to think of their next move. The part of her heart that knew for sure that Berkley was alive was starting to dim since she thought she would've heard from her by now.

"Captain." Devin's voice came through the intercom.

"Come back in, Devin." She motioned for him to close the door. "I need you to assign your most trusted person to Blazer."

"Sure, but why?"

"A small fishing trip." Aidan went on to tell him her plan and made him repeat it before he left to carry out her orders.

"You sure know how to bait a hook, ma'am."

"My real talent comes in gutting and filleting my catch," she said so seriously that it made Devin salute before he left the room.

CHAPTER TWENTY-SEVEN

North Korean Countryside

Dawn came and showed the first signs of a stormy day with sheets of heavy rain falling on the open land, but it only penetrated the trees as a drizzle. Berkley had kept Harvey awake by talking to him softly about all the hunting trips she'd gone on with her father. They'd kept moving through the night but at such a slow pace that the horse hadn't made a sound and kept moving.

Even at that rate they'd covered a lot of miles, and by morning the long stretch of forest barely visible that had seemed to go on for miles in the little moonlight was starting to thin. Berkley told Junior to stop and when he did the horse pawed the ground and shook his head hard enough to douse an already soaked Junior.

"Let's stop here," Berkley said softly. From what she could see through the trees and rain, their cover wasn't just thinning, they were coming to a town. So far the only thing that had gone right was that the rain had completely obliterated their tracks.

Berkley slid off the horse and helped Junior down. The grimace on his face was a good gauge as to how much pain he was in from the hours of riding. "Hang in, and I promise a nice bunk in the ship's hospital ward with a good-looking nurse just for you," she said as she sat him against a tree.

She took another energy bar and handed it all to him, and Junior shook his head and broke it in half. "You can't carry my ass and go without food too."

They chewed slowly and sat together as the rain splattered on their flight suits softly but enough that they were soaked and chilled. Even though the trees were thick, there was no game except for some songbirds in the high branches. That was lucky for them as well since it would make it unlikely that they'd run into a hunting party searching for anything but them.

"Try and get some sleep," Berkley said and stood.

"Where are you going?"

She pointed toward the town. "This is the last of this kind of cover, so I need to see what our best move is once the sun sets."

From the edge of the trees she scanned the area using the binoculars since there was no sun to reflect off the glass. The town didn't appear large, more of a center for the surrounding farmers to bring their crops and farm animals in exchange for supplies.

There were trucks parked next to the largest building, which appeared to be a warehouse of some kind with grain silos along the back. The only cars she spotted looked to belong to police or government officials, and for such a small place it had more of those than seemed normal.

Berkley stayed flat on her belly and watched. If the extra force was out of the ordinary, the lousy weather wasn't going to stop them from their objective if they'd somehow tracked them to the area. After hours of watching, the only brick building she could see from her vantage point, a door opened and a group of men stepped out. Everyone stood in the rain except for one man. The cigarette hanging from his mouth bobbed as he spoke, but stayed dry under the large umbrella the man standing next to him was holding. Whoever he was, the rest of the group leaned in listening to every word, or at least that's what it looked like to Berkley.

After talking briefly with the group, one of the police opened the back door of the large black sedan parked on the street, and the umbrella holder walked the guy to the car. Another three cars quickly pulled up and most of the uniformed men who'd stood silently in the rain left as well, obviously part of the civilian's entourage.

The situation seemed out of the ordinary judging by the way the people huddled around the obvious VIP, but the strangest thing was the one person who'd stood back from the group but had gotten into the car first. It was a woman, and while she was traveling with the man everyone was treating like a god, her body language was that of someone who didn't want to be there.

"From this far away I can't be sure, but that's what it looks like," Berkley said to herself as she adjusted the glasses for the best look possible. After the caravan left, the town went back to normal and the streets had only a few stragglers. The weather kept her from seeing too far into the countryside, but from her spot she could see it was bleak. She could see no clumps of trees and no noticeable hills or rock formations to hide the both of them and a horse.

"The only thing missing is a big red neon sign suspended over us with a blinking arrow that reads *here we are*." Berkley studied the terrain and opened the compass to find the least worse course that wouldn't take them too far out of the way. "Shit."

❖

"You don't look pleased, Comrade Umeko," Lowe said between puffs of his ever-present cigarette. The back of the car was filled with gray smoke, and with the rain the relief of rolling down the window would be impossible.

"I don't understand why you need me with you," Jin said, not caring she wasn't acknowledging his comment.

"Do you feel I'm keeping you from something?" He blew a stream of smoke in her direction before turning his head toward the window.

"I'd think you'd want me to carry out the duty for which I was trained." Jin tried to breath through her nose, her throat raw from the hours of being in Lowe's haze.

They'd left her father and Yong back at the base, and from that moment Lowe had made a slow pace back toward the capital. The only time he'd left Jin alone was when she stepped into the bathroom or when she was locked in a room to rest. He seemed content to ask her bizarre questions about her daily activities and didn't show the least care about finding the two Americans who might've survived the crash. That subject he didn't want to talk about, at least not with her.

"If your memory isn't good, we've done that already and you failed miserably. For now, we'll put someone else in charge of outside aggressors, and you'll pretend you give a damn about what happens to our country," Lowe said in such a casual manner that he could've been talking about the rain. "Tell me how well you get along with your partner, Yong."

The last Jin saw of Yong was when they pulled away from the base. She was standing next to Pak, who appeared made of stone. Her father had never been an emotional man, but Jin expected something from him as she was ordered to leave with Lowe. That she would be blamed for what happened and made to pay for it was a foregone conclusion, so she expected some acknowledgment from Pak that her immediate future was to be fertilizer after Lowe cut her into little pieces and spread her along the fields for the good of the people.

She hoped Yong had taken her advice and run at the first opportunity. She had a feeling Pak would take advantage and rid himself of the one person he felt had held Jin back. Only if she lived and succeeded would Pak regain some standing within the regime, but she also knew Pak would do his best to carry on even if Lowe killed her.

"We work well together," Jin said with conviction.

"Is that all?"

"I've known Yong from the first day I reported for duty. She serves well and works hard. What else is there to say?"

Lowe lowered the window and flicked the small stub of his cigarette out, but raised it again before the fresh air made an impact on the interior. He opened his case and retrieved another one of the many he'd taken the time to roll the night before. They had spent the night in a police station sleeping on uncomfortable bunks in the tiny jail cells. Jin had sat and watched as he meticulously measured out tobacco and rolled each smoke as if it were part of his religion.

"I'm sure there might be plenty, but we'll come back to that. Instead you can tell me about the pride you have for your father, Pak," Lowe said with the smile that made Jin want to slit his throat. "He is a true patriot, don't you think?"

"If there's one thing you can say for General Lee, it's that he has always put country before anything or anyone."

Lowe laughed in a way that sounded like he was truly pleased. "Isn't that the goal of everyone who serves the Great Leader?"

"Some achieve more glory than others."

"Are you deficient in that arena, then?"

Jin closed her eyes and prepared herself for what she was sure would come next. "I'm sure you know all my deficiencies as well as wrongdoings when it comes to my service, Mr. Nam Chil, or is it that you want to hear it from me personally?"

"I have a feeling you won't give me that without a little persuasion," he said and laughed again.

Death beckoned to her in the next few days, and it wouldn't come quietly or gently. The slow drive through the countryside was to allow Lowe to compare her answers with those that would come as he cut away her dignity one little piece at a time.

It wasn't something she looked forward to, and she would endure it only because she knew Pak would as well. Her father deserved to suffer if only to repay the wrongs he'd committed against her mother. While she still had the strength, her plan was to implicate Pak as much as she could so that Lowe would have no choice but to take him to the pit of hell choking on his own blood.

"You've got nothing more to add?" Lowe asked.

Jin didn't answer and didn't open her eyes. In her mind she was in her grandfather's garden with her mother. The sun was shining and it felt like a warm shield on her skin and her mother was telling her how it'd protect her from everything that would try to harm her.

This was the place she would go when Lowe pulled out his tools, and Jin was sure that no matter the pain, her mother would sit and hold her hand until Jin joined her in death. With that reality there was nothing more to say.

CHAPTER TWENTY-EIGHT

USS *Jefferson*

"Come on," Devin said to Blazer when he unlocked the door. "You want to tell your story, now's your chance." He hit the metal door with the flat of his hand hard enough to bring Alan Lewis to his door to look out the small pane of glass.

"It's about goddamn time," Blazer said. He left his shirt on the bed and followed Devin in his T-shirt and pants.

Aidan had the route Blazer had flown cued on the computer again, but she knew no matter what she said or showed him, he wasn't going to crack. For now his behavior didn't bother her. "At ease, Lieutenant."

"Is there some reason you've kept me locked in that room for this long?" He stared at her for a long moment before adding, "Ma'am."

"You do indignant well, but you're not here to ask questions," Aidan said. "So don't give me any encouragement to stick you where I originally wanted. If you ask where that is, we'll cut this short so Devin can accommodate you."

Blazer glared at her briefly before he fixed his eyes like Alan had on the wall. "Do you want to tell us what happened?"

It was as if Alan and Blazer had studied a script. He repeated Alan's story almost verbatim. He relaxed his shoulders when she didn't interrupt, and only when he got to the end did he add anything new.

"Cletus was good, but she was no match for the Korean who came after us." As he said it he glanced down at her and Aidan saw the glee in his eyes. "Because Cletus was shot down over enemy lines, I'd prepare for some sort of reprisal from the North Korean government. Let's hope it isn't on American soil."

"So it was Cletus who turned toward enemy lines?"

"My job, which she kept reminding me at every opportunity, was to follow her lead. I did that and Lewis and I almost got killed."

Aidan shook her head in Devin's direction when he went to say something. "With Cletus's experience I find it surprising that she would've gone looking for a fight. That's not her style."

"I guess she had something to prove and it didn't matter what your orders were. She obviously had other plans."

"Since I don't have any proof otherwise, I guess I'll have to take your word for it." Aidan glanced at Devin again. "You're free to go, and I'll let you know if I have any other questions."

Blazer appeared stunned.

"You're dismissed as soon as Lieutenant Clark escorts you back to gather your things. Step out a moment and I'll have him escort you back."

"Remember, see who our flyboy is chummy with, and it might make your investigation as to who sent Teague a message easier," Aidan said to Devin.

"What about Alan?" Devin asked.

"I want you to deliver the message that Blazer threw him overboard. Make sure you remind him that we gave him every opportunity to tell us what happened and he refused to protect the asshole who gave him up on the first sweep." She stood and stretched her back out. "When you're loyal to a snake, you give him the chance to throw you into the prop."

"And if he wants to talk to you?"

"Make him wait." Aidan stopped at the door that headed toward the bridge. "I've found that desperation and the drive of self-preservation has always been a good motivator, especially when you whip it with fear."

"Is there some reason you didn't tell Blazer what Secretary Orr shared with you?" Devin stood a few feet from her at the head of corridor that would lead him to where he was holding Alan. "That would've gotten a response for sure."

"Patience, Devin, the game isn't over."

"I have a feeling it is, only Blazer is the last person who hasn't figured it out yet."

"That's because he thinks his safety net is still in place, but if I know Drew Orr, Blazer's safe landing spot is somewhere that has one door and no windows." A few sailors passed them and Devin moved closer to her to keep their conversation private. "To loosen things on our end, have that talk with Alan and try to get his attention when you bring Blazer back down to cut him loose."

"You got it, Captain." Devin radioed the guard he'd assigned to Alan and told him to wait five minutes and then ask him something that would bring him to the door. "Let's go," he told Blazer right after.

"Have we started our flight exercises?"

Devin glanced back at Blazer amazed at his audacity mixed with a good dose of stupidity. "The team started yesterday."

"Who's in charge now that the flight god is gone?"

"Commander Levine is missing in action and still your superior, asshole, so check the wisecracks."

"Sorry." Blazer raised his hands and laughed. He laughed harder when Devin clenched his fists.

Devin couldn't have planned it better. In Blazer's lame attempt to taunt him for his loyalty to Aidan, he never looked toward Alan's door. After he picked up the book he'd been reading and his discarded uniform, Blazer threw Devin a casual salute and laughed as he walked away.

The guard at the main door of the area gave Devin a small nod indicating that Blazer was gone. Only then did Devin open the door to Alan's cell.

"It's about damn time," Alan said after he took a step back because Devin was blocking the entryway.

"It's about damn time for what?" Devin repeated and smiled. "You think you're going somewhere, sunshine?"

"Since Blazer just walked out I figured you checked our story and you saw I was telling the truth." Alan pointed in the direction Blazer had headed.

"We did check your stories." Devin leaned against the door frame. "I say stories because Blazer's account had a few different parts to it than yours."

"What are you talking about?"

"They didn't match up because he told us the truth, and his explanation fit the facts better than your version." Devin spread his hands and lifted them as he shrugged. "We both know you turned back toward the north, and we both know that Cletus ordered you to turn around before you cut off the link." Devin knocked on the metal door to make Alan look up. "And I do mean you, Lewis."

"What are you talking about?" Alan's eyes were wide open now as he repeated himself and Devin could almost smell the fear Aidan mentioned on him.

"It was you who wanted to deviate, you who cut the transmission to Cletus, and you who got her and Junior killed. All you, Lewis, and I've got the best witness in the world who'll back it up—your pilot. How'd you get to call all the shots up there? You fucking Blazer?"

"He wouldn't do that," Alan said while he shook his head.

"Your boyfriend took one look at what the captain showed you and he couldn't talk fast enough. That means you're stuck in here for the duration, so get comfortable. When we're stateside the captain will turn you over for a court-martial and they're going to fry you. If you want to avoid that—"

"What, talk?" Alan appeared relieved when Devin spoke again. "I'm not that stupid, Lieutenant."

"Boy, I don't give a rat fuck if you talk." Devin moved forward so fast Alan fell back on the bunk. "What I was going to say was if you want to avoid a trial then give me a reason to fix the problem cheaper. Give my men any shit and I'll fucking kill you myself and save the Navy the trouble."

"You're bluffing. You can't touch me."

"You really are as stupid as Blazer said. If you're talking about your Pentagon boys coming to the rescue, they're already in custody. I'm sure they're telling everyone who'll sit and listen that you're the grand mastermind. Think about it. It's Blazer and his father's word against yours. The odds aren't in your favor." Devin left after that and Alan didn't start screaming until he was in the corridor, but Devin kept going.

"Let's see who's the better bluffer, asshole, you or me," Devin said.

❖

Washington, DC

"Sir, we finished the log search you asked for," Commander Mark

"Rooster" Palmer, head of the security forces for the Pentagon, said and handed Drew a sheet of paper. "The only visit so far that meets the parameters you set is number forty-two."

Drew ran his finger down the page and fell back in his seat when he saw Rodney James's name. He knew the proud man was upset after Peter had forced his retirement, but not enough to participate in whatever Jerry had in mind.

"Did you talk to anyone with the Navy? What's the retired admiral been up to?"

"From my sources, sir, Mr. James has accepted a job with a defense contractor as their liaison with Congress."

"Thanks, Rooster, and remember to not talk about this with anyone," Drew said as a dismissal. When he was alone he picked up the phone and dialed. "Meredith, I need to talk to him."

Peter Khalid came on the line seconds later. "What's up, Drew?"

"Mr. President, I've started an investigation because I think we've got a situation."

"Give me an hour and we'll meet here."

As Drew gathered his information for his meeting the phone rang. It was Rooster again. "I just got a call from the brig, sir, and Teague's demanding a meeting with you."

"I'll be happy to oblige as soon as I get warrants for any building he has a mortgage or lease on. Any movement at his house?"

"Not yet. I had Lucas Rhodes's assistant call and tell his wife he wouldn't be home for a couple of days. He said we'd asked him to stay on because of everything that's going on with the *Jefferson*. I've got his house under surveillance around the clock and we're looking for any other buildings he has regular access to."

"I'm on my way to the White House. Call me if you find anything."

When he arrived at the Oval Office, Peter was on the phone behind his desk and he waved him in when Drew hesitated at the door. The president had not only taken his jacket off, but rolled up his sleeves and taken off his tie.

"Tell me what's giving you heartburn since you have that look on your face," Peter said and took a seat across from him.

Drew gave him all the details he had so far and what he wanted done. "You know Rodney wasn't happy with giving Aidan Sullivan this commission, and less happy with the way his career ended."

"What about the pilot who went down? Any new information?"

"Officially we're listing her and her partner as MIA, but the assumption is that the team is dead. The way the planes were set up to self-destruct on impact, there's going to be very little wreckage for the Koreans to go through. I'm not worried about that. What's bothering me is the information Teague got off the *Jefferson*. It makes what happened suspicious. We need to know if Commander Levine's going down was a loss of war or something aided by assholes with a grudge."

Peter smiled. "I love that you don't think you need to walk on eggshells around me. I'll arrange for whatever warrants you need, but I want daily reports on your progress."

"What about Rodney?"

"Give me something more concrete before you pick him up. I may not care for his attitude on a whole lot of things, but I do respect his service. That has to count for something."

"I'll keep you in the loop." Drew rose to leave. By the time he got back to his office, Rooster and a team from the FBI were searching Jerry's and Adam's homes and the office space they'd leased under the name New Horizon Consultants. The afternoon was spent going through the boxes of information that were collected, and then Drew was ready to meet with Jerry.

"Let's see how he explains most of this stuff, then we'll meet with the weak link in the chain," Drew told Rooster.

"If you're talking about Adam, that should be a short conversation. So far all he's given the guards is his name, date of birth, and social. He gives 'crazy zealot' a whole new meaning."

"That's fine for him, but I wonder how long he'll toe Jerry's line when I threaten him with little Blazer Morris." Drew picked up Blazer's file. "Blaze is a good word to describe what could happen to his son's career if he doesn't cooperate."

❖

North Korean Countryside

"You awake?" Junior asked as the rain got worse and the skies darkened. They'd been sleeping on and off all day, but it had been difficult with the weather. Berkley had told him about their dilemma when she'd returned from her recon and Junior had spent his time awake rubbing his leg above the break.

"It's hard with this water torture going on," Berkley said without lifting her head off the tree she was leaning against. "What's on your mind?"

"How do you think we can move forward?"

"I don't have a good map of the area, so I can't be sure, but I guess the best thing is to wait until at least midnight and then go around this place on the west side." The bottle Berkley had taken was full of rain water, so she offered Junior some. "It's more open than the east, but less populated."

"I thought you said there were cops, or some sort of military."

"I'm not sure what they call them, but they're down there. We're a team, so if you've got an idea tell me."

"The way I see it, we can't stay here, but if the rain clears I think somebody's going to see us."

"If this holds up until dark, you want to get going? There's two ways to look at this. If it's late, there won't be a lot of people around, but at first dark they should be inside, especially on a night like tonight."

"I say we go early, but whatever you decide I'm behind you."

"Actually, you'll be in front driving the horse," Berkley said and they both laughed.

She stretched before she stood and went back to her spot to take another look at the town. It was as if the light had been sucked out of the place. What she hadn't told Junior was that there was no cover for miles and for their survival it wasn't a great thing, but he was right. Staying put wasn't an option.

She planned their route and kept in mind that the other chance they'd have to take was to go slow while they passed the town. Two people galloping through the countryside would be something out of the ordinary, in her opinion. From the little glimpse of what she'd seen of the place from ground level it was bleak—the kind of place where no one moved quickly because there was nothing to rush for.

After she'd memorized the map in her head, she went back and sat with Junior. She untied the splint to ease the pressure on his leg and through the tear in his pants she saw the bruising and red streaks that signaled an infection was setting in. Their time was growing short.

"I want you to keep him at a slow pace and I'll tell you where to head. If anyone stops us, you stay put and I'll take care of it. I don't want to kill anyone, but I also want to get us out of here."

Junior nodded and held his hand up as a request to be helped to his feet. When he was standing, he didn't let go of her. "No matter what, it's been an honor serving with you, Cletus."

"You're a good man, Junior, try and remember that. All that shit you got from assholes like Blazer was just that—shit." She squeezed his hand and put the other one on his shoulder. "So don't go counting us out yet."

"I'm not, but my dad always tells me to never leave anything unsaid if you can help it."

The horse stood still obediently as Berkley pulled Junior up, and they waited until the streets were relatively empty before starting out. They were past the main section of town when a lone walker with a rifle slung across his back headed toward them with his hand up. He obviously didn't feel any alarm yet since he never moved to ready his weapon.

"Stop and relax," Berkley whispered to Junior as she waved to the man who was saying something in a louder than normal voice, but she figured it had to do with the rain more than any excitement over being the one to catch two Americans in the middle of a field. As he got closer, Berkley could see the guy squinting as if trying to make out their faces. "Put your head down," she told Junior and copied his action. The man screamed something to them again, but this time started to ready his weapon. "Start toward him and get there before he gets that thing pointed at us."

They reached him before he could bring the rifle around and Berkley jumped from the horse and landed on top of him. She pulled his arm back and away from his weapon, and slugged him when he started a panicked-sounding dialogue. It stunned him long enough for Berkley to get behind him and wrap her arm around his neck. The bolt of the gun he so desperately tried to use pressed painfully into her chest, but Berkley didn't let go.

She could hear the man trying to squeeze air into his lungs, and he was beating on her arm and kicking his legs. The attempts to free himself became more futile, and after what felt like an eternity to Berkley, he went limp in her arms.

"Is he dead?" Junior asked.

Berkley pressed her finger to his neck and nodded. It was the first time she'd killed someone that wasn't in the cockpit of another plane trying to knock her from the sky, and as upsetting as it was, there was no time to dwell. "Yeah, he is."

"What's he doing out here?"

"This is the country of the million man army, and the visit earlier probably called up the piece that lives here. I'm thinking it's the only time civilians like this are allowed to carry guns." Berkley accepted Junior's hand to remount. "The grass is high, but they'll find him by tomorrow, so put some distance between us and this place."

"You got it." Junior used his good leg to spur the horse into a canter. "This pace should be good and won't tire our ride too much."

The rain never let up and Berkley led them a little farther east than she'd envisioned, but she wanted to keep to the open farmlands as a cover. At three in the morning she pointed to a small stand of trees. "It's not much, but let's take a break."

The three trees stood like gnarled goblins in a sea of yellow grass that had been beaten down by the rain. Their branches started about three feet from the ground, but the foliage wasn't thick. It was as if they were too old to produce many leaves.

"This country is strange, don't you think?" Junior said and sounded glad to be off the horse.

"How so?" Berkley walked the perimeter and tied their ride to one of the low limbs between two of the trees.

"You go for miles without seeing anyone, and yet all the land is empty. All this acreage could be used for wheat or something."

"You aren't getting so bored with my company that you want to see more of the local citizens, are you?" Berkley laughed. "People pick their fate, and sometimes they follow so blindly that they end up screwing their kid's future. I'm sure this wasn't the promise of the revolution they signed up for, but now it's too late to do anything but go along with the saber rattling so it doesn't end up buried in their chests."

The damn weather wouldn't let up and Berkley felt like her fingers were going to stay permanently pruned. There was no way to tell how much distance they had covered, and that they hadn't seen any sign of a search party shocked her. Then almost as if jinxing herself, she heard it.

"Wait," she said when he went to reply to what she'd said. In order to better concentrate and separate the sound from the steady beat of rain, she closed her eyes.

"Fuck," Berkley said as she got to her feet. It was crazy to be in a helicopter right now, but they'd probably found the dead civilian sentry and had no choice but to start the search for who'd killed him.

The sound got louder and the spotlight scanned the area in front of their path. The craft was three hundred yards from them by Berkley's estimate, but she guessed once it was close enough to spot the trees she and Junior would be caught since she doubted she could hold them off with just her pistol.

Her heart beat as fast as the prop as she watched the spotlight get closer like a speeding train screaming out of a tunnel. The light reached the ground about twenty-five feet from where she was standing and kept going.

"Junior, stay put." She followed the path the helicopter had taken.

A quarter mile later the land gave way to a slope that rose to the highest hill Berkley had encountered so far. When she reached the tip her chest burned from the exertion, and she bent over with her hands on her knees to catch her breath. Just as quickly she dropped to her stomach and moved back so her body rested on the incline.

The last thing she expected to see as she crested the hill was a base of some kind with about forty planes lined up on a large tarmac along with a few rows of tanks. Every other light was turned off, but it was enough for Berkley to see two runways and the two men who'd gotten off the helicopter refueling it.

"What the hell?" Berkley said softly after thirty minutes of watching. It felt like she'd entered the rabbit hole, but she got to her feet and ran before the eerie strangeness of the place completely sank in. The helicopter had started up again and was going back in the direction it had come.

The next chance they'd have to take would either get them back to the *Jefferson* or speed up their deaths.

CHAPTER TWENTY-NINE

CIA Facility, Northern Virginia

Jerry Teague appeared ill, but Drew figured it was the orange jumpsuit that had washed all the color from his face. The guards at the plain-looking facility had done a good job of stripping away everything that would've given Jerry a sense of the life that he'd been taken away from.

"I know you didn't care for my political beliefs, Drew, but I never pegged you as a vindictive son of a bitch." Jerry sat in the metal chair his guard had pulled out for him and crossed his legs, which made his sandal fall off his foot. "And here I was worried about my retirement. Once my lawsuit hits federal court I don't think I'll have a problem."

"Tell me about your meeting with Rodney," Drew said as he took his seat. One of his assistants placed a box next to him on the floor before stepping out.

"The admiral and I met on numerous occasions. You'll have to narrow your scope."

"The one that happened right before the *Jefferson* set sail."

"I was giving an honorable man the respect he deserved," Jerry said in a sarcastic tone. "That's something you and your boss need lessons on, because what happened to Admiral James was a disgrace."

"So you were being kind by giving him a shoulder to cry on?" Drew kept his eyes on Jerry's expressions as well as his body language.

"Is this all you're here for?" Jerry put his feet on the floor and slammed his hands on the table. "Someone comes to my office who's under your microscope and suddenly I'm the bad guy?"

"Obviously all my questions have been too difficult for you so far, so let's try something new." Drew took a small notepad from his suit pocket. "Why did you call Captain Aidan Sullivan and Commander Levine to your office before their departure?"

"To wish them well, but that was a waste of time. It only proved Rodney's point about women in combat positions."

"What point is that, since any information about this mission is classified?"

"Please," Jerry said as he looked down. "You know as well as I do that when you work in that stone cave, nothing is classified for long for those of us lucky enough to have a window."

"Talk to me about New Horizons." Drew waved Rooster in with the other box of information he'd need for this interview.

"That's a private business that has nothing to do with my job at the Pentagon."

"Okay." Drew laughed before he took the top off the box. The first folder was in a dark blue binder. "I'd think with the heavy hitters you've got on the first page you'd want to brag." He opened the folder to the page that had *Board Members* as a header.

"And you'd think you'd be smart enough to let me go because of that list," Jerry said and tapped his finger forcibly on the page.

"The threats are going to get old if that's the route you want to take."

Jerry sat back and turned to the side as if his only option was to ignore them both. "You can also admit that you and the poser who got elected are in way over your heads, but the fact you won't is going to get even older over time."

"If the people thought the job you and your friends were doing was so great, the election would've been a landslide in the other direction," Drew said and Jerry turned more away from him. "What you can't stand is that President Khalid called this strike only two months after he got sworn into office. The *weakling* title you tried to pin on him got blown when those plants did. It didn't escape my notice that your old bosses set this up before he was inaugurated to see if he had the balls to go through with it."

"Only you've got a bigger problem now, don't you?" Jerry asked and laughed.

"We'll get to that, but not yet." Drew took out the next folder that had a label on the front that read *Secured Finance*. Drew's eyebrows rose when he saw how much money New Horizon had, but they hadn't found it yet. "I know how much you make, as well as everyone on this list." Drew went back to the board list. "You all must have a heck of a second job. Where's the money coming from?"

"I've got an uncle who loves me," Jerry said then stood. "If you want any other answers then let me go. Keep me here and you can fuck yourself, Secretary Orr, but I say that with all due respect."

"The answers will come without your help because I had you pegged from the first day you got here." As Drew spoke he started taking out all the files in the box and putting them on the table. "You have a picture in your head of how the world should be, and with a little bit of power you almost achieved it. The thing is, your picture doesn't have room for anyone who doesn't think or believe as strongly as you and your buddies."

"It all comes down to an us against them mentality," Jerry said from the door. "The question you have to ask yourself is how many do you have on your side and how dedicated to winning are they? I know the answer, so I'm not worried."

Drew and Rooster nodded to the guard and he escorted Jerry out. "If he's right, Adam will never break no matter what you threaten him with," Rooster said.

"We need to find a couple of things before we talk to Mr. Morris." Drew dragged the financial information from the pile. "What's the old saying—follow the money?"

"My men tore that place apart. If it's real, Jerry did a good job of hiding it."

The list of board members was the next thing Drew reviewed again. "He didn't hide it." His finger stopped at Rodney's name. "He gave it to someone for safekeeping." He tapped his finger on Rodney's name. "But I think I know where to find it."

"Shouldn't we concentrate on what exactly they're up to?" Rooster asked. "It could just be venture capital for their New Horizon company."

"If I'm wrong, then I hope you get along with your new boss," Drew said with a smile. "But I sure love that office the president gave me, so don't think you're going to escort me out anytime soon."

❖

South of Pyongyang, North Korea

Jin hesitated before she got out of the car. They had been on the road for hours and she was stiff from sitting rigidly next to Lowe. The signs with names of towns she'd never been to had gone by like time stamps on what was left of her life.

"You're free to rest for the night," Lowe said from under his umbrella even though the rain had given way to a fine mist. "I've arranged for a phone in your room if you'd like to make any calls."

Her first urge was to laugh at what wasn't some kindness on his part, but another strand in the web he was weaving for her. "Thank you, Comrade," Jin said instead. In her hand was her mother's necklace. A reminder that this was the opportunity she and her mother didn't have.

"I'll call for you in the morning," Lowe said, not moving, looking at her like he was trying to crawl in her head by studying her.

The house where they'd stopped was surrounded by some of the country's elite forces, and they stood so straight in Lowe's presence that Jin thought they'd snap in half if someone tipped them over. Unlike the small dwellings in the countryside outside Pyongyang, this place was rambling with a beautiful garden that even in the dark she could see was for decoration rather than for growing food.

Every twenty feet or so strong spotlights illuminated the surroundings. It was like they'd driven until they'd reached another country. This place was definitely foreign in North Korea.

Lowe continued to stare at Jin as she took in the house. "Is there something wrong?" he asked her.

His question seemed to wake her from a stupor and she shook her head. "No, I'm sorry to keep you waiting."

"Sir, if I could speak with you a moment," the man who opened the door for him said once Lowe had crossed the threshold. Another man behind him pointed down a hallway for Jin to follow him to her room. "You asked for any information that seemed out of the ordinary."

"Let's hear it."

"The head of the volunteer security forces from the village where you stopped earlier called to report a murder."

The room they entered had a wall of glass so when Lowe sat at his desk he could enjoy the view of the small lake the property had. It was the only place he felt he could let his guard down somewhat when he was alone, but with his constant errands for Jong Il there'd been no time to waste gazing at water.

"Disputes over a chicken or an ear of corn don't interest me," Lowe said as he took off his coat and tossed it across a chair and sat down. He immediately picked up a pair of pliers and the man lowered his head as if he was afraid Lowe was about to take his displeasure out on him.

The tool had been a gift from his father, and along with it he told Lowe stories of when and how he'd used it. Lowe kept it on his desk and used it as a nutcracker—one of the only things he was sentimental about. He reached for the bowl of walnuts and crushed one so severely he had to throw it away. His aggravation stemmed from having experience on his side.

After a lifetime of service to Kim Jong Il's father, Lowe's father had trained Lowe not only in his trade but also on how to work for a man who was sometimes blinded by circumstance. He didn't want to get caught in the storm the Great Leader would unleash on those responsible for what he'd lost, because he knew too well what happened to those who did.

"I'm sorry, sir, it didn't have anything to do with village disputes. The man was given a rifle and sent out on patrol. Sometime tonight someone was able to overpower and strangle him before he was able to get the weapon off his shoulder."

"What else did they find in the area? And I'm hoping they actually sent someone trained to investigate and not some farmer with delusions of being a soldier."

"The rain wiped out most of the tracks, but there were still some deep impressions in the mud that the leader of the area said looked like a horse's hoofprints," the man said with his head still lowered. "They lead away from the body toward the southeast. Once they got to the grass, the trail was lost."

Lowe turned on the computer on his desk and opened a map of

the area. There wasn't much there, except for perhaps a nightmare if the security was breached. "Are there any patrols in the vicinity ready to move?"

"Just the small group you spoke with today, sir. If you like, I can call Central Command and have a unit dispatched immediately."

"No," Lowe said, and it came out as panicked as he suddenly felt. Sending men would only lead back to him if there was a problem, and Lowe's plan to put this behind all of them was to offer his boss two sacrifices—Jin and Pak. "You're to tell no one about this. I'll take care of it myself."

"Yes, sir." The man bowed. "Is there anything else?"

"Make sure to bring Captain Umeko and her guest something to eat. I'm sure they'd love to get reacquainted over a meal." The man bowed, again not needing a formal dismissal. When he closed and locked the door, Lowe called the man who'd reported the murder and told him to list it as a local dispute, for security reasons.

The investigation into the plane crash had been given to him personally by the Great Leader, but what had been a fortuitous assignment would signal his own demise if he didn't have answers soon or couldn't prove the pilots of the downed plane were dead. If they were still alive, it would be disastrous if they reached the Haeju site.

"Perhaps Captain Umeko will live longer than I'd planned," Lowe said as he tapped his chin with the phone. It was time to change his plan and give Jin a larger role in his salvation. "Later we'll pay a visit to the scrap heap and see what we find."

CHAPTER THIRTY

The helicopter followed the same route to return to the north and the roving spotlights were nowhere close to Berkley as she returned to where she'd left Junior. She'd checked the time. It was a couple of hours before dawn. If they were going to take a chance, it'd have to be now.

"Time to move." She helped Junior to stand. "But we've got to leave our friend behind."

"What? Why?"

"Over that hill is a huge burial ground, but with a little magic I think we can raise the dead." She turned her back to him so he could climb on.

"If I go quietly will you explain what you're talking about?"

"It's a field full of parked Russian MiGs and old tanks in pieces." She balanced him and started back toward the hill. "My guess is it's a junkyard their military must use for parts."

"Should I mention now that I'm a horrible mechanic?"

Berkley laughed and made a mental note to buy all the maintenance crew back in Fallon a steak dinner when she made it home. "I promise to give you lessons when we get back, but once we get down there all I need is for you to hand me stuff."

When they reached the top of the hill Berkley helped Junior to his stomach and took out the binoculars. "How do you want to go in?" Junior asked.

"The helicopter was the changing of the guard, and all I saw were two guys, so I want you to stay here until I signal you to come down." She took out her pistol and checked the clip.

"No way," Junior said in a loud whisper. "You can't be sure there's only two of them, and you might need me."

"If there's more than that I'll come back, but you can't make it all the way down there on your belly. We don't have time to argue about it, so stay here. The only chance we've got is right now while they're bunked in for the night." She gave him the binoculars and began her crawl.

"They just got here," Harvey said and tapped his finger on the face of his watch to remind her of the time.

"There's no way they're not going to sleep. That's what I would do in the same circumstance."

The fence had posters with lightning bolts and what she assumed were caution signs, but if it was electrified, she'd be shocked. She laughed at the stupid joke she'd thought up and touched the chain links with the bottom of her boot. Her body tensed in anticipation of having to pull back, but nothing happened.

She pulled the fence forward enough for her to roll under in the darkest part of the yard and ran in a crouch all the way to the smaller building. The place was quiet, so like she thought, they were either sleeping or they were waiting for their prey to fall into their trap.

The door creaked a little as she opened it and she left it ajar and hesitated so she could become accustomed to the low light. The room appeared to be an office and kitchen and at the back were two doors. Judging from the outside, that was the extent of the space.

Berkley took a deep breath and thought of Aidan and the hell Blazer had probably put her through and what she needed to do to change that. It was now just a choice of which door to pick first. Let's hope they're both heavy sleepers, she thought as she turned the knob to the one on the right.

This time the door made no sound, but the room had two bunks in it, which meant the other room was the bathroom. The two men were sleeping, the nearer one uncovered and the other one under a couple of blankets as if he were freezing. She didn't hesitate as she picked the first one and brought the butt of her gun down on the side of his head. His grunt woke the other man and to her surprise he was up and out of bed faster than she would've thought possible.

He screamed something and ran right at her. It was not Berkley's intent to kill either of them if she could help it, but before she could aim, he kicked the weapon out of her hand and it slid across the floor to the door. He then ignored her and went for the pistol.

The guard was smaller than her by a foot, but he was fast and made it to the door first. His hand landed on the gun as Berkley landed on his back. She grabbed him by the hair and pulled his head back as she tried to get hold of his other hand before he could get a good enough grip on the gun to fire.

Time seemed to slow down again for Berkley as she tired to slam his head to the floor. She was able to connect but not before he twisted and got a shot off that sliced through the top of her shoulder. The pain was unbearable, but she was able to slam his head and hand down so that this time the pistol came loose and his head hit the concrete floor with a crack that sounded like a melon being dropped from the second floor.

The fight went out of him after that and Berkley went down with him momentarily, breathing hard from the fight and from the stinging in her shoulder. When she sat up she noticed the blood pool that came from under the man was starting to spread. She checked his pulse but found none. Before she could process any thoughts about the second man she'd killed in the span of a day, the other man sat up, shaking his head, then stumbled toward her.

Berkley forgot about her pain as she ran from him, but he was on her so fast it was as if he'd flown across the room. As she rolled over, Berkley saw him lift his fist to attack. His hand was halfway to her face when the bullet from the gun she'd grabbed ripped right through his gut and knocked him backward.

"Shit," she said as she glanced at both of the still men before standing to make sure they were indeed the only two. Her plan had been to bind them and leave them for their relief to find, but like her father had told her, in any situation where there can be only one winner, you killed everything that moved or looked at you funny to guarantee the winner was you.

Another curse went through her head when she went outside and saw Harvey dragging himself under the fence. "I thought I gave you a direct order to stay put."

"And you said you'd come get me if there was trouble, so

reprimand me after we get the fuck out of here." He used his crutches to reach her and almost fell when he saw the blood covering the top of her flight suit. "They shot you?"

"Pathetically, with my own gun," she said and leaned against the building. "I don't have time to bitch about it now, though, so go in there and try to find some kind of first aid kit while I do a quick inventory."

The facility consisted of the building where the guards slept and another larger building fifty feet away. She opened the door expecting to see shelves of parts but instead found a plane that from a quick view was about three fourths of the way put back together, and another one behind it with an empty engine compartment.

Berkley took a minute to look at what the guards slash mechanics had done and what was missing. But before she bothered, she searched for a fuel source, because even if the plane engine was new it'd be useless without the juice. Next to the other plane parked to the rear was a small portable tank that would get them to the *Jefferson* if it was close to being full.

When she dipped a stick into it the mark, was only half of the way up. "Could at least one damn part of this not be a challenge?"

Junior came back with a wet towel and a roll of bandages. "This is the best I could do."

She sat long enough for him to tie the towel in place, then got to work. Putting engines back together was something you never wanted to rush, but Berkley felt like luck was slowly walking out the door and she needed to be done before the bitch disappeared altogether.

"Need me to do anything?" Junior asked from the bottom of the ladder she was standing on.

"Start putting every drop of that fuel in this thing," she said and lifted her head from under the hatch when the phone started ringing. "Once you're done get in and buckle up."

The damn phone rang over fifty times. Each minute no one answered was one minute closer to the alarm being sounded. She got back to work and as she put the final pieces in place, the compass Triton had given her pressed against her thigh where she had it in her pocket. It reminded her of where she needed to get back to and why.

No more lost chances, and no more giving in and walking away without a fight for the things she wanted. "The only thing that'll keep me from breaking my promises is if they blow me out of the sky, baby, and that only happens once," she whispered for Aidan.

Junior struggled but got into this seat and grunted as he tried to accommodate his leg. "Fire it up and let's see what happens," she said as she secured the engine cover. The sun was up and it was almost nine, which meant they'd gone over her goal time by an hour.

It took three times on the ignition switch, but the engine finally came to life. "Do you read Korean?" Junior asked after Berkley climbed in and locked the top in place.

"Fluently." Berkley laughed. "I've just been holding out on you to make it interesting. See what you can do with the radio before we get there and get shot down by friendly fire." She taxied them outside and came close to crossing her fingers that the runway was long enough. "We'll worry about the tailhook when we get there."

"What's wrong with it?"

"Nothing," Berkley said and added, "we don't have one," right before she punched it.

❖

The sun was starting to light the room they had locked Jin in. She shook her head every time Yong opened her mouth to say something. Up to the moment she entered the room she had congratulated herself on how she'd been able to lock away her emotions, and then she'd seen Yong.

It surprised Jin to realize how much Yong represented all the things that were unresolved in her life, and all the things she hadn't had the time or chance to do. The most important, aside from seeing her mother one last time, was to have been in love just once. What she'd shared with Yong had been physical, but Yong had never gotten close to owning her heart.

An all-consuming love would not be her fate, but she owed Yong for what she'd given her. "It's important for you to get back to work and finish your pilot training," she said, finally breaking the hours of silence. They had only stared at each other up to then and Jin had seen the longing in her lover's eyes.

"I tried to do what you asked, but then I thought there was a chance we'd fly together again. Comrade Nam Chil said it would happen."

Jin smiled at her. While Yong wasn't the love of her life, she did feel a tremendous amount of affection for her. "Our leader is lucky to have you in service, Lieutenant, but our time's done. That means you have the chance to advance your career if you work hard."

"You're here, though," Yong said and stopped when Jin's eyes widened. "From what the men here told me, Comrade Nam Chil is impressed with you."

"I'm sure that's why he's bringing me to the capital, but before I can go back to the cockpit I've got to answer for my part in what went wrong." It was as clear as she could be without killing Yong along with her. "That might take a while." She stood and reached out to touch Yong's arm. "Do you understand me?"

"But there's a chance." Yong sounded as if the answer were a life preserver to what was left of her sanity.

"As good a chance as my father gave us," Jin said softly. "Please, for me, go." After that she turned and picked up the phone Lowe had so kindly set up for her.

The connection went through on the first try and Jin waited for her grandfather to come on the line. "Father," she said after he greeted her.

"Your mother wanted me to tell you that you should be at as much peace as she's enjoying. It was important to her that I tell you she wasn't disappointed with you for not being able to make it."

"Thank you." Jin gripped the phone so hard that her fingers were going numb. "I wanted to tell you the same thing, so when the time comes you can explain to Grandmother."

"Jin?" her grandfather asked in a tone that was already thick with grief. "Have your plans changed? You'd been planning on coming home."

"I'm a guest of Lowe Nam Chil."

The short admission made her grandfather sigh. "Your father, did he give you your mother's gift?"

"Yes." The necklace was around her neck and she touched it with her free hand.

"Let it remind you of those who most love you and it'll make your assignment easier to complete."

"I will, but promise me that you'll take care," Jin said as someone knocked on the door. "Send my love to Grandmother. Good-bye." It wasn't what she had in mind for the last words she'd share with the man who'd raised her, but he knew how she felt about him. There wasn't time to elaborate and no real reason to.

"Captain Umeko," the guard said. "Comrade Nam Chil needs to see you."

"Yong," Jin said after she'd nodded to the guard so he'd know she heard him. "Thank you for your friendship." Yong bowed, but Jin knew it was to hide the tears in her eyes.

"I'll do as you asked," Yong whispered as Jin left the room.

In the light of day the scenery at the back of the house was breathtaking, but not as beautiful as some of the furniture that adorned the rooms they walked past. If this was Lowe's personal residence, the only other person living better in the country was Kim Jong Il.

The guard stopped at what appeared to be a sunroom with a large wooden carved door at the opposite wall. They heard the curse and the sound of something breaking even though the door was closed, and it made the man glance back at her before he knocked.

"Captain Umeko," he announced.

"Get her in here and leave," Lowe said.

The opulent office deserved more of her attention than just the quick look she took, but Jin couldn't stop staring at Lowe. For once the cool and cocky sadist appeared exhausted and rattled. At the corner of his desk was a broken phone receiver—and probably what they'd heard break.

"Good morning, Comrade Lowe."

"Have you ever heard of the Haeju site?" he asked and combed his hair back with his fingers.

"I've never been, but one of my father's nephews is one of the soldiers assigned to that post. It's isolated and relatively low security, but manned constantly like the other sites like it around the country." Jin stood with her hands behind her back. "It's a scrap heap for different government vehicles that are stripped for parts. The one you mentioned is for old planes and tanks, I believe, and because of that it's only got a two-man security team who are highly trusted by the government. I suppose it's a good idea since you don't want someone who'll fly one of the planes to the nearest airport on the other side of our borders."

"So you think someone could get one of them flight ready?"

"That is their job. To take the planes that are in the best condition and repair them to make them flight ready, but once they do, they don't get very far since my father said that, despite the trust they have in the personnel, they never keep much fuel on hand. It's only enough to test the engines once they've been rebuilt." At first she thought this was another one of his circular conversations to draw her out, but something wasn't right. "Is there something I can do for you?"

"If I get us a plane, how fast can you get there?"

"It's not far from here. Less than thirty minutes."

The answer made Lowe calm down until he reached for the phone. When the receiver fell from his hand in two pieces he ripped the entire thing out and threw it at the wall of glass. The sound caught Jin by surprise, and she flinched. She had expected the large pane to shatter, but the phone only fell to the ground as if it had hit a chunk of wood. That meant Lowe had spared no expense to protect himself with bulletproof glass.

He shouted for a car and grabbed Jin by the bicep and yanked her up against his body. "You need to understand something," he said, sounding like the madman he was. "I'd threaten you with your life, but I think you're smart enough to know you're so close to the end that I can taste it."

Jin laughed and took pleasure on looking down on him, their slight height difference apparent at this distance. "Finally, you've given me credit for something."

"Don't patronize me, Captain." Lowe let her go, straightened his back, and took a deep breath. He picked up his coat, stared at it, then dropped it back on the chair. "You'll find that I always make it my business to know what motivates the people I have to work with for whatever reason. When you appeared on my screen I knew you wouldn't respond to threats against your life, just like I know you'd probably never crack in my workroom."

"Then what's this about?"

"I've got a plane waiting at the base where you were stationed before your father decided to punish you," he said and started walking.

"I didn't think Pak confided what he considered his failures to anyone." The guard that had followed them to the car slammed the door once Lowe had gotten in after her.

"Pak is the kind of man who catches our leader's eyes because nothing is as important to him as his own success."

Jin glanced out the window to orient herself as to where exactly they were. "If you're trying to vilify Pak to change my mind about him, then you didn't study my file as carefully as you said. I already know what Pak loves, and the only thing he's faithful to is the adornments on his uniform."

"Stop interrupting me," Lowe said and slapped her. "Your biggest problem is that you think you're so much smarter than everyone else, but all you are is an annoying bitch. I know not to threaten you with Pak. If anything, you'd probably encourage me to remove his eyes and feed them to him. Your grandparents, though, that's another thing altogether, isn't it?" He sat back and laughed when Jin looked at him and flattened her hand on her upper thigh. "You can hit me, but you won't live to enjoy the stinging in your hand."

"Stop playing your games and tell me what you want," Jin said, not fearing any reprisal from him since she got the impression he needed her alive now.

"There has been no evidence that the pilots you downed are actually dead, so I gave orders at every one of the stops we made before we arrived at my home to be vigilant but not go out of their way to search." Lowe went on to explain what had been reported to him the night before. "The scrap heap, as you put it, is in the area where this man was found. I've been calling all morning and there's been no answer. Unlike you, the men stationed there know better than to defy orders or abandon their posts."

"So that proves what?" Jin had experienced a brief moment of happiness when they drove past the main gate of the base. In many ways this had been the most consistent home she'd ever had.

"That if these people are actually alive they could be there trying to put together a ride home. I highly doubt it, but I need to know."

"Anything's possible. If I were in the same position, I could have something flightworthy in a day."

Lowe grabbed her by the wrist this time and squeezed. "You'd better hope that isn't the case, but if you need motivation to make sure they actually died this time, if by some chance they're there, I give you my word that I'll let Pak take the blame for all of this alone."

"And Yong and my grandparents?" Jin put her hand over his since he hadn't let her go.

"Yong has been released from my house already, and your grandparents will be cared for until they die of natural causes."

"How do I know that's true?"

Lowe didn't move when the car stopped next to a plane and the door was opened. "You don't, but if you decide to refuse me or you fail at what I'm asking, you *will* know for sure that you brought about their deaths because I *will* make you watch as I take my time with all of them."

CHAPTER THIRTY-ONE

The weather had cleared to a beautiful day with miles of visibility in all directions, which made Berkley laugh at their shitty luck so far. There was only one thing to be grateful for and that was that they hadn't been captured or even pursued from the time they'd crashed. Whatever the reason, they'd have to figure it out after she got Junior back on the ship and handed him over to the care of the *Jefferson*'s doctor.

She took her time getting accustomed to the differences in the small fighter jet but kept her eyes on the skies around her. "You okay back there, Junior?" Their altitude was slightly higher than when they had flown in, but not by much. What she didn't need was to be picked up on radar since she had no weapons on board and no guidance systems that would alert them to anyone in the vicinity trying to put a lock on them.

"I feel like shit, but I'm thrilled to be here, ma'am," he said and laughed. "This will be a great story to tell my grandkids one day."

"Hopefully, this is as exciting as it gets, so keep your fingers crossed." Berkley had the compass in her hand and was flying them in a southwesterly direction figuring that's where she'd find the *Jefferson* once they were in open waters. "How's the radio coming?"

"Give me a few more minutes and see if I can't rewire this thing enough to get out at least one message."

"That's all I can spare, and then I need your eyes on the skies, so if you can't get it let it go and we'll make due when we're close."

"I don't know about you, but getting shot down is something I'd only like to do once," Junior said and she could hear him tapping on something behind her. "The first time we were lucky, but if we fly over the *Jefferson* in this thing and they don't know who we are, they'll need a teaspoon to pick up all the pieces after they're through with us."

"We need to get there before our side can take a shot at us," she reminded him. "If our hosts for the last couple of days find us first, they'll drop a nuclear bomb on us before they let us out of here alive."

"You could give motivational talks once you're out of the Navy."

"Get the radio working, smart-ass, before we're spotted and they shove a bomb up our backside."

❖

USS *Jefferson*

"I understand you'd like to talk to me," Aidan said to Alan Lewis. Devin had brought him back up to the room they'd been using as an interrogation space after the guards complained about him screaming his demands ever since Devin had locked him back up. "I'm not sure why, since you made it clear that you had told the truth and were done talking."

"I wanted to make sure you understood I had nothing to do with what happened to Commander Levine," Alan said and kept his voice calm even though he was hoarse from all the yelling.

"That's for a military court to decide, Lieutenant Lewis. It's not my call."

"I don't know what Blazer told you, but I had nothing to do with anything."

"The fact that I've released him should tell you his story is more plausible than yours, and easier to prove." Aidan never looked up from her paperwork and tried to appear like taking the time to have this meeting was a burden on her schedule. "Secretary of Defense Orr also video conferenced us to say that Jerry Teague and Adam Morris have been detained for questioning and will remain in custody pending an investigation. They're due for further talks today."

"I don't mean any disrespect, ma'am, but I don't believe you."

Aidan glanced up at him and smiled. "None taken, but you should ask yourself what I have to gain by lying about that. If you'd like I can have the video feed of the meeting cued up so you can watch that section of it." She waited to see if he'd respond. "Disobeying a direct order that results in bringing down a fellow officer, as well as breaching enemy lines for no reason, are not things that the U.S. government takes lightly. This will be investigated until everyone involved has all the alphabet of agencies crawl up their ass and figure out who's the easiest person to blame."

"And you think that's me?" Alan said and smiled.

"Thinking isn't necessary, Lieutenant. There are three people we've found so far and they all tell the same tale. You can believe me or not, I don't give a shit, but I'm sure Blazer will write to you while you do life for this. That is, if they don't decide to kill you for Commander Levine and Lieutenant Whittle's deaths." She dropped her head again and went back to the reports scattered across the table. "If that's all, you're free to go back to your cell."

"I want to see the tape," he said and pulled his arm away from Devin when the MP went to escort him out. It took a few minutes of Aidan typing commands into the computer before Drew's face appeared on the screen and repeated what Aidan and Devin had told Alan.

"Anything else you'd like before Devin locks you out of my sight?"

"I'd like to change my account of what happened," Alan said, and now looked visibly nervous. "I have the right, and I don't care if you have to write me up for lying."

"What would make me believe you?" Aidan locked eyes briefly with Devin. "If you're telling me you lied, then what's to keep it from happening again?"

"Because you know I lied and you know what happened. The only reason I'm here is to confirm the facts."

"Captain," Luther Oliver buzzed in on the intercom. "I'm sorry to disturb you, ma'am, but you need to get to the bridge."

"What's happening?"

"We got a partial message on one of our open lines."

Aidan noticed that Devin and Alan both looked at the speaker where the message was coming from. "What was it?"

"Calling the *Jefferson*, this is Commander Berkley Levine, I'm on my way," Luther played back for them and Aidan felt as if her blood had drained out of her feet she was so weak after hearing Berkley's voice.

"Is that all she said?" Aidan asked softly.

"I'm positive there was more, but she got cut off."

"Devin, get this scum out of my sight. I'll deal with this later." She pointed to Alan. "And you, seems like I might not need your story after all. I'm going to get it from the person you tried to screw over."

"I have the right to talk to you," Alan said, sounding like a man facing life in prison.

"You have the right to shut the hell up and let me get to my job," Aidan said and left the room. She ran through the corridor, jumping over the door hatches along the way to the bridge. *Okay, Cletus, I knew you wouldn't let me down, but now it's time to make it the whole way back,* she thought as she climbed the steps that would lead to the command center of her ship and a view of the blue skies outside.

Her crew snapped to attention when she stepped in and she quickly put them at ease. "Call up Vader and Killer and tell them to report deckside. Have Mike bring up six planes and get them in the air now."

"Where do you want them to head, ma'am?" one of the crew assigned to communications asked.

"Don't waste time asking questions. Get it done," Aidan snapped as she put her binoculars to her eyes. The sky was clear in all directions, but she concentrated on the Korean coastline.

"Captain." Vader's voice came on over the intercom and the decks opened to bring up the jets she'd ordered. "I'm ready to go."

"Did you hear the message?" Aidan asked him.

"Yes, I did, and I couldn't be happier."

"If she's on a radio I'm guessing she's in the air somehow, so take a team southwest and, Killer, you sweep up the northwest but stay clear of the northern coastline."

The two men saluted in the direction of the bridge as they buzzed off the deck one after the other.

"Ma'am." One of the other crewmen who kept watch at the door came up and waited to be acknowledged. Aidan felt like she would miss something if she looked away, but she turned and faced him. "Blazer's outside and wants to talk to you."

"Inform him that the best thing he can do right now is to return to his bunk and wait. If he doesn't take that advice, I want you to carry him there and cuff him to the bed."

"Yes, ma'am."

"Anything else?" she asked Luther.

"Not yet, but I've got the line open."

Aidan nodded and thought, and I've got the light on.

❖

"How's it coming, Junior?" Berkley asked as she scanned the skies around her. The plane felt like it had been put together with rubber bands and duct tape, but they were maintaining a good altitude over what she assumed was South Korea. She was still using the compass to navigate.

"I think that last message went through, but then the damn thing went dead again."

"Do you think it's fixable?"

"Considering we're in a plane with North Korean markings flying over the south, I'm promising you that I'll fix it. Like I said, one downing is enough to convince me that I don't ever want to go through the experience again. How's the fuel situation?"

"Depending on where the captain put down anchor, we might get there on fumes."

"You can land this on the *Jefferson*?"

"I didn't say that, did I?" She glanced at the horizon and saw a beautiful sight. The water meant that they were that much closer to getting home. "But I'll figure something out."

"Good to hear. Is that water I see?"

"Take one look at it and then get your eyes on our ass. Is there anything back there?"

"Clear so far. Shit," Junior shouted.

"What?"

"Sorry, not a bogey, I just shocked the hell out of myself. Try it again on the same frequency."

"This is Commander Berkley Levine calling the USS *Jefferson*. Do you copy?"

"Cletus." Aidan's voice came through her headset. "Where are you?"

"I wish I knew, but before this radio craps out again tell the birds you probably put up that we're in a borrowed plane, and if they shoot me down they'd better pray I actually die this time."

"Can you give us a hint?"

"I'm over land at the moment, but I'm about twenty minutes away from the water. If my compass is correct I'm over the southern territory now, so send them a note that we're not the enemy."

"I'm on it, but how are you going to find us if you don't have the ability to pinpoint our coordinates?"

"I can't land onboard even if I could find you, so you're going to have to radio the South Koreans and tell them I'm going to have to land somewhere onshore. Once you find out where, I need Killer or Vader to find me and guide me in." Berkley scanned the horizon again and saw three planes heading toward her, but from their outline they were off the *Jefferson*. "Radio the planes that three of them are about to wreck into me, so give me a wide berth."

"It's Vader," Aidan said after Luther confirmed it for her. "They're going to buddy with you until we locate someplace for you to land."

"Thanks, Captain, and if you could do us one more favor—arrange for a boat escort to the ship once we're on the ground, and get sickbay ready for Junior."

"Is he all right?"

"Broken leg and laceration from our original crash. I want him taken care of before the infection I'm sure he's got gets out of control."

"We'll be ready," Aidan said. "What?" she asked someone obviously standing close to her. "Cletus, tell Junior to stay on the line. We're switching you so you can communicate with Vader and his team."

"Cletus," Vader's voice came over her headset. "Keep flying toward the water and keep your head down. There's a bogey on your ass and they're trying to lock."

"I am over South Korea, correct?" Berkley asked.

"You are, but this fucker doesn't seem to care," Vader said and Berkley figured it was him flying the lead plane that streaked past her.

Before she could concentrate on who was flying on Vader's wing, a missile from the enemy plane shot him down in an impressive explosion that made Berkley want to turn around and hunt down the enemy craft. The only thing that kept her from doing it was that she had no weapons on board, and the only comfort was that Vader had avoided any collision with the flying debris.

"There's more coming in from the north," Vader said. "Killer, break away from your route and get your team over here."

"Cletus," Junior said. "One of the planes has broken off and looks like it's painted a target on us because they aren't backing down."

Berkley turned her head to the left. The way the plane's wings dipped a little before they banked in that same direction made her think of the plane that had shot them down. That pilot had that little habit as well.

"I can't tell if they've locked on us, but they're closing in," Junior said.

"Hang on because it's not like we can shoot back." If she could reach the water she'd feel better about their survival if for no other reason then they were that much closer to the *Jefferson*. "Captain," Berkley said to Aidan.

"Go ahead."

"Get a fix on us and send us some backup. I've got an unwanted friend on my tail that I can't shake."

"Try to stay up there, I've already sent them out."

A few bullets hit the right wing but didn't cause enough damage to impede their flight, but Berkley rolled under the attack and came so close to the water that if the hatch had been open she would have had no problem smelling the salt water below them. As she reached the bottom of her dive she banked hard to the right and picked up enough elevation so that she could just as quickly bank in the opposite direction.

"Talk to me, Junior."

"Still on our tail, but you're moving enough for them to be missing. They're still using their guns, though."

"There's no way they keep missing me," Berkley said to herself. Without something like the cover of the mountains back home there was nowhere to hide, and it wasn't that hard to hit the target you were after. "What are you up to?" she said to the pilot behind her.

CHAPTER THIRTY-TWO

What are you waiting for?" Lowe asked and sounded angry from the back of the plane Jin was flying. "They're right in front of you in a stolen plane. If you want to live, you will bring it down. If you want your family to live, you will bring this bastard down."

"This is something I know, Comrade, so please let me do my job." Her opponent was doomed, but Jin still admired his ability in the sky. He flew like no one Jin had ever seen in the North Korean forces.

As the American broke in the other direction Jin let loose another round of bullets, but this time none of them found their mark and instead hit the water. After only one encounter Jin thought she knew her quarry and instead of waiting for the American to make his next move she anticipated it and banked to the same side again and momentarily lost sight of him when she regained some altitude. When Jin leveled out she almost laughed when she lost them.

The only place the American could've gone was back into the air fight going on back over the coast. One minute Jin had him in a position where she could toy with him, and then the enemy pilot had changed the game of hide and seek in plain sight. In the fray it wouldn't be impossible to pick him out, it would take time—time that she would have to take in the company of the other American pilots who were fighting to reclaim their dominance in the sky.

Wouldn't it be ironic that it'd be one of the people their quarry served with would take away the honor of what Lowe wanted most. Jin turned toward the coast and flew in a waiting pattern, trying to figure out which one of their planes was the stolen one.

"What are you waiting for?" Lowe screamed and it made her jump in her seat since she'd forgotten he was there.

"Would you like me to shoot down everyone, including ours?"

"I want you to do what I asked you, because if you don't our deal is off."

"None of that matters to me anymore," Jin said and continued to watch the action in front of her. "So try and keep your comments to yourself until we finish this."

"Start shooting or I'm going to—"

"What?" Jin was at the end of her patience. "You're going to do what? Sit and shut up, and think about the mistake you made in getting in this plane with me this morning."

"What are you talking about, Captain?"

"That I'm going to get this done and then I'm going to meet my mother."

There was a long pause as Jin spotted one of their planes being chased by an American pilot, but the F-18 wasn't firing at it. "Your mother is dead," Lowe said finally.

"You're not the top aide to Kim Jong Il for nothing, are you?" Jin said and laughed. She turned off the intercom system in the cockpit. She then took her mother's necklace out of her flight suit and kissed the jade piece. "I'm young, but I'm tired, and you always said there was a chance for us to start over and live in peace. If that's true then I'm ready for that."

❖

"Cletus," the pilot behind her said.

"Hang in there and don't lose me," Berkley answered back. Two more planes had gone down, but this time it was the North Koreans that had lost. The fighting was frenzied and the only reason the South Koreans hadn't sent any planes up was because Aidan had convinced them it was a bad idea. "And once we're clear, take point and lead me to the landing location the captain's looking for."

"You got it," the pilot answered.

"There's another plane behind us," Junior said as they were back over the water.

"Besides the one that's supposed to be following us?" Berkley asked. A quick glance back and the plane that had first shown up on the scene was behind them, the call letters on the tail were the same.

"Ma'am, keep going south and I'll take care of this," the pilot said.

"Peel off and try and get behind it," Berkley said. "It's us they're after, and if we're going to get out of this I need you to get in the most defendable position."

The Korean plane brought down a barrage of bullets but Berkley's order had saved her escort from getting hit. Her good wing was now full of bullet holes and a few had hit the flaps so that she'd lost control of that part of the aircraft on the left side. The only good thing was that she'd gained enough altitude that if they had to bail out again they wouldn't just crash into the water before the chutes opened.

"Are you ready to take a shot?" Berkley asked her escort.

"In a minute, we're coming about now."

"If I had a minute I'd be enjoying the scenery, but this son of a bitch's on me like a tick."

"On my mark break to the left," the pilot said.

"Take the shot. I can't break anywhere. My left wing is stuck in this position." Berkley's mind ran through a couple of scenarios—the best one would leave them the most open for a direct hit on the cockpit, but she had no choice. As her finger went to press down on the radio button, an alarm went off.

"What is that?" Junior asked.

"We're almost out of gas. We're about to have a dramatic water landing, so start getting yourself ready." The engines weren't sputtering yet, but once the alarms sounded she knew she had ten minutes tops to find a landing spot.

"Cletus, can you move at all? If I take the shot now I'm going to hit you as well," the pilot came on again.

"Are you familiar with the Fourth of July?" Berkley asked.

"On my mark," he responded.

"Roger that," Berkley fanned her fingers out and regripped the stick.

"Mark," he said suddenly and Berkley pulled back, gaining altitude quickly like a firecracker being shot on the Fourth of July. Her chaser followed with his finger on the trigger, but the angle left him open for attack from the F-18 behind her, which hit the mark from behind the cockpit to the tail.

When they all leveled out, both Russian MiGs were spewing black smoke and were losing altitude slowly. The sudden burst of power needed for the climb had used the last of Berkley's fuel, and the engines were now missing. Below them, all she could see was open water.

"Aidan," she said into her mike.

"Go ahead."

"Do you see us on radar?"

"I have you and two other planes about ten miles west of us."

"Send out the rescue boats," Berkley said and the engines went dead. "Junior, try to stay in one piece this time."

"I'll do my best," he said and laughed, but it sounded more like a nervous gurgle.

She pulled the release lever and the top blew off, then the seats disengaged from the floor of the plane. As they started up, she prayed that whatever soldier had packed the chutes didn't have some grudge against their air force and they would actually open. The fear ended and her stomach roiled as she stopped going up and started her descent. One second they were hurling through the air and the next they stopped abruptly when the chutes opened.

Berkley maneuvered as close to her partner as she could without hitting him. "Junior," she yelled.

"I'm okay," he yelled back.

"Grab hold of those controls and hit the water as soon as you can. The last thing we need is for someone to cut us in half before we start swimming." In the distance she saw the plane that had been shooting at them fly past with its right engine on fire and one of the American jets on its tail.

Berkley twisted around. What seemed like miles from them the Korean plane went down. She squinted against the sun and thought she saw two parachutes gliding down over the crash site. For the moment, they were safe. She turned to find Junior and used her parachute controls to get closer to him.

"You okay?" she asked.

"Don't worry. I ducked this time, so no new injuries."

The water was icy cold when she plunged in, and she kicked to the top feeling like there was only a little time before this would be over. Up to now she'd been anxious to get back, but for the first time she was totally impatient to see Aidan again. She'd gone through the motions of her life for too long and it was time to get back to enjoying it with someone who was willing to share it with her.

At the surface she found Junior and came up behind him and slipped her hands under his arms to pull him to her chest. "Let me do all the work to keep us afloat. That leg is bad enough and I don't want you to get it any more out of whack."

"This will definitely make a good story, don't you think?"

"You bet, and once I get my hands on Blazer and beat the shit out of him you'll have your ending." She kicked slowly to keep them both afloat trying to conserve her energy, not knowing how long it would take a rescue crew to find them. "You did good throughout this whole thing, which is something I want you to promise me you'll tell your dad."

"I'm sure he'll be impressed that you carried my ass out of there."

"You had it over me on the horse. Without that we'd still be making our way through there, and I'm not sure how much longer we'd have lasted without getting caught."

"You hear that?" Junior asked and turned his head to the side.

"Hopefully, it's the good guys." Berkley looked in the same direction the boat motor was coming from and waited. There were three boats in the area and they were skimming the water in a zigzag pattern with two men at each bow with binoculars sweeping the area. "I've never been so glad to see khaki in all my life," Berkley said. "Lift your arms up and wave them over."

❖

Northern Virginia

"Sir," the guard at the security prison where Drew Orr was holding Jerry Teague and Adam Morris said into the phone. "We're ready to bring Mr. Morris up whenever you are."

"I'm waiting with Rooster in interrogation room three. Bring him in." Drew had stopped to take a radio call from Aidan to hear the latest developments. With Berkley Levine about to be rescued, he figured it would make his end of the investigation that much easier now that Cletus would be able to tell them everything.

He'd left Jerry alone even though the guards had said Jerry was pacing his cell like an agitated tiger demanding to see his attorney or the president. After hearing Aidan's report, Drew told her to lock Blazer back up and they'd sort out what had happened together, but he didn't want to give Blazer any more freedom to do further damage if he was working with someone other than Alan Lewis.

"Sir." The voice on the intercom sounded excited. "You need to get down here."

"What the hell now?" Rooster asked.

They made their way down the corridor, and as they went past Jerry's cell they saw his face pressed to the small glass that the guards used to do visual checks. When they reached the open door of Adam's room they found him on the floor next to his bunk with froth oozing out of his mouth.

"You didn't check him when he came in?" Drew asked as he pressed his fingers to Adam's neck to check for a pulse that he knew wasn't there.

"We did, and we also took everything away from him," said the doctor leaning over Adam's body. "The only thing I can think of is that he brought it in rectally. None of us thought he was crazy enough to try something like this."

"Start thinking on the crazy level, gentleman," Drew said as he stood, "because this situation is even more out there than I first believed." He stepped away from Adam's lifeless body and let Rooster in to look over the space. "Have Jerry moved into interrogation again, and cuff him to the chair. Once you let him stew for a few hours, give him a choice to talk to me or Walby Edwards."

"Mr. Edwards is currently assigned in Afghanistan, sir," the guard said.

"I'm well aware of where he is, but one phone call is all it takes, so tell Jerry if he'd like to test my resolve, I'll be happy to make that call and I plan to keep him chained to the chair until Walby gets here. Either way, I'm not the one with my ass in the hot seat so what the fuck do I care, but move him now."

"What do you want to do next?" Rooster asked.

"We're going back to the offices of New Horizons, only this time we're going to take a long look. The answers have to be there, and I just feel that whatever these idiots are involved in is something that is going to blow up in our face if we don't figure it out soon."

Rooster followed him out of the building and into the car waiting right outside. "Jerry was the type of man that the last president valued for his loyalty, but Jerry used that to his advantage and made friends on the extreme right of the spectrum."

"What he did was step on anyone who didn't agree with his politics, and our old boss applauded him for it," Rooster said and Drew nodded. "You know, you were there. When that old son of a bitch got canned, for a while it was like he wasn't gone, there were so many people like Jerry and Adam left behind."

"What we need now is to find out how many weeds he planted before he left, and if it's really Jerry who's responsible for them all." The car sliced through Washington traffic with a police escort and they headed to the offices Jerry and Adam had set up in the suburbs.

"If you want, you can head back and I'll take care of this."

"Just because I have a title now doesn't mean that I'm going to sit behind a desk and wait for someone to try to torpedo President Khalid's character in an effort to discredit him as a leader." He hit his fist on the arm rest. "They tried that shit during the campaign and it didn't fly. They're not getting a second chance."

A team of guards standing at the office entrance moved aside only when Rooster flashed his ID at them. "The files we've found so far that you looked at were in a safe room in the middle of the building."

"The stash we're looking for won't be with that. Those boxes you carried out of here before were window dressing to throw us off their scent." Drew walked in the quiet space and studied the layout from the plans that Rooster had laid out on the receptionist's desk.

"My men went through here slowly and thoroughly. I doubt we missed anything," Rooster said from over his shoulder.

"Which one was Jerry's office?"

Rooster pointed to the big space at the end of the left corridor. "Since he's got a power complex, he picked the big one."

"It looks like the biggest one, but that honor goes to this one." Drew pointed to the one on the opposite side of the plans. "And I'd bet my ass that this one doesn't belong to the late Adam Morris, does it?"

"That one was furnished, but no, Adam's office was this one next to Jerry's." Rooster pointed to a small space with no window access. "You think it's in there?"

"If I know anything about who we're dealing with, I'll need a few things before we go take a look."

"Sir, you only have to ask and we'll get you whatever you like."

Drew made him a list and headed to the mystery office. The furniture was tasteful, but there were no personal touches to give him a clue as to who sat behind the large desk. There were only two pieces of art on the wall, but they were beautifully framed copies of the Declaration of Independence and the Constitution.

From the report Rooster's men had put together he knew every drawer had been opened and every wall searched for a safe or other hiding place. The Declaration print had a safe behind it but it was empty.

"Sir, you have a call on line one," one of Rooster's men said.

"Drew Orr," he said into the receiver as he tried out the comfortable leather desk chair.

"I've gotten about twelve phone calls today from twelve men who went on about how important they were, and they all center around you and your treatment of two patriots you've locked up," Peter Khalid said and laughed.

"Did you write their names down so I can add them to my list of weird shit to look into today?"

"I did one better. I had their files pulled and delivered to your office. Anything new?"

"Adam Morris is dead from a pill he smuggled into the facility in his butt, and I have a corporation swimming in cash, but I can't find it." Drew opened the desk drawers and peered inside to check out what the owner had stocked it with. "But on a good note I'm sure you read my report on what happened today in the Sea of Japan. Our lost lambs have returned to the fold."

"I did and I also read your theory of what's going on with these people at the Pentagon."

Drew laughed and rolled the chair back so he could see all the way to the back of the middle drawer. "Are you sorry yet that you asked me to do this job?"

"No, but all those callers certainly are of a different opinion."

"Don't worry. If the ship goes down, I'll make damn sure I'm the only one on it." He rolled the chair back when he saw the corner of a gilded religious card shoved to the back of the drawer. "You can count on me for that at least."

"What you're telling me then is that you think this job has made me an asshole if you think I'm going to stand for that. Tell me what you want and I'll move things along for you."

Drew took the religious card out and looked at the picture. It didn't have an image of someone with an exaggerated halo on their head, but instead had the image of an old schooner sailing in rough seas. It was the symbol of St. Brendan, patron saint of sailors. The men who'd searched the premises before had most probably seen it but had left it as something not important to the investigation.

"Sir, I need you to trust me."

"Drew, drop the titles, this is me you're talking to, so level with me. What's got to get done and how serious is this?"

"Peter, I need you to stay out of this until we've finished our initial investigation, and as soon as I'm done here I need to see you and Vice President Michaels."

"Take your time. I'll call Olivia for a meeting early tonight."

Drew hung up the phone and tapped his finger on the St. Brendan stamp. "Only a sailor would keep this. Rooster," he called out the door.

"Found something?"

Drew held up the stamp. "This is part of the answer we're looking for, so maybe the other part is here as well. Did my request get here yet?"

"Our answer is to pray?" Rooster asked and laughed.

"I have a feeling they've already been answered."

"You ready?" Rooster waved in the Marines who were right behind him when Drew nodded.

They walked in and rolled in an x-ray machine. "Cover every inch of the floor that doesn't have a heavy piece of furniture on it," Drew said and stood to get out of their way. "Once you're done, use the wand and cover the walls."

The scan took only a few minutes before the men rolled up the rug in front of the desk and took a crowbar to the wide wood planks that made up the floor. The compartment held a metal box that resembled one that banks used in their safety deposit vaults.

"Wait outside," Rooster told the Marines.

When the door closed Drew opened the box. "Have them go through the rest of the building inch by inch, and tell the surveillance team you have on Rodney James's house to be extra vigilant." He shut the lid and picked up the evidence. "Come on. We have a meeting at the White House."

CHAPTER THIRTY-THREE

Sea of Japan

The waves were starting to pick up so Berkley couldn't tell who was on the vessel headed toward them. Only when they were about a hundred yards out did she see the blond hair on top of the binoculars glued to the eyes she knew were blue. "We're almost home, Junior." She started kicking toward the boat.

"Hello, sailor," she yelled up to Aidan when she was close enough. The divers had hit the water as soon as the engine was cut and they took Junior from her arms and put him in a stretcher so they could lift him onboard.

"You're late," Aidan said, her voice cracking at the end.

"You know how much I love to sightsee. We even went horseback riding. It was like camp." Berkley smiled up at her. "In the end it was your pie that motivated us to get moving, so we borrowed a plane."

"I'll make one as soon as you're back onboard, but for now get up here." Aidan shielded her eyes from the sun but couldn't take her eyes off Berkley, who saluted her from the water.

"Glad you could make it out here to greet us," Berkley said when she made it up. She smiled, knowing from the expression on her face that Aidan wanted to touch her as much as Berkley wanted to take her into her arms, but this wasn't the time.

As soon as they got Junior out of the water Aidan gave them the sign to move out. "Get us back and then get back on patrol," Aidan told the men on the rescue boat. "We saw another set of parachutes deploy after the second plane started to go down, and I want to get to whoever it is before the Koreans get to them."

"Let me see to my partner and I'll be happy to tell you what we've been up to as soon as we get back." Berkley, now wrapped in a warm blanket, sat next to Junior, who was similarly swaddled. "How you feeling?"

"Like I've crashed twice in a lifetime. Thanks for getting us out of that hellhole."

"Glad to do it, and now I'll see what I can do about that nurse I promised you."

The trip back to the carrier didn't take long, and the medics waiting for Junior wheeled him away as soon as they hit the deck.

"Welcome back, Commander," Devin said and shook Berkley's hand. "Whenever you're ready I'd like to debrief you."

"Give me a chance to take a shower and I'll be happy to answer any questions."

"Could you answer a couple before that if I promise I won't take a lot of your time?"

Berkley glanced at Aidan before answering.

"Is that yours?" Aidan pointed to the blood on Berkley's shoulder where the blanket had slipped down. When she got no immediate answer she shook her head. "I know the perfect place for you to ask all the questions you want, Devin."

They entered one of the exam rooms in the infirmary and Aidan covered Berkley with a warm, dry blanket after Berkley peeled away her flight suit. They'd left Devin outside until the doctor had a chance to examine the injury. "You should plan to stay down here until that's healed," she told Berkley.

"In good time, Captain." Berkley adjusted the blanket and waved Devin in. "But for now I want to know what you've done with the team that went with me. Did Blazer and Alan make it back here?"

"We still have Alan in custody, and the captain let Blazer go for reasons she'll explain to you."

"Not anymore," Aidan added. "He's back in custody."

Devin nodded and turned his attention back to Berkley. "As you know, we didn't have radio contact with you while you were gone unless it was necessary and with your plane down, we didn't have the conversations between you and Junior. The only two left to fill in the blanks of what happened were Blazer and Lewis," Devin said.

Berkley then gave them a rundown of how the mission had

progressed up to the destruction of the North Korean plant. "Before that, the little punk tried to test me, but he did his role well until we were on the way back. As we turned for home the North got a plane up and Blazer disobeyed a direct order to not turn and engage. He did and almost got his ass handed to him, so I had no choice but to bail him out. What I can't prove was what happened next. I told him to bank in one direction and he went the opposite way, leaving me hanging. We got shot down, and with more than one plane on him by then, he decided to do what I ordered him to in the first place."

"What, run back here with his tail between his legs, leaving his team leader behind?" Devin asked.

"He's an ass, that's for sure, but I'm not convinced that his performance in the heat of battle wasn't more shaped by nerves than anything sinister on his part."

"There's more," Aidan said and told her about the message that had gotten to Jerry. "The defense secretary is starting his own investigation stateside, but we haven't found who got the message out or how. There's no record of it."

"The communications systems on the jets are capable of getting out a message in code if someone really wants to get specific about it," Berkley said. "They're satellite linked, so a message going out from here to the Pentagon wouldn't raise too many eyebrows on the other end if the person they delivered it to didn't act surprised."

"We checked everything that can raise a signal onboard and found nothing."

"Look for someone who is a little more than computer literate. It would've taken some time, but it's possible to get something out, then erase it from the system if you know your way around the program. That's one way to do it. The other way is much more simplistic and that's sending it in Morse Code. Not everyone is a techie these days, so no one ever thinks to check something so low tech." Berkley shivered and wrapped the blanket around her more tightly. "Alan didn't tell you what you wanted when you showed him your cards? If Jerry Teague and Adam Morris are in custody, I'd talk if I was involved somehow, because there's no way Morris lets his kid go down."

"He was about to when you got the first message through. I put him back in lockup until we got you back," Aidan said.

"Wouldn't the message they received at the Pentagon have had some sort of code of where it originated from?" Devin asked. "A specific radio, I mean."

"Like I said, there's ways around anything if you know what you're doing. For now my suggestion is to go through everyone's records. We want to talk to anyone with higher than normal computer skills and we'll work down from there, but first I want to talk to butthead and bigger butthead."

"Captain Aidan had already mentioned everyone's service files, so I'll take care of finishing that," Devin said. "And if you don't mind I'd like to be there when you talk to Blazer and Alan."

"Sure, but make certain you don't have him anywhere around Alan. That's who I want to talk to first," Aidan added when Devin went to leave.

❖

Berkley sat beside Aidan and pushed her drying hair back off her forehead. "You can fuss at me later, but first I want to tell you something."

"What makes you think I'd fuss at you? All I want to do is touch you to make sure I'm not dreaming."

"You live with and love a woman long enough and you learn certain things about her." Berkley laughed.

"That was the old Aidan you bunked with in Hawaii." She stood and locked the door. "This is the new and improved version." She pointed to her chest. When Aidan reached Berkley she sat in her lap and kissed her like Berkley's lips held the nectar of life. "Please don't ever scare me like that again," she said when their lips parted. "I thought I'd lost my chance to prove to you what you mean to me."

"I didn't make it through that to show what a survivor I am, baby. I did it because my fear was that I'd miss the chance to tell you that despite our stupidity and what happened in the past, I love you. Don't live another moment thinking you have to prove anything to me." Berkley framed her face with her hands and kissed her forehead.

"Ma'am." The intercom on the wall buzzed.

"Yes," Aidan said and sounded frustrated that work had intruded on them.

"The rescue boats radioed in and said they've found two more survivors and are bringing them back."

"Who are they?" Aidan asked.

"A female pilot and a civilian, from what they said. Should I tell them that you'll be up to take care of where to put them?"

"Have Devin handle it and for now take care of any wounds they might have and then put them in the brig." Aidan tapped her finger on the side of the radio and turned back to Berkley. "Friends of yours?"

"If I'm right, I think it's the pilot that shot me down, but it was a lucky shot. Anything else you want to know you're going to have to wait until the interrogators get a hold of them."

"Do you think they'll keep so we can finish our talk?"

"I thought we were done?" Berkley met her half way when Aidan moved back toward her. "The picket fence and dog are in our future, but for now we've got a lot left to do around here."

"Just like that?" Aidan asked and gladly parted her lips when Berkley kissed her.

"If you want me to play hard to get I will, but no matter what, there's no denying what I feel for you. Life is too short sometimes, and before anything else happens to keep me from you I wanted you to know what was in here so there'd be nothing left undone between us." Berkley tapped over her own heart.

"Unless I get the sixty plus years I asked for, there's always going to be something left undone between us."

"That might be true when it comes to memories, but not to anything left unsaid. I love you, and I'm going to say it enough times to make you believe that I truly feel that way about you."

"You scared the hell out of me, Cletus," Aidan said and pressed her face against Berkley's chest. "It's taken all I have to get out of bed in the morning, which makes me think that I've had enough of this life where I have to hide who I really am and who I love."

"All in good time, love, but for now we're going to finish what we started and we're going to do it so we make the two old guys we left at home proud."

"Will you at least turn in early so I can finally sleep through the night, and if I wake up in tears it's going to be because I'm thrilled you're back?" She kissed the blanket over Berkley's heart.

"Didn't you read what I left for you?" Berkley asked.

"Honey, I wanted to die when Blazer told me you'd been shot down and were lost. The last thing I wanted was to do something that would cement that in my heart."

"Let me talk to Blazer and we might get somewhere. Then we can start erasing some of those bad feelings, and we'll start right here." Berkley kissed her again.

"That sounds like a colossal waste of time since he hasn't said much since getting back, but knock yourself out." Hearing a quick tap on the door, Aidan unlocked it to let the doctor in.

"There's talking to Blazer the way the Navy dictates in situations like this, and there's me talking to him with none of you around." Berkley pushed the blanket from her shoulder so the doctor could tend to her wound. It took longer than Berkley was ready to sit for, but he stitched it and told her to keep it dry for a couple of days. She'd been lucky since the bullet hadn't hit any bone or tendon, so the recovery would be short.

They walked back to their quarters and Aidan watched as Berkley got into the shower. "You aren't supposed to get that wet. Now finish what you were saying about Blazer."

"After the little bastard got me shot down, I want twenty minutes alone with him. I think I at least deserve that."

"If you bruise him it's going to be hard to explain."

"If he's missing because he fell off the ship, that would be hard to explain. Bruises mean he fell into the door repeatedly from the bad case of seasickness he's suffered from since coming aboard."

"What did he have to gain from all this?" Aidan sat on the bunk and winked at her when Berkley faced her naked before getting under the steaming water.

"He's good. If he wasn't, no one from the president on down would've convinced me to put him on the team. Blazer's immature, though, and it either has to do with that or it might be this message that someone got off to that asshole we met with before we left." Berkley rushed through her shower and toweled off. "Whatever it is, like I said, it's going to be hard to prove that what he did, except for the part where he turned back to engage, was an action more against me than toward the MiG on our ass."

"What's your first impression?"

"That there's a chance that we'll never find out."

CHAPTER THIRTY-FOUR

Washington, DC

"Mr. President," Rooster said as he shook Peter's hand in the Oval Office. "Thank you for allowing me to attend, sir."

"Anyone want coffee or something?" Peter asked.

"No, sir, but we did find something, so if the vice president could join us we can proceed," Drew said.

"Olivia's on her way," Peter said, his attention on the box Drew had carried in.

"Sorry I'm late," Olivia Michaels said. The ex-senator from Massachusetts had been one of Peter's strongest opponents in the campaign, but after being asked had turned into his strongest asset in winning over the undecided voters around the country. "If I have to attend one more healthcare meeting, I might end up needing a doctor." All the men stood and laughed. "Nice to see you again, Drew."

"Madame Vice President, it's a pleasure."

"I read the report you sent over, but could you give us a brief recap, if you don't mind?"

"No problem, ma'am. As you know we launched the *Jefferson* to carry out the operation against North Korea. With the massive amount of intelligence going in, we never thought the mission would end with one of our pilots going off his rails and trying to engage the enemy over their territory against the direct orders from his commanding officer."

"That part was in the initial report. What I need to know is, what is this conspiracy that's brewing down the street under all our noses?"

She cut to the main course. "Or at least that's what these stupid bastards would like to think, that we're totally clueless."

"After we went through most of this information, I've formed an opinion, and when I tell you I promise you'll think I'm off my tracks as well."

"Everyone already knows that about you, buddy, so let's hear it since you've piqued my interest," Peter said. "This meeting will never be made public because it has to do with national security, and I'm sure Olivia would love to know why she's here."

"I believe that New Horizon is some sort of organization that Jerry Teague and Adam Morris were front men for, but the big fish are still swimming in lazy circles watching us chase shadows."

"What type of organization?" Olivia asked.

"The last president took us to war, and a lot of his friends profited from the unnecessary action. Under new leadership that promised an end to that, I think they fabricated an incident that has the potential to embarrass you and Peter to the point the public loses faith in your ability to protect this country."

Peter laughed. "And I'm supposed to act like a scared puppy and run back to the old masters of the universe who controlled the Pentagon and get them to help me?" He laughed harder. "You're right. That's ludicrous."

"I'm not joking, and if we don't smoke them all out of their holes we're going to be chasing our tails for your entire term instead of trying to bring about the change you promised."

"War is hell, Peter, but it's also a moneymaker for a lot of people," Olivia said. "Drew's right. We need to find out if there really is any fire to go along with all this smoke."

"What did you have in mind?" Peter asked.

"The first thing is you need to stay clear of this and what needs to be done," Drew said. "But before I leave here today I'd like a blind warrant for Rodney James's house. I want to bring him in and I want to sweat him like the pig he's acted like the last few months."

"We discussed this," Peter said and pointed his finger at Drew.

"We did, but"—he put the box on the coffee table that separated them—"this tells me that we have a lot of money in play." Drew took out the bundle of bank books bound together with a rubber band. "The financials that we found in Jerry's office weren't some pie-in-the-sky wish numbers. They're real."

"What's he going to finance with all this?" Olivia asked when she glanced down at the amounts.

"That's a good question, and the first thing that comes to mind is payment to someone like Blazer to do something incredibly stupid. He's allegedly involved in what happened to Commander Levine and her partner. My theory on that is that his superiors figured this would cause the type of international incident that would embarrass this administration enough that the power shift would be more permanent next time."

"Four years is a long time to wait," Rooster said.

"Not really," Peter countered. "When you consider if you're patient enough and the situation is sold to the American public in a way that spells our doom if drastic measures aren't taken, it makes their mindset more tolerant when one fringe group or another wants to take over. War and vengeance is the way to go for a lot of people, and once you get there and the reality of the loss of troops and money can't be hidden, that's when the stupor of the overblown sense of getting payback wears off. Everything in life comes with a cost, and this time it was higher than most people thought."

"Yes, sir, and you were the hangover treatment the public settled on this time. Only people like Jerry, Adam, and Rodney aren't about to give up without causing an incident that would make everyone lose confidence in you as commander in chief."

"What do we do so that doesn't happen?" Olivia asked.

"I need to go through Rodney James's house and to bring him in for questioning," Drew said and smiled when Rooster's eyebrows shot up. "I need you to make it the kind that lets me hang on to him for a while."

"Did you get what I asked for?" Peter said. "The bank information is compelling, but there's no way to prove they belong to Rodney, or that he's ever seen them."

Drew handed him the religious stamp and sat back down. "There's your proof, and I know it's not much, but it's all I got besides my gut telling me that he's involved."

Olivia took the picture. "The patron saint of sailors isn't exactly the smoking gun I think Peter wanted, but knowing you, I'm here for a reason. My first guess is I play the scapegoat if you're wrong."

"If you were in Peter's position and had chosen me for the job I have now, I'd still play it this way with whoever you'd picked to be your second."

"I can buy you maybe a month before this is front-page news, and that'll depend on Mrs. Retired Admiral Rodney James. If she's the boisterous kind then the gig is up and we'll see it as the six o'clock lead-off tomorrow morning." Olivia stood and waved to the side door when Drew and Rooster popped up after her. "Peter, as far as you're concerned, this isn't a problem for you anymore. When we find something I'll come by for tea and we'll have another one of these get-togethers."

"Thanks, but don't treat me like I'm in a bubble. I want regular updates and the consequences be damned."

"For once, Peter, listen to the people trying to help you out," Drew said and shook hands with him. "This isn't just about you anymore. What I'm doing is for the country I love and am sworn to serve. That's a different animal than the world people like Jerry and Rodney want to create."

"Godspeed, then."

❖

USS *Jefferson*

Blazer was standing in front of the door with a smirk when he saw Berkley with the key in her hand. The smug smile disappeared quickly when she swung the door open and it hit him square in the face, cutting his brow and lip.

"You bitch," he said seemingly not caring that the insult could get him court-martialed.

Berkley grabbed him by the hair and slammed his face into the steel wall adding another cut to his chin. "Miss me?" He landed on the floor next to the bunk.

"Keep it up and I'll bury you." The blood was coating his teeth when he smiled at her.

"Maybe they'll put me next to your father," Berkley said as she stood over him, her hands behind her back.

"What the hell are you talking about? My father is who's going to get you kicked out of the military, but not before you do some serious time for this." He laughed and spit a big red glob close to her feet.

"I'm sorry to have to be the one to tell you, but your father's in the morgue at the prison the CIA runs in Virginia that really doesn't exist."

"Yeah right, I'm supposed to believe that." Blazer laughed and lifted his middle finger at her.

"The great patriot took the coward's way out after he saw what kind of jam he was in." She delivered the news with no sense of satisfaction since whatever she thought about Blazer, his father was dead. "It would've surprised me, but after dealing with you I can see that your lack of spine is hereditary, so I shouldn't hold your shortcomings against you."

"Fucking shut up about my father. Compared to him you're a disgrace to that uniform."

"Heroes who commit suicide with a pill crushed between their teeth don't get buried at Arlington, Lieutenant. I might not like you, but let me be the first to offer you my condolences for your loss. Of course in this case, your loss is only compounded by the fact that you thought Daddy was going to back you up on what you did." The image of what must have gone through Blazer's head as her plane went down made Berkley pull her hand back and slap him. "That's a reminder that it's my turn to take a shot at you, only I'm going to make sure I follow through."

"He told me you'd try and fuck with my head. You and your kind don't deserve to be here," he screamed and beat his fists on the tops of his thighs.

"Only someone sick in the head would tell you your father is dead to get you to cooperate, Lieutenant Morris." Berkley bent down and touched his shoulder only to have Blazer pull away so violently that he ended up cracking his head into the side of the toilet. "I'm sure you didn't want to get this kind of news from me, but I thought you'd want to know that before you speak to the captain again. If you were waiting for his influence at the Pentagon to get you out of trouble, that's not going to happen."

"Get the fuck out of here, and tell Captain Sullivan I demand a call."

"Watch your language, Lieutenant," Aidan said from outside and smiled at Berkley when she snapped to attention. "If you'd like a call, I'd love to accommodate you, but for now that's impossible. We've gotten word from Command that we're on high alert and have to concentrate on patrols instead of personal calls."

"She told me my father's dead."

"I give you my word that the information she shared with you is accurate. I'm sorry, but we received word along with our new orders. Your father and Jerry Teague were in custody as part of an investigation that started when Commander Levine's plane went down. Sometimes it takes an action like that to uncover something much uglier, so in a way I should thank you for being so uncooperative."

Blazer screamed and scrambled toward Aidan in what looked like an attempt to attack her until he ran into Berkley's fist, which dropped him cold. "That one you can chalk up to defense of a superior officer, Captain," Berkley said as she shook her hand. "When did Command call you, or were you in here checking up on me?"

"I'm not known for my flights of fantasy. They did call." Aidan stuck her tongue out at her and stepped back as Berkley moved around Blazer and locked the door. "From what little they said it sounded like the little guy we picked up with your girlfriend is someone important and they want him back. If they don't get him—"

"It'll be our doom?" Berkley finished for her.

"I know you have a vivid imagination, Commander, but you're really not James Bond, and it isn't Goldfinger down the hall. From what the admiral said, the North Korean consulate is demanding his return or they will engage us."

"They're not worried about the pilot?"

"So far she hasn't said a word, but they didn't mention her."

"Do you mind if I try?" Berkley stopped inside the door so they were out of the line of vision of the prisoners and the guards.

"Aren't you tired? We do have other people onboard who can manage to get the questioning done."

"I'm not trying to step on your shoulder decorations, Captain." Berkley tapped the emblems of Aidan's rank. "But I would like to talk to the pilot. Maybe I can get her to open up a little."

"Five minutes, but you need to take Devin with you." Aidan put her hand up. "I trust you, but my orders are to lift anchor, and when I do these people are coming with us. That means State and a whole bunch of the spooks are waiting to get their hands on them so they can take turns dissecting their brains. The five minute mark is to protect you from being accused of screwing that up for them."

"Thanks, and I'll be good. I promise."

❖

Jin was lying on the small cot in her cell with her eyes closed, and she didn't open them when she heard the lock disengage. It wasn't out of defiance but from her failure. Before she took off she'd disengaged the parachute system so when she ejected them she thought it was her ticket to join her mother. But whatever she'd done, Lowe had found a way to undo.

"Excuse me," the female officer said from the door. "Do you speak English?"

Jin opened her eyes and stared at the woman standing in the open hatch. "Very little, but don't waste your time. I have nothing to say."

"My name is Commander Berkley Levine. Can you tell me who we have in the next cell?" she asked and handed Jin a bottle of water. "The man with you."

"You have caught a big fish, Commander." Jin took a sip and flipped her head back. "Call your intelligence people and tell them you have Lowe Nam Chil. I'm sure you won't need any further information."

"You're willing to give him up so easily?" Berkley stepped aside when one of the mess hall workers came in with a tray. Both Jin and Berkley looked at the delivery girl when she lingered too long for what was necessary. "Lieutenant, are you moonlighting?" Berkley asked the woman carrying in her food, waking her from the stupor she seemed to be in.

"Call me when the tray is empty," Erika said and walked out.

"I'm sorry for the interruption, Captain. Do you remember the question?"

"My comrade has much to answer for, and I don't fear death, so it's only fair that you and your people have fun with him."

"Death isn't on the table, but I'll pass along your message."

Berkley bowed again. "If you need anything, tell the guard and I'll come by."

"Thank you," Jin said and bowed in return. "If it makes it easier on you, my name is Captain Jin Umeko."

"You made that look easy," Devin said as they left the area.

"I'll give my mother all the credit. She always says politeness pays off."

Drew led her back to the communications room that was set up for live feed from Washington, and asked, "Who do you think this Lowe character is?"

"I'm sure the spooks have a file on him, but if the secretary is videoconferencing in today, maybe he's got a clue." The usual attendees were already sitting at the table when they arrived and Aidan shared a glance with her as Berkley sat down. "Our guest is being surprisingly cooperative and she gave up her backseat's name."

"Save it for about three minutes so you don't have to repeat it all," Aidan told her.

"Commander," Drew said the minute his face was visible on the screen. "Welcome back and job well done getting yourself and Lieutenant Whittle out of harm's way. Your captain sent word of your safe return."

"Thank you, Mr. Secretary. I'm sure you would've done the same in similar circumstances. I've got a name for you to check out." Berkley glanced at Devin to see if he wanted to give the report, but he shook his head. "The pilot we rescued is Captain Jin Umeko of the North Korean air force and the man with her is Lowe Nam Chil, is how she pronounced it."

"Lowe Nam Chil, are you sure?"

"I'm not sure why she's being so cooperative, but that's what she said, and followed it with that you'd know who Lowe was."

"If it's who we've heard about, he's Kim Jong Il's main henchman and interrogator. Thank you, Commander." Drew turned his eyes to Aidan. "Any luck on finding who sent that message, Captain?"

"We've got some new channels to investigate, sir, but so far no luck. The one thing we have done is inform Blazer that his father is dead. He didn't take it well, and I'm not really sure he believes us, but his partner Alan Lewis has been much more forthcoming since Cletus's return. Devin sat with him again, and he told us that Blazer didn't share with him if what happened was an accident or on purpose, but Blazer did make him swear not to tell that they hadn't gone back to check if their team members had made it out. All those actions followed the first call to ignore the order Cletus had given him not to engage."

"You need to hang in a few more days and make sure that Nam Chil doesn't cause any harm to himself. I've got Naval Command bringing in some backup to stabilize the area, then I want you to lift anchor and sail for the West Coast. Somewhere along the way I'll make arrangements for Nam Chil's departure from the *Jefferson*."

"And if we're engaged by the North Koreans?" Aidan asked.

"Have your pilots set up patrol and you have the green light that if fired on you engage. I'm hoping with the high tension now that they end up backing down before we're done, but there's a possibility that they won't."

"We'll handle it and make preparation to sail. Thanks for the update, and if we have anything new on our end I'll contact you immediately."

"Will do, Washington out," Drew said and the screen went black.

"Devin, you might want to do a full cavity search of our guest considering what happened with Adam Morris," Aidan said.

"Aye, Captain, that sounds like a blast," he said in a deadpan voice.

"And you get some rest and don't get any wild ideas about doing any patrols yourself tonight," Aidan said to Berkley. "Vader's got everything under control, and I told him you can meet tomorrow morning to set up our defenses."

"Let me check on Junior and I'll bunk down for the night," Berkley said and saluted Aidan before she left.

CHAPTER THIRTY-FIVE

Junior was sleeping off his anesthesia when Berkley checked on him. They'd had to sedate him to reset his leg. The doctor had told her that there was a chance that he'd have a slight limp, but he was lucky his leg had been saved at all considering the infection that had set in.

When she locked the door to her quarters she headed to the chest in front of her bunk and sat to take her boots off, but her eyes stayed on Aidan and the way she was following her around the room with her gaze.

"Are you off duty for the night, Captain?"

"It's still light outside, but I made an executive decision and took a few hours off to put you to sleep and then I have to go back to work for a little while. Unless someone drops a bomb on the ship tonight, I'm going to sleep in your arms."

For once, Berkley didn't bother being neat and dropped her uniform where she stood. It hadn't technically been that long since she'd left Aidan's bed, but when their bodies met skin to skin, it felt like a lifetime had passed her by since she'd felt something that wonderful. She rolled Aidan over and enjoyed the sensation of the simple touch, only to have Aidan start crying.

"Don't." Berkley wiped Aidan's face with the tips of her fingers. "I hate seeing you in pain."

"The pain I could live with," Aidan sniffled. "I bore it for the years we were apart, but this time it was the numbness I couldn't stand. When I thought you weren't coming back I thought that's all the sensation I'd ever feel again—nothing."

"I'm here." Berkley rolled them again so she could hover over Aidan and kiss her tears as they tracked down her cheeks. "And I want you to feel me."

She moved to Aidan's lips as her hand cupped the breast closer to her, and she smiled when she heard Aidan's moan. "Let me in," she whispered as her hand went lower. "Show me how much you missed me."

Aidan was smaller than her, but her body was strong and Berkley could feel her muscles twitch. In the Korean countryside she'd thought about how to touch Aidan when she made it back and thought she'd have the discipline to go slow. But it was impossible.

Berkley placed Aidan's leg over hers so she could see the blond hair that covered her goal. "I dreamed about this," Berkley said as her fingers dipped into Aidan's sex and found her wet. With Aidan lying naked next to her, Berkley took her time to admire the expanse of soft skin and luscious curves that had made her burn since their first time together.

"Go inside." Aidan grabbed her wrist. "I need to know you're here."

Berkley ran her fingers along the wetness until they were covered in Aidan's essence. Her movements were slow enough to make Aidan squeeze her wrist hard.

"Baby," Aidan said right before Berkley entered her in one fast motion and buried her fingers inside her. "Oh God."

Aidan's clit was hard under her thumb and the way her hips started rocking right away encouraged her to pump her fingers faster. The moment might have proven to Aidan that she was back, but it freed Berkley's heart from the past. This woman who gave herself so willingly to her touch was the one who would give her the kind of life worth living.

When she came, Aidan grabbed her wrist again to get her to stop moving her hand, but also to keep her inside. "I love you," she said, her voice low.

"I love you too, sweetheart, and I'm looking forward to that picket fence you keep talking about."

"It means retirement, Cletus," Aidan said and her sex squeezed Berkley's fingers. "Are you ready for that?"

"The toys aren't as fun in the civilian world, that I admit, but there are other things to life than fast planes." Berkley kissed the tip of Aidan's nose.

"Like what?"

"Fast women," she teased, and Aidan retaliated with a pinch to her nipple. "Okay, fast woman. You're the only one I need, and we're going to be fine. No matter what people like Blazer think of our service, we've given enough."

"I've got another year." Aidan sighed. "I don't know if I could handle being away from you that long."

"You're in command of a carrier and I'm a pilot, sweet pea. I think things are going to work out for us."

"Enough about that. I'm supposed to be putting you to sleep," Aidan said before she kissed her. "Would you like to hear a bedtime story?"

"Does it have any dirty words in it?"

"It's more of an acted-out story without a lot of dialogue, but feel free to express your thoughts as we get through it." Aidan kissed her again and moved down the bed after Berkley's fingers finally left their warm haven. "I don't know if this will give you the same thrill as when you're in that bat from hell, but I'll do my best." Aidan sucked in Berkley's clit so hard she came close to losing control instantly.

They linked their hands together and Berkley closed her eyes as the tingling sensation washed over her. She fought the urge to scream at how good she felt. It didn't take long for the orgasm to reach a point that she couldn't stop. Aidan must have sensed the change in her breathing and put her tongue at the base without breaking the suction of her lips. It made Berkley's resolve to make it last longer shatter.

"The F-18's got nothing on you, baby," she said when her breathing slowed to a pant.

"Let's hope you feel that way when I'm fussing at you to go and cut the grass." Aidan moved up so she was covering Berkley's body with her own. Their lazy kiss was interrupted by the alarm going off and the bridge announcing that they had incoming MiGs from the northwest.

"Back to work, Captain," Berkley said and slapped Aidan's ass to get her moving. She picked up the receiver in her room and called up to the tarmac. "Vader, get your team in the air and keep the bastards away from the ship. If you have a shot, take it. I doubt they're here to pay a social call."

"You got it, boss."

Berkley called Mike Dyer next and told him to find her a backseat, which made Aidan stop dressing. The glare she shot her made Berkley put her hands up.

"You and I both know this is my job. If you want us to stay together, you need to let me do it, and have faith that I'll come back."

"No one's going to say shit if you stay behind, least of all me."

"I know that, but it's not in me to stay behind, and remember that was the thing about me that attracted you in the first place." Berkley moved closer to her and placed her hands along Aidan's jaw and kissed her. "I love you. That's what I fight for, and that's what gives me the will to come home when I'm done."

"Promise me again," Aidan said and Berkley could tell she did her best to smile.

"I'll be right back, so keep the light on."

Minutes later Berkley was next to her new plane and found a young woman already in the backseat. Berkley didn't waste time getting in and saluting the ground crew that secured the hatch. Once they were in the air she saw that the Koreans had sent about twenty planes and they were flying in a wide circle around the *Jefferson* but making no attempt to engage their planes, which were creating a buffer between the enemy and the ship.

"What's your name?" Berkley asked.

"Hattie Skinner, Commander."

"Up here it's Cletus, and I promised the captain that I would try my best not to destroy any more expensive government property, so speak up, okay?"

"You got it."

"Vader, what's up?" she radioed him next.

"We're locked in a game of ring-around-the-rosy, but they haven't made any hostile movements."

Berkley gained altitude and decided to go around to the other side of the ring the Koreans had formed. "How many planes did you send up?"

"We've got eighteen in the air now and I have more on deck ready to go if we need it."

"Cletus." Aidan's voice came through the radio. "We're getting a message from their government. So far they said if we let the two people onboard go they'll call their fighters back."

"What's Command on our side saying?"

"They've sent the formal response and it was no, so heads up, everyone. If it's true that they'll engage, I need everyone vigilant."

"What frequency are they on, Captain?" Berkley asked.

Aidan gave them all the correct channel so the planes could adjust their communications equipment. "This is Commander Levine of the USS *Jefferson*," Berkley said slowly. "You are engaged in hostile activities in international waters. Break your pattern or you *will* be fired upon."

Silence followed, but the computer beeped that one of the planes had locked on her. "Acknowledge that you understand, or we will engage." Again, there was only silence.

"Cletus, we're locked," Hattie said.

"Got it," Berkley answered and changed back to the channel where she could talk to Vader and Killer. "Broken wing formation. Lock on someone and be careful of incoming fire from the boys on deck."

She waited for the plane that had locked on her to act. If it did, it would end up disastrously for the North Koreans. The pilot let his missile go and Berkley took evasive action by gaining altitude and allowing one of her pilots to shoot down the missile.

"Fire at will, everyone," she told her pilots. It was still dusk, but the sky came alive with gunfire and rocket explosions. In less than two minutes five of the Korean planes had been downed. "Cease fire," Berkley ordered, and even the Koreans listened. "This is Commander Levine. Stand down and turn it around or we'll down the rest of your men." She was flying above the fray now and kept an eye on her radar screen.

As she was about to ask for acknowledgment of her warning, the remaining planes broke to the left and circled back toward the north. "Killer, an escort to the coast, please."

"Copy. Beta team, follow my lead."

In the realm of combat it wasn't exactly a battle, but Berkley wasn't complaining. She lined up for landing and thought about the next year of her life. Unless the new administration changed course dramatically this is where she'd be. Her teaching days were over.

"Thank you, Hattie," she said as she brought them in.

"Anytime, ma'am. I'll be here until Junior is back on his feet."

Landing on a carrier always took Berkley's breath away. There wasn't another experience that came close to the rush it gave her when the tailhook stopped her momentum cold. She laughed as she waited for the crew to bring the ladder and get them out once they were secured. The takeoffs and landings made her hair stand on end, but nothing compared to what Aidan had done earlier.

❖

She made her way to the bridge when they were done and asked to speak to Aidan. "Once Killer and Vader land, send up the remaining planes and we'll set up a watch pattern for now. I think you should get with Command, though, and find out who this is we're holding. The last thing we need is a nightly visit from the regime trying to get their boy back."

"You think they'll tell us? You know how the alphabet soup works."

"Tell them we've already lost one plane over this and I'd like to avoid any unnecessary damage if we can help it." Berkley put her body between Aidan and the rest of the people working around them. "Think about it, Aidan. We've stuck a big-ass stick in a hornet's nest, and these are the type of hornets with something to prove. Until they order us to lift anchor, we're sitting ducks out here."

"I'll try my best."

Their orders were to lift anchor and start for the West Coast. It wouldn't take long for the *Jefferson* to be far enough from shore for the North Koreans to no longer be a problem. The fate of Jin and Lowe would be decided somewhere en route.

"This is like no other mission I've been on," Aidan told Berkley when she made it back to her private office. "There's something strange about this whole thing, don't you think?"

"What I can't understand is why was Lowe with Jin? If he's that important to their government he would've been kept in a bunker somewhere."

"And from what I've read about this regime, the small show of force doesn't add up. The reason they were never engaged was the fear of what the retaliation would be." She rolled her chair back and pushed Berkley into it so she could sit in her lap.

"That's for the spooks to figure out, but there was something else I've been meaning to ask you. What's Erika doing serving meals?"

Aidan gave her the rundown on what had happened, and she felt Berkley tense. "She didn't think I'd do it, but I didn't have the patience to sort out her bullshit."

"After you dismissed her as your assistant, did she spend any time in the cargo area?"

"I could ask. I didn't think about her at all once I sent her to the kitchen."

"Save my place, I'll be back." Berkley jogged to the cargo hold where the jets were stored and brought on deck by hydraulic lifts when they were needed. The planes that had just landed were being refueled and checked over by Mike and his maintenance crew, which included Hattie Skinner.

"Did you forget something, Commander?" Hattie asked as she put her clipboard with her checklist under her arm.

"A minute with Mike," Berkley said and smiled. "Thanks again for filling in tonight."

"Hey, Cletus, you're not going up again so quickly, are you?" Mike Dyer asked.

"Not until morning. What I need to know is if Lieutenant Erika Gibson's been down here."

Mike wiped his hands on the rag in his hand and glanced back at Hattie. Devin was closing in on them with a couple of his men. "When she got reassigned she came down and talked to a couple of people to vent off some steam about what happened. I kept it respectful, though, but I thought she had a right." He stuffed the rag in his back pocket and cocked his cap back. "Is there a problem with that?"

"Devin's going to need a list of everyone who she came in contact with." Berkley leaned in and lowered her voice. "This is serious shit, Mike, so mention it to your crew that you *do not* want to get caught lying. People lose their careers over shit like this."

"The last thing I need is to get caught up in some kind of witch hunt." Mike turned around and waved Hattie over. "Hattie, aside from you, who else did Erika talk to while she was down here?"

"Only a couple of the guys, but after she started delivering meals down here, we hit it off. Is there a problem?"

"Did you by chance take her for a spin in one of the jets?" Berkley asked, and Devin moved closer.

"I don't think I could've gotten away with that, Commander," Hattie said with a laugh. "Mike and the pilots don't like it when anyone takes the planes off the ship without permission."

"I'm talking about sitting her in one and showing her all the fancy buttons." Berkley put her hand on her shoulder and forced herself to smile. "Did you do that?"

"She was interested, and as long as she didn't actually touch anything I didn't see anything wrong with that." Hattie sounded less relaxed.

"Okay, so you're telling me that you were the one who spent the most time with Erika, and befriended her?"

"Yeah, she was always nice—despite what happened."

"About her job you mean?"

"Yeah," Hattie said and Berkley glanced at Devin over Hattie's shoulder to keep him in place. "It was a demotion she didn't feel that she deserved, but she tried to make the best of it."

"Hattie, I need you to come with us and answer a few more questions." Berkley moved her hand until it was wrapped around Hattie's bicep.

"I told you all you wanted to know." Hattie tried to break Berkley's hold. "She didn't touch anything."

"I believe you," Berkley responded and let her go, but Devin's men moved in. "You can come on your own or not. That choice is up to you, but you are coming."

The MPs stepped closer, but Hattie put her hands up and followed Berkley quietly. The room Aidan had been using as an interrogation room was empty, and one of the guards went in with Hattie while Devin called for Aidan outside with Berkley.

"What's your plan?" Devin asked Berkley after he was finished on the phone.

"She said she showed Erika the cockpit but she didn't touch

anything. That I believe is true, but Erika didn't need to touch anything. She had someone do it for her, and it turns out to be a nice kid from Kansas who didn't realize she was being played."

"You think Hattie sent the message that Mr. Teague got?"

"If you let me I'll try and find out for you, but I don't want to step on your toes."

"Knock yourself out," Devin said and casually saluted when Aidan arrived.

"Just for my benefit, do I need to do anything?" Aidan said after Berkley told her what she was thinking and asked to speak to Hattie.

"Follow my lead and agree with everything I say," Berkley said and winked at Aidan before opening the door. "Hattie, I realize how devoted you are to the service, but we have a problem."

"I told you, Erika complained, but in my opinion it was to be expected."

"She does have the right to bitch and really that isn't against policy, but when she asked you to send a message for her, that crossed the line." Berkley knocked on the table to keep her quiet when Hattie took a deep breath and opened her mouth. "I'm not asking you if you sent it, I'm telling you I know you did it. The reason you're here is for you to explain to me why you did it so that Captain Sullivan can decide what charges to bring you up on, if that's necessary."

"You're already in deep, Hattie, so don't add lying to the trouble you're in," Aidan said going along with Berkley.

"She told me it was a favor for a friend," Hattie said in a rush, "and the reason it had to be sent is because Captain Sullivan needed help." When she finished there were tears in her eyes.

"Hattie, I want you to go back to work and for now don't worry about this, but don't share what you said with anyone. Do you think you can do that?"

"You're going to throw me out for this, aren't you?" Hattie asked Aidan.

"I don't want to, but you have to understand that when Erika asked, the correct course of action should've been to go to your superior. Right now what we need is for you to go back to work and keep your mouth shut." Aidan was stern but finished by patting Hattie on the hand. "I'll have Devin walk you back and tell Mike there's nothing wrong."

Alone again, Aidan turned to Berkley and laughed. "Devin and I ran around here trying to find who did that, and you get it done in five minutes. Maybe they should've given you this commission."

"Honey, you had a few things on your mind, starting with being upset about what you thought had happened to me. It was luck on my part that I figured it out so quick. Now it's up to you to see if Erika was involved with Blazer or if it was something she did to get back at you after she played delivery girl with his meals." Berkley took Aidan's hand in hers briefly. "Not that it matters much now, since we'll all probably be detained once we get back, but I want you to have as much information as possible once we dock."

"Do you think she'd be that vindictive?"

"Are you kidding me, cute stuff? If you'd rebuffed me I'd take down everyone in sight." Berkley kissed her forehead.

"Get some rest and I'll bring Erika in and beat her with a wet noodle and see what she has to say."

"Don't be long." Berkley kissed her again and helped Aidan out of her chair.

"I'll need to find out if she had any contact with Blazer, then I need to finish up with Alan." Aidan pressed her hand to Berkley's chest over her heart and smiled. "If you haven't figured it out yet, I'm thrilled that you're back."

"Glad to be back. Now get to work so I can have my turn at you asking me hard questions," Berkley joked.

CHAPTER THIRTY-SIX

The questioning took hours and ended with Erika in the cell next to Blazer's, but from what Aidan could tell it was more of Erika doing him a favor than her being a part of whatever he was wrapped up in. So far they had been lucky with the weather and with the two North Koreans they had on board, who mostly lay in their bunks and stirred only when meals were delivered.

Aidan had stopped to introduce herself and to take any statement they wanted to make, but both Lowe and Jin had looked at her as if they could see through her. Only Lowe had demanded in reasonably good English to be brought back, but when Aidan shook her head he had become totally unresponsive.

After giving orders for the night watch and strict warnings to wake her if anything even slightly out of the ordinary happened, Aidan retired and found Berkley in her room asleep. "You were always one to break the rules, Cletus, but I think it's what appealed to my goody two-shoes self when we met." She sat on the edge of her bunk and ran her fingers lightly through Berkley's hair. "You were it for me from that first day, and this is like a dream that you're here."

"I'll only get better with age, Captain, so get in here," Berkley said in a raspy voice, making Aidan laugh.

"You weren't supposed to hear all that." Aidan lay down with her back pressed against Berkley's front.

"If you want me to change my rule-breaking ways, you let me know and I'll try my best. The rest is something that's good to hear, so don't be embarrassed."

Berkley sat up a little and kissed her good night. "Get some sleep."

"I guess you didn't miss me that much." Aidan reached back and slapped Berkley's butt.

"I missed you plenty, but the next time I get you naked it's going to be somewhere with room service and thick walls. Once we're there you're going to lock yourself in the bathroom to get away from me, and you should consider that fair warning."

"Fair enough." Aidan put her hands over Berkley's and closed her eyes. It felt like she had just gone to sleep when a voice came over her intercom.

"Captain," the man said after the damn thing gave off a short, shrill beep.

"Yes," Aidan said but didn't move.

"I wanted you to know that we were able to get through to Washington to give Blazer his call he asked for."

"Put an extra watch on him and have Devin send someone in and do a cavity check for any type of medication he might have on him. Tell him to check the room carefully as well."

"Aye, ma'am, sorry to disturb you."

"No, thank you for letting me know."

With the engines churning at full speed, they were well out of range by the time Aidan fell asleep again. She had checked the navigational maps before she'd gone to bed and it made her relax even more. The only danger they would face now would be bad weather, but even that appeared to be cooperating, with calm waters predicted all the way to San Diego.

For once, there was no sense of foreboding with all that information in her head and Berkley's arms around her. With every mile they put between them and Asia, the better she felt, but there was always the part of Aidan's brain that never slept. It was the part that had made her so successful in her years of service.

❖

Northern Virginia

"Let me go back to my cell. There's nothing I have to say, and I don't care what you do to me," Jerry Teague told Rooster and Walby

Edwards, one of the best interrogators the CIA had. Drew had checked with the agency to see when Walby was returning from the Middle East and was surprised to learn he was already back. After one short phone call he was ready to help them.

"I took a nap today, Jerry, so I've got as much time as it takes." Walby sounded as if he'd really just woken up from a restful night's sleep. "If I do get tired I've lined up a few of my friends to take my place since I wouldn't want you to think we'd skimp on you."

"Could you be any lamer?"

Walby laughed and cracked open a can of diet soda. He'd ordered Jerry's food and liquids cut off the night before. "I'm making conversation, Jerry." He took a sip and sighed as if it was the best thing he'd ever put in his mouth. "I've got so much time that the only thing that'll get in our way is my retirement."

"What was the question again?" Jerry's eyes followed the path of the can to Walby's lips after he asked. It was as if all of a sudden he couldn't make enough saliva to keep his mouth wet. He'd read all the reports of when they'd sent Walby in to question someone and had thought how weak the people had been for talking without Walby laying a hand on them.

"Tell me about the missing slots on this list you got going here." Walby held up the board of directors list from New Horizon.

"You don't want to know about the money? That's what Drew went on and on about."

"I'll talk about whatever you want, but that's not my priority at the moment. You know, we aren't completely inept like the media says. We've got some folks working on those financials you had at the office, and it's only a matter of time before we find the cash."

"Ha, like hell you will. My business is set up on a code that won't ever be cracked."

"That's rather humorous," Walby said and finished the can in one long draw. "The problem with that theory is that you trusted people like Adam Morris."

"He killed himself rather than break the code."

"He killed himself because he didn't want to compromise his son, and because he was crazy." Walby drew an invisible circle around his ear and laughed. He wasn't there to be politically correct. "If you want my advice, there's two instances you don't put your faith in crazy people—when you have a secret business and when you have an affair. Those two instances are disastrous when you go the crazy route."

"You're a riot, but it's not going to work. Take me back to my cell."

"The only reason we brought you here is to help yourself out. It's only a matter of time before people like Drew and Rooster break your precious code and whoever you think is on your side is going to fold so fast it's going to put you in jail for life before you get used to that nice orange color."

Jerry laughed and rubbed his index finger over a small scar on his forearm. "People like Drew and Rooster aren't true patriots, and you aren't what I thought, either. The sad thing is, all three of you don't know what a true American really is because you work for someone like Peter Khalid." He stood as much as he could with the restraints that were holding him to the chair and shouted, "The last time a travesty like this happened in our country, true heroes fought to take it back."

"Uh-huh." Walby yawned. "That sounds like Adam Morris wasn't the only crazy upholding the code."

"Fuck you," Jerry said and grunted when one of the guards pushed him back in the chair. "We were given a gift by our founding fathers, and the people pissed all over that by putting someone with so little honor in the highest office in the land. Because of that they've lost the right to be a part of fixing what's broken with this country."

"Sounds like you're planning a revolution, Jerry. Is that what's on your mind, and the reason you've got such a fat bank account?" Rooster asked.

"Take me back to my cell and do with me what you will, but I'm not going to break. I'm not afraid of what you can dish out because I know before too long I'll be a free man and a hero to the country I love."

"It was nice talking to you, Jerry, and I'll be back later." Walby stood. "I hope you have a good time with some of the people I'm training for that retirement I'm looking forward to. That means you're going to be here for a while, and I wouldn't waste my breath asking to be returned to my cell."

Drew sat in the room next to the interview room and was staring at the monitors when Rooster and Walby walked in. "How long before you start to get anything useful?" he asked Walby.

"Might be tomorrow, but you never know. Since this constitutes a national security threat, we're clear to use a lot of measures we don't usually consider. I'll let you know as we move along."

They were all watching the screen as Jerry turned to the side and tried his best to ignore the next group of people Walby had sent in. "And nothing new on all that load of paper?" Drew asked Rooster.

"I left you my report this morning while you were dealing with the *Jefferson*. The interrogation teams are ready for the two Koreans the *Jefferson* fished out of the water. All we need is the go-ahead from you and they'll be on their way. Any luck with Rodney?"

"It's like he's got a switch in his head that he can turn off and on at will. He bitched for an hour after we brought him in, and then nothing."

"Does he know you're ripping his house to shreds to find something?" Walby said.

"I could have told him his wife was giving it all up, and I still wouldn't have gotten a reaction out of him." Drew turned away from the screen and swore under his breath. He hated being in the dark, especially when it came to players like Rodney and Jerry. They represented to him the worst kind of person who was entrusted with a little power. They tried their best to trample the Constitution to change the world to fit what they wanted.

"You want me to talk to him?" Walby said.

"I want you to take turns talking to both of them. You weren't just pissing in the wind in there when you said we have people working on this money and where it's coming from."

"Where are you taking Nam Chil and the pilot we scooped out of the water?" Walby asked.

"I'm having a jet meet them while they're still out of the seven-mile limit and having them transported to Gitmo. Once they arrive I'll have you sent back," Drew told Walby. "Think you can break the breaker?"

"I might have to ask him for some pointers before I ask him anything else. What I don't know is if the crew of the *Jefferson* realizes who exactly they have on board."

"I didn't mention it. I put him on suicide watch since all we have around us are patriots who love their countries to death," Drew said. "I'm on my way to meet with the forensic accountants I've got on this. Let me know if you find out anything."

"Compared to us, those are the people they should be scared shitless of," Walby said.

❖

USS *Jefferson*

"All's clear, ma'am," one of Aidan's commanders on the bridge said when she stepped in as the sun was starting to rise. She'd parted ways with Berkley as she headed to the infirmary to visit Junior.

They were a couple of days away from docking, and she figured they'd be in port for a minimum of three weeks while adjustments were made and their supplies were restocked. Once that was done, their next stop would most probably be to join the fleet stationed off Iraq as backup operation.

"Thank you." She scanned the reports on the engine performance and nodded her approval. "I'm going to take a walk through the lower decks and talk to the engine room and plane storage areas to get their status reports. Call me if you need anything."

"Will do, ma'am," the man said and saluted.

The alarm went off when Aidan's hand landed on the main door to the engine room. "Bogeys coming in from twelve o'clock. They aren't responding to any call to identify themselves," the bridge commander said. "From what we can see they're armed to the teeth."

"What the hell?" Aidan said as she sprinted to the bridge. The only place someone could launch an attack from was either Canada or Mexico, and if that happened it meant the world had gone mad—why would it be coming from their own soil? "Repeat, bogeys at twelve o'clock," he repeated the whole message again.

As Aidan reached the deck below the bridge she heard the first of the planes leave the deck and her chest tightened that she hadn't had a chance to see Berkley before she left. And if she knew Berkley, she was one of the first off the carrier.

"Who in the hell is this?" she asked as she picked up her glasses and pointed them to the east.

"It's strange, ma'am. The planes are painted black like the ones we used on this mission and they aren't responding to any call to identify themselves."

"Captain," Berkley's voice came over the radio.

"Go ahead, Commander."

"There's actually about twenty of them and they've split into an attack formation. Do I have permission to fire?"

"Let me try to raise them one more time and if they don't respond, blow them out of the sky," Aidan said and nodded to Luther to try to communicate with them again. He did, and there was only silence. "Cletus, consider this a hostile action against the *Jefferson*. You and your team may fire at will."

"Ma'am, I have Naval Command on the line," Luther said.

"Aidan, this is Edgar Caldwell," the man said.

"Edgar, good to hear your voice." Aidan kept her eyes on the horizon where the black planes spread out and tried to get past Berkley and the others. "You want to tell me who the hell's trying to take me out so close to the U.S. shoreline?"

"We have tight radar security sitting on top of you, but we had a temporary glitch in the system, and it's like they came out of nowhere. They weren't there one second, then all of a sudden the screen came to life. We count twenty-five so far."

"And you've got no idea of who they are or where they came from?"

"We've got a team leaving here to take a look, so try and hang on. You do have the green light in case they actually are stupid enough to fire on you."

"Thanks, Edgar, I'll keep the line open so you can hear what's going on."

❖

Berkley flew into the throat of the formation headed toward them and was impressed at how they dropped and split so she couldn't easily come back and get behind them. "Vader, spilt left and, Killer, you take the right. I'll keep up the middle. I need the rest of you to keep close to the ship. Whoever lets a bullet land on that deck will be running laps for months."

"Cletus, two broke away with us," Hattie said.

Berkley had been joking with Junior when the alarm sounded, and had it been possible she would've loaded him up. He was young, but he'd proven himself enough to make Berkley miss his voice in the situation. Hattie had been waiting when Berkley made it to her jet.

"Let's see what they have in mind," Berkley and the three planes that were on her team started their maneuvers to try to lose their tails.

Berkley gained altitude and went through a series of acrobatics that made it hard for her own team to keep up. She decided to climb because she didn't want to give whoever this was any chance to get close to the ship.

"Captain," Berkley radioed the *Jefferson*.

"Go ahead," Aidan responded immediately.

"What we're looking at is a team of jets that appear to come out of the old Eastern Bloc. They're all of various models that were sold after the Soviet Union broke apart. They're older but in great shape, and whoever's flying them aren't novices."

"Have they engaged?" Aidan said.

Berkley broke left to make everyone behind her follow, and then just as quickly she went right into a loop. It wasn't that she thought she'd lose the lot of them, but it was to draw them farther away from the ship and to see how well armed they were.

"Not yet," she answered when they leveled out, "but it's not for lack of firepower."

"There's backup coming from onshore," Aidan said.

The plane behind her accelerated and did an impressive set of rolls so it could come alongside Berkley. When she realized that was his motive, she adjusted her speed. "Commander," a man's voice came over the radio. "There's no chance of surrender."

"Who is this asshole?" Berkley asked.

"No need to be insulting, Cletus," the man said and chuckled.

"I'd like to know who I'm talking to," Berkley said.

"My name as far as you're concerned is the Grim Reaper, and as I was saying, there's no chance of surrender."

"Interesting thing to say when you're in the air with some of the most elite Naval aviators serving today." Berkley frantically tried to place the voice but came up empty. It didn't sound familiar, but he knew her.

"Nothing like bragging about yourself, Commander."

"I'm not referring to myself, Grim. The team I picked is talented, and I'm proud to have them on my side." Berkley glanced to her left where the guy she assumed was speaking was close to her, but the cockpit was tinted so dark that she couldn't make out any of his features. "Aside from not allowing us to surrender, is there some reason you're here?"

"To fight for my country and rid her of the cancer that's weakening her enough that she's lost her dignity."

"Vader." Berkley changed frequency momentarily while keeping the line open with her shadow. She muted the transmission so he wouldn't hear her orders.

"Go ahead, Cletus."

"Get everyone in position to take all these idiots out." As she gave directions Grim kept pace with her. "A country free to give everyone a chance is worthy of fighting for, but that's not your problem with the situation, is it?" she asked going back to her conversation with Grim.

"Everyone does need to serve, but this isn't your place," Grim said.

"What? I'm supposed to be barefoot and pregnant, or better yet, in the secretarial pool?"

"You can laugh, Cletus, but I'm no different than Paul Revere. I'm warning my people that it's time to take back what's ours."

"Cletus," Hattie broke in. "The plane behind us is trying to lock."

"Shots fired," Killer said.

Berkley flew right into Grim's airspace, and he had no choice but to get out of the way. It was a gamble on her part because if he was that fanatical it'd be like playing chicken with a kamikaze pilot, but Berkley guessed right. Grim was a fanatic but he didn't want to commit outright suicide.

"Let's see what we can do about lighting your lantern, Paul Revere," she said for her own benefit.

The move toward Grim made the plane behind her break his pattern and got her closer to Grim, but Berkley kept driving Grim to her left in an effort to break him from his pack. "What's going on back there, Hattie?" The force of keeping up with Grim was making the bullet wound in her shoulder throb.

"They broke with us, but they haven't tried to take a shot."

"Hang on." Berkley accelerated like she was trying to catch up to Grim to hit him. She was playing the odds again and trying to make him do what most people with fighter pilot training would do. The problem was, she didn't know if he'd had as complete an education as hers from people like her father and Will.

As she got closer he wobbled a bit, then put on a burst of speed to get away from her. She wouldn't do this for the rest of his group, but this one she wanted to down so he'd survive.

She opened her guns when he got in front of her and made a line of puncture marks from his right wing through the tail section. He tried to bank again to get away from her, and she opened fire again, shredding the left wing as well. It didn't take long for the black smoke to color the sky, and he started losing altitude.

"*Jefferson*, radar mark where this plane goes down," Berkley radioed the ship. "As soon as the situation is controlled, send rescue out."

"Roger that, Cletus."

Berkley started another set of rolls to lessen her chances at becoming a target since she figured the rest of the hostiles would come after them now that their leader was going down. Grim was trying to head inland, but he was losing too much altitude to make it back to the U.S. coastline if that's where he'd come from.

For someone used to the unexpected in combat situations, the plane behind her changing directions and blowing Grim out of the sky came as a surprise. They had come to engage, but not let themselves be captured. Since the target had become Grim, it put the pack flying with him at a disadvantage and Berkley took out Grim's killer first.

When Berkley doubled back, her team was engaged with the few remaining planes they hadn't downed yet, but the *Jefferson* pilots hadn't sustained any causalities. From what Berkley could see of the remaining force, Grim had been their best pilot, and he had led his people to slaughter.

"Team leaders," Berkley said, this time not bothering to try to keep her orders from the idiots who'd come to take on her men. "Finish them off, but cut at least three loose."

"Independence force, break away," another pilot said when Berkley was finished. "I repeat, break away." At that, the six remaining planes retreated.

"We need one alive," Berkley said as she turned to give chase. She opened fire on the first plane she came to, trying her best not to hit his fuel tanks. "Target going down, radar mark, please."

The force from the *Jefferson* targeted the other five and fired in the same way—to bring them down but not totally destroy them. As soon as the sky was clear, Berkley flew close to the water in the area the planes went down. She was able to spot three of the six and was disgusted to see not one of them had exited their aircraft.

"Fuck me," she said. "They're choosing to sink." By the time she flew past again, the jets had disappeared into the waters of the Pacific. "Captain, release the boats. The divers might have some luck."

"They're being launched now, Cletus," Aidan said.

"Alpha team on patrol," Berkley said to the planes assigned to her.

"Hour sessions, boss?" Vader asked.

"Sounds good," Berkley said and headed back to the *Jefferson* to make sure it was covered from all sides.

When she landed an hour later the rescue boats were being loaded back on board, and the divers appeared frustrated. Aidan was waiting on deck with her hands on her hips as she stared in her direction.

"You do realize you're wounded, right?" Aidan asked.

"I wouldn't have gone if I didn't think I could do my job. The doctor checked it out while I was visiting Junior."

"He cleared you to fly this much?" Aidan asked and closed her eyes slightly as if daring Berkley to lie. "Because if he did, I didn't get that memo, and I'm not forgetting that yesterday I cut you some slack because of the circumstances."

"I'm back and I'm fine, so don't chew the poor bastard out." Berkley smiled, but judging by Aidan's posture it would take more than charm to cajole her out of her anger. "Any luck on finding anyone so we can figure out where they came from?"

"They picked a good spot to scuttle those things. It's too deep around here for the salvage capabilities we've got on board. A half day closer and I'd put down anchor and let the dive team work."

Berkley nodded her thanks to Hattie and pointed Aiden inside.

"I'm sure they realized that." When they were in the corridor she whispered, "Get pissed at me when we get back to shore, but for now I'm not going to let some lowlifes put a blemish on your record. They can send all they want and I'm going to give them a Stinger enema."

"A girl can't ask for a better knight, baby, but get your ass back to the infirmary if you really don't want me to be pissed." The area had too many people around for Berkley to touch Aidan, but she did look at her like she wanted to lick her from her head on down. "If you don't get down there and stop looking at me that way, you're going to have to break a promise to my father."

"I'll do that, then we need to finish talking to all the crazy people we've got on this boat." Berkley tried to stretch her shoulder without wincing and came close. "It's like they stacked the deck against you to see how well you'd perform under pressure."

"That's why I'm glad you're here, Cletus, if only to let me blow off a little steam." Aidan ran her nail up the zipper of Berkley's flight suit.

CHAPTER THIRTY-SEVEN

Washington, DC

"I want to know what the hell happened, and I want to know who's responsible for this." Peter Khalid stood in the situation room surrounded by his military advisers and Olivia Michaels. "How is it possible for a pack of planes to suddenly appear on the radar and try to destroy an American carrier? I want someone to explain that to me."

"Sir." Sawyer Garner, the man Peter had tapped to take Rodney's place, stood and spoke. "We are looking into that now. With the type of aircraft Commander Levine reported seeing, we've calculated the range of where they could've come from."

"And you've narrowed it down to where exactly?"

"It has to be somewhere close to the west coast. Our best guess for now they came from either the Oregon or Washington coast. Some of those areas are sparsely populated, so it wouldn't be hard to get them in the air with only a few fishermen seeing a force that large flying low enough to evade radar."

"After 9-11 I would think you'd have every area off our coast covered from a hundred feet underwater to infinity, Admiral." Peter glared at the other commanders in the room. "I realize I didn't choose the military route to get here, but I would think one of you would've thought that might've been a good idea."

"We did, sir, and those measures were in place."

"Then I repeat my question of how this happened. Is it that you saw them and thought it would be a good exercise for Commander Levine and the pilots of the *Jefferson*?" Peter closed his eyes briefly. He was trying to rein in his temper, but listening to the exchange between Berkley and the others had as they brought down the hostile planes had driven up his blood pressure.

"Sir, the measures we had put in place were changed this morning," Sawyer said and waited a beat before going on. "The order came from Secretary Orr's office and was verified by Deputy Secretary Lucas Rhodes. It brought the radar down momentarily, then someone changed the radar floor to ten thousand feet."

"That's impossible," Peter said.

"I know that, and Secretary Orr would be the first to tell you that. What we're trying to find now is who hacked into his personal files to figure out his passwords to carry something like this out. It was caught immediately when the men assigned as watchers called in with the change in the system. It took less than half an hour to find the mistake, but it was enough time to get the hostile birds in the air."

"What's your best guess on how that happened, Drew?" Peter asked.

"From what the geek squad I have going through the system said, it was a backdoor left from the previous administration. It gave someone access to not only my password but to everything that's on our network at the Pentagon." Drew sighed after he delivered the news. "The other development is that Jerry Teague died this morning."

"I thought he was under twenty-four hour surveillance?" Peter asked.

"He was, but like Adam Morris he was able to poison himself, only this time the capsule was implanted under the skin of his forearm. We have him on video when he pressed into the spot as if trying to relieve a cramp or something and a few minutes later he was dead."

"Mr. President, we are, in my opinion, under attack, but not from foreign terrorists, but homegrown nuts who must think we are the Antichrist." Olivia pointed to Peter and herself. "If you want my input, until we can prove otherwise, this is the work of Jerry Teague, Adam Morris, and a few of the crew members of the *Jefferson* who are all a part of this New Horizon that Drew and Rooster found. I'm not naïve enough though to believe that they're the masterminds behind this."

"No Joe Blow off the street, no matter how good a hacker they are, could've broken the security firewalls at the Pentagon unless they were working from the inside, with the help of someone high enough to let them into the secure areas to put in the worm they used to change the protocol orders today," Drew said.

"Olivia, I need you on Capitol Hill today to meet with the leadership of the defense committees of both houses and give them a brief report of what's happened," Peter said. "Don't go into great detail yet, and if they bitch tell them we don't know who to trust yet. The members of New Horizon are still a mystery and I hope to God once we do find the key that none of their names are on it."

"I'll be happy to do that," Olivia said.

"What about Rodney?" Peter asked Drew.

"We have him in custody, but he refuses to talk, and in view of what happened with Jerry this morning we've had him scanned for any implants. The prison doctor removed a device like Jerry's from his forearm." Drew put a picture of the item on the screen. "Whoever they were working for, there can be no room for betrayal of their cause even if it means death."

"Starting today, I want everyone working at the Pentagon to undergo a polygraph. I realize they're not reliable, but get it done, and give no one the option of opting out of it. Before something like this happens again I want to know who these people are, who they have as moles, and I want to know where those planes took off from." Peter stared out at nodding heads, but he took the time to look them all in the eye.

"Consider it done, sir," Sawyer said.

"That order also applies to everyone in this room," Peter said and waited for a reaction. "What happened today is treason, plain and simple. If you know of or are a part of this, my suggestion is to turn yourself in. I've said this many times, but I mean it. I might not have been your choice for this job, but I take the oath I swore to very seriously. *Do not* test my resolve on how swiftly or decisively I'll act when I find who is responsible."

The people in uniform in the room stood immediately and snapped to attention.

"Thank you, and you're dismissed until twenty hundred tonight. We'll reconvene to go over what new information we find."

Everyone left except for Drew and Olivia, and they moved closer to Peter. "Did you find what I asked?" Peter asked Drew.

"In the last two years of your predecessor's term, he replaced Don

Rogers as Secretary of Defense with someone who would be a pawn for the real power brokers in the administration, but would appease the public's thirst for Rogers's blood," Drew said.

"I know that part," Peter cut in.

"I realize that too, but the answer you want requires a little history." Drew produced the visitor logs from the Pentagon for the day Rogers had been replaced. "The new secretary met with Don for four hours as his first item of business, but the meeting was also attended by former Vice President Dick Chandler."

"The man is an ass who got us into a lot of the messes Olivia and I'll have to clean up, hopefully in the next eight years, but there's no way he's involved in this," Peter said with a laugh.

"I'm not saying he is, Peter, but I do think that day was when the worm was put in place, and I'm sure it was sold to the new simpleton as being important to national security. Dick didn't spend all that time in his bunker alone. He had some of the best technical minds in there trying to help him rule the world."

"And you think he had one of those computer geeks put in something so he could keep tabs on what was happening over there after Don left? Wait, don't answer that," he said as if something had dawned on him in that moment. "It wasn't a problem when they put the replacement in, it was what came after. Even if my opponent in the election had won, there was no way he'd let Dick and his cronies anywhere near the important information again."

"I don't have proof of that, sir, but that's exactly what I think happened. Even after you started putting people in, someone has been monitoring all the information coming through the Pentagon's system and cherry-picking the items that would cause the most damage to you."

"If that's true, we need to build a solid case against everyone involved because we'll only get one bite at the apple while it's still on the branch. Screw it up and some of these bastards will walk, and they'll destroy any information that'll connect them to anything," Peter said.

"The answers lie with Rodney for now, and the key to getting them is Walby," Drew said. "I'll make sure he knows he has the green light to turn that key as many times as he needs to get the lock to open."

❖

USS *Jefferson*

"Miss me?" Berkley asked Blazer once she unlocked his cell door. "I've been doing nothing but thinking of you since the last time I saw you."

"I hate to disappoint you, but you haven't crossed my mind." Blazer sat on his bunk, and despite the normal temperature, his shirt was wet with sweat. "What happened to the force that just attacked?"

"They challenged an American carrier, what do you think happened to them?" Berkley stood with her fists on her hips which made the khaki shirt pull across her shoulders. She chose the posture because she could take up as much space as possible.

"Considering what happened on our mission, maybe they thought it'd be an easy thing."

"Actually, it was easy on our part, and when you get a lot of help from the people supposedly attacking you, it was a breeze."

"What are you talking about?" Blazer leaned forward so far it looked like his stomach hurt.

"I shot down their leader so he'd have to eject because I wanted to meet this Grim Reaper, but his own man blew him away." Berkley watched as Blazer's usual sour demeanor cracked into a picture of pain, and he started to rock on his bunk.

"He's dead?" Blazer asked with tears soaking his cheeks.

"Friend of yours?" Berkley asked, shocked at his reaction to the news.

"Get out," Blazer screamed. "Leave me alone."

"There's one more thing." Berkley decided to put aside the questions and anger at what he'd done to her and Junior. "I understand Devin and the captain told you about the information we received about your father. You might not believe me, but I am sorry for your loss, and once we're in port, representatives from the Pentagon will inform you of the details since he was in their custody when he decided on the route he did."

"Get out," Blazer repeated but without the volume. "Leave me alone."

"What the hell was that?" Devin asked as soon as Blazer's door was closed.

"I've got a good guess, but let's talk to Hattie one more time," Berkley said and called Aidan to meet them.

"You think Hattie held out?" Devin asked and had to almost jog to keep up with Berkley.

"Hattie's a sweet kid who's confused as to what side she's fighting for, and she's going to tell Aidan everything or I'm going to fling her ass off this boat myself."

The interrogation room was empty, but Devin sat next to Berkley. "This Grim Reaper was related to Blazer, wasn't he?" Devin asked and then sent a request to the Navy for the personnel section of Blazer's file.

"When you get that," Berkley said and pointed at the screen, "I'll give you a month's salary if he doesn't have a brother who's either too young or has something physically wrong that kept him out of the aviation program."

A picture popped up on the screen of a nice-looking young man with blond hair and eyes so blue they resembled lasers. The small paragraph included with it identified Travis Morris, age eighteen, who was on the list to enter the Naval Academy when he graduated from high school. Blazer's younger brother bore no family resemblance to him and it made Berkley wonder what his mother looked like.

"What's up?" Aidan asked when she arrived. "You're supposed to be resting," she told Berkley.

"Ma'am, we've got some developments." Devin told her about Berkley's meeting with Blazer and showed her Travis's picture.

"You think this kid was in one of those planes?" Aidan asked Berkley.

"Not only was he in one of the planes, I think you're looking at Grim Reaper. When I was up there and he was taunting me, there was something familiar about his moves. It didn't dawn on me until now because I haven't spent enough time in the air with Blazer, but he was definitely one of Travis's flight instructors."

"That I get, but what does Hattie have to do with all this?" Aidan asked.

"Maybe nothing and maybe everything. When I talked to Blazer he knew those planes were coming, and I don't believe any of Devin's men gave him the heads up. Am I right?" Berkley asked Devin.

"My orders were to keep them locked up and to give them no information unless it was approved by the captain."

"Then how did he know, and why did he have such a bad reaction when I told him what happened? The information to attack came from someone on the mainland, but we have to be absolutely sure about that, and that's why we need to talk to our messenger pigeon."

"The world's off-kilter if we're being attacked by our own people," Aidan said with a shake of her head. "What's there to gain from that?"

"That's someone else's job to find out, but they'd better hurry. Whoever sent those kids to their deaths for nothing deserves to rot in a hole somewhere."

"You requested to see me again, Commander?" Hattie said a few minutes later.

"Have a seat," Aidan said.

"Hattie, I'm going to warn you about lying before we start, but I have faith it's not necessary and you're going to do the right thing here," Berkley said, trying her best to be nice. "Was the message you got out for Erika the only one?"

Hattie sat back and sighed. Instead of answering she grabbed two handfuls of hair and acted as if she was going to cry. It was Aidan who lost patience first.

"You may feel like we're picking on you, but before you answer you should ask yourself if we already know the answer," Aidan said.

"If you know already, ma'am, why am I here?" Hattie asked.

"Because Commander Levine thinks you deserve a chance to redeem yourself for doing something you didn't realize was so harmful," Aidan said. She glanced at Berkley, who stood behind Hattie and had her thumb up. "Blazer knew we were attacked, yet he's confined with no communications except for anyone approved by me. Since I know none of Devin's men told him anything, how'd he know that?"

"I didn't send anything out, and I don't care what you think you know. It wasn't me." Hattie dropped her head and was gripping the edge of the table as if she'd slide away if she let go. "You might be in charge, but I know I've got rights, so I'm going back to work. If you've really got all this evidence against me I guess you'll lock me up too." Hattie stood.

"Sit your ass down," Berkley said loudly. "You go when you're dismissed and not before." With the information Devin had given her, she now knew she'd been wrong about Hattie. "No one said anything about you sending a message out."

"It's good to know you realize I'm not that stupid," Hattie said.

"But you did get one and deliver it to Blazer," Berkley said, now sure that's what had happened. "You chose this idiot over your country because you thought he had a right to bitch? Isn't that what you said about Erika? What you should've asked yourself is why he was in trouble in the first place."

"The message came through a couple of days after Erika asked me to send the first one. She told me those planes were part of a secret exercise sanctioned by the Navy to test our preparedness. They weren't supposed to shoot at anyone."

"For your sake aren't you glad I'm better than the pilots we faced? If not, your stupidity could've really cost you." Berkley felt the anger build in her chest, and Hattie was only a small reason why. She was most upset with herself. "Since you can't do enough for Blazer and Erika, I think you should join them."

"Captain, isn't that your call?" Hattie asked.

"Commander Levine saved me the trouble," Aidan said. "Devin, take her down and we'll turn over the lot of them once we make port." Hattie stood and started to move before Devin could touch her. "What the hell happened to respect for your superior officers?" Aidan asked Berkley when they were alone again.

"I was thinking the same thing and something finally dawned on me." Berkley stared at the closed door distractedly.

"You're doing pretty good so far if you ask me, so I can't wait to hear what else you figured out."

"That's why whatever all this is has worked so well." Berkley fell in a chair, suddenly feeling very tired.

"What are you talking about?"

"Think about the service and the security forces today and how they've all changed since September Eleventh. It's tight and the security measures are ridiculously redundant. For someone from the outside to break them would be next to impossible, so whoever the puppet master is—"

"Controls on the lowest level," Aidan finished for her.

"Makes sense, doesn't it?" Berkley asked and nodded. "People like you give orders, but you don't actually send the messages or follow the chain of who gets the orders. This crap we've faced worked because their boss recruited the worker bees, not too many people in command."

"How do we find them all then?"

"It depends on the level of organization and what they hope to accomplish. This might only be resolved from the top down."

"How else would they do it?"

"For something like this, finding the top will be as difficult as trying to round up everyone like Hattie." Berkley stretched and winced when it pulled at her wound. "The fleet of jets they sent against us proves they've got money and a gaggle of recruits. What I don't understand is why challenge us at all?"

"I'll leave that up to men like Drew Orr."

"The problem with that, Captain, is that people like Drew Orr will expect the answers from someone like you. If I'm right about that, you have to prepare yourself for your retirement to be delayed."

"I love it when you're right, but I hope to hell you're way off target this time." Aidan gazed at her and opened her mouth a couple of times before finally speaking. "If you're not though, what happens then?"

"We get free clothes and cool toys for a couple more years." Berkley smiled. "Whatever happens, I think we proved ourselves adequately enough that we can serve together."

"Then we get the picket fence?"

"I even come with a dog."

"Which reminds me..." Aidan glanced at her watch and started to get up. "You promised me a story about the name Cletus."

"I thought you would've figured it out when Dad christened Harvey with Junior."

They walked to the mess hall together and greeted quite a few people along the way. "Isn't your dog's name Junior?" Aidan asked.

Berkley nodded and handed her a tray. "Junior is *our* dog," she whispered, "and he comes from a long line of champion hunters, so it's in his blood to find his prey. Dad thought it'd bring Harvey luck to share his name."

"And Cletus?"

"That'd be Junior's great-granddaddy, and Dad's favorite dog of all time. The day I got my wings he thought I deserved the name, and not before."

Aidan laughed as she loaded up her tray. "Not exactly ferocious sounding, but it suits you."

"Maybe later you could pet me," Berkley whispered again and made Aidan stumble with her tray.

The rest of their trip was uneventful. Berkley tried to talk to Jin a few more times before they reached the rendezvous point. Jin was polite, accepted the food Berkley brought, but didn't answer any question except to say she was fine.

When the Marine Osprey landed, Berkley walked Jin to the craft and wished her well. Jin bowed and shook Berkley's hand before boarding without a problem. Lowe wasn't nearly as cooperative.

The short, portly man had to be carried on as he screamed obscenities in both Korean and English. When the craft lifted off Berkley felt as if this wasn't the last she'd see of Jin, and if it wasn't, she looked forward to having a real conversation with her when Jin felt comfortable enough to go beyond the niceties.

CHAPTER THIRTY-EIGHT

Northern Virginia

"Anything yet?" Rooster asked when he joined Drew at the monitor. The room the feed was coming from had three interrogators working with Walby, but their target, Rodney James, still had his jaw set in a defiant pose. It'd been three days and he was still nowhere close to cracking.

"We've learned new and inventive ways to use the standard curse words," Drew said.

"How did we get here?" Rooster asked and tapped the screen over Rodney's forearm, which was covered with a bandage where the poison device had been removed. "This kook was advising the president not that long ago."

Drew put his hand up when Walby opened a file on New Horizons. "Hang on, and see if he changes his story any."

"Rodney, we've picked up and questioned all the people on the list, and you're the only one with the grape Kool-Aid sewn into his arm," Walby said. He was way beyond trying to be polite. "They've never heard of all this, and have agreed to cooperate however they can." He slammed the file in front of Rodney so hard that he jumped in his seat. "You listed over thirty wild goose chases and it's time to tell us why. Think about your family and everything you stood for."

"That's what I'm doing." Rodney picked up the folder and flung it at Walby's head. "It's time to stand up for what's right."

Walby and his men laughed. "In case it hasn't sunk in, you're standing alone. Your buddies decided to desert you in spectacular fashion. Jerry and Adam cracked after ten minutes of questioning, not exactly what you were looking for in some allies, I'm guessing."

"Eventually, they'll have their reward when things change."

Walby walked around the table and put his hands on Rodney. "When what changes?" he asked as he squeezed Rodney's shoulders. "I'm sure you're sick of being in here, but not as tired as I am asking you the same goddamn thing over and over." He let him go and moved so Rodney could see him. "So hopefully your last answer is a signal that you're willing to make this easy on yourself."

"Walby, you're a traitor to the cause." Rodney stood and walked toward the door as if daring anyone to stop him.

"Wilfred, the monitors please," Walby said and the video feed Drew and Rooster were watching went dark. "Don't say I didn't warn you, Rodney."

"You wouldn't dare touch me," Rodney said with contempt.

"The president needs answers and it's my duty to get them," Walby said. Behind him the men with him readied a board. On the floor was a bucket of water with a towel floating in it.

"That pansy doesn't have the balls to deal with threats the way we did," Rodney said, but his eyes were glued to the bucket.

"When a force tried to sink one of our carriers, he knew the rules changed, but I give him credit for trying to give you the respect you don't deserve," Walby said and cocked his head in Rodney's direction.

Despite the facility's thick walls, Drew and Rooster heard Rodney's muffled cries. It took less than thirty minutes for Walby to get the answers he needed. When he gave Drew the information, he watched the shock register as much as when he'd first heard it.

"You think the information is reliable?" Drew asked.

"It doesn't take much to get people to talk, and we'll verify what he said in a few hours with another interview. The last thing Rodney wants is to repeat the last hour, so he'll talk. Our job is to compare stories." One of Walby's team delivered a written report of what Walby had said. "If you want my opinion—he's telling the truth. At least enough of the truth that he's missing his little implant. I understand their purpose now more than ever."

"Keep at it, and we'll check with you at midnight," Drew said. "With this information, our meeting with the president has to be tonight, but I need Aidan and Commander Levine here and that's about how much time they'll need to make the trip."

"For the first time in all the years I've been doing this, I hope I'm wrong," Walby said.

"Me too, but we've got no choice other than to stop this before it takes hold with anyone else," Drew said.

"Sir, we have a call coming in for you on a secure line," one of the guards said from the door to Drew. "It's not anyone we can ID yet, so we're trying to trace the call."

"Secretary Orr," Drew said and listened for anything strange or identifying in the background.

"You have four of my people in custody." The voice was being manipulated to sound metallic so there was no way to know if it was a man or woman. "You have ten minutes to release them or there'll be a consequence you won't like."

"Would you like to give me a hint as to who that might be, or should I release everyone in custody across the country?" Drew said.

"The three on the *Jefferson* I could almost understand, but Rodney James is a decorated hero and deserved a lot more respect than what you've shown so far."

"Who is this?" Drew locked eyes with Rooster and Walby, who were listening, but they both shook their heads. The trace the team was running was on the screen but it was bouncing off towers across the globe.

"In good time, Mr. Secretary, but right now you're on the clock. You have ten minutes to release Rodney James, Lieutenant David Morris, Lieutenant Alan Lewis, and Lieutenant Erika Gibson. My demands have also been sent to the White House, so consider yourself and your boss warned."

The line went dead. "Anything?" Drew asked.

"No, sir," one of the technical team answered. "Whoever it was has some sophisticated anti-tracing equipment."

"I thought we plugged the leaks in here?" Rooster said.

"The computers were sealed, or so the geek squad said, and that might be true," Walby added. "But there are more ways than the Internet to gather information."

"Way ahead of you," Drew said and handed the phone to Rooster.

"Tell your men to match up names to all phone calls made out of the office. I want to know who was on the other end." He picked up another line and put out the red alert, calling up their national security forces.

"Sir, President Khalid on line one."

"What the hell is going on?" Peter sounded angry. "If these people are trying to make us look like incompetent idiots, we're doing everything we can to accommodate them."

"We're working on finding the caller and I've got the planes in the air and troops on standby, sir," Drew said. He took the report from their national radar grid from Rooster. There wasn't anything in the air so far that didn't belong there.

"We'll see how ready we are in five minutes," Peter said.

Drew felt as if he could do more from his office, but there was no time. When the mark hit three minutes, the caller was back on the line. "I've received no calls and I take it none are forthcoming."

"If you're familiar with American policy, you have to know we *do not* negotiate with terrorists," Drew said. The line was being traced again as Drew's team and the president's office listened in. "There'll be no release of anyone in custody."

"I knew that when I gave you the ten minutes," the mechanical voice said.

"Then why waste your time making threats?" Drew asked.

"I made no threat, Mr. Secretary, it was a promise. Khalid thought he could promote some people like you and show the public how fair-minded he is, but all he's done is weaken our military to the point that we'll lose the respect we fought so hard to gain in the last eight years."

"The last eight years have been nothing but an exercise in weakening our military. Promoting people who want to serve with honor is helping to rebuild it," Drew countered as he watched the signal bounce from one tower to the next around the world. This guy was probably down the street having coffee as he made his idle threats.

"Then I dedicate my next action to you, Khalid, Captain Aidan Sullivan, and Commander Berkley Levine," the voice said and the line went dead before they could pinpoint the location of the call.

"Anything?" Drew asked when he put the phone down.

"Nothing yet, sir," one of the guards reported, his radio alive with chatter but no sign of alarm yet.

"Let's get back to the office for now so we can monitor the situation and work on our report for tonight's meeting with the joint chiefs," Drew told Rooster. As the driver reached the door that led to Drew's office, his phone rang and the excited voice on the other end told him that the caller's threats were real and an area south of Coos Bay, Oregon, had been bombed.

"Any injuries?" Drew asked as he and Rooster jogged into the building.

"We're sending people into the area now, sir. We called the local police and National Guard to seal off the area until our forensic teams can get in there."

"Where in the hell did this come from?" Drew asked the staff assembled in his office.

"The strike didn't come from the air. From the first accounts we've gotten, we think it came from the water. I've got water patrol searching for anything that could launch something big enough to destroy the swath of land we're talking about here," Admiral Sawyer Garner said. "The president's been informed and everyone's been put on the investigation into where these assholes got this much firepower to begin with."

"Start with an inventory of our own stocks. I want it finished by tonight." The phone rang on Drew's desk and the technician sitting at the tracking computer pointed to the phone. "Drew Orr," he said when he picked up the receiver.

"Now you know I'm serious," the mechanical voice said and laughed.

"What I know now is that you're a terrorist who's killed I don't know how many innocent lives yet, and for no good reason."

"Nonsense, Secretary Orr, you know as well as I do that some innocent lives must be lost in war. It's not pretty, but no different than when our founding fathers started their quest for freedom." Drew watched the screen again as the bastard spoke and knew there was no way they'd catch him by conventional means. "New Horizon isn't really new but a return to the way things are supposed to be before the gullible American public was seduced by the Antichrist they've put in the Oval Office."

"If you're such a patriot of the people, why go through such lengths to disguise yourself?" Drew asked.

"All in good time, but you should stop wasting your time with Rodney and the others. They've all taken an oath not to talk."

"We found their nice little surgical enhancements, so the only two of you who are permanently silent are Adam and Jerry. The others are in our hands now and I'll do whatever it takes to break them, so enjoy your sick game while you can, but we *will* find you."

"The only way that's going to happen is if I turn myself in." The aggravating laugh came again. "You're in over your head, as is your boss, but I'm getting ready to rectify that by showing the public what true order really means. That they can go to bed at night and sleep well knowing that they are tucked safely under the blanket of safety that exists only if people like you are shown the door."

"My kind? What exactly does that mean?"

"The kind of man who puts two incompetent bitches in charge of a mission that had disastrous results, and the kind of man who thinks that's progress. Your boss also took out the most devoted men working at the Pentagon and replaced them with doves like you. Any progress that was made, you gave away so that our enemies will see us only as the weakling you and your kind represent."

"You blew up American soil because the *Jefferson* has a woman at the helm and I'm not a warmonger? Are you insane or totally stupid?"

"What I am is generous." The inflection never changed, but the volume went up. "I'm telling you that the war has begun whether you want to acknowledge it or not, and I'll continue to hit you until the seduction I mentioned ends and the public begs me to take charge so the bleeding will stop. And the two I'll begin with are your little poster girls you've put before us as the two shining examples of the new military. That's a bigger joke than when Khalid was sworn in."

The line went down again and Drew didn't bother to ask if there'd been any luck on the trace. Instead he asked to be patched to the *Jefferson*, then to the president.

❖

USS *Jefferson*

"The captain needs you on the bridge," Devin told Berkley. She was standing at the railing on the main deck talking to the other pilots.

"You ready to take me flying?" Aidan asked when Berkley stood next to her and waited to be acknowledged. "Secretary Orr expects us in Washington by tonight if possible."

"Did they find where all those jets flew out of?"

"There was a private airstrip in the middle of a thick stretch of forest in Oregon. We believe they destroyed it with four missiles fired from a ship off the coast." Aidan gave control of navigation over to her second and started for the deck. "The team the FBI sent in said there was space for seventy planes, but the place was deserted, which kept the casualties to zero. A small wood mill nearby didn't fare as well."

"When it came to the airstrip, was it a case of wishful thinking or good planning?" Berkley thought about what kind of damage another heavily armed forty-five planes could do around the country if they really existed. "No other clues left behind?"

"I'm sure the twenty people who died because they had the bad luck of being at work today are considered a ton of evidence, but that's it. Whoever's responsible called Secretary Orr before and after it happened. The shit storm that caused is why he wants to talk to us." Aidan turned her face to the cool breezed coming off the water. "My father's known Drew for years, so I'm not surprised at how many resources he's dumping into this. We're beyond a couple of disgruntled people playing soldier, I think."

"Who are you going to put in charge here? Because you leaving now isn't exactly how it's supposed to work."

"I've put a team together with people like Devin and Luther, and they know what to do. I trust them."

"Okay then," Berkley said.

It seemed to Aidan that the words had just left her lover's lips when she was in the backseat of Berkley's jet lined up for takeoff.

Five hours and a few pit stops later they landed outside Washington and were met by Rooster and some of his men.

"Thank you for getting here so quickly." Rooster shook hands with them. "We're going directly to the meeting and then we'll put you up for the night."

"Sounds good," Aidan said as Berkley nodded next to her holding their bags. "But I've got an apartment here, so when we're done I'd rather stay there."

"Consider it done, Captain." Rooster waved up the driver. "Now, if you're ready." He held open the back door.

"Am I alone in feeling that there's a big sack of shit hovering over us and somebody's getting ready to drop it on us?" Aidan asked Berkley in a low voice.

"It's when you wish you had a total security clearance to know everything that's going on."

"Careful what you wish for, Cletus, because too much information is sometimes worse than none at all."

"I doubt we're getting that, so I'm not worried."

"Uh-huh," Aidan said without conviction.

When the vehicle stopped, it occurred to Berkley that they hadn't had the chance to call their parents and tell them they were back. "Depends on what this is, but if we can, we should go see your folks tomorrow," she told Aidan.

"My father's already crazy about you, but I'm sure once I tell him what you said it'll knock you up a few notches."

The guard at the White House gate asked everyone for their IDs before they were allowed in. Their escorts moved them quickly through the door and into the basement situation room where Drew and Rooster were already waiting.

"Madame Vice President," Aidan said when another door opened and Olivia Michaels stepped in. "It's a pleasure to meet you, ma'am."

"Sorry to drag you off the *Jefferson* before you had the chance to dock her." The vice president shook Aidan's hand and then Berkley's. "Commander, I'm glad to see you doing so well. How's the shoulder?" The invited military personnel filed in as the vice president was speaking.

"Healing nicely, ma'am," Berkley said.

"Aidan." Drew stepped up and gave her a warm hug. "Great job on picking a good crew and getting out with so little casualties considering what was thrown at you." Drew shook Berkley's hand with both of his. "It's an honor, Commander."

"Thanks, and likewise," Berkley said and glanced around quickly at the rest of the people who'd arrived. "Considering your guests tonight, can I ask why we're here?"

"Protecting our country is about to become a different animal, and—"

"We need all the help we can get," President Khalid finished for him. "At ease, everyone, and let's get to it."

Drew pulled two chairs for Aidan and Berkley before he sat next to the president. "We talked with Rodney right before the terrorist with the little voice changer called, and he finally filled in some blanks for us," Drew said.

"He's referring to retired Admiral Rodney James," the vice president filled in for Aidan and Berkley.

"The meeting confirmed the bits of information we've been able to collect after what happened to Commander Levine."

"What did Rodney cough up?" Vice President Michaels asked.

"New Horizons is more of a movement than a business. It has a command structure much like our military, but their mission is to put in place a much more dictatorial government."

"They want to overthrow the government?" one of the generals asked. "That's ludicrous, and more like Rodney having some fun at your expense."

"I'd agree with you, but consider where we are right now." Drew stood. "We are fighting two wars and deployed in other hot spots around the world. What was supposed to be a short stint in Iraq has become a quagmire."

"A perfect storm since the people entrusted with our safety are at their most fatigued, that's true." The president leaned back in his chair. "Still, that doesn't compute in my mind as to how Rodney, or whoever he's working with, thinks they can be successful."

"Storms can be tracked, but they're still a guessing game as to where and when they'll hit until they're right on you. In this case the storm was carefully created and controlled until Commander Levine dropped those bombs on her target. Not until then was the plan unleashed," Drew said.

"What exactly is that?" Vice President Michaels asked.

"It was supposed to start with the sinking of the *Jefferson* by their air corps once the ship was in range of the U.S. coastline, followed by some wishful thinking in hoping for retaliation from North Korea on American soil." Drew could feel the frustration growing in the room. "That was the plan, and I'm not trying to hold back, but you all need to have a complete picture."

"What I've heard so far is shit," the general said.

"What we have, sir, is millions of dollars missing from the Pentagon's budget and put into blind accounts that are going to take months to find," Drew said. "That money obviously was used to finance New Horizon's revolution. What I don't know yet is if there are any weapons missing as well as the cash, but since they don't sell guided missiles at your local supermarket, I'm going with the assumption that they stole some of those as well."

"Granted, having a unit of jets go against our people was crazy," Rodney's replacement Sawyer Garner said, "but there's no sign of any militia that organized working within our borders."

"Not yet. But remember those who lived here for years leading unassuming lives until they decided to bring down the Towers," Drew said. "And before any of you start preaching about how that can never happen again, know that Rodney wasn't the top man, and we don't have a clue as to how many runts like Blazer they have. But the reason we're here is to decide on a course of action to deal with who Rodney said *is* in charge. If he's telling the truth, then the cleared patch of land in Oregon will be the first of many."

"He cracked on that?" Olivia said.

"Rodney did give us a name, yes." Drew took a deep breath. "The leader and creator of New Horizon is Dick Chandler."

"The former vice president?" Peter asked incredulously. "Tell me you're joking."

"When Rodney said his name, a lot of this made more sense," Drew said. "It had to be someone with power to put all this together, especially when it came to the people he was able to recruit. The wrench in all this not moving as fast as Dick had planned was you, Aidan."

"How so?" Aidan asked.

"The initial message sent to Jerry Teague mentioned you were being a problem, and whether you knew at the time, you managed to lock away some of the people put onboard to give you the most headaches."

"You were also a problem for them, Commander," Rooster told Berkley. "Their main battle cry was to use you as an example of what needs to be changed under a new rule. Too bad you not only lived but you carried your partner out of there, which didn't exactly fit with their theory of where women belong or don't."

"Are they still questioning Rodney?" Peter asked.

"That'll continue for some time," Drew said. "I'm having the detainees moved to the facility for questioning as well. We need to get answers and fast before we have any more incidents like Coos Bay, and I think we should use any means necessary to do that."

"To review then, the money comes from the Pentagon, and Rodney's named Dick Chandler as the mastermind," Peter said.

"That's correct, sir," Drew answered. "I really don't want to believe it, but it's the only scenario that makes sense to me the more I think about it. No matter how you look at this, Chandler's involvement and the power he held under the last administration was the only way he could've infiltrated the way he did. That he surrounded himself with people like Jerry Teague and Adam Morris explains the recruits willing to give up their lives, and that he gave people like Rodney free rein for so long explains a lot as well."

"We'll go with that assumption then that Chandler is indeed behind this, but I want him brought in under the radar. If there's a leak I'm going to assume it came from someone in this room and you'll find yourself without a place at this table if anyone decides to go that route," Peter said. "If the information gathered so far is correct, then the terrorist's game has changed, but this is no Ruby Ridge or Waco."

Peter pointed to Duke Stiel, the current head of the FBI, who had so far nodded at everything he'd said. "I want you to split this investigation between your agency and Drew's people, Duke."

"It might be better if we bring Mr. Chandler in for questioning since he's still advising Congress on energy matters. We can tell him that we need his help with some vetting issues." Duke paused as if to see if there would be any objections. "This is a man with deep connections in every branch of government, industry, and foreign entities, so we have to tread carefully."

"If he's guilty then he's going down, I don't care who he knows," Sawyer said.

"I'll be glad to be the one who escorts him to a small cell one day, but we need to have all the facts we can get our hands on before we accuse someone like this of treason and terrorism. Shoot blind and he'll drive anyone working for him underground so deep it'll take dynamite to find them," Duke said and pointed at Sawyer. "Do you want that?"

"I think we can all agree that something has to be done, and all the evidence collected as soon as we can," Peter said. He knocked on the table once with his knuckles to bring the meeting back under control. "I want you to break into teams and get this done."

"Sir, I don't mean to interrupt, but what would you like from Commander Levine and me?" Aidan asked.

The president gazed at her and smiled. "Everyone, if you could excuse us a minute, I'd like to speak to Capitan Sullivan and Commander Levine," he said and everyone headed for the door. "Drew, please join us."

"Mr. President, before we begin I'd like to thank you for the privilege you honored me with when you gave me the helm of the *Jefferson*. I realize that things didn't turn out like we planned, but it'll be the highlight of my career," Aidan said.

"Aidan, I hope that you don't mind me calling you that," the president said and Aidan nodded. "I'm not here to tell you what a bad job you did, because from the reports I've gotten what you were able to do in this situation is beyond the call and deserves congratulations from a grateful nation. You and Berkley epitomize what's right with the military."

"Thank you, sir," Berkley said.

"Before I answer you as to why you're here, let me tell you a little story." The president waved them closer. "I promise I don't bite," he joked. "I started my career working in the inner city with kids no one gave a damn about, and that got me to the city council and eventually to the state house. The senate was a fluke chance that worked out for me in the end, and I was able to get a pretty good promotion from the American people. Through it all what I learned on the streets held true no matter what office I held."

"What's that, sir?" Berkley asked.

"That people who think like Rodney and Dick Chandler, if that's who he's working for, take one look at segments of society and totally dismiss them because of their beliefs. It's only a woman, or a black man, or whoever they think is beneath them and they move on."

The president talked in his usual elegant but calm style even though his audience was so small, and Berkley found herself nodding. "You might come from New York, sir, but my father volunteers his time in New Orleans working with the kids you were just talking about. You can decide to dismiss them if you like, but if you turn your back on any of them you'll find yourself wising you'd paid more attention."

"Then you understand where I'm coming from," the president said. "This is going to play out one of two ways. If this is Dick, he's either going to totally ignore you as a non-threat, or having you two involved will make him concentrate his people into bringing you down."

"So our new official role will be bait?" Aidan asked.

"I'm not taking your commission away from you, Aidan, but I'm asking you to come ashore for a bit and lead this investigation with Berkley. If I sign the order, the choice will be out of your hands, but I'd rather it be voluntary on both your parts." The president stood and held out his hand. "So to answer your question, you can consider yourself bait, but if I'm right this time around the shark will find himself on the dock gutted and filleted, hating himself for not paying closer attention."

"That's very complimentary, sir, thank you." Berkley stood and shook his hand. It wasn't the job she'd signed up for when she decided to follow Aidan, but the president was right. Shaking his hand made it a binding agreement, but the different agencies and people they'd have to work with would know it was something they took on. For morale later on if things didn't go well, that would go a longer way than if the team the president put together thought they were working with someone forced to be at their side.

"We'll do our best not to let you down," Aidan added.

"Considering what I've asked of you already, I'm not worried. You've earned your spots at this table, and Drew will see that you get the support you need to do what's necessary," the president said and told them good night.

"If it's not something you really want to do, I'll talk to him," Drew said when the president left.

"Do you really think the former vice president is planning a coup against the government?" Berkley asked.

"You wouldn't be here if I didn't think that," Drew said. "The country has become a place people like Dick don't recognize anymore, and it's being led by a man who doesn't fit their mold of someone who deserves the office. Things like that make a man crazy, and we're in for some insane times."

"Don't worry, Drew, we're going to work with you," Aidan said.

"That makes me feel better since I know I can trust you, and with who's been recruited for the other side, that level of trust has been in short supply lately."

"Let's get to it, then," Berkley said.

Chapter Thirty-nine

D uke Stiel pulled his jacket down as the agent driving turned into the long, winding driveway that led to former Vice President Chandler's Virginia estate. The charcoal suit suddenly felt too tight on him as he contemplated having to bring in the man a good number of people in the high levels of government and some of the public thought was the real brains behind the last administration. Dick might've been unpopular with the general public, but in law enforcement circles like the FBI, he held near hero status because he'd fought so hard to lower the standards to make cases or actually question someone.

"Is he expecting us, sir?" the agent asked.

This wasn't the first time Duke had been to the farm, as Dick referred to it, and they had never followed the drive to the front door. That was only for guests who weren't friends of the former vice president, and they were welcomed but kept at arm's length. Duke's visits had never started at the front door but rather around back where the large mahogany paneled study had its own private entrance.

"No. So go around front," Duke said, willing to carry out the president's orders but also wanting to give his old friend a warning that this wasn't a friendly visit.

The big house came into view and the strategically placed lights illuminated the stately columns that lined the front of the two-story house that sat nestled in a stand of large trees. It was lit but there was no movement to alert them that anyone was home, and Duke almost let out a relieved breath.

They'd brought along only two cars. Enough to accommodate the Secret Service men assigned to Dick and his wife if she wanted to accompany him, so Duke put his hand up to keep them in their seats.

With one last tug at his clothing, Duke climbed the ten steps to the door and hesitated before he pressed the doorbell, listening for any sound from inside. The only noise was the hum of the Suburbans behind him and the call of an owl in the distance.

When he pressed the bell there was only a sudden but brief excruciating pain.

❖

Aidan stood in the middle of her bedroom toweling off her hair after the long, hot shower she'd shared with Berkley. The apartment that had for so long seemed like a storage unit for her clothes and bed felt more like a home with Berkley walking around the place in a robe, waiting for the pizza they'd ordered.

They had chosen to put off any discussion of their surreal day until they'd eaten and slept for at least six hours. "This seems weird, doesn't it?" she called out to Berkley.

The phone rang and the doorman gave her notice that the pizza delivery man was on his way up. "What?" Berkley asked when she came in to retrieve her wallet.

"Pay the guy and then I'll tell you," Aidan said and laughed when Berkley tweaked her nipple and closed the door behind her. "It's a good thing she still doesn't like to share," Aidan told her reflection when she went back into the bathroom to hang up the wet towel. She joined Berkley at the counter that separated her den from the kitchen and sat next to her on one of the tall stools in a pair of sleep pants and T-shirt with *Navy* stitched across her chest.

Berkley opened the refrigerator and opened two cold beers before she sat down. "What's strange aside from the fact that there are big chunks of pineapple on my pizza?" Berkley asked.

"That's not strange, baby, so quit complaining and try it." Aidan held up her piece to Berkley's mouth. "What I was talking about is that this is such a normal night here with you, doing what I'm sure a lot of people are right now, and yet there's all this stuff going on. Do you think their theory is too out there?"

"I'm sure we'll have a better idea once we get to read all the info they collected now that we have those dandy all-clearance decoder rings the president gave us." Berkley laughed. "Seriously, though, I'd tell you it's all bullshit, but nothing surprises me anymore. People don't feel right about something these days and they pick up a gun instead of uttering a word."

"I have a few words for you." Aidan fed Berkley some more pizza. She gladly put it down when Berkley gently batted her hand away and kissed her. When Berkley's tongue passed her lips, all the stress that had built up from the moment they left the *Jefferson*'s deck gave way and another feeling altogether flourished in her groin.

This was what she missed about Berkley the most. Her lover was to most a hardnosed military pilot who had a habit of knocking you on your ass if you were out of line, but then there was this side of her that only a few had ever experienced. Berkley had a way of building a desire in you that robbed you of any reason or caution that could arise in your brain.

The leather sofa in her den felt cold under her back for only a moment when Berkley put her down after carrying her there, but the discomfort was short lived when Berkley snaked her hand under her shirt and squeezed her breast and sucked her nipple through the garment. The television was on, but the soft murmurs of MSNBC were easy to ignore as Berkley lay next to her.

"I don't want to wait," Aidan said out of breath. "Please, baby."

"I thought about this when I was walking through that barren landscape praying that I'd see you again," Berkley said softly before she moved to the other breast. "That I'd get to do this again." She flattened her hand and ran it down Aidan's stomach and under the elastic of her sleep pants.

Aidan closed her eyes and let the deep voice fill the cold, empty places in her like hot chocolate on a winter's day. Her skin felt like it was on fire and the pressure in her groin was building to the point that she thought she'd come the second Berkley put her hand between her legs.

"That's what scared me the most," Berkley said, her hand stopped on the top of Aidan's sex.

"What?" Aidan opened her eyes and placed her hands on Berkley's face after she heard the rawness in her voice. "You can tell me."

"That I wouldn't ever get the chance again to show you how much I love you." Her hand went lower and Aidan saw the pure bliss in Berkley's eyes when she felt how wet she was. "But most of all that I'd squandered this gift with my own stubbornness. I love you," she whispered before lowering her head and kissing Aidan as her fingers slipped inside.

To Aidan, it was where Berkley belonged. In that place that existed in her that held the deepest of her truths, she knew she'd never belong to anyone as fully as she did to Berkley. It wasn't because of the great sex, or what Berkley brought to her life, but that Berkley was the one. The only person who'd hold the essence of who she was in the palm of those big hands, and it'd be safe forever.

"I love you so much." Aidan let out a grunt when the pad of Berkley's thumb hit her clitoris. Trying to stop the reaction it caused in her body was like trying to turn back a tsunami. Her hips rose in rhythm with Berkley's hand until the orgasm brought tears to her eyes. "Thank you for coming back to me."

"You don't really ever lose anything that belongs to you, my beautiful girl." Berkley carefully wiped her tears.

Aidan smiled at the poetic side of Berkley and was going to chastise her for turning her head toward the television, but stopped when she saw what Berkley was staring at. The reporter was standing in front of a blazing inferno, talking excitedly with his hands. Berkley reached for the remote and turned up the volume.

"From our accounts the explosion happened approximately an hour ago, completely destroying former Vice President Chandler's home and surrounding buildings. There is no word yet whether Mr. and Mrs. Chandler were home at the time, but the FBI confirms that Director Duke Stiel was one of the agents killed in the blast." The reporter pointed to the metal shell of the car. "What Director Stiel and the other agents were doing here has not been disclosed yet, but our colleague at the White House is investigating."

They both looked on in shock and then the phone rang.

"Are you watching the news?" Drew asked before Aidan could say anything.

"What happened?"

"The bastard is gone and left no trail. He must've known we were coming and rigged the bombs to go off when whoever we sent pressed the doorbell. We have to wait for the fire to be put out before we can do anything, but I need you and Berkley ready to go in the morning."

"We'll be there," Aidan said and disconnected the line. "There was no sign of Chandler," she told Berkley.

"Ready or not, love, it's begun."

About the Author

Ali lives right outside New Orleans with her partner of many years. As a writer, she couldn't ask for a better more beautiful place—so full of real-life characters to fuel the imagination. When she isn't writing, working in the yard, cheering for the LSU Tigers, or riding her bicycle, she makes a living in the nonprofit sector.

Ali has written *The Devil Inside, The Devil Unleashed, Deal With the Devil, Carly's Sound, Second Season, Calling the Dead, Blue Skies*, and the soon-to-be-released *The Devil Be Damned*.

Books Available From Bold Strokes Books

No Leavin' Love by Larkin Rose. Beautiful, successful Mercedes Miller thinks she can resume her affair with ranch foreman Sydney Campbell, but the rules have changed. (978-1-60282-079-1)

Between the Lines by Bobbi Marolt. When romance writer Gail Prescott meets actress Tannen Albright, she develops feelings that she usually only experiences through her characters. (978-1-60282-078-4)

Blue Skies by Ali Vali. Commander Berkley Levine leads an elite group of pilots on missions ordered by her ex-lover Captain Aidan Sullivan and everything is on the line—including love. (978-1-60282-077-7)

The Lure by Felice Picano. When Noel Cummings is recruited by the police to go undercover to find a killer, his life will never be the same. (978-1-60282-076-0)

Death of a Dying Man by J.M. Redmann. Mickey Knight, Private Eye and partner of Dr. Cordelia James, doesn't need a drop-dead gorgeous assistant—not until nature steps in. (978-1-60282-075-3)

Justice for All by Radclyffe. Dell Mitchell goes undercover to expose a human traffic ring and ends up in the middle of an even deadlier conspiracy. (978-1-60282-074-6)

Sanctuary by I. Beacham. Cate Canton faces one major obstacle to her goal of crushing her business rival, Dita Newton—her uncontrollable attraction to Dita. (978-1-60282-055-5)

The Sublime and Spirited Voyage of Original Sin by Colette Moody. Pirate Gayle Malvern finds the presence of an abducted seamstress, Celia Pierce, a welcome distraction until the captive comes to mean more to her than is wise. (978-1-60282-054-8)

Suspect Passions by VK Powell. Can two women, a city attorney and a beat cop, put aside their differences long enough to see that they're perfect for each other? (978-1-60282-053-1)